"Michael, if anything happens to me, there's a letter in my bag. Please—"

His heart skipped a panicked beat, and he lowered his face to hers. "Listen to me. You're going to be fine. Both you and the baby. So don't talk—"

"I've written it all—" The rest of what Sadie was about to say was cut off by her anguished cry.

"Now come on, push. Your baby is anxious to meet you."

A grueling fifteen minutes later, they welcomed a baby girl with shouts of joy.

Sadie looked at him and smiled. "I don't know what I would have done without you, Michael."

He gently moved her sweat-dampened hair from her face. "You were incredible. She's beautiful, and so are you." His face warmed as the words rolled off his tongue. It was how he felt, but not something he should say to a woman he'd known for little more than an hour. But in that moment, he felt close to Sadie, closer than he'd ever felt to a woman before.

ALSO BY DEBBIE MASON

The Highland Falls series
Summer on Honeysuckle Ridge
Christmas on Reindeer Road

The Harmony Harbor series
Mistletoe Cottage
Christmas with an Angel (short story)
Starlight Bridge
Primrose Lane
Sugarplum Way
Driftwood Cove
Sandpiper Shore
The Corner of Holly and Ivy
Barefoot Beach
Christmas in Harmony Harbor

The Christmas, Colorado series
The Trouble with Christmas
Christmas in July
It Happened at Christmas
Wedding Bells in Christmas
Snowbound at Christmas
Kiss Me in Christmas
Happy Ever After in Christmas
Marry Me at Christmas (short story)
Miracle at Christmas (novella)
One Night in Christmas (novella)

Falling in Love on Willow Creek

DEBBIE MASON

A Highland Falls Novel

FOREVER
New York   Boston

Copyright © 2021 by Debbie Mazzuca

Cover design by Daniela Medina. Cover photographs © Shutterstock. Cover copyright © 2021 by Hachette Book Group, Inc.

Bonus novella *A Wedding on Honeysuckle Ridge* by Debbie Mason © 2021 by Debbie Mazzuca

Forever
Hachette Book Group
1290 Avenue of the Americas, New York, NY 10104
read-forever.com
twitter.com/readforeverpub

First Edition: June 2021

Forever is an imprint of Grand Central Publishing. The Forever name and logo are trademarks of Hachette Book Group, Inc.

The publisher is not responsible for websites (or their content) that are not owned by the publisher.

The Hachette Speakers Bureau provides a wide range of authors for speaking events. To find out more, go to www.hachettespeakersbureau.com or call (866) 376-6591.

ISBNs: 978-1-5387-1700-4 (mass market), 978-1-5387-1698-4 (ebook)

Printed in the United States of America

CW

10 9 8 7 6 5 4 3 2 1

To all my readers,

Thank you for sharing your love of my stories with your friends and family. Your enthusiasm, encouragement, and support mean the world to me. You are, without a doubt, the most wonderful readers an author could ask for.

A big thank-you also to two members of my readers' group, Maureen Barry and Marcia Hill Quinn, for naming Finn and Lula Belle the unicorn.

Falling in Love
on Willow Creek

Chapter One

♥

When you grew up in a small town with a grandmother who believed in unicorns and a baby brother who frequently found himself on the wrong side of the law, the last thing you wanted was to draw attention to yourself. But as Sadie Gray knew from experience, sometimes that was easier said than done.

At that moment, she stood in the display window of I Believe in Unicorns, her grandmother's store in Highland Falls, North Carolina, wearing a hairband adorned with pastel ribbons, pointed ears, and a gold unicorn horn.

If she were eight instead of twenty-eight, she might have been able to pull off the look. She'd said as much to her grandmother when she'd dragged a pink unicorn sweatshirt over Sadie's ginormous baby bump and then stuck the hairband on her head.

People made the mistake of thinking Agnes MacLeod, the adorable Betty White look-alike with a soft Scottish burr, was a pushover. Sadie knew better. She'd been raised by her grandmother, after all. And when Agnes MacLeod made up her mind, good luck trying to change it. Which was why Sadie hadn't bothered putting up a fight. At least not much of one.

"All right now, add a few more heart and unicorn balloons in the window. Though mind that you don't block the *Blowout Valentine's Day Sale* sign," Agnes directed Sadie from where she sat on the stool behind the cash register enjoying a cup of tea.

Her grandmother wore a red velour jogging suit, a hairband decorated with blinking hearts, and sneakers that lit up when she tapped her feet to the Irish Rovers singing "The Unicorn Song."

Sadie didn't know whether it was the light show or "The Unicorn Song" on a constant loop that was making her queasy or if the nausea was due to lack of sleep. The baby had spent the better part of the night kicking her in the back and tap-dancing on her bladder. Still, no matter how queasy, uncomfortable, and sleep-deprived she might be, she refused to complain. There was nothing she wanted more than this baby. And nothing that she wanted less in her life than her baby's daddy.

Her queasiness intensified at the thought of Drew, the afore-mentioned baby daddy. Maybe it wasn't just lack of sleep, "The Unicorn Song," or the light show making her feel sick. Maybe it was the stress of knowing she had to confront Drew when she went home to Charlotte later today.

She had a rebranding project due first thing tomorrow. A project that she prayed would put her on her boss's radar for the art director position at the advertising agency where she'd worked for the past six months. Now more than ever, thanks to Drew, she needed the increase in salary that the promotion would bring.

"Your sale would have been more effective if you'd held it last weekend instead of on the actual day, Granny," Sadie grumbled. She'd arrived two days ago to spend the weekend with Agnes at her grandmother's apartment above the store. If not for the sale, Sadie would have been on her way home. Instead, she was making a spectacle of herself in the window display of I Believe in Unicorns on a dark and dreary Sunday morning.

Her grandmother simply smiled at Sadie's grumpy observation

and picked up the ringing landline, wishing the caller a happy Valentine's Day.

Cursing Cupid in her head, Sadie blew a stream of hot, cranky air into a heart-shaped balloon. Her stomach expanded like the Goodyear blimp, pressing her baby bump against the cold glass. She stepped back from the window, and the unicorn knight rescuing the unicorn princess in the castle's turret stabbed Sadie in the butt with his plastic sword. On an *ouch*, she let go of the balloon to rub her butt, and the red heart shot toward the window, taking out the sale sign before sputtering, deflated, at her feet.

With a hand on her lower back, Sadie stuck the knight in the turret and gave the unicorn princess the sword. There might have been a time—twenty years ago—when she believed in fairy tales, but no longer. None of the frogs she'd kissed as a little girl had turned into princes as advertised, and she hadn't fared any better as an adult who should have known better.

She bent to retrieve the sale sign from the floor but her stomach got in the way as much as the wooden replica of Edinburgh Castle behind her. If it were up to her, the castle would end up in the storage room, along with half the store's merchandise.

Unicorn-themed clothes, stuffed animals, books, toys, and tchotchkes fought for space on shelves draped in white fairy lights. Seasonal gifts were crowded on tables with bases carved to resemble trees while whimsical children's furniture sat on the white oak floor. Gold-glitter stars, pastel-colored rainbows, and inspirational unicorn art adorned the walls as angel unicorns rode across the ceiling on white cardboard clouds.

When she was much younger, she'd loved hanging out at the store with her grandmother. Sadie had been into unicorns, glitter, and rainbows as much as Agnes back then. But that had been before the kids at school found out that not only did Sadie's grandmother believe in unicorns, she also had the second sight.

Sadie glanced at Agnes, hoping for some help retrieving the

signage, but whoever was on the other end of the phone had captured her grandmother's full attention. Sadie straightened and put a hand on the glass for balance as she attempted to get the tape on the sign to stick to her sneaker. After three tries that left her sweaty and frustrated, she managed to raise the sign a few inches off the floor. It didn't help so she kicked the sign up and into the air and made a grab for it.

As she reached out to snag the sign, she noticed a man across the road leaning against a dark sedan. In the open black dress coat he wore over his dark suit, he looked like he'd stepped off the cover of *GQ* magazine. And while she might not have been able to make out the color of his eyes from that distance, she definitely felt the intensity of his stare. He studied her like she was a bug under a microscope.

And maybe because his cool, calculating gaze flustered her, she lost her balance at the same time she snagged the sign. Using the window to save herself from falling, she ended up like a pregnant starfish plastered against the glass. A cute couple walking hand in hand on the sidewalk in front of the store smiled up at her. She managed the semblance of a smile in return, the left side of her mouth ticking up.

The cute couple looked down and laughed. She chuckled and rolled her eyes like she was in on the joke and raised a mocking hand to her hairband. Except they were looking down, not up. Another couple joined them. Cute couple number one pointed at Sadie, and the four of them shared a laugh at her expense.

She followed their gazes but couldn't see past the top of her stomach. Frustrated, but no less stubborn than her grandmother, she acknowledged their friendly waves with a finger-wave of her own. Then, once they were out of sight, she lifted the hem of the sweatshirt to see what they'd been looking at.

Her eyes went wide. "Granny, you've got me stuck in the front window wearing a sweatshirt that says I'm horny!"

Suddenly remembering that the cute couples hadn't been her only audience, her gaze shot to the man across the road. At the sight of the huge, naked, and stretch-marked stomach she'd just flashed him, she was surprised not to see a grossed-out expression on his incredibly handsome face. Like the one Drew made whenever he caught a glimpse of her naked. Something that happened more frequently than she wanted because the man was still living with—off—her, and her place wasn't big enough for the almost-three of them. It was her fault they were still cohabitating after the crap he'd pulled. She blamed it on her fatal flaw.

Despite all the men in her life proving that they couldn't be trusted, she'd let herself get sucked in by Drew. She'd bought his half-truths and lies of omission, but no longer. She was done with him. Done with men in general. She'd raise her baby on her own. She'd devote herself to building a beautiful, drama-free life for just the two of them.

Tugging down her sweatshirt without giving the man across the road a second glance, she called to her grandmother. "Granny, did you hear me?"

Agnes responded with a distracted "I didn't have any *Hoping for a Unicorn* sweatshirts left in your size." Then she went back to stuffing twenty-dollar bills from the open cash drawer into an envelope.

Sadie frowned. "What are you doing?"

"Nothing." Her grandmother slid the envelope behind her back and lifted her chin at the door. "We're in for it now. Brooklyn Sutherland is headed our way. I told the girls they should have invited her to your shower but no one listened to me. That's what happens when you get old. No one—"

"I'm onto you, Granny. Don't bother trying to distract me. I'm not taking your money. I'm fine, so put the twenties back in the cash drawer." Sadie had been venting about Drew to her best friends at the surprise baby shower they'd hosted for her the night before, and Agnes had overheard her tale of woe.

Drew had gotten fired for drinking on the job last month, a circumstance he blamed on being stressed about the baby. On top of that, just hours before the shower, she'd discovered he'd maxed out her credit card while online shopping because, he'd whined, he was bored.

The front door chimed, and Sadie glanced over her shoulder. Her grandmother hadn't been lying. Brooklyn walked in with a thin-lipped smile on her pageant-winning face. They'd been frenemies since grade school. Brooklyn had recently moved back to Highland Falls to open Spill the Tea on Main Street with her mother, who was the biggest gossip in town.

"I hear your baby shower was the event of the season," Brooklyn said with a hint of the South in her voice as she flicked her long auburn hair over the shoulder of her plaid-lined trench coat. She'd always been blunt and to the point, traits that had once annoyed Sadie but that she now found herself admiring. At least Brooklyn was honest.

"Congratulations, by the way," her grade school frenemy continued. "I haven't seen you since I've been home."

"Thanks. About the shower," Sadie said, placing a hand on the knight's head to gingerly climb out of the display window. "It was a surprise, so I didn't have a say in the guest list, and my friends, Abby and Mallory, they haven't been in town long. They wouldn't have known to invite you. But hey, it saved you from having to buy a shower gift." She smiled, then gestured at the shop under construction across the road to distract Brooklyn from her obviously hurt feelings, which made Sadie feel horrible. "Congrats to you too."

Sadie noticed *GQ* guy was still hanging around, only now he had a cell phone pressed to his ear. It annoyed her that her attention kept going back to the man. It shouldn't matter that he was drop-dead gorgeous.

Moving so he was out of her line of sight, she refocused on Brooklyn. "Granny says you're getting lots of buzz. When's the opening?"

"April, if everything goes as planned." Brooklyn gave her an ingratiating smile. "I was actually hoping you could get your friend Abby to feature us on her YouTube channel. She does such a great job promoting Highland Falls."

There was nothing that Abby liked better than promoting local events and businesses, but she might have an issue with some of the gossip Brooklyn's mother had been spreading around town. Sadie didn't want to commit without talking to her first.

"Of course she will," Agnes chimed in as she closed the cash drawer, the twenties suspiciously missing. "You won't hear it from my granddaughter, but she's Abby's partner, more or less."

Less. Sadie worked part-time for Abby but her grandmother was obviously trying to distract Sadie from what she was up to with the cash.

"She does all her design work and takes care of the technical end of things as well," Agnes continued, ignoring Sadie's *please stop talking* stare. "Our Sadie's a computer whiz, you know. Just like her brother and her father. Not that I approved of how her father used his technical wizardry, mind you, but Sadie, she's always used her skills for the greater good. She takes after the MacLeod side in that, she does."

Sadie gaped at her grandmother, wondering what had possessed her to talk about Sadie's father in front of Brooklyn. It had taken years to live down the damage Jeremiah Gray had done to their family's reputation. They hadn't spoken about him in fourteen years.

She also found it telling—but not surprising—that her grandmother didn't lump Sadie's brother Elijah in with their father. Agnes couldn't see past Elijah's sparkling honey-brown eyes and mischievous toothpaste-commercial grin to the petty criminal who lay within.

"If you can put in a good word with Abby for us, I'd really appreciate it." Brooklyn's smile had gone from ingratiating to uncomfortable. "We're looking forward to the airing of your birth day video. Although I was kind of surprised that you agreed to let your baby's birth be filmed. You were always so private. Abby must be a very persuasive woman. But I'm sure she won't show, you know, *everything*." She waved her hand in the general vicinity of Sadie's baby bump.

She now understood Brooklyn's strained smile. "Trust me, my birth plan does not include lights, cameras, and Abby calling action."

Sadie wanted a home delivery with calming music, lavender-scented candles burning, the lights turned down low, and her soft-spoken midwife lovingly guiding Sadie's baby into the world. "Where did you hear about the episode?"

"You know Momma, she always gets the inside scoop. She'll be the one spilling the tea at the store, and I'll be the one making it," Brooklyn said, deepening her Southern drawl.

"Making the actual tea or giving your momma something to gossip about?" Sadie asked, knowing full well what Brooklyn meant but wanting her to think about what being on the receiving end of her mother's storytelling would be like.

Brooklyn lifted a shoulder. "I don't have a life, so I'm safe."

But no one else was. "Well, this time, your momma scooped up some fake news." Sadie planned to call Abby as soon as Brooklyn left, and not just about the birth day episode.

They had to have a serious conversation about whether Abby should be promoting Spill the Tea. Sadie might have been young when her own family became grist for Babs Sutherland's rumor mill, but that didn't mean she didn't remember what it had been like.

Sadie waited for her grandmother to chime in. It had been a difficult time for all of them. But Agnes didn't say a word. Sadie glanced at her, only to discover her grandmother was in the middle of a stealthy getaway.

"Ah, Granny, where do you think you're going?" Sadie couldn't hold down the fort on her own. At this stage in her pregnancy, she needed more bathroom breaks than her grandmother.

Agnes waved her hand behind her head—a hand that held an envelope. "I'll be right back."

Huh, so the money wasn't for Sadie after all. She leaned past Brooklyn to get a look at the woman her grandmother was trying to keep out of the store.

"I wouldn't mind warming up for a bit before I head back home, Mrs. MacLeod. It's cold enough to freeze the teats off a frog." Tall with beachy blond waves, the twentysomething woman muscled her way past Sadie's grandmother. The blonde wore a puffy, iridescent-blue jacket, a denim skirt, and thigh-high black leather boots. She took one look at Sadie and spun around, snatching the envelope from Agnes's hand before heading out the door at a fast clip.

"Granny, who was that?" Sadie asked with a sense of foreboding.

"Oh, just a lass who does alterations for me," her grandmother said, eyeing the younger woman's progress through the window.

"It's Payton Howard," Brooklyn whispered. Then, probably seeing that the name meant nothing to Sadie, she added, "She was dating your brother before he...before he left town last summer. He was spotted around Willow Creek two days ago, and someone saw him leaving Payton's house late last night."

Sadie and her grandmother hadn't seen or heard from her brother since last summer. Truth be told, even before Elijah had gone on the run, Sadie had rarely heard from him. He called when he needed money or a favor or a fall guy—in her case, a fall girl. She was just lucky his actions hadn't landed her in jail.

She'd been bailing her baby brother out of trouble for years. But last summer, she couldn't—wouldn't—help him. He'd gotten involved with drugs. She didn't know the whole story. He hadn't deigned to share it with her. Even when he'd been blackmailing her for cash.

She had to get rid of Brooklyn without seeming rude. Sadie needed to talk to her grandmother alone. Agnes was keeping something from her.

Sadie rubbed the sore spot just above her tailbone. "I should probably sit down and rest for a bit." She wasn't faking. The earlier ache had worsened, spreading across her lower back. "But don't worry, I'll put in a good word for you with Abby. I'm sure she can fit you in before your grand opening."

"Thank you, that would be great," Brooklyn said but didn't make a move to leave. She chewed on her bottom lip while looking at Sadie's grandmother, who was rearranging the sale sign in the display window, no doubt hoping to avoid a confrontation with Sadie. Brooklyn glanced at Sadie. "Um, you know how your grandmother has the second sight?"

Oh no, she did not just go there. Brooklyn had teased Sadie mercilessly when word got out in grade school about Agnes's *gift*. It was bad enough Sadie had a grandmother who believed in unicorns, but to have a grandmother who could tell someone's future simply by holding their hand…Eyebrow raised, Sadie crossed her arms.

Brooklyn winced. "I know, and I'm sorry. I was just jealous that all the boys liked you."

Sadie snorted. "They did not."

"Trust me, they did. You were cool and smart and had no idea how pretty you were. We were all about clothes and makeup and boys, and you were all about soccer, nature hikes, and photography." Brooklyn glanced at Agnes, who looked like she planned to spend the rest of the day in the display window. She was waving at passersby while doing an impression of Vanna White, pointing out sale items in the window. "I'm really nervous about the store opening, and I was hoping your grandmother could, you know, tell me if Spill the Tea will be a success."

"Speaking from personal experience, you might not like what you hear. Granny has no control over her gift."

"But her predictions come true, don't they?"

"Sometimes, but not always in the way you expect or want them to," Sadie said, thinking back to her grandmother's latest prediction for her.

In December, she'd told Sadie that she'd experience an all-consuming pain and love on the day of hearts. With everything going on, Sadie had forgotten about it until now. In a way, it looked like part of her grandmother's prediction had come true. Elijah was back, which would no doubt cause Sadie pain, and she'd once loved her brother with all her heart.

But that hadn't been the end of her grandmother's prophecy. Agnes had also said a man would come from the shadows to deliver Sadie from the pain, but in the end, he'd bring her more because he wasn't who he said he was. Either her brother or Drew qualified for the role.

Happy Valentine's Day to me, she thought.

Chapter Two

♥

FBI agent Chase Roberts stood ankle-deep in wet snow in the middle of the woods outside of Highland Falls. He'd rather be sitting in his car with the heat on high, watching the antics of Elijah Gray's sister in the window of I Believe in Unicorns. Instead, he was freezing his ass off waiting for an agent from the North Carolina State Bureau of Investigation to arrive.

On the request of NCSBI agent Nathan Black, a man he'd never met, Chase had spent the better part of his Sunday morning surveilling the unicorn store on Main Street in Highland Falls. He'd been about to make contact with Sadie Gray and her grandmother when Black called to say plans had changed, directing him to a cottage on Willow Creek owned by the Grays. An hour later, he'd received another call from Black, asking him to check out Payton Howard's house on Chestnut Lane.

Now here Chase stood at meeting place number four with no sign of the other agent.

Chase wasn't impressed, with the man or the location. He was so far out of his comfort zone that he might as well be standing on the moon in the middle of a geomagnetic storm. He was big-city born and raised and wanted nothing more than to get transferred back to DC. But other than in a body bag, the fastest way out of this backwater was to tag a career-making case. From the little he'd learned about Elijah Gray, this case wasn't it.

No, he thought, as a disheveled, long-haired man with a heavy beard tromped through the dark, desolate woods toward him, this was Chase's payback for DC. His new boss didn't like him any better than his old one had.

"Hey, man, sorry I'm late. I'm undercover and couldn't get away without drawing attention." Dressed like he rode with a biker gang, the guy was a behemoth, an easy six-five with two hundred and forty pounds of muscle bulking up his broad-shouldered frame. Chase didn't need his BS meter to go off to tell him the other agent was bad news. He wouldn't trust this guy as far as he could throw him.

"You're twenty minutes late, Black. You have lipstick on your neck, your hair doesn't look like you've combed it in a week, your eyes are bloodshot, and you smell like you drank your weight in bourbon last night. So my guess is you've spent the better part of the day in bed nursing a hangover"—he reached over and tugged a long hair from the zipper of Black's leather jacket—"with a blonde to keep you company while you sent me all over Highland Falls to see if Elijah Gray had made an appearance."

Black grinned, shooting a finger at him. "Got it in one. Guess I shouldn't be surprised. Word is you're a freaking genius. The guy who brought in America's Most Wanted all by his lonesome. By the book and uncompromising, with a work ethic that puts your fellow agents to shame, you have more enemies than friends at the bureau." Black crouched, picked up a stick to move some snow-covered leaves around, and then glanced up at Chase with a flash of white teeth through his heavy beard. He looked like a wolf.

"Me," the other agent continued, "I'm as good as you but the exact opposite. Everyone in law enforcement loves me. I know better than to write up my boss for skirting the rules to crack a case. So play your cards right, and I might be able to get you that transfer back to DC that you want so bad."

Law enforcement agents were a small, incestuous bunch. They gossiped more than a table of seniors at a small-town church social. So Chase had no idea why he was remotely surprised that, despite being assigned to the field office in North Carolina only ten days ago, he'd already become fodder for the rumor mill.

What proved a bigger mystery—and one he occasionally tried to solve when the spirit moved him, which wasn't often—was why his dedication to seeking justice and upholding the law was considered a character flaw in the eyes of his fellow agents and bosses. Maybe if he cared what other people thought about him, he'd spend more than a few minutes thinking about it. But all he really cared about were the case files awaiting him on his desk.

And DC, he reminded himself. He cared about going home. So maybe he had to work on his people skills. The thought gave him a headache.

"I won't be riding back to DC on the coattails of this case, no matter how cozy you are with the powers that be, Black. It's not big enough. Elijah Gray's a petty criminal who made the mistake of thinking the gang he was running drugs for wouldn't miss a few blocks of cocaine. Talk to the Jackson County sheriff. The Whiteside Mountain Gang are in his jurisdiction."

"I can't talk to the sheriff. That's why I wanted a face-to-face. It's why I requested you." Black stood up, dropped the stick he'd been using to move around the leaves, and shoved his hands in his pockets. He searched Chase's face as though gauging whether he could trust him or not.

A damp wind whistled through the leafless trees, the iced branches clicking together like wind chimes—the only movement and sound in the utterly still and quiet forest.

Chase lifted the collar of his coat against the bitter breeze, waiting while Black struggled with whatever he was about to say. This was more than just a case for the other agent. This was personal.

"Three days ago, a friend reached out. He's a deputy with the Jackson County Sheriff's Department," Black said. "We were supposed to meet here two days ago." He looked down at the ground as though searching for a clue. "Brodie never showed, and I haven't been able to reach him."

"Since you won't take this to the sheriff and I spent the better part of the day tracking Elijah Gray's last-known movements, I'm guessing your friend has intel that links the Jackson County Sheriff's Department to the Whiteside Mountain Gang." And the fact that the deputy had been missing for the past two days didn't bode well for him.

Black nodded. "He got the intel from Elijah Gray. He was Brodie's confidential informant. Gray approached Brodie for help when the drugs he was delivering for the Whiteside Mountain Gang went"—Black made air quotes—"*missing* last summer. But when the situation got too hot for him to handle, Gray took off. Brodie finally managed to track him down a few weeks ago. Apparently Gray wasn't having much fun on the run and hoped to trade information to get out of the mess he was in."

"And your friend believed his intel was reliable?"

"I know what you're thinking. I thought the same. Gray isn't exactly a stand-up guy. He had no qualms leaving his sister holding the bag. She was just lucky Highland Falls' chief of police was a former New York City homicide detective and good at his job, otherwise she'd be having her baby in jail."

Chase thought about the woman with the long dark hair standing spread-eagle in the window of I Believe in Unicorns. He'd looked into her, not too deeply, but deep enough to gather Sadie Gray was smart, ambitious, reliable, and well liked by her colleagues but perhaps not the best judge of character given her previous and current romantic relationships. Still, she'd been brought in for questioning last summer for a reason.

"Or she's just good at hiding who she really is," Chase said. "She might have been involved from the beginning. She left a well-paid job to operate the tour bus for her brother last summer." Highland Tours was how Gray had delivered the product for the gang.

"Then there's the fact that Elijah's girlfriend, Payton Howard, stopped by the family's store this morning," Chase continued. "She didn't stick around for long and came out holding an envelope. My bet is it contained cash. Either to pass on to Elijah or to keep Payton quiet. I checked out her place and didn't see any sign Gray was there. But there were signs someone had been staying at the cottage on Willow Creek. You might want to pass that on to Highland Falls' chief of police."

"I want to hold off on that. I think I can trust the guy, but I don't want to take a chance the Jackson County Sheriff's Department gets wind that I'm looking into Brodie's disappearance. Gray told Brodie he had evidence the sheriff was involved. From things Brodie witnessed last year, he thinks other deputies might be on the take as well." He blew out a breath and scrubbed his face. "I need to find him."

"You know the odds, Black. It's been forty-eight hours..." He held up his hand at the other man's tortured expression. "You're right, there's a chance your friend is fine and lying low." Chase calculated there was about a ten-percent chance the deputy wasn't buried in a shallow grave.

"So you'll help me? No one, including your special agent in charge, can know what we're looking into."

"Wait a minute. What does my boss think I'm doing with you?"

"He owes me. I called in my marker. He has no idea what I need you for, only that I needed a partner."

That didn't make sense. This went well beyond interagency cooperation. There was more to this, more to Nathan Black, than Chase knew, and he didn't like it. Maybe he'd been right after all—his boss had found a way to get rid of him.

To confirm his suspicions, Chase considered asking Black how many of his partners had wound up in the hospital or the morgue but decided to let it go. No matter his concerns about Black or how dangerous the assignment might be, Chase was now convinced he'd found a case big enough to get him back to DC.

"All right, Granny," Sadie said. "There's no one in the store so now's your chance to tell me why you gave Payton Howard an envelope filled with twenty-dollar bills."

Sadie knew only too well that Agnes had been putting her off for the past several hours. At first, her grandmother had used Brooklyn as an excuse, pretending she was having a hard time reading her. Poor Brooklyn thought it meant she didn't have a future. But when Agnes began spouting readings without going into a trancelike state, there'd been no doubt in Sadie's mind that her grandmother was faking it. The question was why, but that was a question Sadie would save for another time, because Agnes had seemed genuinely distressed at her inability to do a reading.

Sadie didn't have the bandwidth to deal with two dramas today. As soon as Brooklyn had left the store, they'd been inundated with customers, ensuring that Sadie remained on her feet all day. Her back was killing her, she was tired, and she had a four-hour drive ahead of her in crappy weather. The rain had changed to sleet about fifteen minutes ago and now was changing to snow.

She rubbed her lower back, thinking of the work awaiting her when she got home. She still had several hours to put into tomorrow's presentation. And then there was Drew to deal with. She eyed the whimsical pink couch in the corner of the store, barely resisting the urge to walk over and curl up on it and sleep for a week.

"Oh now, it's nothing. Just helping the lass out is all. She's fallen on hard times, and we take care of own. She's...she was our Elijah's girl." Avoiding Sadie's narrowed gaze, her grandmother walked to the window. "You'd best be on your way. We can't have you driving the mountain roads in the snow at dark, now can we?"

She was right, and it was obvious Sadie wasn't going to get more out of her. And if she was being honest with herself, she didn't want to spend another minute thinking or arguing about her brother.

"I'll let this go for now, Granny. But I'm calling Gabe. I'll let him know that Elijah has been spotted around Payton's house and the cottage." As well as being Highland Falls' chief of police, Gabe was her best friend Mallory's fiancé. "So don't even think about helping Elijah out. You'd be charged with aiding and abetting." She walked over and kissed her grandmother's powder-scented cheek. "I don't want to visit you in prison."

Ten minutes later, Sadie was on her way. It didn't take long for her to realize she'd made a mistake. Despite the frantic *swish* of the wipers, snow was building up on her windshield. But if she turned back now, she could kiss the art director position goodbye. She thought about the additional credit card debt Drew had saddled her with and took several deep, calming breaths. She had to keep going. Her SUV had four-wheel drive and winter tires.

Leaning forward to peer past the snow pelting her windshield, she murmured, "Just a few more miles and we'll be through the worst of it, baby."

Maybe not the worst of the weather, but the road would widen and straighten. There'd be more traffic too. At that moment, she was the only one on the road, her high beams all that were visible through the wall of white. The trees on either side of the road were already coated with snow. She might have appreciated the winter wonderland more if she weren't driving. Her stomach tightened as though to remind her she had a baby on board. She gasped when the cramp didn't immediately subside, instead deepening and lengthening.

She breathed through the pain. "It's just Braxton Hicks contractions. Nothing to worry about. Perfectly normal at this stage. But if you could make them stop until we get back to Charlotte, I'd really..." Her tires hit a patch of ice, and she sunk her teeth in her lower lip to stifle a scream. Tightening her grip on the steering wheel, she struggled to regain control of the car.

Several terrifying seconds later, her tires were headed in the right direction. She glanced out the passenger-side window. A dark sedan and an army-green jeep were pulled off the road.

And that's when she decided that no matter how much was at stake, she couldn't take the risk. She continued driving, looking for a safe place to turn around. Her stomach tightened with another cramp, this one stronger than the last.

Her pained groan turned into a strangled gasp as her tires once again hit an icy patch. She tried to breathe through the contraction while fighting to keep the car on the road but it was getting harder to do as one contraction rolled into another. A gush of water ran down her legs onto the mat and the pedals. Her foot slid onto the gas, causing the car to spin.

She took her foot off the gas. The car kept going, plowing into the guardrail on the opposite side of the road, jolting her hard against the seatbelt and then throwing her back against the seat. A plume of white thumped down on the windshield.

She tried to calm her breathing as she smoothed her palms over her rock-hard stomach, searching for a sign her baby was all right. But even as she did, she knew there'd be no tiny flutters or kicks to alleviate her fears. She was in labor.

Fingers shaking, she undid her seatbelt and spotted her cell phone on the passenger-side floor. She leaned on her side across the middle console, stretching her fingers to grab it, gritting her teeth in frustration when it slid out of reach. The console pressed against her stomach as she rolled onto it to get closer, a small sigh of relief pushing past her lips when her fingers closed around her phone. When she finally managed to get herself in an upright position, she turned it on. Her heartbeat stuttered. No bars. She powered down her window, snow rushing inside the SUV as she stuck her phone outside, searching for a signal.

She swallowed a sob and her panic. Neither would do her or her baby any good. She had to stay calm and figure a way out of this. At the sound of tree branches snapping, she looked toward the dark woods.

From the shadows a form took shape.

It was a man.

Chapter Three

♥

Chase stopped to stare at the woman peering at him through the falling snow. He brushed the wet flakes from his eyes, positive they were messing with his vision. But no, the snow hadn't fooled him into thinking the face belonged to Sadie Gray. It was her. The woman from the window. The sister of their prime suspect in the disappearance of Black's friend. What were the odds of her showing up at the same time they searched the woods for Brodie?

Chase didn't put much stock in coincidences, but for some reason, in this instance, he wished he did. Maybe he just didn't want to believe that a pregnant woman who looked sweetly innocent wearing a unicorn headband could be involved in Brodie's disappearance or that she'd followed Chase here to discover what he'd learned. If she was involved, she would have been on her guard, looking for any sign the police were onto them.

It wouldn't have been a stretch for her to figure out that Chase was law enforcement. He might not have been flashing his badge around or making small talk with the locals while he was there, but he hadn't hidden the fact he was surveilling the store. At that point, Black hadn't warned him of the necessity of keeping this quiet.

The smell of cigarette smoke and the clatter of frozen branches suggested the other agent was coming his way. His eyes still locked with Sadie Gray's, Chase pulled out his phone to warn Black. They couldn't be seen together, especially by her. As Chase went to send a text, his eyes left her face. He noted the sizzle of steam through the falling snow, the crumpled front bumper, the tire hanging off the rim.

"Are you okay?" he yelled, slipping and sliding down the frozen incline to reach her. He didn't care if she'd run into the guardrail because she was checking up on them for her brother. She was pregnant, and not just a little pregnant, as he'd clearly seen for himself.

She blinked several times as though coming out of a trance. "No. I'm not okay. I'm pretty sure I'm having my baby." She groaned and pulled her head back inside the window to lean it against the headrest.

Chase froze with his foot halfway over the guardrail. "Now? You're having your baby now?" Panic had raised his voice an octave, and he searched the long, winding road for a sign that help was on the way.

Except instead of sirens, all he heard was the creaking of branches and the crunch of snow. And instead of help on its way in the form of swirling lights and high beams, he saw Black creeping toward his jeep. The agent glanced his way. Even from this distance, Black's fear for his friend was evident in his strained expression. They hadn't found Brodie or any sign that he'd shown up for the meet. Black put the blame squarely on Elijah Gray.

Chase gestured for him to stay put anyway and then glanced at Sadie, who'd yet to respond. Her eyes were squeezed shut, her lips were pressed tight, and she was moaning low in her throat.

Good God, she really was having her baby. "Did you call 911? Just nod or shake your head." *Please nod.*

"I—" She grimaced. "I can't get a signal."

He looked at his cell phone. No bars on the screen. Holding it up as he searched for a signal, he walked to the driver's-side door.

"It'll be all right," he told her. He didn't believe for a single second that it would be but reassuring her seemed to be what the situation required. "I'm calling 911," he yelled for Black's benefit, hoping against hope the other agent had a better service provider than Chase and Sadie.

Raising his phone higher, Chase walked carefully into the middle of the ice-slicked, desolate road. Nothing. Not even one bar.

The passenger-side window went down, and he brought the phone to his ear.

"Did you—" She whimpered, then took a couple seconds to catch her breath. "Did you get through?"

He held up a finger, pretending to talk to a dispatcher. "Yes. Definitely in labor. She's..." He rested the phone on his shoulder. "She wants to know how far apart the contractions are."

"Three min—"

What! "Her contractions are three minutes apart," he yelled into his dead phone while looking in the direction of Black's jeep. There was no sign of him. Chase ducked his head. There was no sign of him because he was in his jeep.

"I, um, I think I better lie down," she said, her face drained of color.

"No, I don't think you should. If you lie down, the baby might think it's time to come out."

"Trust me, this baby's coming whether we want it to or not."

"Not," he said, in case she thought he was on board with delivering her baby.

Her eyes moved over his face, and then she bowed her head and groaned.

"Don't worry, they'll be here soon. Really soon," he lied, his voice going in and out as he jumped up and down, waving his arms to get Black's attention. If the other agent started up his engine, Chase would shoot out his tires. A door creaked open. He stopped jumping. He was just about to utter a *thank God* when he realized Sadie had opened the car door, not Black.

"What do you think you're doing?" Chase sprinted around the back of the SUV. *Ice. Crap.* His feet went out from under him but he threw himself against the vehicle to keep himself upright.

Her arms wrapped around her stomach, Sadie gave him a raised-eyebrow look. "You didn't get through to 911."

"How did you know?" he asked, gingerly making his way to her side.

"Lots of practice with men not telling me the truth."

"I'm sorry," he said, and he was. "I didn't want you to freak out."

Her lips twitched, and her pretty hazel eyes smiled. "You're freaked out enough for the both of us." She winced and bent over. "My car's not going anywhere anytime soon. I need a ride to the hospital."

"Right, of course." He mentally kicked his ass. He'd allowed panic to hijack his common sense. He didn't have to deliver her baby; he just had to get her to the hospital on time. He thought about the files neatly piled on his front seat and the FBI jacket in the back.

She took a step, and he reached for her. "Careful, it's icy." He slid an arm around her waist, glancing from his car to hers. "I have a better idea." He leaned around her to power up the windows and then he opened the back passenger-side door and helped her sit inside. "I'll bring my car up alongside yours. That way we minimize the risk of you falling."

"Okay." She nodded, clenching her jaw as if to stop her teeth from chattering.

Delivering a baby might be completely out of his wheelhouse, but seeing to someone's care and comfort wasn't. This he could handle. "Do you have an emergency winter kit in your trunk?"

She gave him a blank look.

"Blankets, extra clothes, that sort of thing." When his explanation didn't appear to register, he said, "Don't worry about it. I do." The FBI's motto was Fidelity, Bravery, Integrity, which he wholeheartedly subscribed to. But he had a motto of his own: Be Prepared. He looked down at his ruined shoes. In his defense, Black had told him they'd meet on Main Street. "I'll be right back."

She grabbed his arm. "Please, don't go. I have baby blankets in my trunk."

"We need something a little bigger than that. I promise. I won't be long." He gave her a reassuring smile and went to remove her hand from his arm but something in her eyes stopped him. He recognized the pure, unadulterated panic he saw there, and maybe because he did, the next words out of his mouth were calm and in control. "We won't makc it to the hospital, will we?"

"I'm new to this too, but I don't think so." She bit her lip, and her eyes filled with tears.

"It'll be fine...honey," he said instead of calling her by her name, which he very nearly did. "We can do this. Trust me."

A tear rolled down her cheek. "I...I had it all planned. Lights down low, spa-like music, and a lavender-scented..." She trailed off, hiccupping on a sob.

"I'm sorry it didn't work out the way you planned." He helped her lie down on the backseat, wedging himself inside to pull the door closed. "I'm sorry you're stuck with me instead of your baby's daddy. But I'll—"

She shook her head as she struggled out of her puffy red jacket. "It's better that he's not here. I might tell him exactly what I think of him when I'm pushing out our sweet, innocent child, and the last thing I want my baby to hear is me cursing their father for putting me deeper in debt."

He knew Drew was a piece of work from the cursory background check he'd done after discovering he lived with Sadie. Chase didn't understand why someone like her would put up with a guy who had a drinking problem and couldn't hold down a job. Then again, the man seemed to have a talent for attracting women to take care of him.

Still, she was getting agitated, and Chase figured she had more important things to concern herself with. "Don't think about him then. You can deal with him later. Kick him to the curb. Get a restraining order so he doesn't harass you. Change all your passwords and the locks on your door," he said as he began removing her boots.

He stopped. She was staring at him. He'd said too much. Of course he had. Because once he started looking into something, he couldn't stop. He'd looked into the other women Drew had been involved with in the past and knew it wouldn't be easy for Sadie to get rid of him.

Her forehead creased. "Who are you?"

He knew what she meant but tried to distract her. "You're right. We should probably introduce ourselves. I'm Michael Knight." It wasn't a complete lie. His middle name was Michael, and his maternal grandfather, Jonathan Knight, referred to by most as *the judge*, had adopted Chase and his little brother when they were eight and five.

Gritting her teeth, she held up a finger, then closed her eyes. He gently removed her jacket from her clenched fist and folded it, waiting for the contraction to subside before placing it beneath her head.

"Thanks. I'm Sadie. Sadie Gray. But that's not what I meant. I saw you today on Main Street. You were there for a while. You were, uh, looking at me."

"Watching you." He corrected with a smile. "You were enter-taining. I was going to buy something for a friend's little girl. But when I ran the idea by her, she informed me her daughter was too old for unicorns."

The trick to lying was to add some truth. Three months ago, he'd had a woman in his life. However, she no longer considered him a friend. She'd accused him of being emotionally unavail-able and a workaholic. They'd been friends with benefits so he hadn't met her daughter.

"You should have brought her with you. My grandmother would have enjoyed the challenge." She looked at him from under her long lashes. "I'm sorry I flashed you. I didn't realize I was standing in the window wearing a sweatshirt that said I was horny. I thought it said *Hoping for a unicorn*. Which I'm not. Hoping for a unicorn, I mean. My grandmother is the one who believes in unicorns, not me." She wrinkled her nose. "Sorry for babbling. I'm just embarrassed I flashed you."

"Don't worry about it. And feel free to babble. It's better than having you go into shock. Besides, I'll be seeing a lot more than your stomach...Oh, ah." He scratched his head. "That wasn't helpful, was it?"

Caught up in a contraction, she didn't register his apology. Hopefully, she also hadn't registered why he'd had to make one in the first place. He took off his coat, careful not to reveal the shoulder holster and gun beneath his suit jacket.

"Thank you," she said when he laid it over her. She inhaled deeply and closed her eyes. Then she opened them to reward him with a breath-stealing smile. "Your cologne smells amazing. It's even better than lavender."

"I'm glad you like it. And it looks like you'll also get your wish for low light." He nodded at the darkening sky out the window. "Now all that's left is the music." He opened the back passenger-side door. "I'll take care of that now. Don't worry,

I'm not going further than the front seat," he said as he got out and opened the driver's-side door. He slid behind the wheel and started the engine, turning the heat to high. As he searched for a radio station that met her requirement, he glanced in the rearview mirror. Black had decided to grace them with his presence.

Before he did though, Chase had to ensure the agent was holding it together. The more they'd searched and the more they talked, the more obvious it became that Black was losing hope his friend was alive. Chase didn't want him interrogating Sadie.

He found a station with some New Age music and figured it would work. "Sadie, a jeep pulled off the road around the same time as me, and it looks like the driver is coming to see if we need a hand. He looks a little rough, so I want to check him out first."

She cast him a dubious glance.

He stopped with a foot out the door. "What? You don't think I can handle myself?"

"Well, you're pretty…" She rolled her eyes, presumably at herself, because he hadn't said or done anything. "I mean beautiful." She dragged in a deep breath through her nostrils. "You know what I mean."

He really didn't, which she must have noticed because she added, "You're like a cross between Brad Pitt in *Meet Joe Black* and Charlie Hunnam in *Sons of Anarchy*. Only when Jax got out of prison in the third season. Maybe it was season four. And don't be offended, but I really wish you weren't off-the-charts good-looking. I'd prefer an unattractive man to deliver my baby. Unattractive but kin—" A contraction cut her off.

He leaned over the seat to give her hand a squeeze, then grabbed his key fob from the pocket of his coat. "Relax and focus on your breathing. I'll be back in two minutes. Right before your next contraction."

She opened one eye. He probably shouldn't have reminded her how close her contractions were. He'd been timing them.

Chase met Black a couple yards from Sadie's SUV.

"What the hell's taking you so long? Did you get anything out of her?"

"The only thing we're getting out of her is a baby." Chase took the other agent by the arm. "I need a couple things from my trunk. She doesn't know I'm FBI, and we're going to keep it that way." He beeped the unlock button on his fob. "Do you have any blankets or bottles of water?"

"No. I mean, yeah. I've got both." He looked from Sadie's SUV to Chase. "Do you even have a clue what you're doing?"

"No idea." He cocked his head; there was something in Black's voice that said he might. "Have you delivered a baby before?"

"I have five older sisters. They have a baseball team between them. Four of them wouldn't have a baby at a hospital if you paid them, and they made sure, if I was in town, I was in on the action. No matter how much I did not want or need to see my sisters' hoo-has." He shuddered, then lifted a shoulder. "I wouldn't have missed helping bring my nieces into the world though. I just block out that part."

Chase smiled. He'd just found the answer to Sadie's last wish—an unattractive man to deliver her baby. Under all that hair, Black was probably a good-looking guy, but right now, he qualified. "Great. You can deliver the baby. Do you have hand sanitizer?"

Five minutes later, when Chase opened the front passenger door, unloading blankets, a battery-operated lantern, and the baby stuff he'd gotten out of Sadie's trunk, she half yelled, half sobbed at him, "You were gone for two contractions. I thought you weren't coming back!"

"I'm here now, and I've got good news," he said as Black opened the back door. "I found someone to deliver your baby, and he knows what he's doing. Sadie, meet Eddie Taylor."

Black gave Chase a look before smiling at Sadie. Eddie Taylor was the man who had been on top of the FBI's Most Wanted list before Chase had apprehended him.

As Sadie and Black got acquainted, Chase got to work on the front passenger seat. He removed the two bolts at the back of the seat and on the front side rails and then disconnected the battery. He was half listening to Black and Sadie's conversation, blocking out parts like *transitioning* and *crowning*. By the time he lifted the seat out and set it on the side of the road, Sadie was panting.

"Don't push," Black ordered.

Chase shut the car door and got situated on the floor. He turned on the lantern, adjusting the light to low. Then he turned up the music, the sounds of Enya's "Watermark" filling the SUV.

Ignoring Black's raised-eyebrow glance, Chase took Sadie's hand between his. "Just breathe, honey. You've got—sweet mother of God." She squeezed the life out of his fingers. She had the grip of a rock climber. A three-hundred-pound rock climber.

Black chuckled, then said, "Just a little longer, Sadie. You've got this, honey."

Chase speared the agent with a look. Black grinned and then ducked his head under the blanket. Chase shuddered, and his legs went weak. Black might not be the type of partner Chase would have wished for, but he was sincerely glad he was here to help Sadie.

"Michael, if anything happens to me, there's a letter in my bag. Please—"

His heart skipped a panicked beat, and he scooted closer to slide an arm beneath her neck and cradle her against his chest. He lowered his face to hers. "Listen to me. You're going to be fine. Both you and the baby. So don't talk—"

"Please, just promise me you won't let Drew have custody of my child. I want my friend Abby or my cousin Ellie to take the baby. I've written it all—" The rest of what she was about to say was cut off by her anguished cry.

"Push, Sadie," Black said, but she wasn't listening to him. She was holding Chase's gaze and breaking his hand.

"I promise. He won't get near your baby." Or Sadie. As soon as she and the baby were safe and in the hospital, Chase would ensure that Drew was out of their lives for good. "Now come on, push. Your baby is anxious to meet you."

A grueling fifteen minutes later, they welcomed Sadie's baby girl with shouts of joy.

"It's not a unicorn," he said, his voice gruff with emotion.

She looked at him and smiled. "Thank God, and thank you. I don't know what I would have done without you, Michael. Without either of you."

Chase gently moved her sweat-dampened hair from her face. "You were incredible. She's beautiful, and so are you." His face warmed as the words rolled off his tongue. It was how he felt, but not something he should say to a woman he'd known for little more than an hour, a woman he was surveilling for a case. But in that moment, he felt close to Sadie, closer than he'd ever felt to a woman before.

Black handed Chase the red-faced, squalling infant. "Swaddle her in the blanket," the agent directed.

Pulse racing, Chase stared down at the baby, who fit in his two hands. She squirmed, arching her spine as she howled at the top of her lungs, and he nearly lost his grip. His hands were sweaty, and she was slippery. Tiny too, with delicate little bones. Bones he could crush if he held her too tight, but he didn't dare loosen his grip. If she fell, she'd break. He shot a panicked glance at Sadie and Black. What had the agent been thinking handing him the baby? Chase had no idea what to do.

Sadie met his eyes, a soft smile on her face. She was looking at him like he was her hero, and he didn't want to disappoint her. All he needed was to look up advice on Google or a video to watch. He'd absorb the information in a nanosecond, and he could live up to Sadie's expectations. But they were in the middle of nowhere, and none of them had service on their cell phones. He had to improvise. He couldn't ask for Black's advice or for Sadie's. She might freak out if she knew she'd entrusted her precious child to a man who didn't have a clue what to do with it. He couldn't even keep a plant alive.

But he did have an IQ of 160 so surely he could figure out how to swaddle a baby in a blanket. He picked up the blanket and looked from it to the screaming child.

Black sighed and lifted his head. "Think of a burrito," he said, then went back to doing whatever he was doing down there.

Chase nearly let his relief show and thanked Black, but then he remembered how Sadie had looked at him. "I know what swaddling means." He glanced from the blanket to the passenger-side seat. "I was just working out how best to hold her and lay out the blanket at the same time." Not bad. He might even buy the excuse. Then he caught Sadie's eye. She looked like she didn't know whether to laugh or cry.

Laugh, he decided when she pressed her lips together and they curved in a grin. "Hold her against your chest with one hand and use your other hand to lay out the blanket."

"Right. Good idea." As he ever so slowly brought the baby to his chest, he imagined what it must be like for her after spending so many months curled inside her mother's warm, dark womb. No wonder she was screaming. He'd be screaming too. Feeling like he now had some insight into the problem, he used his hand and forearm to hold the baby against his chest, then reached for the white blanket with his other hand.

But instead of laying the blanket on the seat, he completely covered the baby with it—head and all—and held her tight. He thought of the sounds and motion she'd be familiar with and, next to her ear, made a low shushing sound while rocking her in his arms. Her screams subsided, and she made soft snuffling noises as she nestled against him. He smiled against the blanket and the side of her little head, as proud of comforting her as he'd been of bringing in Eddie Taylor.

His world shrank until it was just him and the baby sitting in the warm glow of the lantern. He couldn't remember ever feeling this peaceful.

"Would you mind swaddling her now?" Sadie's voice penetrated the bubble of contentment. "I mean, I'm grateful you got her to stop crying, but I'd really like to hold her."

"Right. Of course." As he moved the baby away from his chest and looked into that tiny, heart-shaped face, it felt like the hard shell around his heart quivered and then splintered, letting in an emotion he'd never felt before.

He wondered if it was love.

Chapter Four

♥

Sadie glanced up at the man holding her and her newborn baby in the backseat of his car as if they meant the world to him. Michael Knight, her knight in shining armor. Maybe it was a rush of hormones after giving birth, but that's how she thought of him. He was sweet, kind, and considerate, and yes, with the light from the streetlights playing off his chiseled cheekbones and square, beard-stubbled jaw, drop-dead gorgeous.

She didn't want to contemplate what she looked like right now. Although from the admiration in Michael's eyes, you'd think she was a reigning beauty queen or a warrior princess returning from battle.

"You doing okay? Any pain?" he asked, tucking the blankets around her and her daughter.

"No, I'm good. We're good." She smiled at the baby asleep on her chest, Michael's hand splayed across her daughter's back.

She looked so peaceful and angelic now. Unlike fifteen minutes ago when Eddie and Michael had moved them into the backseat of his car to make the trip to the hospital. It was as if Michael and her daughter had forged a bond in the moments after Sadie had given birth. The baby hadn't settled until he'd wrapped them in his arms and rested that big, strong hand of his on her tiny back.

Sadie imagined the baby felt like she did—protected and loved. Cared for, she quickly amended. The flood of endorphins had definitely done a number on her if she was fancying herself in love with the man holding her so close, so tenderly.

How that thought brought up an image of Drew in her head, she had no idea. But there he was, the real father of her baby. No matter how difficult the past few months had been or how much crap he'd recently pulled, he deserved to know he had a daughter. He deserved to share in the happiness of the moment.

"Michael, would you mind grabbing my phone?" While Eddie had gone to get the car, Michael had meticulously catalogued every item he'd collected off the floor and seat of the SUV to put in her purse. If she didn't know better, she might have thought he was looking for something. Either that or he couldn't believe how much crap she could fit in her purse. "I need to call Drew."

"Sure," Michael said with an edge to his voice, which made her wonder just how much she'd told him about her relationship with her baby's daddy. She didn't think she'd overshared. But honestly, the last thirty minutes of labor and delivery were kind of a blur. All she really remembered were Michael's words of encouragement and praise.

He reached into her purse on the floor. Retrieving her phone, he handed it to her, sharing a glance with Eddie in the rearview mirror. Okay, so that settled it. She'd totally overshared.

"I can't remember exactly what I said about Drew to you guys, but he's not that bad," she said, addressing the elephant in the car.

"Any man who sits around drinking beer and shopping online while his pregnant partner works to keep a roof over their heads and pays for the debt he's racking up on her credit card is the definition of a *bad* guy, Sadie," Michael said.

"And his pregnant partner is an idiot for letting him take advantage of her," she murmured against her daughter's head.

She'd tried to end their relationship last December. She'd even hired a lawyer. Then, a week before the holidays, Drew had followed her to Highland Falls. The things he'd done and said had worried her. She'd been afraid he'd do something stupid and follow through with his threat that life wasn't worth living without her. It didn't take long for her to realize he'd simply figured out what buttons to push to get her to let him stay. But by then she was too tired to deal with him, and he was out of work.

"He's really messed with your head, hasn't he?" Michael said. "He doesn't deserve you, Sadie, and he doesn't deserve her."

"Michael's right. If any of my sisters' partners treated them the way he treated you, I'd make them disappear. You want, I can take care of that for you," Eddie said, sounding as if he meant it.

"He's joking. He—" Michael began, no doubt picking up on her concern.

"No, he isn't, brother. He's very serious." Eddie stopped at a red light and looked back at her, the scary expression on his face leaving little doubt that he was.

Don't worry, Michael mouthed, rolling his eyes as if the big man up front was as harmless as a fly. "Eyes on the road, Eddie. The light's green, and you're holding up traffic." The blast of a horn punctuated Michael's remark.

"Thank you. I appreciate your concern, Eddie. Yours too, Michael. I know my relationship with Drew isn't healthy, and I will take care of it. But it doesn't negate the fact he's the father of my daughter and deserves to be part of this."

The grunts coming from Michael and Eddie indicated they didn't feel the same.

"Okay, you guys are entitled to your opinions, but if you don't mind, I'd appreciate you keeping them to yourself. I'm going to FaceTime Drew so he can see the baby. His daughter," she reminded them.

Their muttered *fine*s weren't all that convincing. But as she had come to learn in the short time they'd been together, they were good guys, caring guys, and she was pretty sure they'd abide by her wishes.

She held up the phone and groaned when she saw herself. Her hair was a long, sweaty mess and plastered to her head.

As she went to fluff her hair, Michael took her hand and lowered it, saying quietly, "You don't need to fix your hair. You're beautiful just the way you are, Sadie."

She wished it was him she was FaceTiming. "I can actually see what I look like, but that's sweet of you to say."

She angled the phone to get the baby on the screen and pressed the FaceTime icon. It wasn't until Michael put his finger on the edge of her phone and angled it down, that she realized he'd been in the shot.

Drew's haggard face and bloodshot eyes filled the screen. "Hey, where are you? I'm starving."

The inside of the car went electric with unhappy male vibes.

She didn't blame them. She wasn't happy either. "So am I, Drew. I'm also exhausted from just giving birth to my daughter." She should say *our*, she knew she should, but she just couldn't bring herself to do it. Michael's arms tightened around her as if offering support.

"What do you mean you had the baby? I don't under...wait, did you say daughter? I thought we were having a boy. I really was hoping for a boy, you know."

Michael angled toward the front seat and whispered, "I'll help you bury the body."

"I'll do it myself," she muttered.

"What did you say?" Drew craned his neck to get a look at the baby. "Is that it?"

"If by *it* you mean your daughter, then yes, it is." His cavalier attitude broke her heart. They didn't need him. They'd be fine on their own, better than fine. "Drew, I have to go. We'll be at Jackson County Hospital if you want to meet your daughter."

"Okay, I might be able to make it tomorrow. Weather's still pretty crappy though. I'll let you know." He leaned in, and she thought for a minute he might say something that would make up for his hurtful reaction. She knew she'd forgive him if he did. She'd chalk it up to shock or the beer she swore she could smell through the screen. "You look like you could use some rest anyhow. Get—"

She pressed End, hard. "Don't say anything," she said into the heavy silence.

She could feel the tension coming off Michael in waves, his chest expanding like he was having trouble containing his anger. But instead of venting, he simply kissed Sadie's head and kept his thoughts to himself.

Ten minutes later, Eddie broke the silence. "We're here. Stay put. I'll grab somebody."

Michael eased her out of his arms. "Do you have anyone you want me to call? Your grandmother? Friends?"

She didn't think she could get the words past the lump in her throat and shook her head instead of trying to answer. She didn't know when she'd ever felt so lonely. But then her daughter wriggled and snuffled, letting out a mewling cry, reminding Sadie she wasn't alone and there wouldn't be time to feel lonely.

"I don't want to bother them. It's late." She managed a smile as the baby's cries grew more insistent, raising her voice to say, "I'll call them in the morning."

"Sadie, I—" Michael broke off as the car door opened. "Looks like your ride's here, ladies." The baby stopped crying the minute he scooped her into his arms. He smiled, nuzzling her daughter's cheek.

"You'll be able to do that all you want later, daddy. Right now, we need to get this little sweetie inside and checked over," a nurse said as she expertly retrieved the baby from Michael and placed her into a clear bassinet on wheels. She was off before they had a chance to correct her. Michael shrugged and gave Sadie a lopsided grin, as if secretly pleased by the misunderstanding.

Eddie rolled his eyes and elbowed Michael out of the way, scooping Sadie into his arms before she realized what he was up to. The big man laughed at something Michael said under his breath, then gently deposited Sadie on the hospital gurney.

Michael nudged the orderly out of the way and tucked her purse in beside her. "We'll let you get settled in your room. Do you want me to grab you something to eat?"

She smiled, relieved that he wasn't going to leave. "I wouldn't mind a soup and sandwich if the cafeteria's still open."

"Sorry, folks. We have to get going," the orderly said at the sound of sirens headed their way.

Michael and Eddie jogged alongside her as she was whisked through the emergency room doors. They glanced over their shoulders when an ambulance, siren blaring, lights flashing, pulled up to the doors, a Jackson County sheriff's car following close behind. Sadie caught the two men sharing a glance. She didn't have time to wonder at their silent exchange. Michael leaned in when the orderly stopped the gurney at the nurses' station, her thoughts scattering when the magnetic woodsy fragrance enveloped her and he pressed his warm lips to her forehead.

He opened his mouth to say something as he eased away but the orderly interrupted him. "You can give the nurses the information, sir," he said, and then wheeled Sadie down the hall and past the elevators. When the orderly took a right down a long, sterile corridor, she turned her head to look for Michael but he and Eddie were nowhere to be seen.

It took at least an hour before she and her daughter were examined and then settled in a room. Sadie smiled at the sandwich, a bowl of soup, and a vase with two pink roses sitting on a small table beside the bed. Her smile fell when she looked around. The hospital room was empty.

"Did you see the man who brought these?" she asked the gray-haired nurse.

"I certainly did," the woman said with a twinkle in her eyes.

Sadie smiled. "Do you know where he went?"

"I don't but I'm sure someone is bound to know. The nurses were tracking his every move."

Sadie tucked into the sandwich while the nurse went off in search of Michael and Eddie. She had polished off everything by the time the woman returned.

"Sorry, pet. No one's seen hide nor hair of him or his friend."

"Michael...They didn't leave a note?" she asked past the lump in her throat.

"No, I checked at the nurses' station. There, there." She patted Sadie's arm, obviously sensing her distress. "I'm sure they'll—" She broke off with a smile when Sadie's grandmother and her best friends, Mallory and Abby, walked into the room carrying balloons and stuffed unicorns.

Sadie took one look at the stuffed unicorn knight and burst into tears.

The next night, Chase sat across from Sadie's apartment in Charlotte, waiting for Drew to come home. He hadn't gone to see Sadie or his newborn daughter. Chase had checked. The nurse he'd paid to keep an eye on Sadie kept him well informed. No one other than her grandmother and friends had come to visit her.

Pretending that he was on staff at the Jackson County Hospital, Chase had called her grandmother before pulling out of the hospital parking lot. He couldn't bear the thought of leaving Sadie alone, and he had to stay away from her until the case was solved. Once it was, it wasn't likely she'd want anything to do with him. He ignored the dull ache in his chest and looked up at the apartment building. At least he could take care of Drew for her.

A hulking shadow moving to the side of the building caught his attention. Nathan Black. Chase sighed and pulled out onto the road, making a U-turn to drive up to the front of the building. He powered down the passenger-side window.

"What do you think you're doing?" he asked as his partner stepped from the shadows.

Black wore a patched motorcycle jacket, his hair and beard just as long and unkempt as when Chase had dropped him at his jeep yesterday. "Taking care of Drew for Sadie. Same thing as you, I'd wager."

"I don't know about that. I plan on threatening him with jail time unless he leaves Sadie and the baby alone."

It wasn't an idle threat. The guy had racked up complaints of stalking and harassment from women throughout North Carolina and Tennessee. He seemed to be good at disappearing when things got hot. The complaints weren't serious enough to warrant Chase tracking him down, but Drew didn't know that. There was also the matter of him using Sadie's credit card without her permission, which Chase could use against him. Chase bet Sadie wasn't the only one who'd found herself up to her eyeballs in debt thanks to the man.

Black rolled his eyes. "Okay, choirboy, you do it your way, and I'll do it mine."

"Yeah, what are you going to do? Make him disappear?" He narrowed his eyes when Black grinned.

"You want me to work Brodie's case with you, we do it my way," Chase said. "I don't want this blowing back on Sadie. She's got enough to deal with."

"Fine." Black looked up at the building. "Doesn't look like he's going to be back for a while. Any idea where he might be?"

"Yeah. Follow me."

They found him at the second strip club on Chase's list. As agreed, Black went in ahead of him. Chase waited an extra five minutes before going inside. Black sat at the far end of the bar. Everyone gave him a wide berth. He met Chase's gaze and nodded at a table where Drew sat with a scantily clad redhead on his lap, leaning toward the stage with a fistful of twenties. Chase was tempted to let Black do what he wanted with him. Instead, he walked to the table and grabbed the twenties from Drew's hand before he stuffed them in the G-string of the blonde on the stage.

"Sorry, he's got a baby at home to feed," Chase told the blonde.

"Hey, wait a minute. Who do you think you are?" Drew blustered at Chase.

"Your worst nightmare if you don't do exactly as I say."

Chapter Five

♥

Three months later

Every head in Spill the Tea turned when Sadie walked into the bubblegum-pink tea shop. She looked down at herself, checking for spit-up or spilled coffee. No stains, which was kind of amazing. As amazing as looking semi-presentable in a crocheted green top and a khaki skirt paired with wedge sandals.

The effort to get dressed and get out had exhausted her. But she was on her own for the first time in three months, and she planned to soak up every second of peace and quiet as if her life depended on it. Because lately, she felt like it did.

She glanced around, avoiding eye contact with the women stuffed into pink velvet booths with clear acrylic tables between them and the women sitting precariously on pink leather–topped stools with ballet-slippered feet, who leaned in to catch every word of the latest gossip from Babs Sutherland's red-slicked lips. From where she stood behind the shiny, white tea bar, Babs, a buxom fiftysomething blonde, glanced at Sadie, nodding at the other women in a way that seemed to say, *Look at her, out for tea without her darling baby girl.*

Sadie's cheeks warmed. Everyone knew, that's why they were looking at her. They all knew her daughter hated her.

She was about to head out the door and across the street to I Believe in Unicorns, where her grandmother was looking after Michaela, when she spotted a familiar head of long, curly red hair in the far right-hand corner. Sadie made a beeline for her best friend Abby.

"Oh my gosh," Abby cried as Sadie slid across from her in the booth. "Are you okay? I was so worried about you."

"I'm fine. You know my grandmother, she exaggerates. I didn't have a crying jag, and I'm not suffering from postpartum depression." When Abby frowned, Sadie elaborated. "She caught me at a bad time. It wasn't easy moving back home. To be honest, I feel like a failure."

Abby reached for her hands. "That wasn't what I was talking about, sweetie. But you're not a failure. You're a single mommy, who needs the support of her friends and family. You certainly weren't getting any from Drew."

Wasn't that the truth. After a brief hospital stay without a word from Drew, she'd arrived home with their daughter to find he'd cleared out of her apartment in Charlotte. The only thing he'd taken that didn't belong to him—well, aside from the items he'd maxed out her credit card to buy—was her TV. He'd sounded terrified when she'd finally tracked him down. The next morning, she'd opened her door to find her TV. He hadn't even stuck around to see Michaela.

"And don't get me started on your boss," Abby said. "You'd think a woman would be more understanding about the difficulty of finding reliable, affordable childcare. You can't just leave your baby with anyone."

True, and it wasn't like Sadie had intentionally blown her presentation by having Michaela early. But if she was honest, her lack of childcare prospects wasn't her only problem. It was like her brain had gone on vacation. The simplest tasks were beyond her.

She couldn't do anything right, even breastfeed her daughter. At Michaela's first-week checkup, the pediatrician had suggested that Sadie supplement with formula. Michaela had lost weight and had jaundice. Within days, it became obvious that her daughter preferred the bottle to Sadie's boob.

"You're right," Sadie said, "but at that point, I was at my wits' end and would have settled for Drew as her caregiver. Not that he volunteered. But I can't complain. She offered to lay me off instead of firing me and gave me some good leads on contract work."

"You don't need contracts. You're as much a part of the success of *Abby Does Highland Falls* as I am, and I have more than enough work for you."

"You're the reason you're a success. You and only you, Abby. I've hardly done any work for you in the past six months. And as much as I love you and appreciate what you're trying to do, I can't take charity."

"Charity? Sweetie, you'd be doing me a favor. You know how busy I am with the channel in the summer. I have a ton of stuff planned. Don't I, Bella Boo?" she said to the eight-pound gold-and-tan Yorkshire terrier that popped out of her purse. Wearing a dress that matched the pink-velvet booth, Bella scampered onto Abby's lap. "We have Summer Solstice, Fourth of July, the Highland Games, and don't get me started on the *Outlander* stuff. The Bel Air Babes are driving me crazy. It's like *Abby Does Highland Falls* has become their favorite tool in their Droughtlander survival kit."

The Bel Air Babes, who were huge fans of Diana Gabaldon's *Outlander*, were Abby's friends from her Hollywood days. She used to be a big-deal influencer until she divorced her husband. They were business partners now, with profits from Honeysuckle Farm shampoo going directly into the charity Abby had established in her aunt's name.

"And those are just, you know, what subscribers expect to see," Abby continued as she dug a gourmet doggie treat from her purse and gave it to Bella. "If I'm going to grow...if *we're* going to grow," Abby corrected with a smile, "I have to come up with a couple of fantabulous ideas every season. So what do you think of"—she held up her hands like she was holding a sign—"Falling in Love on Willow Creek?"

Abby had enough sparkle in her green eyes to make Sadie nervous. "Falling in love with what?"

"You, silly. We'll do our own version of *The Bachelorette*. We'll start auditioning—"

"No way. Not happening." Sadie glanced around for a waitress. She could only leave her grandmother alone with Michaela for so long. Not that Sadie didn't trust Agnes; she didn't trust her daughter not to exhaust her grandmother.

"Trust me," Sadie continued. "Even if I wanted a man in my life, which I really, really don't, no one would sign up with me as your bachelorette. I'm a mess, and not a hot one."

She wasn't being completely honest though. Not about being a mess—she definitely was. But she wasn't telling the truth about not wanting a man in her life. Except she didn't want just any man. She wanted one man, and one man only. Michael Knight.

What she wouldn't give for him to magically appear in her life. She'd even prayed, and she hadn't done that in a long time. She'd prayed that, just like he'd walked out of the woods on Valentine's Day and come to her rescue, he'd walk back into her life again. And it had nothing to do with the man being drop-dead gorgeous. He'd made her feel like she could conquer the world on her own but that she wasn't alone. He'd been there for her to lean on.

She thought about him constantly. When she paced the floors at night, trying to calm her daughter or get her to sleep, she'd talk to him, in her head and sometimes out loud. She had no way of contacting him, him or Eddie. Michael didn't know she'd named her daughter after him, a man she'd fallen in love with.

She didn't believe in love at first sight. Honestly, she hadn't thought she was capable of falling in love with a man. Sure, she'd had relationships with men, plenty of them. But they were short-term relationships, like one month short, and she'd never been invested enough to care when they ended.

Her relationship with Drew had lasted the longest, and the only reason it had was because she got pregnant. She'd been ecstatic, completely over the moon at the news, and she'd made the mistake of conflating her happiness about the baby with her happiness with the baby's daddy. Looking back, she'd never been happy with Drew. He must have felt the same since he'd upped and walked away without a word or explanation. Which didn't bother her. But it did bother her that he didn't care enough about his daughter to stick around.

She glanced at Abby, who was looking at her as though seeing her for the first time. "You're not a mess. You're ... We'll schedule it for July." She chewed on her bottom lip. "Maybe August. You won't look so pale and ... drawn then. You'll be all glowy with a nice tan, and your hair will be even more gorgeous than it is now with all those fantastic highlights."

Sadie glanced at the hank of long, dull chestnut locks falling limply over her shoulder. "I have a mirror, Abs. I know what I look like." And she didn't care. She didn't care about a lot these days.

"You're just tired, sweetie. And I'm not trying to body-shame you or anything, but you've lost your baby weight and then some. You need to stop dieting."

She looked down at herself. "I'm not dieting. The weight's just kind of melting off me." Half the time she was too tired to eat, let alone cook.

"No wonder you look like death warmed over. You need to eat." Abby waved over the waitress, who happened to be Brooklyn. She looked like Brunette Barbie with her frosted-pink lipstick, pink ruffled dress, and hot pink stilettos.

With a smile pasted on her face, Abby said through clenched teeth, "I also have to do *another* segment on Spill the Tea because Babs took over the first one and spilled the beans about Brooklyn's breakup, which, by the way, was messier than mine and yours, so now my subscribers want her back on."

"What does…Oh, hi, Brooklyn," Sadie said, surprised she'd made it to their table that quickly in those heels. "How are you?"

"I'm fine, but what about you, darlin'? You must be absolutely terrified."

"I was a little terrified at the beginning. I think most new moms are, but we're starting to get the hang of it." A derisive snort almost popped out of her mouth. Like heck she was getting the hang of it.

Brooklyn frowned and glanced at Abby, raising a questioning brow.

"I don't think she knows," Abby said to Brooklyn, reaching for Sadie's hands like she had when she'd first sat down. "Sweetie, this is why I asked you if you were okay earlier. They—" She looked around and leaned closer, lowering her voice. "They found a body in the woods near your cottage last night. Didn't you hear the sirens or see the police?"

"Uh, no? Should I have?" She tried to think back but the night was a blur. Everything seemed like a blur since she'd had Michaela, and it had only gotten worse when she'd moved into the cottage three days ago. She'd yet to unpack ninety-nine percent of the moving boxes.

From Brooklyn and Abby's expressions, they expected her to have heard something. "I have blackout drapes on all the windows, and I keep them shut." The last thing she wanted after managing to get Michaela to sleep was for light or sound to wake her up. "Was it a hiker? Did they fall?"

"No, it was a deputy from the Jackson County Sheriff's Department," Abby said.

"He was murdered. Execution-style," Brooklyn stage-whispered.

Sadie glanced around. Everyone was looking at her while at the same time pretending that they weren't. "They don't think I did it, do they?" she asked Abby.

At least Sadie knew why everyone at Spill the Tea had been staring at her when she walked in. Surprisingly, she was relieved that they hadn't been staring at her because they thought she was a bad mother but because they thought she'd killed someone.

Chase took a seat at the table with Agent Black and Highland Falls' chief of police, Gabriel Buchanan. To ensure they weren't seen together, Buchanan had suggested they meet at his father-in-law's place. Located halfway up the mountain, the log house was miles from anyone. Chase wasn't comfortable bringing someone else in, but he'd acquiesced to the chief's request.

"Thanks for letting us use your home to meet, Mr. Carlisle. I'm sure the chief has impressed upon you the need for your utmost discretion in this matter," Chase said.

The older man turned with a coffeepot in hand. Tall with a rangy build, he had a full head of dark hair just starting to silver at the temples. He looked younger than his sixty-two years.

"Call me Boyd, and yes, he has. I've got things to do out in the shed if you'd prefer me to get gone," he offered, filling Black's mug with the aromatic dark brew.

Chase's partner hadn't said much since they'd arrived. He looked different now than he had three months ago, his dark hair cut military short, his strong jaw no longer covered in a long, bushy beard.

"Sorry for your loss, son," Boyd said to Black as he moved to fill Chase's mug.

Brodie's body had been found in the woods near the Grays' cottage on Willow Creek. Neither he nor Black had discussed the coincidence of Sadie moving into the cottage just two days before the discovery. They would though. They had to lay out everything for Buchanan. The body was found in his jurisdiction. If they were working a case undercover in his backyard, they'd need him to sign on.

"I'd like you to stay, Boyd," Chief Buchanan said. Then he added, for Chase and Black's benefit, "My father-in-law knows the area and the players. I think his expertise could be beneficial to your case."

"What Gabe is too polite to say is I used to have an illegal still." Boyd patted his son-in-law's shoulder. "I had customers from Jackson County. Once in a while, I ran moonshine out Whiteside Mountain way. I had a couple run-ins with the boys you're looking at. Gotta say, I'm surprised they'd be involved in something like this. They might have new players though."

The chief sat back in his chair and raised an eyebrow at Chase. "He hasn't sold shine in more than a year."

"I never said anything," Chase protested.

"You didn't have to," Black said. He turned to Chief Buchanan. "He can't help himself. He's by the book and doesn't play well with others. He likes to do things on his own. Sort of like the Lone Ranger."

"As I understand it, that's mostly worked out for him," Buchanan said. He raised his mug, moving it between Chase and Black with a grin. "You two as partners? I'm having a harder time seeing."

"You looked into us." Chase didn't like it, but he would have done the same in Chief Buchanan's position.

"Yeah, but don't worry. I know how to do it without raising

suspicions." He glanced at his cell phone vibrating on the table. "Sorry, I have to take this. Hey, Teddy, what's up?" The chief's mouth twitched. "Is that right? Well, you tell your brothers you won the bet fair and square so they have to do what you say. Within reason, buddy. Put Mom on the phone. Hey, honey, everything okay there? A spa?" He laughed. "I'm sure it did. Tell the boys I'll make it up to them later. I shouldn't be long."

Something tugged inside Chase's chest at the way Buchanan's face softened when he spoke to his wife. Love and family, the man had it all. Instead of examining why the thought caused a twinge in his chest, Chase went over what he'd found out about the chief. Buchanan wasn't the only one who'd run a background check.

The former New York City homicide detective had married Boyd's daughter last month, not long after they'd met. They were a blended family. Three boys from his previous marriage and two from hers. They had a baby due in the fall, the reason for fast-tracking the wedding, Chase supposed.

Buchanan listened to his wife and nodded, his gaze moving from Chase to Black. "Yeah, I'll stop by and check on her. You know I can't discuss an ongoing investigation. Yes, I know that too." He sighed. "Honey, don't call Eden. Sadie doesn't need a lawyer."

Chase shared a glance with Black. They may not have had the opportunity to discuss the possibility of Sadie's involvement in Brodie's death, but they both knew, no matter the experience the three of them had shared, they had to look into her—Chase because that's who he was, and Black because nothing, not even the bond that had developed between Chase, Nate, and Sadie that day back in February, would stand in the way of him finding out who'd murdered Brodie.

Buchanan caught their silent exchange and sighed. "I've got to go, honey. Take care of my girls." He disconnected. "You can't seriously be looking at Sadie Gray for this."

"We can't not," Chase said. "You have to bring her in for questioning. For her sake as much as for the sake of the case."

"Easy for you to say. She's one of my wife's closest friends."

"Is that why she hasn't been questioned?" Given the proximity of the body to the cottage, Chase had found it odd that no one had talked to her yet. At the very least, she should have been asked what she'd seen and heard.

"No. She's going through a tough time. She had a baby..." He trailed off. He must have read something on their faces. Probably Black's—the man didn't hide his emotions as well as Chase. Maybe because he had more emotions than Chase. "You've got to be kidding me. It was the two of you who helped deliver her baby, wasn't it?"

Lowering his gaze to his mug, Chase nodded. "Yeah."

Then they'd walked away and left her alone. It had been one of the hardest things he'd ever done, but he hadn't had a choice. They couldn't risk being seen, and, as Black had warned Chase on the way back to his jeep that night, they couldn't risk Sadie discovering who they were. At least not until they'd closed the case.

"And she doesn't have a clue who you are." It wasn't a question. Buchanan scrubbed his face. "And you don't want her to. So how do you want to play this?"

Black gave the chief a brief rundown of their suspicions about the sheriff and Elijah's involvement. "Chase and I've been working other cases while we were working this one. But now...now that Brodie's been found, we, ah..." Black's voice cracked with emotion, and he bowed his head.

Chase glanced from his partner back to his coffee mug. He knew he should do something but he'd never handled emotional situations well. His grandfather hadn't been an emotional or demonstrative man either.

"We've both taken personal time." Chase's boss had granted

his request with no questions asked, which had been somewhat surprising. Then again, he'd probably been glad to get rid of him. Chase had cleared all his cases and had been in the process of reviewing his fellow agents' ongoing investigations. "We're here until this is done. Elijah Gray is the key. With the body left so close to the cottage on Willow Creek, it could be a message from Elijah or to him. Staying close to the family is our best chance of finding him." Chase ignored the uptick in his pulse at the thought of being close to Sadie again.

He hadn't been able to get her off his mind. All he did was think about her and the baby. Wondering how they were, wondering if Sadie thought about him as much as he thought about her. Wondering if he'd done the right thing by ensuring Drew was gone from her life for good. Black would have done the same. Only Chase doubted he would have gone by the book.

"It'll be tough for you to stay close to them without raising suspicion. It's a small town. Everyone pretty much knows everyone else's business." He glanced at his father-in-law. "Any suggestions?"

"What about one of them going undercover as a park ranger? Jensen's set to retire at the end of the week. One of them could replace him. Easy to keep an eye out for Elijah while at the same time protecting Sadie and her baby."

The chief nodded. "I can set that up easily enough. No one other than Boyd and I will know," he assured Chase. "And I think I have a way to get one of you in undercover at I Believe in Unicorns. We have a program to help ex-offenders reintegrate into society. Some of the businesses in town have signed up. I Believe in Unicorns is one of them." Buchanan grinned. "So, which one of you is going to sell stuffed unicorns and which one of you is going to track black bears?"

Chapter Six

♥

Sadie held her breath as she inched the yellow cottage door closed behind her, grimacing at what sounded to her like an overly loud click. A quick glance at her daughter revealed she remained asleep in her carrier. *One hurdle down, about twenty-five to go*, Sadie thought as she headed for her SUV parked on the gravel driveway.

Gently swinging the carrier, she looked across the dirt road to the woods beyond the meadow. It was a beautiful, warm spring morning under a bright, cloudless blue sky, the sweet scent of clover and the low buzz of bees filling the air. The idyllic scene made it easy to forget that just a week ago a body had been found in the woods. At the reminder, she turned and walked back up the stone path that meandered through what had once been a wildflower garden to the front door.

Gabe had stopped by earlier in the week to check on her. He'd reminded her to keep her door locked at all times. He'd questioned her too. Nothing that made her feel like she was a suspect, just that she may have witnessed something that would help their investigation into that poor man's murder.

She was a little more honest with Gabe than she had been with

Abby and Brooklyn about why she hadn't seen or heard a single thing the night the man died. Not only because Gabe was chief of police but also because he'd raised three boys on his own when he'd lost his first wife, so he would understand the soul-crushing exhaustion that came with being a single parent.

What he didn't seem to understand was why she had reservations about Project HOPE (Helping Offenders Pursue Excellence)—or, more to the point, using her grandmother's store to kick off the program in Highland Falls. It wasn't that Sadie was against an ex-offender getting a second chance, it was just that she'd prefer a business other than her grandmother's provide it. Knowing Gabe had personally vetted the ex-offender didn't make her feel any better. It should, but it didn't. Her grandmother was too trusting for her own good. Case in point: Agnes's inability to see past her own grandson's boyish charm to his larcenous ways.

But apparently, Gabe had disregarded Sadie's concerns, because Agnes had informed her that she had a new employee starting today. An employee who'd come highly recommended by none other than the chief of police. Of course her grandmother didn't add that her highly recommended new employee's most recent occupation had most likely been working in the prison library.

It showed just how concerned Sadie was that she risked Michaela waking up from a nap. *Cat nap* was a more apt name for what her daughter did, but those moments were more precious than gold and diamonds. Within that brief window of peace and quiet, Sadie was able to grab a shower and savor a mouthful of coffee. She measured her days in increments of twenty-minute naps, forty-five if she'd been especially blessed.

They were currently at the fifteen-minute mark. She glanced at her sleeping child, surprised as always at how utterly angelic Michaela looked while sleeping. Her mouth was a perfect rosebud, her cheeks sweetly rounded and pink, her soft curls as shiny and bright as a new copper penny.

Saying a silent prayer that Michaela's pretty blue eyes remained closed for at least another twenty minutes, Sadie inserted the key into the cottage's yellow door and slowly turned it, in hopes of avoiding the loud *thunk* of the tumblers locking into place.

Success. She smiled. Door successfully locked, and baby still asleep. It didn't take much to make her happy these days. Although what she was feeling right now probably didn't reach the level of happiness. *Mildly relieved* might be a more accurate description.

As she turned to walk to her car, a blast of gunfire rang out from the woods. Sadie gasped, dropping to a crouch. She curled over the carrier to protect Michaela. Black birds shot up from the tops of the trees, squawking their displeasure. Her daughter did the same.

"It's okay, baby. Mommy's here." Rocking the carrier, she nuzzled Michaela's soft cheek. Her soothing words and kisses did little to comfort her daughter. Over Michaela's ear-piercing shrieks, Sadie listened for a return of gunfire.

Pretty sure that she hadn't heard any, she cautiously lifted her head to search the tree line. A tall, broad-shouldered man in a ball cap ran backward from the woods. At the familiar sight of his sage-green park ranger uniform, she relaxed. He had a gun in his hand and didn't appear injured.

When the park ranger took off his hat and dragged a hand through his dark blond hair instead of removing the radio off his belt or giving chase, Sadie slowly inched up.

"Hello!" she yelled to make herself heard over her daughter's angry cries. The ranger straightened but didn't respond or turn her way. She came to her feet, thinking her voice wasn't projecting from that close to the ground. Maybe she should be more specific too. After all, she could be calling *hello* to anyone.

"Excuse me, sir? Mr. Park Ranger! Over here."

He slowly turned.

Her heart skipped a beat when his face came into view. She raised a hand to shield her eyes, afraid the sun was messing with her vision, fooling her into believing the man of her dreams was slowly walking across the meadow toward her.

"Michael." His name came out on a sob. It was him. It was really him. "Michael," she cried again, louder this time.

He raised a hand, a half smile on his gorgeous face.

She grabbed the carrier's handle and raced across the road with her crying child. She didn't stop running until she reached him.

"It's you. It's really you," she whispered, reaching out to touch his face. It wasn't enough. She needed more. She needed him, and she hadn't realized how much until this very moment. "You left us!" she cried, throwing an arm around his neck.

Burying her face against his chest, she breathed him in. He smelled as incredible as she remembered—like warm amber and worn leather. She bit her lip, determined not to cry, but inside she wailed as loudly as her daughter. All her fears, the panic and insecurities that had been building inside her over the past three months, were seconds from pouring out of her. It was like she'd been walking on a tightrope across a gorge without a safety net, and now Michael was here to provide one.

He put his arm around her, his bicep flexing against her back. His chest was hard and muscled, his shirt warm and soft. "I'm sorry," he said, his low voice rumbling against her cheek. "I, uh, thought I'd be in the way."

He sounded uncomfortable, and why wouldn't he be? He had an emotional woman he barely knew clinging to him as if he were the answer to her prayers. It didn't matter that he kind of was. Michael Knight had no idea that, in her mind, he'd become her knight in shining armor. It didn't matter that Eddie had been the one who'd actually delivered her daughter. Michael had won hero status and her undying gratitude the moment he'd attempted to re-create the spa-like atmosphere she'd dreamed of for her baby's birth. And all the intimate moments during and after Michaela's arrival. Sadie's memories of that night were encased in a warm bubble of love and joy, in stark contrast to the reality of her past three months.

The weight of the carrier no longer pulled on her arm, and she panicked, thinking that, in her happiness at seeing Michael, at being held by him, she'd completely forgotten about the baby and...dropped her. But no, as she glanced down, she saw that Michael had taken the carrier from her and was gazing at her daughter with the same look of wonder she'd seen on his face the night she was born. That look right there, she thought, had been what had won her heart.

She reluctantly stepped back but couldn't stop herself from keeping a hand on his chest. The steady beat of his heart beneath her fingers reassured her. This was real, not a figment of her imagination. He was here. She hadn't completely lost her mind.

He stepped back, lifting the carrier so that her screaming child was eye level with him, dislodging Sadie's hand from his chest in the process. She was tempted to cling to his shirt with the tips of her fingers but had enough self-respect left to let go.

"She's beautiful," he said in an awestruck voice, looking at Sadie with a tender smile that had absolutely nothing to do with her. He turned back to her daughter. "There now, don't cry, sweetheart. That's right. There's a good girl," he said, his voice so soothing even Sadie felt comforted.

She stared at her daughter, no doubt with a *what the heck?* expression on her face. Michaela had stopped screaming. She was utterly and completely silent, staring at the man who smiled at her like she was some miraculous little being. Michaela appeared mesmerized by his stunning good looks. Like mother, like daughter.

Michaela's mouth trembled, and Sadie prepared herself for an eardrum-shattering scream. She was about to warn Michael to do the same, and then the inconceivable happened. Her daughter...smiled.

Michael's smile grew, and so did Michaela's. She looked like the sun had come out to shine down on her and her alone, a big, bright, gurgling smile on her face. Michael laughed, a delighted laugh, and her daughter did the same. The more he laughed, the more Michaela did, until her daughter was laughing so hard that she was hiccupping.

And right there, in the middle of the meadow on a picture-perfect spring day with the man she'd fancied herself in love with and her daughter who'd never smiled or laughed at her, Sadie broke down and cried.

Michael and Michaela stopped laughing to stare at her.

Sadie raised a hand. "Don't mind me," she mumbled through a mortified sob. "It's just hormones. They're all over the place." Which she proved seconds later when her sobs turned into guffaws of laughter at her daughter's and Michael's wide-eyed expressions. They were looking at her like she'd lost her mind. "Sorry." She waved her hands in front of her face.

This time Michael's tender smile was for her. "Don't. I should be the one apologizing." He took her hand. "The gunshot must have terrified both of you."

"Right, the gunshot," she said, with only a slight gurgle of laughter left in her voice. "What happened?"

"Snake. A really big snake," he said, looking around the tall grass. He shuddered, his tender smile turning tense. "We should probably get out of here."

"You shot a snake?"

"Mm-hmm." He nodded. "Don't worry. It didn't suffer. I shot it right between the eyes."

"You shot a snake right between the eyes?"

"Yes. I'm an excellent shot." He frowned. "You seem surprised."

"Well, it's just that your job is to protect wildlife, isn't it?"

"Right, of course. Oh, I see what you're getting at. But my job is also to protect humans. I think the snake had...rabies."

"Snakes don't get rabies," she said as they reached the road. She'd grown up in these woods and had more than a passing knowledge about the wildlife that inhabited them.

"Right. Of course, I know that. Seeing you and the baby flustered me, I guess. I wasn't thinking straight. I meant to say poisonous. The snake was poisonous."

"Well, yes, we have six types of venomous snakes in the area, but they're pro—"

He shot a horrified glance at the woods. "Six?"

"Michael, don't be offended, but exactly how long have you been a park ranger?"

He lifted the carrier he'd been lightly swinging at his side to glance at his watch. "An hour and forty-five minutes and five seconds."

"I suppose that explains it, but don't you have to have some sort of training?"

"A valid driver's license and a bachelor's degree in natural sciences," he said as they reached her driveway.

"And you have a bachelor's degree in natural sciences?"

"No." He took a deep breath, looking like he was weighing whether or not to tell her something. "You have to promise you won't tell anyone what I'm about to share with you."

"I promise. I won't say anything."

"I'm assistant to the director of the Fish and Wildlife Service in Washington, DC. I'm on assignment. An undercover assignment. I can't tell you what it is, but it's important."

"And you've never had an up-close encounter with a snake before, have you?"

"Other than the snakes at my office? No."

"So was that why you were in the woods on Valentine's Day?"

"Yes. I'd come on a scouting expedition." He glanced at her while setting the carrier on the hood of the SUV. "Do you mind if I take her out for a minute?"

"No, not at all." She went to help him but he'd already figured out the finicky mechanism and was lifting her daughter into his arms.

"Look at you," he said, cradling Michaela against his chest. "You're so big now." He smiled at Sadie. "She really is beautiful."

"Now she is, and when she's sleeping, which isn't a lot." Sadie leaned against the SUV beside Michael and stroked Michaela's chubby leg. "That's the first time I've seen her smile or laugh. She cries all the time, Michael. She hates me."

He put his arm around her, tucking her against his side. "She doesn't hate you. No one could hate you, Sadie Gray." He kissed the top of her head and then frowned as if surprised at himself for doing so before continuing. "I'm sorry I left without saying goodbye. I was late for my flight back to DC."

"You could have left me a note, a number." She squeezed her eyes shut at the plaintive tone in her voice. "Sorry. I don't mean to sound needy. It's just that you were with me on one of the scariest, most incredible nights of my life." She lifted a shoulder instead of telling him how much that had meant to her, how much he meant to her.

"It meant something to me too, Sadie." He opened his mouth and then closed it, a moment passing before he smiled at her and said, "It's a night I won't forget. And you don't sound needy, you sound exhausted. How much sleep did you get last night?"

"Same as always. A couple of hours here and there. I think she has her nights and days mixed up. Not that she sleeps much in the..." She trailed off, looking at her daughter, who'd fallen asleep with her hand curled around Michael's finger, a drooly smile on her face.

Sadie sighed. "Her name's Michaela," she said, as if that explained everything.

"You named her after me?" He looked stunned and, if she wasn't mistaken, a little sad.

Of course he felt sorry for her. She was pathetic. She'd named her daughter after a man she barely knew, a man she wanted to wrap her arms around and never let go.

Chapter Seven

♥

Chase looked from Sadie to her daughter. Knowing she'd named her after him made him feel even closer to the pretty copper-haired baby sleeping peacefully in his arms.

Closer to her mother too, he thought, returning his gaze to Sadie.

She made an embarrassed face. "I was going to name her Isabelle. Then I thought she looked like a Michaela. Okay, so she looked more like E.T. than a Michaela when she was born." She sighed. "Fine, I named her after you. You were amazing and, for one minute—just one quick minute so don't freak out or anything—I wished you were her daddy. You were considerate and kind, and I wanted that so badly for her. For her to have a good, honest man in her life. I had second thoughts after you abandoned us but then I looked up the meaning of Michael. It comes from the angel Michael. When I first found out I was pregnant, that's exactly how I felt. Like she was a gift from heaven. Lately, I've begun to wonder if she's a gift from Satan instead."

The idea of Sadie wishing he was Michaela's daddy didn't freak him out at all. Instead it filled him with a longing that surprised him, and that freaked him out. Just a little. But more troubling was Sadie's perception of him as a good, honest man.

He had a difficult time working up an amused smile knowing how she'd feel about him when she learned the truth. "No way. Look at her. She's an angel."

"You do know that Satan was an angel before he got kicked out of heaven, right?"

The smile that curved his lips now grew with genuine amusement. "You don't have to be embarrassed you named her after me, Sadie. I'm touched."

"Really?"

"Honestly. I'm honored." So much so that, when all this was over, he'd go by Michael instead of Chase if she wanted him to. Except it was unlikely she'd want anything to do with him once this was wrapped up.

And thinking of why he was really there, he had no choice but to take advantage of the opportunity to see just how much Sadie knew. The sooner they found and brought in her brother, the better. Chase didn't relish the idea of spending any more time in the woods than he had to. As both he and Sadie had discovered, he made a lousy park ranger. He shuddered at the memory of the snake he'd shot. He supposed he should feel bad, but the thing had been terrifyingly huge.

He glanced at Sadie as she fixed the baby's bootie. She seemed to know more about the wildlife around Highland Falls than he did, which wasn't hard, but still, maybe they could work something out that benefited them both.

He took in her shadowed eyes and pale face; she was exhausted. Still beautiful though. He pushed the inappropriate thought aside. He was investigating a corrupt sheriff's department and the murder of a deputy, Black's friend. He had to keep his head in the game and not on Sadie or her daughter.

It didn't mean he couldn't use the situation to both their

advantages though. "You know, I'll probably be here for a few weeks and wouldn't mind picking your brain about life in the wilds of Highland Falls. In exchange, I could help out with my namesake." He tried to gauge Sadie's reaction. "You could catch up on some sleep while I watch her."

"Sleep." She sounded like he'd offered her the moon and the stars. Then she rewarded him with a grateful smile that made him feel like she'd given him the moon and the stars. And for the first time in his career, he thought he might be in over his head. As a man who put his job above all else, that was a thought that gave him pause.

"You have no idea how much I want to take advantage of your offer," she said, "but it wouldn't be fair. This is just some weird anomaly. You have no idea what she's really like."

Apparently, Sadie's happiness trumped his worry about his feelings for her. "You can take advantage of me anytime. How about now?"

She laughed. "Okay, don't say I didn't warn you. But while I'd love nothing more than to crawl into bed and pull the covers over my head for an hour while you look after my demon child, I have to rescue my grandmother."

Chase frowned. Buchanan had said everything was a go for Black at I Believe in Unicorns. Then again, Chase's partner hadn't met Agnes MacLeod yet. Chase hoped Black hadn't managed to mess things up. They needed to keep the grandmother and her store covered as much as they did Sadie and the cottage.

"Nothing serious, I hope," he said.

"Oh, it's serious, all right. Gabe—he's the chief of police— pulled a fast one on me. Don't get me wrong, he's a great guy. He's also an amazing husband and father, and I know this because he's married to one of my closest friends. So I really do trust that he has the best interests of the community and my grandmother at heart, and the idea of giving ex-offenders a second chance is not only admirable but necessary. He just needs to find another local business to launch his pilot project."

Obviously, Sadie wasn't on board with Project HOPE. Something Gabe had kept to himself. "How does your grandmother feel about it?"

"She's seventy-six and gullible, Michael. I don't care how she feels about it. It's not happening."

Michaela startled at her mother's raised voice, her eyes popping open, her mouth puckering as if to cry. Michael made soft crooning sounds and rocked her, feeling relieved when she stuck her thumb in her mouth and closed her eyes. He needed to get Sadie on board with Project HOPE.

She looked from the baby to him. "How did you do that? I've never been able to get her back to sleep once she wakes up. And I mean never."

There was a touch of hurt, and maybe a little resentment, in her voice. The last thing he needed right now was Sadie ticked at him. It wouldn't help the case he had to make for Project HOPE. "It's not me, it's her." He nodded at her thumb in her mouth.

Sadie tilted her head. "You're right. She's never sucked her thumb before. Wow. Maybe things are finally turning around." She gave him another heart-stopping smile.

Which meant his answer came out a little delayed. He hoped she didn't notice. "I'm sure they are. Now, about your grandmother. Maybe having someone helping out at the store is a good thing. Saves you from going in, right?"

"I don't know. Lately I've been feeling like she's keeping something from me. I need to spend more time there, but it's been hard with Michaela. Her crying jags are not exactly conducive to a pleasant shopping experience."

She'd just handed him the perfect opportunity to find out what she knew about her brother. "What about other family members?

Do you have any brothers or sisters who can help out and keep an eye on things?"

"I have a brother. Elijah. But as far as him helping out, that would be a big fat no." She sighed. "Out of any family in town, I guess ours should be leading the effort to give ex-offenders a second chance, seeing as my brother will no doubt end up one."

"Your brother's in trouble with the law?" He worked to keep the smile of relief from his face. Whatever Elijah Gray was involved in, given her response, Sadie wasn't. Chase would stake his career on it.

She pulled a face. "Sorry. The last thing I want is to air out my family's dirty laundry, but you'll hear about it anyway so you might as well hear it from me." She crossed her arms and looked toward a weeping willow tree, its branches swaying and dipping into the fast-moving creek. "Elijah's been in and out of trouble with the law since he was a teenager. Petty crimes, nothing really serious: stealing a bike, letting someone's cattle out, vandalizing the town's water tower. The problem is, other than the chief of police talking to him, there were no consequences. My grandmother made sure there weren't."

"Is that why you said your grandmother's gullible? Your brother was able to convince her to intervene?"

"No, not back then. She just felt sorry for him. He'd started acting out when my parents died."

"I'm sorry about your parents."

She gave him a half smile. "Thanks. It was a long time ago, and they hadn't lived with us for a while anyhow. My grandmother basically raised us."

He knew why Agnes MacLeod had stepped in to raise her grandchildren but it wasn't something he could bring up without arousing Sadie's suspicions. Maybe a week from now—when it was plausible he would have heard the gossip around town— he'd bring up the infamous Jeremiah Gray, world-class hacker, who'd gone to prison for hacking into US retailers and stealing upwards of a hundred and eighty million dollars.

"So I'm guessing, from what you said, that your brother isn't exactly on the straight and narrow."

"Understatement." She toed the stones on the driveway, eyes lifting to a large bird soaring overhead. She smiled. "Beautiful, isn't it? It's a hawk, in case you're wondering."

"And the thing dangling from his mouth I'm assuming is a mouse."

"Good job. You don't miss much, do you?"

"No, I don't." He nudged her foot with his. "It bothers you about your brother turning to a life of crime, doesn't it?"

She nodded. "I feel like I failed him somehow. He's my baby brother. I felt—feel—responsible for him. Honestly, I blame my grandmother for being too lenient and constantly making excuses for him, but I'm no better. I've spent the past ten years bailing him out of his get-rich-quick schemes. Last summer, I nearly went to jail because of him. He's no longer involved in petty crimes. He's graduated to the big leagues, and I want nothing to do with him. As far as I'm concerned, he's dead to me." She grimaced. "Sorry, I didn't mean to go off like that. It's just..."

"Just what?" he asked when she trailed off.

"The feeling I was mentioning to you. That something was going on with my grandmother. I think that something is my brother. She knows how I feel about him, so if he's come sniffing around for money again, she won't tell me. Sorry, I don't know what's gotten into me. You're easy to talk to, I guess. Thanks for listening. I'd better get going and see what Agnes is up to."

"Don't apologize. You can talk to me about your brother anytime. I understand more than you know, Sadie. My brother got mixed up with the wrong crowd. He ruined not only his own life but several others'." It wasn't true. Although if you asked his grandfather, he'd say it was. Chase's brother was a venture capitalist.

"So you probably think I'm terrible, not being more supportive of Project HOPE."

"I wouldn't say that. But maybe you should give it a shot. Let things play out and see how it goes. You never know, this guy might be able to give you some insight into Elijah that will be helpful."

"If he can convince Granny not to send money whenever my brother asks, I'll give him a raise. Then again, I might be worrying over nothing. Maybe my grandmother isn't sending Elijah money like I suspect, and Gabe's protégé will take one look around the store and head for the door."

She picked up the baby's carrier and moved to the back passenger-side door, glancing at him as she opened it. "Doesn't it seem strange to you that a man would want to work at I Believe in Unicorns? I know I'm being sexist, but it's beyond me why he'd choose my grandmother's store over Highland Brew or the hardware store. I know for a fact they've both signed up for the program."

She was right. It did seem odd. They should have thought about that. They couldn't risk her getting suspicious. "He's probably gay."

He smiled, thinking of how Black would react to the news.

"I'm definitely a unicorn in this here town." The dark-haired man offered Sadie a winning grin as he pointed to the unicorn stretched across the triple-XL pink sweatshirt he wore. Thankfully the sweatshirt said *I'm a unicorn* and not *I'm horny*, otherwise the three seventy-something female customers eyeing him hungrily from the children's furniture section might have rushed him.

The man was charming and very good-looking. From her

grandmother's preening smile when she introduced them, Nate had won her over in the short time he'd been there: two hours, according to Sadie's cell phone. Good luck trying to get rid of him now.

It was her own fault, she thought, swinging the carrier to avoid another crying jag. Michaela had started wailing the moment she'd strapped her into her carrier in the backseat. She hadn't stopped until Sadie pulled into the parking spot beside the store five minutes ago, when she promptly fell into an exhausted sleep.

That would teach Sadie to think her luck was changing. It was Michael. He'd imprinted himself on Michaela the night she was born. He'd bonded with her before Sadie had, and somehow her daughter remembered him. Maybe it was his low, sexy voice or his pheromone-inducing cologne.

No, that would be what she remembered, not her three-month-old daughter.

"Isn't she a little beauty," the man said, looking down at Michaela, who was snuffling in her sleep.

Sadie frowned. There was something familiar about Nate's voice. She couldn't quite put her finger on who, but he reminded her of someone.

Before she could ask whether they'd met before, her grandmother beamed up at him with a speculative gleam in her eye. "My granddaughter's single, you know."

Sadie should have known that's where she'd go. Granny was as bad as Abby. God help her if her grandmother found out about Abby's bachelorette idea.

"You can't kid a kidder, Granny," Nate said. "No way someone hasn't snapped up this stunning woman."

"You can save your charm for the customers, Nate. I'm immune," Sadie said, heading toward the office.

He followed her. "You're not my type, if you know what

I mean. I prefer tall, dark, and handsome to long, lean, and gorgeous."

So Michael was right. That made her feel a little better at least. She would have been more concerned that Nate had an ulterior motive for choosing a unicorn store run by a gullible old lady if he were straight.

"Good to know. Now let's get your paperwork filled out, and you can tell me a bit about yourself." She glanced back and caught his grimace, which she would have commented on if she hadn't spotted Mr. Teller, the bank manager, walking into the store with a grim expression on his face.

Sometimes it sucked to be right. She'd known her grandmother was up to something, and she was sure that something had to do with Elijah. Even more so when her grandmother looped her arm through Mr. Teller's and yelled over her shoulder, "I'll leave you two to mind the store. Fred and I are going to Spill the Tea."

"Oh no, you're not. Don't take another step toward that door, Granny. You either, Mr. Teller." She handed the carrier handle to Nate. "Keep swinging if you value your hearing."

Chapter Eight

♥

Chase leaned against the blue industrial garbage bin in the alley behind I Believe in Unicorns. Black had called for the meet. Chase had a story worked out in case Sadie took them by surprise—there was a moose loose on the streets of Highland Falls.

As Chase had discovered, large wild animals wandering down Main Street wasn't out of the realm of possibility. It had happened as recently as last month, according to the *Highland Falls Herald*. After embarrassing himself with Sadie, Chase had spent the past three hours learning everything he could about wildlife in the area while surveilling the cottage. Though he planned to keep some of his newfound knowledge to himself. He needed a believable excuse to hang out with Sadie.

Black exited I Believe in Unicorns as if he'd seen the cousin of the snake Chase had shot in the woods. The sound of Michaela crying in the store abruptly cut off when the back door swung closed behind his partner as he made his way into the alley. Black slumped against the garbage bin Chase stood half-hidden behind.

"How can something that little be so loud? And cranky? Sadie's right, the kid's possessed." As he tapped a cigarette from a pack into his massive palm, Black scowled at Chase. "What are you smirking at?"

"Pink suits you."

"Har har." He stuck the cigarette between his teeth and pulled out his sweatshirt to look down at the unicorn. "Gotta admit though, going gay was a good call. Although it doesn't seem to deter the old ladies."

"Sadie's grandmother made a move on you?"

"No, three of her friends did. Agnes is too busy trying to set me up with Sadie. Unlike Sadie's friend Abby, who has a guy in mind for me, and several in mind for Sadie, who she's trying to convince to do a version of *The Bachelorette* on her YouTube channel." He rubbed his ear as though he'd lost his hearing. "I think Abby might be a problem."

"Yeah, so do I. Sadie doesn't need a man. She needs to sleep."

Black cocked his head. "Interesting that you would go there, but that's not the problem I was referring to. Abby wants to use me to promote Project HOPE on her YouTube channel. I can't risk her blowing my cover."

"We could have her channel shut down for a couple weeks, but I don't like the idea of impacting her income."

"Yeah, it sounds like she does a lot of good promoting the community. Local businesses might suffer."

"We'll talk to Gabe. See if he has any suggestions on how to get her to back off."

"If Sadie agreed to do the bachelorette thing for her, it's a good bet Abby would—"

Chase's pulse kicked up. He had to cut this off now and in such a way that Black wouldn't question his motives. He was doing that enough for the both of them. "As much as I agree Abby poses a threat, that wasn't why you called. You said you needed my help to distract Sadie so you could get a look at the computer. What's going on?"

"Between Satan's spawn screaming the store down and—"

"Don't call her that," Chase said, defensive on the baby's behalf. "Her name's Michaela."

"Don't look so smug. It's not like Sadie could name her after me-slash-Eddie, the *real* hero of the day. No one names—"

"We have more important things to discuss than Sadie choosing to name her baby after me and not you. Were you able to follow up on whether Agnes is funneling money through the store to Elijah?" The moment Sadie pulled out of her driveway, Chase had called to share his suspicion and to inform Black that he had to pretend he was gay.

"I don't have any hard evidence yet, but Sadie seems to think so. At least I'm pretty sure she said his name when she was ushering Agnes and the bank manager into the office for a chat. It was a little hard to hear through the closed office door and over the demon...baby crying while also helping out customers. It was quite the shitshow. Literally. I had to change her diaper, and that's on you." Black's dark eyes narrowed. "Don't think I haven't figured out that you played me. The only reason I'm not patrolling the woods and communing with nature is because you're a card shark."

As they'd both called dibs on the park ranger job—Chase because he wanted to stay close to Sadie, Black because...he probably wanted to stay close to Sadie too, which ticked Chase off—they'd played a game of blackjack. Chase won, as he knew he would. Counting cards wasn't especially difficult. After watching a short instructional video while pretending to be returning an email outside Boyd's cabin, he'd figured it out.

But if Black thought he got the short end of the straw... "You think it's easy playing park ranger? I'd take Michaela and flirty seventysomething women over what I saw in the woods this morning. I swear, the thing must have been ten feet—"

Black chuckled and blew out a couple smoke rings. "Come on, you out of anybody can't believe Bigfoot actually exists."

"I wasn't talking about...Wait a minute, there've been sightings of Bigfoot in these woods?" He shuddered, catching the gleam of amusement in Black's eyes. No way was Chase going to mention his run-in with the snake now. But he was definitely looking into Bigfoot sightings at some point. He waved his hand. "Of course I don't believe in Bigfoot. I was just having some fun with you."

"Is that right? I'm surprised. You're not what I think of as a fun-loving guy."

"All right, Black. Just tell me where we stand and why you think you'll find the information on the computer. Agnes strikes me as old-school. I don't see her banking online. Not to mention I'm pretty sure I witnessed a cash payoff between her and Elijah's girlfriend back in February."

They'd dug into Payton Howard but there were no red flags, other than minor run-ins with the law as a teenager and the fact that she'd dated Elijah. A few weeks of surveillance hadn't gotten them any closer to finding the guy. It was like he was a ghost.

"I agree. But after the meeting—which went on for over an hour, I might add—Sadie was chomping at the bit to get on the computer but the baby needed to be fed. If you can believe it, she tried to get me to give the kid a bottle but one of Agnes's friends needed a hand with her bags."

"Why wouldn't she get her grandmother to feed Michaela?"

"The meeting didn't go well. Both Sadie and Agnes were upset. At each other, if I'm reading it right. I think the store's in financial trouble. Sadie promised the bank manager she'd have a business plan to him by the end of the week."

"She doesn't need this right now," Chase said, thinking out loud. At the look Black gave him, he decided he should have kept the thought to himself.

"And how exactly would you know that, Roberts? Have you been spending time with Sadie without telling me?"

"I told you, I ran into her this morning. I was going to debrief you tonight. Like we agreed, remember?"

"No, I think it's more than that. You could have told me when you called this morning."

He could have, but he'd been afraid Black might hear something in his voice that would make him wonder about Chase's feelings for Sadie. "After talking to her, I was ninety percent certain we could take her off our suspect list. I wanted to search the cottage before telling you. There were no signs of her brother being there or that she's in touch with him. But aside from her telling me, there were plenty of signs she's struggling. She moved back to Highland Falls ten days ago and hasn't unpacked."

"It's no wonder. The kid never sleeps, from the sound of it."

Chase didn't share how bad it actually was. He also didn't want to share everything Sadie had told him or that she'd cried in his arms. It was private, a special moment he wanted to keep to himself. It had nothing to do with the case.

"But you can't fool a player, Roberts." Black tossed his cigarette, grinding it into the pavement with the toe of his boot. "So here's the deal. Neither of us makes a move on her while we're working the case."

Damn it, he'd been right. Black was interested in Sadie too, and there was nothing Chase could say without giving himself away.

"Honestly, I'm surprised I'd even have to reiterate that with you, Mr. By-the-Book," Black continued. "Come to think of it, I'm surprised you searched Sadie's cottage without a warrant."

"You don't have to reiterate it with me, Black. I'd never jeopardize a case"—or his chance to get back to DC—"by getting involved with a member of the suspect's family." He ignored the weight lying heavy in his stomach. "You, on the other hand..."

"Trust me, I'd never do anything to jeopardize a case, particularly this one. I owe it to Brodie to go by the book."

"I'm glad to hear it, and just so you know, technically, I didn't break into the cottage. The patio door, including the screen door, was open."

"That's not good."

"No, it's not." He glanced at the back door to the store. "Now that I think about it, I can use it as an excuse to get Sadie out of your way. I should be able to stall her at the cottage for at least an hour." Maybe she'd let him unpack some boxes for her. He'd had a hard time not doing so while he was there. "Does that work for you?"

"Yeah, if you can do it. I've been trying to get her to leave for the past hour. That's why I finally caved and called you."

"All right, I'll stick around here for another few minutes before going around to the front of the store. That way it won't look suspicious."

"Good. You know, this partnership might just work out after all, Roberts." Black grinned, offering his hand.

Less than a second after Chase had clasped Black's hand, the agent tightened his grip. Chase knew never to trust that grin again. He firmed his own grip, glad to see the other man wince. Seconds later, Black did the same. And so it continued until Chase finally gave in for the sake of expediency and their cover. "Am I supposed to say uncle?"

Black chuckled and released Chase's hand. "You surprise me, Roberts. I didn't know you had it in you. But I'm glad to know I'll have more than just that big brain of yours backing me up."

Fifteen minutes later, Chase walked into I Believe in Unicorns. Both Black and Sadie turned to him, expressions of relief and gratitude lighting up their faces. He'd stopped by Spill the Tea to pick up something for Sadie, but he had a feeling her relief had nothing to do with the blueberry scones and tea in the tray. Spine arched, arms flailing, Michaela screamed at the top of her lungs in Sadie's arms.

Chase imagined Black's relief didn't only have to do with

Michaela. Abby Everhart looked like she'd been trying to sell his partner on something, or someone. Chase recognized the petite redhead from her YouTube channel. He'd watched it to get a feel for Highland Falls and Sadie, who'd made a couple appearances on the show. Although she apparently worked more behind the scenes than in front of them.

Sadie rushed over with a red-faced, sweaty Michaela. "You are not leaving here without giving me your cell phone number." She pushed the baby at him. "Please, work your magic. She'll make herself sick if she doesn't stop crying."

He wished they didn't have an audience. With her bloodshot eyes and pale face, Sadie looked like she needed a hug. And he wanted to give her one, which would have been incredibly difficult for him to process if he hadn't wanted to hug her before. It was a good thing that he didn't believe in magic and fairies like half the citizens of Highland Falls claimed to, or he might think she'd cast a spell on him.

"Okay, I've got her." Cradling Michaela against his chest with one arm, he held out the tray from Spill the Tea to Sadie. "Go sit and have your tea and scones while Michaela and I take a tour of the store. Let's go see the unicorns, shall we?" he said to the baby, who'd stopped crying to blink at him.

Sniffling, her muffled sobs shaking her little body, she buried her face in his neck and sighed.

"Oh my gosh, he's a baby whisperer." Abby approached with a grin that reminded him a little of Black's, putting him on instant alert. "And he comes bearing gifts."

Tapping her lips with her finger, she looked from him to Sadie. "Is there something you're not telling me, girlfriend? Is he the reason you don't want to do Falling in Love on Willow Creek? That's the working title for this summer's main attraction on my YouTube channel, *Abby Does Highland Falls*," she explained to Chase. "I'm Abby, by the way."

He smiled. "Michael Knight."

Abby's mouth dropped open. "Sadie, it's him. It's your knight in shining armor."

From where she sat on a stool behind the cash register, Sadie choked on a bite of her scone. Grabbing her tea, she took a sip. Face flushed as she cleared her throat, Sadie nodded. "Yes, it's him."

"Oh, wow, it's so wonderful to meet you." Abby closed the distance between them, wrapping her arms around him and Michaela. The baby stiffened at the same time Michael did. Apparently, he only felt comfortable when Sadie hugged him. Interesting. And concerning.

Black looked concerned too, but mostly put out that he didn't get a mention. Chase smiled.

"Oh my gosh, so he is totally the reason why you don't want to do my bachelorette event. You're together."

Sadie slowly lowered the to-go cup of tea from her mouth, looked from him to Abby, and nodded.

His smile fell. Wait. What?

Black shot him a *what the hell is going on?* look.

He shot back an *I don't have a clue* look. But while he may not have had a clue, after the initial shock of Sadie saying they were together had worn off, a bolt of happiness lit him up inside.

Black's eyes narrowed.

So maybe that warm glow wasn't only lighting up Chase on the inside. His next thought extinguished the warm glow completely. He'd made a promise to Black, and he had to keep it. No matter how difficult it would be to do so.

"As happy as I am for you, now I have to fill that slot with something equally fun and entertaining." She glanced at Black and smiled. "And I think I know exactly who can do that. So, Nate, what do you think about From Behind Bars to the Wilds of Highland Falls?"

"I'm not exactly sure I Believe in Unicorns qualifies as the wilds of Highland Falls," Black said, sending Chase a desperate *do something* glance.

"Sadie and I aren't really *together* together, so, you know, she could star in Falling in Love on Willow Creek. No offense to Nate, but she'd be a much bigger draw."

Chapter Nine

♥

Sadie gasped, inhaling the fruity tea she'd just taken a sip of. It went down the wrong way, causing her to choke and spew brilliant blue liquid down the front of her short-sleeved white blouse and white capri pants. She should have known better than to wear white.

Setting the cup of blueberry tea on the counter, she reached for a roll of paper towels on the shelf while staring at Michael. He gave her what appeared to be an apologetic wince.

As if she'd accept his apology.

She hadn't thought she had the cognitive bandwidth to come up with a believable excuse that Abby wouldn't be able to argue with. So when Abby assumed Sadie and Michael were together, she'd latched on to it. She'd been mentally celebrating, hiding her self-satisfied smile by taking a sip of tea, when Michael went and ruined everything.

"Here, let me help." Abby pulled a travel-size stain removal spray from her bag. "Mallory's rubbing off on me," she said, referring to their mutual best friend's habit of carrying everything but the kitchen sink in her oversize purse.

"Thank..." Sadie trailed off as she discovered another reason

not to wear white. The spray had rendered her top see-through.
Abby must not have noticed because she kept squirting.

"That's good. All good, thanks." Sadie ripped off several
squares of paper towel. Her gaze met Michael's as she used them
to cover the front of her top.

Sorry, he mouthed.

She might have forgiven him—he'd rocked her daughter
into a peaceful slumber, after all—if Abby hadn't chosen that
moment to give Sadie a big, bright smile and say, "I'm so happy
we're doing this. It'll be fabulous. We'll just—" She broke off
at the sound of an alarm beeping on her phone. "Oops, gotta
go. I have to pick up Bella from her spa day at Penelope's Pet
Emporium, but I'll give you a call tonight and we can work out
the details. And you, Mr. Park Ranger, are going to be one of
the lucky bachelors that gets a chance to fall in love with my
incredible best friend."

"Um, I don't think that will be—"

Abby cut Michael off with a wave of her hand. "I won't take
no for an answer," she said, and headed for the door.

Sadie opened her mouth to point out that the man wasn't even
interested enough to fake-date her. She wasn't going to think
about the dull ache in her chest that accompanied the thought. It
was no doubt due to embarrassment.

"From either of you," Abby added. "Whether you realize it
or not, you two have major chemistry. Plus, you're hot, and my
subscribers will adore you as much as my goddaughter does.
Although for entirely different reasons." She blew Sadie a kiss,
waving goodbye as the door closed behind her.

"I can see why her channel does well," Nate observed. "Her
brain goes as fast as her mouth. She sure can talk."

"She can," Sadie agreed, wishing she had half of Abby's
energy. "Can you hold down the fort, Nate? I need to talk
to Michael for a moment. Sorry, I didn't introduce you guys.

Michael, Nate. Nate, Michael. He's a park ranger and the only person on the planet my daughter likes."

"Hey." Nate gave Michael a chin lift before saying to Sadie, "If you want, you can go home and change. I'm sure Agnes will come down when…" He trailed off with a grimace.

"When I leave?" she finished for him, and then sighed. "I'm sorry you had to be here for that, Nate. But I have too much to do to go home. I'll be in the office if you need me. I'll let my grandmother know the coast is clear."

Sadie waved Michael to the office down the short hallway on their left, a hallway that also led to the door to her grandmother's apartment above the store. "I can't believe you threw me under the bus like that," Sadie said as she pulled the door closed behind them—quietly, so as not to wake her daughter still sleeping soundly in his arms.

"I'm sorry. I wasn't thinking. I just didn't want you to miss the opportunity to meet the right guy for you and Michaela." He looked away. "And, uh, I'm only here for a few weeks."

"Oh no, I didn't mean what I said to Abby." Had Sadie wished she and Michael were a couple more than once today? Of course she had. Why wouldn't she? He'd been the one bright spot in an otherwise disastrous day. But she wasn't completely delusional.

"About us being together," she clarified. "I was just using you as an excuse. I don't really think there's anything between us, other than my daughter, who loves you more than me." She sat at the desk and scrubbed her face with her hands, unable to stifle a yawn.

"She doesn't love me more than you, Sadie," Michael said as he walked to the cradle in the corner of the office.

"Please, don't put her down. I just need a few more minutes of peace—" Too late. He was already lowering Michaela into the cradle.

Sadie closed her eyes and gritted her teeth, preparing for her daughter's eardrum-shattering scream. She knew it wasn't fair to ask Michael to stay any longer than he already had but she honestly didn't know how to deal with everything on her plate right now. Her chest was so tight that she wondered if she might have a heart attack. More likely a breakdown, she decided when her eyes grew hot and her vision blurred.

But her daughter's cries didn't shatter the quiet of the office. The only sound was the rhythmic creak of the cradle against the oak floorboards. Sadie's breathing assumed the restful cadence of the rocking cradle, and the tightness in her chest eased. She relaxed against the back of the chair with relief and gratitude, her eyes growing heavy.

Large, warm hands came to rest on her shoulders, strong fingers gently kneading the last of her tension away. It was like floating in the creek beneath the weeping willow, the movement of the water gently rocking her to sleep as she lay beneath a dark, starlit sky.

The intoxicating scent of amber and leather filled her senses as a low, deep voice said near her ear, "You need to sleep, Sadie."

I need this. You. She blinked, swimming up from that dark, calming pool. Afraid she'd said the words out loud. She'd felt them right down to her soul.

"I can't." She sounded like her mouth was filled with cotton wool.

His hands left her shoulders to gently turn the chair to face him. He crouched at her feet. "You can't go on like this. You'll wind up in the hospital."

"You don't understand."

"Make me understand then."

"I can't. I can't dump everything on you." It embarrassed her that she wanted to. She hated asking for help. Hated that she needed it. It made her feel weak.

"You can, but I understand if you don't want to." He looked away, as if debating whether to tell her something.

"What is it?" she asked, although suddenly leery of what he might say.

"When I picked up your scones and tea—"

She clapped a hand over her mouth. "I'm so sorry. I didn't even thank—"

"Sadie, stop. It's fine. But from what I overheard the woman in Spill the Tea saying, business at I Believe in Unicorns isn't fine."

She blew out a long, frustrated breath. "Granny's friends must have run right over there after my little scene with her and Mr. Teller. Honestly, you can't keep anything in this town a secret."

But she couldn't put the blame entirely on her grandmother's friends and Babs Sutherland. Sadie knew better than to air the family's dirty laundry in the middle of the store. She might as well have taken out a billboard on Main Street.

"So it's true? The store is in financial trouble?"

She nodded, taking a minute to regain control of the panic welling up inside her. "If I don't figure out a way to turn things around, the bank will foreclose. I promised Mr. Teller, the bank manager, that I'd come up with a business plan by the end of this week." Afraid she'd start blubbering any minute, she pressed her fingers to her lips.

"Hey." He gently took her chin between his fingers, getting her to look at him. "You don't have to hide your tears with me, Sadie. Let them out. It might help."

Her laugh caught on a sob. "Just what you need, another Gray crying all over you."

He smiled, but it didn't reach his intent blue gaze. "You were worried your grandmother was hiding something from you. Was this it?"

"Yes, it was exactly what I was afraid of, and for the past three months, I've put off confronting her, because I didn't want to deal with it. I buried my head in the sand while my brother bled this business and my grandmother dry." She blinked back tears. "She could lose the store and her home because of me."

"No. Don't take the blame for this. Put it where it belongs. On your brother." He grimaced at the snuffling sound coming from the cradle and came to his feet. He walked to the cradle, rocking it with one hand while stroking Michaela's copper curls with the other.

"You're right. It is Elijah's fault. But it's not like he can bail out Granny." She kept her voice low so as not to wake her daughter. "It falls on me, just like it always does. Only this time, I don't have a clue how to solve the problem."

He kept an eye on Michaela as he stopped rocking the cradle. Then, seemingly satisfied that she was once more in a deep sleep, he came over and leaned against the desk, crossing his arms. Distracted by the bulge of his biceps, it took her a minute to realize he'd been talking to her. "Sorry, what was that?"

"I offered to help. I don't know anything about operating a retail business or selling unicorns, but I can act as a sounding board."

"That's sweet of you to offer, but for you to act as a sounding board, I'd actually need ideas to bounce off you, and I've got nothing."

"Because you're exhausted."

Her phone pinged. She glanced at the screen and groaned. "It's Abby with a list of bachelors." She blinked. "She even put Nate on there. Why would she—" There was another ping. "Of course, he's hot too. She thinks the two of you will not only attract a lot of attention from her subscribers but also from the single ladies in this county. She obviously doesn't care that he's gay."

"Is he?"

"Is he what? Gay?"

"No. Hot?" He shook his head. "Never mind. Forget I asked. Just tell Abby you don't want to do it."

"I should. In fact, I think I have. I guess I wasn't firm enough. It's not my forte. I have a problem saying no to people. Don't you?"

"Not at all."

"So if someone asks you to do something you don't want to do, you just say no? No excuses, no nothing?"

"That's right." He nodded at her phone. "Call Abby and tell her you have too much on your plate if you don't want to do it. You don't, do you?"

"Gosh, no. On top of everything else, the last thing I need is this. Honestly, I'd want no part of it even if my world wasn't imploding." She handed him her phone. "You tell her. I'm sure the last thing either you or Nate want is to appear on a reality dating show."

"It won't matter if Nate and I say no. You're the star of the show. Trust me, Abby will have no problem finding guys who want to date you. You need to call her and say no, Sadie. Not me. You. Do it now. You'll feel better."

"But she's so excited about it. I hate to disappoint her. And the thing is, Abby's channel has been a boon to Highland Falls. She promotes the heck out of the area, and local businesses have benefited big time. So in a way, I wouldn't just be letting her down. I'd be letting the whole town down. I can't win."

"What if you come up with something better? Something that benefits I Believe in Unicorns and Abby. She seems to have a good heart, and there's no doubt she cares about you and Michaela. If you told her the truth—"

"I can't. I can't tell her what Elijah's done or that we could lose the store. I'll figure out something." She always did. But it had never been this bad. Her stomach pitched like she'd gone bungee jumping at Deadman's Gorge, twice, on a full stomach. She eyed the garbage can.

"I hate to be the bearer of bad news, but I think the town already has a fairly good idea what's going on."

"How could I forget? My fight with Granny went viral." She winced, remembering the stricken look on her grandmother's face. Until Mr. Teller had shown up, Agnes hadn't known how deep in the hole Elijah had put her and the store. They'd both been burying their heads in the sand—Sadie by not asking the questions that needed to be asked, her grandmother by filing her bank statements unopened.

"Now that she knows, you can work together. Come up with a plan to turn the store around. Is there anyone your grandmother can ask for a loan?"

"My uncle Bryan. But he's the last person my grandmother would want to find out that she's in financial trouble."

"Maybe Mr. Teller will let you take out a second mortgage based on your... your credit. Sorry, I forgot. You mentioned your ex had tanked your credit when you were in labor."

"Yes, and I also don't have a job that pays a living wage. Unless you count my contract work with Abby, which she probably won't have to give me when I pull the plug on her bachelorette idea. As to my grandmother working with me, that won't happen anytime soon. She wouldn't even speak to me after I laid into her about bleeding the store dry for Elijah."

Her comment was met with a loud *thunk* from the apartment above. She sighed and lifted her chin at the ceiling. "Granny's probably listening in through the vent."

Michael pushed off the desk and cocked his head. Sadie thought he was holding his breath waiting for Michaela to wake up, but he looked more interested in what was going on in the apartment upstairs than in the cradle. She heard it now too, the sound of heavy footfalls followed by lighter footsteps. Agnes wasn't alone.

"Sadie, you don't think your grandmother has been hiding your brother all along, do you?"

Chapter Ten

♥

Sadie reacted to Chase's question by jumping from the chair and heading for the door.

"Wait. Let me go with you, Sadie. You could be walking into a dangerous situation." While he no longer believed she was involved in her brother's crimes in any way, Chase didn't trust that her anger at Elijah outweighed their family ties.

"Michaela is more dangerous than my brother," she scoffed, nodding at the gun in his holster. "And you have a twitchy finger."

"I don't have a twitchy finger. I've been in situations far more dangerous than..." He trailed off. Chase had but Michael hadn't.

He wasn't very good at undercover work. He had a difficult time lying. But he knew exactly what had to be done in this instance. They couldn't break cover. If Agnes MacLeod had been hiding Elijah all along, they couldn't take him down in the apartment. It would be better if he ran and they grabbed him without anyone the wiser.

Chase pulled his cell phone from his back pocket and glanced at the screen, acting like it had been on vibrate. "Just give me a

second. I have to respond to this." He shot off a quick text to a
man who had no problem lying.

Strong possibility Elijah Gray in upstairs apartment. Will
investigate. Keep an eye on exits. Let Gabe know.

The police station was on Main Street. The chief wouldn't
alert his officers but he'd keep an eye out on his own. He knew
the importance of keeping Elijah's capture on the downlow.
The last thing they wanted was the Jackson County Sheriff's
Department knowing they had him in custody.

"You shot a snake, Michael."

He raised his head. She'd never let him live that down. "Trust
me, navigating office politics in DC is far more dangerous than
dealing with the wild animals of Highland Falls. And while you
may not consider your brother dangerous, you don't know how
he'd react if cornered. The best move is for you to call your
grandmother. Tell her you need to speak with her. Once she's out
of the apartment, I'll go up and take a look around."

"She won't want to talk to me now that I know that she's been
helping out Elijah this entire time." Sadie shook her head. "I'm
so mad at her right now. I get the whole standing-by-your-family
thing, but she's gone too far this time. My brother was moving
drugs for a gang, Michael. I still have a hard time believing
he got himself mixed up in something like that. He...Anyway,
I have to deal with it." She glanced at her daughter sleeping
in the cradle and then back at Michael. "I promise, I shouldn't
be more than twenty minutes. I know I've already taken up
too much of your time..." She frowned. "They can't fire you,
can they?"

"Technically, they could. They don't know I'm undercover
for Fish and Wildlife. I'm supposed to be looking for a moose
on Main Street."

She laughed. "They're pulling your leg. We don't have moose here."

"Yes, you do." He swiped the screen on his cell phone and showed her the photo from the front page of the *Highland Falls Herald*. "Look, it says so right here."

"It's an elk. They look similar but a moose is a lot bigger. They can weigh as much as eighteen hundred pounds. The newspaper owner's granddaughter wrote the story. She was doing a spring internship. She's from New York City and obviously as well acquainted with wildlife as you are."

His phone pinged. He checked the screen. It was a message from Black.

No sign of him. Gabe's patrolling Main Street. What's your status?

Trying to stall Sadie. Text her grandmother. Tell her Sadie's gone and that you need her help.

"You should head out. I don't want you to get fired. I'll take Michaela with me," she said, taking a step toward the cradle.

"Are you kidding me right now?" He caught the surprise in her eyes at the anger in his voice. He was a little surprised himself. Even his colleagues, who were far from his number one fans, credited him with being unshakable, calm, and level-headed in any situation. Although they'd follow up the compliment with a comment about him having a chunk of ice where his heart should be.

He rubbed his jaw. "I'm sorry. I shouldn't have used that tone of voice with you. I'm just afraid you're underestimating your brother and what he's capable of, Sadie."

"I know my brother, Michael. He wouldn't hurt a fly. I mean that literally. Elijah is a pacifist."

"A pacifist who moved drugs for a gang. Sorry, but come on. Drug dealers aren't exactly singing 'Kumbaya' and roasting marshmallows in the woods."

"Okay, you've made your point. I'll call Gran—" She turned at the sound of the door opening at the end of the hall. "That must be her now."

Obviously, Black had done as Chase asked and told Agnes that Sadie had left, which he'd hoped would be the case at this point. But Sadie had distracted him, and she was now one step ahead of him.

"Sadie, wait," he said when she went to open the office door. "I'm not sure confronting your grandmother is the best—" He sighed when she opened the door and rushed into the hall.

"How could you, Granny? How could you be hiding Elijah all this time?" she called to her grandmother's back.

Agnes whirled around, looking sweetly innocent in a pink sweatshirt, white pants, and pink sneakers. She pressed a hand to her chest. "Oh now, you just about gave me heart failure. Nate said—"

Sadie cut off her grandmother. "We're even then. My heart has just about stopped twice today thanks to you. Is Elijah in the apartment now? Don't lie to me, Granny."

While the two women were distracted, Chase moved to the door at the end of the hall. He had his hand on the knob when he heard the sound of sirens, and not just one. Something big was happening in Highland Falls. He hoped that something big didn't involve an Elijah Gray sighting and the entire police department wasn't about to converge on the store.

Black appeared behind Sadie's grandmother and met Chase's questioning gaze with a negative head shake. He hadn't seen Gray.

"No, of course he's not in my apartment. Whatever gave you that idea?" Sadie's grandmother protested, frowning when she spotted Chase. "Whoa there, laddie. Where do you think you're going? Sadie, stop that young man." The older woman's voice followed Chase as he disappeared up the stairs and into the apartment above the store, accompanied by his partner buying him time.

"There you are, Mrs. M. I couldn't get the cash register to open, and one of your customers thought I was robbing the place. I hope she hasn't gone and called the police on me."

Sadie had a fairly good idea who had called the police, and it wasn't a customer. It was her brother. It would be just like Elijah to set up a distraction so he could make a clean getaway. She glanced over her shoulder. Michael had obviously gone to search the apartment, exactly like he'd intended on doing all along. She appreciated him being protective of her and Michaela, but this was her problem, not his.

"Nate, I need to have a word with my grandmother. She'll be with you in a minute." Sadie made a mental note to check out his story after she'd grilled her grandmother. Something about it didn't quite jibe with her.

"Sure, no problem," Nate said, but he didn't move.

She was about to add *in private* when her grandmother said, "You told me Sadie had gone home, Nate." Agnes sounded disappointed in her new hire.

Sadie narrowed her eyes at the man, feeling like her earlier suspicions about him had just been validated. "You knew I was in the office, Nate. Why would you tell my grandmother I went home?"

"I didn't want to disturb you and your *friend*." He gave her a broad wink as though he thought she and Michael had been making out. "And you and your gran had just had a falling-out so . . . " He trailed off as if that explained everything.

Her grandmother pressed her hands to her chest. "Now is that not a fine piece of news to get on a day like today? You have a boyfriend, and a handsome one at that." Agnes's delighted smile fell. "But I don't appreciate him going up to my apartment uninvited, Sadie."

At any other time, her matchmaking grandmother believing she had a boyfriend would have concerned Sadie, but right now she had bigger worries to contend with and couldn't afford to waste any more time. Obviously, from the lack of commotion overhead, Elijah was gone, as Sadie had suspected he would be. "Granny, give me your cell phone."

"Sorry, dear, I don't have it on me." Her grandmother's rubber-soled sneakers squeaked on the wood floor as she tried to make a getaway. "I'll just check on the cash register with Nate. I won't be but a minute." Her Scottish burr had thickened, something it did when she was nervous.

"White pants show everything, Granny. Including the outline of your phone in your front pocket. Hand it over." Sadie made a *gimme* gesture with her fingers.

"Sorry, but there are things on my phone I'd rather you not see. My friend Mr. Murphy has been getting a little flirty in his texts, if you know what I mean."

Sadie rolled her eyes. "Good try. Now hand it over."

"You know, you've gotten very bossy since you had a baby. Where is Michaela, by the way?"

"Don't try and distract me, Granny. It won't work. She's sleeping in the office."

"Isn't that wonderful!" her grandmother yelled as if Sadie had suddenly become hard of hearing.

Sadie's eyes went wide at the sound of sniffling coming from the office. "I can't believe you did that. Is there anything you won't do to protect Elijah?"

"One of us has to protect him." She grimaced at the sound of

Michaela crying. "I'm sorry. I shouldn't have done that, but I'm at my wits' end. Your brother's in trouble, serious trouble."

"Of his own making, and now he's dragging you down with him."

Agnes's bottom lip quivered.

Sadie briefly closed her eyes. The sight of her grandmother fighting to contain her tears and fears got to her. "Nate, do me a favor and rock the cradle," Sadie said to the man listening intently to their conversation.

"Uh, okay." He walked past her like he was on his way to the electric chair.

"Thank you. There's a bottle made up for her in the mini-fridge if she doesn't settle right away." She closed the office door on his *God help me* expression.

"All right, I'll hear Elijah out. But to do that, I need to talk to him. Where is he, Granny?"

"I don't know. I don't," she repeated when Sadie raised an eyebrow.

"Okay, if that's true, then the only way for me to get in touch with him is on your phone." She sighed when her grandmother looked like she didn't have a clue what Sadie was talking about. "I know my brother, Granny. I know how he thinks and how he operates. You also know I can easily hack your phone so you might as well hand it over."

"Fine." She dug the phone out of her pocket and reluctantly handed it over. "But you have to promise me you won't turn him in. Not until you hear him out. He knows he messed up, Sadie. He's just trying to make it right. He's scared."

"He should be scared. He's gotten himself mixed up with some very bad people. You should be scared too. Because if those same people discover you've been hiding him, they might come looking for him here." She honestly hadn't considered that her grandmother might be in danger until that very moment.

The thought rattled her nerves, and she jumped when the door opened at the end of the hall. It was Michael. He glanced from her to her grandmother. "Everything okay here?" he asked, walking toward them. His concerned gaze went to the office. Michaela's crying was audible through the closed door.

Her grandmother crossed her arms. "No, laddie, it's not. You entered my apartment without my permission."

"I'm sorry about that, ma'am. Sadie was worried about you. She thought her brother might be hiding in your apartment without you being aware of it."

"Well, as you saw for yourself, she was worrying for nothing." She gave Michael a speculative look. "But it seems my granddaughter has been keeping secrets from me. I didn't know she had a young man in her life. I can't understand why she's been hiding you away though. You're—"

"Granny, Michael's a friend, not a boyfriend." Sadie prayed that he didn't think she'd inferred otherwise.

She couldn't tell by his expression because he'd turned when Nate opened the door with a wailing Michaela in the crook of his arm, holding up the bottle with his other hand. "She won't stop crying long enough for me to get the bottle in her mouth."

"Here, give her to me." Michael reached for her daughter.

Sadie felt guilty for not being the one to take Michaela but right now finding Elijah won out over comforting her crying child. Besides, she had no doubt her daughter preferred being in Michael's arms to being in hers. She watched him snuggle Michaela against his chest and gently pat her back, Michaela's cries subsiding to soft whimpers. Sadie didn't blame her. She wouldn't mind being in his arms either.

"I don't get it," Nate muttered. Sharing a glance with Michael that Sadie couldn't read, he added, "If you don't mind, I think I'll take a break, Mrs. M. Have a smoke and calm my nerves."

"Take all the time you need, Nate. With all the commotion, you didn't get your lunch break," her grandmother said distractedly, her attention on Michael and Michaela. She looked intrigued, which at any other time would have had Sadie grabbing her daughter and Michael and heading for the door.

"I might just take you up on that, Mrs. M. Thanks." He handed Michael the bottle.

As their new employee went to walk away, Sadie asked, "Nate, before you go, do you remember the customer that you thought might have called the police?"

"Not off the top of my head. I'll give it some thought while I'm on my break."

"I'll take a look at the cash register. It can be finicky." Her grandmother followed Nate down the hall, glancing over her shoulder at Sadie, probably expecting her to call her back so she could continue her interrogation. But Sadie knew her grandmother well enough to know she wouldn't get anything else out of her.

"Do you mind hanging around a little while longer?" Sadie asked Michael. "Maybe give Michaela her bottle? There's something I need to take care of."

She hated to ask. She already owed him so much. But getting in touch with her brother was too important to put off. Hopefully, Michael's boss still assumed he was off chasing a "moose" down Main Street. They wouldn't expect him back anytime soon.

"Does that something have to do with your brother?" He glanced at the phone in her hand. Unlike Sadie's plain black phone case, her grandmother's case was sparkly and embossed with unicorns.

"No, just store business. Trying to keep the lights on, you know." She held his gaze, hoping he'd miss her sliding her grandmother's phone into her pocket as she did so. "Why would you ask?"

"I think the better question is why didn't you ask what I found in your grandmother's apartment?"

"I just assumed you didn't find anything. You didn't, did you?"

"There's definitely been two people in the apartment. There were two cups of tea on the coffee table. One with lipstick and one without. The tea was lukewarm."

"I don't want to discount your powers of observation, but one of my grandmother's friends could have stopped by for a cup of tea. In fact, I'd say there was a ninety-nine-point-nine percent chance that's what happened. They'd want the inside scoop to take back to their mutual friends."

"That might be, but there was a razor on the bathroom counter that was filled with auburn stubble. So unless your grandmother has short strands of auburn hair growing from her face or legs, I think we can safely rule her out. I also can't see your grandmother owning an Xbox on which she plays *Fortnite*. And not only does she play the game, she goes by Godric Gryffindor and her team is the top scorer on the leaderboard. There's also a very large steak in the fridge and the faint smell of marijuana in the air."

"Two for three. The marijuana could go either way. Agnes has been known to smoke pot on occasion for her arthritis. Elijah's a vegan but Granny loves her steak. You got my brother on the razor and *Fortnite* game. Although Granny does play, and she's probably a member of his team. Elijah goes by Godric Gryffindor online. He's a big Harry Potter fan. And you're impressively observant for someone who was in my grandmother's apartment for under ten minutes." She smiled.

He didn't return her smile. "I am, which is how I know you're hiding something. What's going on, Sadie?"

"Nothing. Nothing at all. I just need a few minutes." Before he could ask anything else, she walked into the office and closed the door. She leaned her back against it and retrieved her grandmother's phone, scrolling through the call log. Just like she'd thought, there were a whole lot of calls to Payton Howard. Her brother had been using her grandmother's cell phone.

Sadie went to retrieve her own phone and frowned at her purse lying open on the desk. She didn't remember leaving it like that. Her first thought was Nate. She grabbed her wallet. Her credit card was still there and so was the twenty-dollar bill she'd taken out last Sunday. Okay, one outlaw at a time, she thought, and took a screenshot of Payton's number. Then she went through her grandmother's most recent texts.

Agnes hadn't been lying. Sadie was just glad her grandmother's attempts at sexting with Mr. Murphy were more G-rated than X-rated. She scrolled to the text messages between Agnes and Payton. They were way worse and most definitely from her brother.

"You sound like you're seventeen and in love for the first time, baby brother," Sadie murmured, embarrassed for him. He seemed a lot more invested in their relationship than Payton was. Sadly, Sadie could relate—on Payton's end, not Elijah's.

"Okay, baby brother, let's see if I'm right and you spoofed Granny's phone." She sent a text message to her grandmother.

> Granny says you're trying to make things right. Give me one reason to believe you.

She didn't say everything she wanted to. She didn't tell him how angry she was at him for putting their grandmother in danger, for putting I Believe in Unicorns and the apartment upstairs at risk.

Dots showed up on her screen and then disappeared before showing up again moments later.

> I'm sorry about Granny. I didn't know what else to do or who to turn to. Meet me at the rock in the woods at ten tonight. I'll tell you everything. Come alone. BTW, you'll need to buy Granny a new phone.

The screen went black. He'd trashed the data and any evidence that was on the phone. She should have anticipated that he would. If her brain had been functioning instead of being half-asleep, she would have. It had been his endgame all along, which meant the only reason he hadn't trashed the phone earlier is because he was waiting for her to contact him.

They'd played her. They were in on this together. She wished she could throw up her hands and walk away. They knew she wouldn't. Honestly, she must have a neon *sucker* sign stuck on her forehead. Everyone saw her coming from a mile away.

She sighed, forcing a smile as she opened the door. At the sight of Michaela, head lolling with the bottle in her mouth, the smile was no longer forced. She glanced at Michael. "I have a feeling I'll be up late tonight. Any chance you feel like hanging out? We can work on improving your knowledge of Highland Falls' flora and fauna. Unless you have other plans."

"No, I'm free for the night."

"Great. How does nine forty-five sound?" If she hung around with him for too long before her scheduled meet with Elijah, she was afraid she'd tell him the truth. She'd already seen how well that worked out.

"Suspiciously specific."

Chapter Eleven

♥

Chase sat in his car on the side of the road, just out of view from the cottage on Willow Creek. He'd been there for more than an hour. His cell phone rang. It was Black. He put him on speaker.

"What's up?" Chase asked.

Black was sitting in his jeep across from I Believe in Unicorns. Both of them were feeling the sting of underestimating Sadie's grandmother. They didn't plan on letting it happen again.

"I've just had a visit from our friendly neighborhood chief of police. Seems he's been getting calls about me from the concerned citizens of Highland Falls. Here I thought I looked all friendly and trustworthy without the beard and the hair. I even put on my best law-abiding-citizen act, smiling and waving at the passersby."

Chase snorted. "They probably thought you were casing the joint."

"Yeah, that's what Gabe said."

"Has he been able to track down the location where the bomb threat came from?" Someone had called in the threat around the same time Sadie's grandmother had left her apartment to come down to the store.

"Not yet, and if it was Elijah as we both suspect, I doubt they'll be able to."

"You're probably right."

"You could have made our job a hell of a lot easier if you'd just bugged Mrs. M's apartment. I don't know how I ended up with a by-the-book partner."

"We're even then. I don't know how I ended up with a partner whose brain works more like a criminal than law enforcement."

"Good thing I like you, Mikey." Black laughed. "Anything happening on your end?"

"No, all quiet here. I take that back," he said as something howled in the woods, drowning out the incessant croaking of frogs and chirping of crickets. "Did you hear that?"

"Yeah. Coyotes making you nervous, city boy?"

"No, of course not." He powered up the window, deciding a change of subject was in order. "If Sadie made contact with Elijah to arrange a meet, it doesn't look like it's happening tonight."

"We know she reached out to him, and we know she used her grandmother's phone to do so. Thanks to Mrs. M, we also know she somehow managed to wipe the evidence from her grandmother's phone. Which, just for the record, puts a big question mark beside Sadie's name in my book."

"You didn't see her face when she realized her grandmother's been hiding Elijah all along or when she discovered Agnes is at risk of losing her home and business because of him. Other than trying to protect her grandmother, she's not involved in this, Black."

"So, if you're right, why do you think she set up a meet with her brother instead of handing over her grandmother's phone to Gabe? I talked to him. He hasn't heard boo from her. I would have been able to tell if he had."

The fact that she hadn't reached out to her best friend's husband bothered Chase too.

"Don't let your feelings for her get in the way, Roberts."

"I don't have feelings for her, Black. Not in the way you're suggesting."

"Yeah? So you don't mind me asking her out when this is over?"

His gut clenched. "You just said you suspect her of being involved in Brodie's death, yet you want to date her? I really don't get you."

"Good try, Mikey. We both know she had nothing to do with Brodie's murder. But what we don't know is how far she'd go to protect her brother."

Chase pushed down the emotions roiling inside him at the thought of Black dating Sadie. The other agent was right: Chase couldn't let his feelings for her get in the way of bringing Elijah and the Jackson County Sheriff's Department to justice. It wasn't just about the successful culmination of the case being his ticket back to DC. He was invested now. He wanted to see justice done for Brodie. There was nothing he hated more than dirty law enforcement.

"She'll go far enough to put herself at risk of ending up in jail for aiding and abetting," Chase said. She already had one strike against her. She'd destroyed evidence in their investigation. For her sake as well as her daughter's, he had to make sure she didn't go further.

"Mrs. M's already got that one covered. I still can't believe that sweet little old lady fooled us all."

"It's always the sweet ones you've got to watch out for," Chase said, thinking of Sadie. "I'd better go. Stay close to your phone. I might need you." The silence on the other end dragged on. "Black?"

"Yeah, I heard you. Looks like Mrs. M has a gentleman caller. I'm going to check it out."

"Let me know what you find out." Chase disconnected and

pulled away from the side of the dirt road. He was ten minutes early for their study date. Study night, he corrected, giving himself a mental shake. It wasn't a date. He had to get his head on straight. He had a feeling he'd need all his wits about him when dealing with Sadie. The woman was running on empty yet she'd still managed to outmaneuver them. It was probably in their best interests if she remained sleep-deprived. Otherwise, she'd run circles around them.

The curtain in the front window of the white stucco cottage moved as Chase pulled alongside Sadie's SUV in the driveway. It was hard to tell whether the silhouette was male or female. Chase hadn't been able to reach the cottage to see if her brother was inside before she got home that afternoon, which is why he arrived ten minutes before she wanted him to. He stepped out of the car, listening for the sound of Elijah making his escape.

The yellow door opened, the outside light shining down on Sadie's long dark hair. She had Michaela in her arms, bouncing the baby on her hip. They both looked exhausted and maybe a little frantic.

"Sorry, I'm early." He held up a takeaway bag from the local bakery, Bites of Bliss. "I was told brownies and fudge were your favorites."

When he'd walked into the bakery, the owner, along with several of her customers, had greeted him like he was a hero. It seemed Abby had stopped in on her way to pick up her dog from the spa and shared that Chase, or Michael as she knew him, had been Sadie's knight in shining armor on Valentine's Day. The owner and her customers couldn't have been friendlier or more welcoming, but he'd been uncomfortable with the attention. He disliked lying to them almost as much as he disliked lying to Sadie. But he wasn't above taking advantage of the situation or the Highland Falls rumor mill.

The women had no problem answering his subtle questions

about Sadie. They were worried about her, her and Agnes. Their feelings on Elijah were mixed, which worried Chase. He didn't trust that they'd turn him in if they saw him.

She made a face. "What else did Bliss tell you?" she asked, handing him the baby to take the bag. She opened it and peeked inside, humming with what sounded like pleasure.

"Just that she and your friends are worried about you." He followed Sadie inside, smiling at Michaela, who was trying to shove her hand in his mouth. He nibbled on her fingers.

At her daughter's giggle, Sadie shook her head and sighed. "You probably won't believe this, but less than two minutes before you arrived, she was in the middle of a crying fit."

Noting Sadie's red-rimmed eyes, he said, "It looks like you were too. Why don't you sit down and put your feet..." He trailed off, unable to find the couch or coffee table he'd seen when he searched the cottage earlier that morning. It looked like she'd started to unpack. The couch and coffee table were buried under piles of clothes, bedding, and towels, while empty boxes were tossed haphazardly on the floor.

She glanced around, biting on her bottom lip like she was holding back tears.

"Don't cry," he said, a note of panic in his voice. Crying babies he could handle, but he didn't think he could handle a crying Sadie without taking her in his arms to comfort her.

Holding her, touching her, had become something of a habit for him. His go-to response when she was upset. It was a habit he couldn't afford, especially now.

She looked surprised. "I wasn't going to cry. I was going to laugh. Maybe a laugh laced with hysteria, but a laugh just the same. In my book, that's a step above tears. We've cried enough for one day, haven't we, baby?" She leaned in to nibble on the hand her daughter had just stuck in Chase's mouth.

She froze, her eyes wide as she looked up at him. She was so close that he could count the gold flecks in her irises and see the slight curl at the ends of her eyelashes. Instead of jerking back like he fully expected her to, she surprised him by burying her face in his neck. He didn't know which was worse—her warm, soft lips touching his mouth, or her warm, soft lips pressed against his neck.

Even while he savored the feel of Sadie's lips on his skin and the way her body felt pressed against his side, his brain was holding up a stop sign, flashing all the reasons why he should step away from her. Right now. This very minute. For the sake of the case. But before he had a chance, Michaela intervened. She took her hand from his mouth to grab a hunk of Sadie's hair, and pulled.

"Ouch." Sadie jerked back, releasing an even louder *ouch*.

"Hang on a sec," Chase said, working to free the long, silky chestnut strands from Michaela's grip. "Let go of Mommy's hair, sweetheart. That's a good girl." She let go of her mother's hair to gurgle up at him and pat his face.

Sadie rubbed her head, staring at him and her daughter. "She's jealous. She's decided you belong to her, and Lord help the person that gets in her way."

"I don't think she's jealous. Maybe just a little territorial." He grimaced when Michaela planted her mouth on his cheek and sucked. "I think she might be more hungry than jealous. She's eating my face."

"I figured it out."

"Umm, I think I did. I just told you she's hungry, remember?"

She waved her hand. "Not about that. I figured out why she's so attached to you. It's your cologne. Scent is powerful in creating memories. She remembers yours from the night she was born. You were the one who comforted her that night, not me."

"Wait a sec," he said, taking in her crossed arms. She wore a form-fitting long-sleeved black T-shirt with black leggings. "Are you mad at me?"

"No... Okay, maybe a little. But only because I want her to love me like she loves you." Keeping an eye on her daughter, she took a hesitant step toward him.

"Uh, Sadie, what are you doing?" he asked when she began rubbing her head on his chest. "I don't think this is a good idea." He nearly swallowed his tongue when she took advantage of her daughter sucking on his face by doing a full body rub against him. "Sadie, you need to stop." Before he embarrassed himself.

"There. Now let's see if it worked." She stepped back and held out her arms. "Give her to me."

"Sure." He tried to pry Michaela off him. "I might need some help here." She was climbing him like he was a tree, her tiny but strong fingers fisted in his hair. He held back a groan when Sadie did as he asked, pressing against him while trying to free Michaela's hands from his hair.

"Come on, baby. Let go of Michael's hair. You're going to make him cry. Pretend you're crying."

"Babies don't develop empathy until they're two, Sadie. I'm not pretending I'm crying. Just—"

She stepped back, her hands falling to her sides. "How do you know they don't? Do you have children? You aren't married, are you?"

"No to both your questions. I've been reading about child development, that's all." His face warmed at the admission. Sadie and the baby had been on his mind a lot in those first few weeks. In an odd way, reading baby books gave him a connection to them. He liked knowing what stages Michaela would be going through. He supposed it helped him to feel close to them.

Sadie's shoulders slumped. "It's not your cologne at all. You love her, and she knows you do."

"She knows you love her too, Sadie."

"Sometimes I'm not sure that I do." She looked away, obviously embarrassed. "And just like she senses you love her, she senses that..." She shook her head as if willing the words away. "I've dreamed about having a baby ever since I was a little girl. When I hit my late twenties, I started to worry I'd never be a mommy. It's the one thing I wanted more than anything else. And now that I am...It's nothing like I imagined. I can't do anything right."

"You're being too hard on yourself. You've had a lot to deal with on your own. It's not easy being a single parent."

She gave him a weak smile. "You sound like you speak from experience."

"In a way, I guess I do. I never knew my father. My mother raised me and my brother on her own." Until she gave up on herself, and on them. Sadie didn't need to know that though.

"You turned out pretty well. Maybe there's hope for me yet."

He wondered if she'd still think that when she eventually learned the truth. "You can tell me to mind my own business if you want, but why haven't you let your friends help? From what Bliss at the bakery said, you have plenty of people who would love to lend you a hand."

She gestured at the half-opened boxes littering the kitchen and living room floor. "And let them see this? All I'd need is for it to get around town how badly I'm failing at motherhood."

"You let me in, and I don't see a woman who's failing." He finally managed to pry Michaela's fingers from his hair and repositioned her on his hip. "I see a woman who could use a hand unpacking a few boxes, that's all." He didn't think now was the time to mention everything else she had yet to deal with. Little steps at a time were probably all she could manage at the moment. "I don't mind helping out, you know. You can sit at the table and eat your brownies and educate me on the flora and fauna of Highland Falls while I unpack. No." He held up his hand when she went to object. "You'd actually be doing me a favor. There's nothing I like more than organizing a space." It was the absolute truth. The mess was giving him a headache.

He walked over to the playpen in front of the patio doors that had been open this morning, relieved to see they were now shut and locked. As he bent to put Michaela into the playpen, she dug her fingers into his arms, letting loose an ear-piercing scream. "Okay, so that's not going to work."

Sadie smiled as she bit into a brownie. "Here," she said around it, wiping her chocolate-coated fingers on her T-shirt before reaching for something on top of the box.

He stared at the smears of chocolate, wondering if she even realized what she'd done.

She walked over. "Put her in here." He did as she suggested, fitting the baby's legs in the holes of the striped fabric. "Now hold out your arms." She slid the straps over his arms, placing them on his shoulders. Once she'd fastened the strap at his back, she patted his arm and leaned in to kiss Michaela's cheek. Sadie drew back and cocked her head. "That's my phone. I better grab it."

"I don't hear anything," he said to her retreating back. He shrugged when she didn't respond and looked down at the baby. "Okay, you be a good girl for me, sweetheart, and we can have this place shipshape in no time."

He bent down to pick up a handful of clothes off the couch, and Michaela gurgled around a smile. Perfect, she thought it was a game. By the time Sadie returned, he had the couch and coffee table cleared of clothes and bedding.

"Sorry about that. It was Abby. I did what you suggested and told her the truth. She called Mallory, exactly like I knew she would. They want to meet up tonight."

"Now? It's almost ten o'clock."

She wouldn't meet his eyes as she walked to the entryway and slipped on a pair of sneakers. "It's the only time Mallory can make it. She has five boys and a full-time job. Once Abby gets an idea in her head, she won't sleep until we come up with a plan. I promise, I won't be long." She was out the door before he could stop her.

It didn't mean he didn't try. He ran to the entryway, grabbing the door just before it closed behind her. She must have run down the walkway to the SUV because she was already sliding behind the wheel. "Sadie, wait. What am I supposed to do with Michaela?"

"Bottles are in the fridge, diapers and onesies on her changing table. First door on the left," she said in response to what she must have assumed was a blank look instead of a panicked one.

"Sadie, I've never changed a diaper before." And he didn't want to learn now. Either she didn't hear him or she was ignoring him, because she started up the SUV's engine, waved, and backed out of the driveway.

Chase retrieved his cell phone from his pocket. He'd been had. "Hey, Chief, Chase Roberts here. Is your wife at home with you?"

"Yeah. She just went to bed. Why?"

"This is going to sound odd, but would you mind checking that she's in bed and not sneaking out a window?"

"What's going on?"

As he relayed what Sadie had told him and his own suspicions, the creak of floorboards and then the sound of a door opening came through the phone. "Honey, did Abby mention anything about meeting with Sadie when you talked to her tonight?" Gabe sighed. "Thanks. No, everything's okay. I have to go out for a bit. I shouldn't be long." A door closed and floorboards once again creaked before the chief came back on the line. "Sounds like you're right, and Sadie's meeting with Elijah. I'll head over your way, see if I can spot her SUV."

"Thanks, Gabe. I'll call Nate. Knowing him, he probably put a tracker on Sadie's car."

Chapter Twelve

♥

Sadie tried to put her daughter and Michael out of her head as she shut off the engine a couple hundred yards from the cottage. But the image of his handsome face smiling at her daughter, who gurgled up at him from where she was strapped to his chest, wasn't easily dismissed. Her feelings for him even less so. It wasn't only her daughter who was entranced by the man. And just like Michaela's feelings for him, Sadie didn't know where her own came from or why.

She couldn't just put it down to him being with her the night Michaela was born. Eddie had been there too, and she didn't fantasize about him. Or rub against him, she thought with a sigh. Not one of her best moments.

Then again, she hadn't had many best moments these past three months. Admittedly, if she'd had any at all, the two people she was trying not to think about played starring roles. And she'd left them and that cozy family scene to traipse through the woods in the dark of night to meet with her brother, who'd caused her no end of heartache. She could only imagine what Michael would think if he knew the truth.

The last thing she wanted was to lie to him but she didn't feel like she had a choice. He would have stopped her if he'd known what she was up to. Tried to stop her, she amended. Because there wasn't a reason he could come up with that she hadn't already thought of herself. It was a risk she had to take. For her grandmother's sake, not her brother's.

Elijah was waiting for her at the big rock they used to chip away at as kids, positive the ridges that sparkled and shone were bands of gold. Even back then, her brother was looking for a get-rich-quick scheme.

She leaned across the console to retrieve her hiking boots and flashlight off the passenger seat. She had put them in the car long before Michael had arrived so they'd be ready for her to sneak off into the night. He'd have no idea how much she would have preferred to stay at the cottage with him and Michaela.

With the flashlight on her lap, Sadie opened the driver's-side door and swung her legs around. She slipped off her sneakers and then pulled on the well-worn hiking boots, listening to the crickets in the meadow, the bullfrogs down by the creek, and the yip of the coyotes in the woods.

She sat for a minute, taking it all in, the melodic sounds of spring, the sweet scent of the flowers in the meadow. The last thing she'd wanted was to come home to Highland Falls. So far everything, other than Michael, had proven she'd been right to make a life in Charlotte instead of here. But this—the sights and sounds and the beauty of this place she'd called home. She hadn't known how much she'd missed it until that moment.

An owl hooted from a tree across the road, pulling her out of her reverie. She grabbed her windbreaker and her black canvas backpack and got out of the SUV. *Old habits die hard*, she thought as she put on the dark, lightweight jacket and then slid the straps of the heavy backpack she'd filled for her brother over her shoulders. She was still looking after him. She supposed she couldn't be mad at her grandmother for doing the same. But she was furious at her brother for putting Agnes at risk, physically and financially.

She shut the door of the SUV, harder than was smart. Sound carried out here. The last thing she wanted was to draw attention to herself. The situation her brother had dragged them into was dangerous.

She put her hand in the pocket of her jacket, closing her fingers around the gun. It gave her a measure of comfort. She knew how to use it. Her brother didn't. But Sadie fully intended that he'd be a half-decent shot before the night was out.

The quarter moon shining down from the star-littered sky didn't do much to light her way through the meadow. She turned on the flashlight, keeping the beam low to the ground. She kept her ears open, listening for sounds that didn't belong as she walked into the woods.

In the distance, she thought she heard the crunch of tires on gravel and turned, scanning the long, winding dirt road. No car lights, no other sounds. She waited a few seconds longer before continuing on the long-remembered trail to the big rock. A branch snapped, bringing her head up. She moved the beam of light through the trees. There was nothing there. Except she couldn't shake the feeling something or someone was watching her.

You're sleep-deprived, she reminded herself. Still, she shut off the flashlight and crouched down, letting her eyes adjust. There was a rustle of leaves. Something small, maybe a snake. The thought made her smile. She hadn't educated Michael on the flora and fauna of Highland Falls as promised. She'd make it up to him. In the short time she'd known him, she had a lot to make up to him for. After tonight, she'd have even more.

As she straightened from the crouch, she saw a faint glow of light through the trees. She sniffed the air and sighed. Elijah. He'd started a campfire. She turned on her flashlight, once again keeping the beam low to the ground, close to her feet. Ferns erased the path she and her brother had tromped along all those years ago. They'd been close back then but time had erased the bond they shared just as easily as the ferns had erased the path.

She saw him before he saw her. His hands were cupped above the small flame, tiny embers floating around his head, turning the chestnut-colored hair they shared to red.

"If someone is looking for you, you've made it easy for them to find you, Elijah." It worried her that she'd gotten this close without him being aware of her presence.

His head shot up, the fear she saw on his face turning to relief. He stood, wiping his palms on his jeans. They were worn and torn.

"You came," he said. "I didn't think you would."

She opened her mouth to tell him she'd come for their grandmother, not for him. It was the truth, but she couldn't bring herself to say the words. He looked young, and scared. The expression on his face was similar to the one he'd worn the night they realized their parents weren't coming back for them.

She slid the backpack off her shoulders. "I don't know why. I've always kept my word to you."

He nodded, dragging a hand down the side of his face. "I messed up, Sadie. I didn't mean for any of this to happen. Honest, I didn't. I just wanted to make a few extra bucks. I thought I could make a go of Highland Tours. All I needed was to come up with a few thousand until I made a name for myself."

"That's what you told me when I gave you two thousand dollars, Elijah." Money she'd been saving to buy a place of her own. She'd invested so much of her hard-earned money into her brother's schemes that there'd never been anything left to make her own dreams come true. That had been the last time, she'd promised herself then. It was a promise she meant to keep.

"I know, I know. But it wasn't enough. I told you it wouldn't be."

"So you tried doubling it by gambling online. And lost it all," she guessed. Although knowing her brother as well as she did, it was an educated guess. And apparently she'd guessed correctly, given the dejected slump of his shoulders.

"If you just came to remind me that I'm a screwup, you might as well go. I know I am."

She tossed him the backpack. "There's a change of clothes, a jacket, some food, and two hundred dollars. It's all I can spare. Don't ask Granny for any more money, Elijah. She's broke."

His eyes glistened in the firelight. "I didn't know how bad it was. She said the store was doing well. You have to know I wouldn't have taken it from her if I'd known."

Sadie wanted to believe him, but she didn't. "Now you do, so I don't want to see your girlfriend in the store begging for cash. I'll be there with Granny from now on."

"Don't blame Payton. She didn't know where to turn. She's pregnant. We're having a baby, Sadie." He smiled, like she should be happy about the news.

"Congratulations. I have a baby, you know. Her name's Michaela."

"Right, yeah." He winced and then gave her a quiet smile. "You always wanted to be a mom. I bet you're a great one."

It would probably cheer him up to hear how spectacularly she was failing at motherhood. He'd always thought life came easily to her. "Why am I here, Elijah? What do you need from me?"

"Do you have to say it like that, Sadie? Don't you think I feel bad enough? I tried to get out of it. I tried to do the right thing."

"You agreed to distribute drugs and then you decided to keep some for yourself. How, in your mind, does that equate to doing the right thing?"

"You don't know the whole story." He shook his head. "I don't know why I thought you'd help me."

"Don't pull your woe-is-me act, Elijah. Just give it to me straight. Where are the drugs?"

"I don't know."

"How can you not—"

"I was scared. I wanted out, and once you're in, you're in. The only way you get out is in a body bag. So I thought I could make a deal. They let me out, and I give them their cocaine back." He looked away and mumbled something.

"What did you just say?"

"I got wasted. I was scared and panicked and started drinking and smoking a little weed. I don't remember what I did with the drugs." He nodded at a shovel leaning against the rock. "I thought it might be here but it's not." His voice cracked. "I don't know what to do. They're after me, Sadie. I told Granny I was in trouble, but it's worse than that. They want me dead. I know too much."

She searched his face. He wasn't lying. "From where I'm standing, you have only one choice to make, and that's to go to the police. Gabe is a friend of mine. He's a good guy. We'll—"

"No. You don't understand, Sadie. I can't go to the police. I already did, and that man is dead because of me."

A chill tiptoed down her spine. "What do you mean?"

"The guy they found dead in the woods a little more than a week ago? He was a deputy with the Jackson County Sheriff's Department. His name was Brodie. I was his CI—his confidential informant. He—" A gunshot blast rent the night air.

Sadie threw herself at her brother, bringing him to the ground as a bullet whizzed past their heads. She grabbed Elijah by his shirt and the backpack by the strap, dragging them with her as she belly-crawled behind the rock. Another blast of gunfire came from the opposite direction, the bullet pinging off the front of the rock.

"There's two of them," she whispered, taking the gun from her pocket. She didn't bother asking her brother if he was armed so she was surprised when he lifted his T-shirt to pull a gun from the back of his jeans.

He shrugged. "Granny made me take her gun when I went on the run last summer."

Two consecutive shotgun blasts echoed in the woods, the

bullets hitting the top of the boulder, sending shards of granite onto their heads.

"Do you know how to use it?" she whispered while digging a water bottle out of the backpack.

"Yeah, I've been practicing," he whispered back.

"Good. Pick up one of those rocks and toss it hard to your right." As he did as she directed, Sadie leaned around the boulder to toss the water on the fire. The flame sputtered and then winked out at the same time one of the shooters fired where Elijah had tossed the rock.

Her heart racing, she leaned back against the boulder, taking a moment before whispering to her brother, "On the count of three, shoot once, then get off a second shot to the right of your first one." If they gave the impression that there were more than just the two of them, maybe the shooters would back off.

She counted down and fired on three. Elijah's gun jammed. Seconds later, she got off another shot. Her brother managed to get off one too. Bullets pinged off either side of the rock. Her plan hadn't worked. The shooters weren't backing off. If anything, they were getting closer.

Sadie patted the ground, her fingers closing over the rocks that had been digging into her thigh. She handed one to her brother. "I'm going to throw mine, and then you're going to throw yours. Once you do, I want you to run low and fast, but not in a straight line, Elijah. Go to the caves."

He shook his head. "I'm not leaving you."

"It's you they want. Here." She handed him her gun. It was more reliable than her grandmother's. Another shot rang out, the bullet shredding the bark of the tree she'd gauged the person shooting at her to be hiding behind.

A man swore and a radio crackled.

She wondered if his partner had nearly shot him. Or were there now more than two shooters? She didn't have time to figure it out or what it meant for them. "Be careful, Elijah," she said and drew back her arm.

They threw the rocks within seconds of each other. Elijah's skipped along the ground. It sounded like someone was running through the woods while hers sounded like someone had run into a tree. He'd always had a good arm—and a soft heart, she thought at the sight of tears shining on his cheeks. "I love you, Sadie. You and Granny. Don't die," he said, then sprinted into the woods.

She didn't have time to respond or to think about the danger they were in. She had to cover his back. She inched up and got off a shot down the middle of where she suspected the two men were positioned, ducking down when they returned fire. Only the gunshots weren't directed at her. They seemed to be directed at the initial shooters...or had they gone after her brother? The snap of branches and crackle of leaves indicated they were on the run.

"Stay safe, baby brother," she whispered. She should have told him she loved him. It might have been her only chance. She pushed away the dark thoughts and leaned as far to the left as she could without making herself a target. Raising the gun, she aimed it in the direction the last shot had come from and pulled the trigger. The gun jammed again.

Branches snapped under heavy footfalls. Someone was coming her way. She closed her eyes and prayed. Then she aimed in the direction of the sound. She pulled the trigger. The gun jammed.

In the distance, she heard rapid shots of gunfire. Someone returned fire, and then someone yelled out in pain. The gunfire and the cry didn't come from her brother, she was sure of it. The caves were in the opposite direction. But the heavy footfalls had closed in on her.

She scrambled for the flashlight. Turning it on, she smothered the beam of light on her thigh, searching the ground for a good-size rock. Finding one near the base of the boulder, she hefted it in her hand. She'd let them get close enough, shine the light in their eyes, and hit them with the rock. Then she'd take off and pray she'd bought herself enough time to get away.

She shot to her feet, shining the light directly into a man's face. She raised her hand with the rock.

"Sadie, it's me. It's Gabe."

Fighting back a sob, she let her hand fall to her side. "Thank God."

An hour later, as she sat on the couch in the cottage, she wished anyone but Gabe had found her. She hated to lie to him but she wouldn't put him in danger. The last law enforcement officer her brother had confided in had died.

"I'm sorry. I wish I could tell you more, Gabe. But like I said, I'd barely gotten to say two words to my brother when they started shooting at us."

"You left here at nine-fifty," Michael said. "According to Gabe, reports of gunfire came in at ten-ten. Surely you would have had time to share more than a few words with your brother." His intent stare hadn't left her face from the moment she walked in with Gabe. It was like he was judging her every move, every word, and he clearly found them lacking in sincerity.

He was angry—at her. He didn't have to say so with words; his expression told her everything she needed to know.

"You missed your calling, Michael. You should have been in law enforcement." She tried for a flippant tone instead of a guilty one.

"I am."

Gabe glanced at him.

He shrugged. "Park rangers fall under the purview of law enforcement." His gaze returned to her face, no doubt waiting for her answer.

"I don't know what you want from me. I can't tell you any more than I already have. The people you should be questioning are the ones who shot at me and my brother."

"They were shooting at your brother. If you hadn't gone off to meet with him, you wouldn't have been in danger, and your daughter wouldn't have been at risk of losing her mother." Michael shoved his hands in the pockets of his chinos and looked away, his jaw clenched.

Those were the words that she'd been waiting for from the moment she'd walked through the door. "I know. I'm sorry I lied to you, Michael. I didn't know what else to do."

"Use your head," he said, then winced. "I should probably go."

"Me too. I'll follow up with you tomorrow, Sadie. You might remember something after you've had some rest. I'm leaving one of my deputies. They'll be outside in their patrol car."

"Thank you." She stood up to see them to the door. It wasn't until she did that she realized the boxes that had filled her living room and kitchen were gone. "Michael, wait. Can you stay a minute?"

She thought he might ignore her and keep walking as Gabe opened the front door. But he stopped, murmured something to Gabe, and then turned to her.

Gabe glanced from Michael to her, a pained grimace on his face as he shut the door behind him.

"What did you want to say, Sadie?"

"I just wanted to thank you for everything you've done, looking after Michaela, unpacking and putting everything away. I can't tell you how much I appreciate it." She gave him a tentative smile.

He didn't return it. "You're welcome." He reached for the door and glanced back at her. "Goodbye, Sadie."

There was a coldness, a finality in his words, and her heart tumbled to her toes.

"I'm not going to see you again, am I?" she asked.

"I'm sorry. But no, you won't."

Chapter Thirteen

♥

No way. You're not telling Sadie who we are. We can't trust her. Look what she pulled last night." Black tossed his cigarette, grinding it into the asphalt with the toe of his sneaker.

Thanks to his partner, the area around the industrial waste bin behind I Believe in Unicorns was littered with cigarette butts. Chase toed them into a small mound. "You should clean this up."

"You're talking about blowing our cover to a woman who just showed us her true colors, and you're worried about a couple cigarette butts lying around on the ground?"

"There aren't a couple of butts, there are twenty-two. You smoke too much. It's bad for your health—and mine, since you continue to smoke around me even when I ask you not to. Death from secondary smoke has been scientifically proven, Black."

His partner shook his head. "I don't get you, Mikey. I really don't."

"That doesn't surprise me, but what does surprise me is you can't see the benefit in telling Sadie who we are."

"Enlighten me, O brilliant one."

Chase pinched the bridge of his nose between his thumb and

forefinger in an attempt to alleviate a headache that came from lack of sleep, worry over Sadie and the baby, and indirectly inhaling two cigarettes. He wondered, and not for the first time that morning, how he'd gotten saddled with this man for a partner.

"If—and that's a big if for me—she's working with her brother, we're more likely to get her to turn on him if she realizes we've been surveilling her and her grandmother and that we have the authority to make a deal. The last thing she wants is to end up in prison." His chest tightened at the image of Michaela being ripped from her mother's arms as they led Sadie away in handcuffs, just as it had last night when he'd learned she'd lied to him and could have been killed.

She'd put herself in danger without any regard for the consequences. Whoever shot at her and her brother last night, they'd assume she was involved, just like his partner had. Both Sadie and Michaela were in danger, and the only way Chase knew how to protect them was to tell her the truth. He was honest enough with himself to admit that the fact he'd no longer have to lie to her played into his decision.

But there was another reason he wanted to tell Sadie the truth, one he wouldn't—couldn't—share with his partner. By Chase's calculations, Black should have come upon Sadie and her brother within minutes of the gunmen. Black was former special ops. From everything Chase had read in the agent's military file, Nathan Black's targets shouldn't have been able to get away from him as he'd claimed when Chase and Gabe had questioned him at the rock in the woods last night. Chase also didn't believe Black's claim that his shots went wide.

Black had a night scope on his rifle, something he obviously didn't know Chase was aware of. But Chase made it his mission to know every last detail about the men and women he worked with. However, one detail about Black eluded him—what was his endgame?

Chase had a feeling his partner's brand of justice wasn't the same as his. He didn't want Sadie caught in the crossfire. When she was at her grandmother's store, she'd be under his partner's protection. She needed to know Black's true identity so he couldn't play her. There was the added benefit that she'd tell Chase if she saw or heard something suspicious.

If she ever talked to him again. He didn't fool himself that his confession would go over well.

"What if Sadie is the mastermind and not her brother? Hear me out," Black said when Chase opened his mouth to shut him down. "Like I told you and Gabe last night, I didn't hear or see much, but it was obvious Sadie was calling the shots. She knew exactly what she was doing. She's smart and one hell of a shot."

Admittedly, learning that Sadie had been armed and knew how to use a gun had concerned him. Although practically everyone in the small town owned a gun, according to Gabe.

"Look, I know you have this Madonna fantasy going on but just because she's a yummy mummy doesn't mean she doesn't also have the brains and motivation to be behind this. It's in her DNA. This isn't the first time she'd find herself on the wrong side of the law either. There was that incident with her father. She was the one who helped him escape police."

"Allegedly. They never found any proof." Not that he'd admit it to Black, but the thought had also crossed Chase's mind.

Jeremiah Gray had put Sadie, a thirteen-year-old at the time, in an untenable position. So had her brother. Just like in her romantic relationships, Sadie had placed her trust in the wrong men. Men who had no scruples when it came to taking advantage of her innate goodness. He ignored the voice in his head that said he'd basically done the same.

"Because they underestimated her, the same as you are. In my experience, women can be just as manipulative and deadly as men. Maybe more so."

"Whether I've misjudged her or not, this is our best play moving forward. We've wasted months looking for Elijah, and now that he's gone to ground again, we need to ensure we don't waste more time. Sadie will lead us to him."

"And why did we waste three months?" Black cupped his hand behind his ear. "Come on, let me hear you say it. No? Then I'll say it for you. Because we underestimated Agnes MacLeod. We never suspected that our Betty White look-alike was hiding her grandson."

"Neither did Sadie, and Agnes raised her," Chase said, still flummoxed, and irritated that Sadie's grandmother had managed to pull the wool over their eyes.

"But did she really? Maybe the three of them are in on it together."

"Either you need more sleep or your filthy habit has starved your brain of oxygen one time too many if you actually believe that." He toed the last of the cigarette butts into the tidy mound. "We're going with my plan, Black. Meet me at the cottage after work. We'll tell Sadie then. Keep a close eye on them today. Let me know—" he began as he went to walk away.

Black grabbed him by the arm, whipped him around, and pulled him up hard against his chest.

"What the—" Chase got out just before Black angled his head as if to kiss him.

Sadie stood at the back door of I Believe in Unicorns, staring at Michael and Nate. She rubbed her sleep-deprived eyes. She knew she was tired but imagining the two men were kissing was ridiculous. They couldn't be...

She blinked them back into focus. They still looked like they were kissing from where she was standing. The man she'd spent the past three months fantasizing about was kissing another man.

If she needed further proof her brain synapses weren't firing on all cylinders, it had just been handed to her on a big, shiny silver platter. Even now, images from yesterday, moments when she thought there might be something between them, played out behind her eyes. She was lucky Gabe had been in the driveway last night, otherwise she might have chased after Michael and declared her feelings for him, anything to make him stay.

She was about to turn away and give them their privacy when Michael pushed Nate away. Then, as though Michael sensed her standing there, he raised his gaze. His lips flattened, and he shoved Nate again. "I don't believe you," he said to the other man.

Nate glanced back at her and shook his head before saying something to Michael that she couldn't hear.

"Too bad. You brought me in on this. We're playing it my way," Michael said to Nate, then walked toward her. "Sadie, we need to talk."

What did he mean by *You brought me in on this*? Something wasn't right. She had a feeling she wasn't going to like what he told her. She thought back to Michael's interactions with Nate yesterday. "You two know each other, don't you?"

Michael nodded, glancing over his shoulder at Nate, who'd lit another cigarette. "We do. You know him too."

Nate muttered something, took a long drag of his cigarette, and then tossed it.

"Of course I do. My grandmother hired him." Her voice hitched as Nate joined Michael. The ex-offender seemed different. His easygoing demeanor was missing. He looked a little scary.

The garbage truck rattled into the alley. "We should probably take this inside," Michael said.

"Oh yeah, we should. Unless you intend to out us to everyone in Highland Falls," Nate muttered.

Okay, so it sounded like her brain had been going in the wrong direction after all. This *was* about the two of them coming out as gay. A much better scenario than the one that had her thinking she should slam the door and run. They weren't working for the Jackson County Sheriff's Department like she'd begun to suspect.

She gave them an understanding smile. "Small towns get a bad rap. People aren't as closed-minded as you think. You don't have to worry how people in town will react to you guys being partners."

"We're partners, Sadie, but we're not gay." Michael held the door open, lifting his chin for her to lead the way.

She turned to face them, blocking the entrance. "No, you're not getting anywhere near my grandmother or daughter until I know who you are. Show me some ID." She slid her hand into the pocket of her jeans, closing her fingers around her phone. Gabe or one of his deputies could be at the store in under four minutes. All she'd have to do is yell for her grandmother to get Michaela out of the store. The knowledge gave Sadie the confidence to lift her chin and hold Michael's intent blue gaze.

"You don't have to be scared. We're not going to hurt you. We're here to protect you, Sadie." He took his wallet from his sage-green uniform pants and flipped it open.

She stared at the badge. "FBI," she whispered, lifting her gaze to his. "You're an FBI agent?"

He nodded, pocketing his ID before she could examine it. "Nate's an agent with the North Carolina State Bureau of Investigation."

The man she'd believed to be an ex-offender flashed his badge. This time she was more careful. She didn't let the sight of the badge distract her from matching the face and the name to the man towering over her.

"We're investigating the murder of my friend. He was a deputy with the Jackson County Sheriff's Department."

"The man found in the woods near the cottage?" The man who'd been trying to help her brother. The man who was killed because he knew too much. "I'm very sorry for your loss," she said at his clipped nod.

Turning, she walked back into the store and forced a smile for her grandmother, who was rocking Michaela in a chair by the display window. "Hey, Granny, I need to talk to Nate and Michael for a minute. Are you okay with Michaela?"

"And why wouldn't I be? Look at her, sleeping like an angel."

Of course she was. The moment Michael and Gabe had pulled out of her driveway last night, Michaela had woken up. Sadie was lucky if she'd managed forty-five minutes of uninterrupted sleep. Between that and panic, she was struggling to come up with a way to deal with this situation. How much of what her brother had told her should she share?

Calm down, she told herself as she walked down the hall to the office with Michael and Nate following close behind. She'd need all her wits about her. Both she and her grandmother could face charges of aiding and abetting a known felon. She'd been in this position before. Only then she'd been a terrified thirteen-year-old who'd made the mistake of trusting her father.

She opened the office door, praying they didn't notice her fingers trembling on the knob. Wishful thinking on her part, she thought, catching Michael glancing at her hands. She folded her arms across the pink unicorn T-shirt she had on. Nate wore the same only several sizes larger. The office seemed crowded, the air charged and stifling—perhaps the reason she was having trouble breathing and felt faint.

"You should probably sit down, Sadie," Michael suggested.

She wondered if he could tell her hands weren't the only thing shaking—so were her legs. But she wouldn't give them the satisfaction of appearing weak or intimidated. She leaned back against the edge of the desk instead of sitting down. "I'm fine. Why are you telling me who you are now?" she asked, buying time while playing through her options in her head.

"Yeah, Mikey, remind me again why we're breaking our cover?" His arms crossed over his broad chest, Nate glared at his partner.

A partner who ignored him. "By meeting with your brother, you put yourself at risk, Sadie. The men who are looking for him could use you to draw him out."

"Or they might come to the conclusion they've been looking for the wrong Gray all along," Nate said.

"Either way, you're in danger," Michael said without correcting his partner.

"You think I had something to do with the drugs and shooting the deputy?" She pulled out the chair from the desk and sat down before her legs gave out. She wasn't expecting to have to defend herself against charges of drug dealing and murder. Against aiding and abetting, yes, but never this.

"We should have the ballistics report back on your grandmother's gun within the next seventy-two hours. We'll know if it was used to kill Brodie then," Nate said.

The gun she'd turned over to Gabe last night. The gun that had been in her brother's possession since last summer.

"So you might as well come clean now," Nate added, while Michael stayed perfectly still and quiet.

He was leaning against the wall, watching her. Like he'd watched her back in February from across the road. The day of hearts. Her grandmother's prediction hadn't been about Elijah or Drew after all. It had been about Michael.

"I didn't shoot your friend, and I had nothing to do with stealing the drugs from the Whiteside Mountain Gang. You believe me, don't you?" she asked Michael. "I'd just moved back to Highland Falls. I—"

"The autopsy came back last week. Brodie was shot in February," Nate clipped out as if the words were hard for him to say.

"There's no way I could have been involved in his shooting. I was almost nine months pregnant. You know that, Michael. You were..." She narrowed her eyes at him. "Why were you there that day? Did you do something to the road, to my car? Did you set it up so I'd crash?"

"Of course not. Brodie had set up a meet with Nate there a few days before." He glanced at the other agent. "We were searching for him, for clues."

Her eyes went wide. "You," she said to Nate. "You're Eddie Taylor."

He gave her a slight bow. "At your service."

She shook her head. She'd thought they were her heroes, that Michael was her knight in shining armor, and all along they were lying to her. "What do you want from me?" Her voice was strained from holding back her emotions.

"We want to know where Elijah is," Michael said.

"I don't know. I don't," she repeated when he raised an eyebrow. It was true. She hadn't heard from Elijah. He could be anywhere by now.

"After last night, you must know he's in danger, Sadie. If they find him before we do, he doesn't stand a chance."

"And I'm supposed to believe he stands a chance with you, with him?" She lifted her chin at Nate. "You've tried and convicted him."

"Are you saying that he didn't steal the cocaine or kill Brodie?" Michael asked.

"Before you answer, you might want to remember that we're the only ones who stand in the way of you going to jail for aiding and abetting. Same goes for your grandmother," Nate said.

"Ease up, Black." Michael pushed off the wall. "Look, Sadie, I know this is a lot to take in. But we're"—he glanced at his partner and then back at her—"I'm on your side. I know how you felt about your brother stealing the drugs. You told me. So no, I don't believe you're involved. But you have to look at this from our perspective, and right now, all the evidence is pointing at your brother shooting Brodie."

"He didn't. He didn't kill Brodie. He—" She closed her mouth. She'd said too much. She was angry that Michael had been lying to her but she didn't want him to end up dead like Brodie. She'd never forgive herself. She imagined that's how her brother felt.

"He told you who he thinks killed Brodie, didn't he?" When she remained silent, Michael said, "Sadie, we know Brodie and your brother believed the Jackson County Sheriff's Department is somehow involved in all of this. That's why we're undercover, and it's why we have to stay that way. None of what we've said to you can leave this room."

"So Nate is going to continue working at the store?" she asked, avoiding meeting the other agent's hard stare. He didn't trust her. She supposed she didn't blame him. He believed her brother killed his friend. He wasn't open to the possibility Elijah might not have had anything to do with Brodie's death. But Michael seemed to be.

Michael nodded. "Yes, he'll be here to protect your grandmother, and you and Michaela when you're here. For that reason, I'd like you to suggest to your grandmother that she rent the second bedroom in her apartment to Nate. It shouldn't be a tough sell. She needs the money."

Her grandmother probably wouldn't be difficult to convince, but Nate looked like he would be. Her life, their lives, were spiraling out of control, which might have been why she almost missed Michael's quietly stated "I'll be staying with you."

She gaped at him. "Staying with me, as in moving in with me?" Her brain seemed to have missed the memo that she shouldn't be happy about this turn of events. She blamed it on sleep deprivation.

"Yes, Abby has already created a cover story about us that by now half the town has bought into."

"And what cover story is that?" Sadie asked, thinking this was very close to what she'd wished for last night before Michael closed the door on her hopes and dreams. Now she knew why they said *Be careful what you wish for*.

Nate clasped his hands to his chest, raising his voice to a grating falsetto. "Michael Knight is Sadie's knight in shining armor. He helped deliver that precious child of hers into the world and the two of them fell madly in love." Nate rolled his eyes. "What a pile of fairy-tale bullcrap. I wouldn't have believed it myself if I hadn't heard it almost verbatim from at least ten different sources." He waggled his eyebrows at Michael. "Too bad his real name is Chase Roberts and not Michael Knight."

Chapter Fourteen

♥

Chase stared at his partner, who simply shrugged like what he'd just told Sadie was no big deal. But it was a big deal. To Chase, and to her. "Sadie, I can—"

She held up a hand. "Don't bother. There's nothing you can say that I want to hear." Her eyes met his. They were cold, and the expression on her face was one of icy disdain. "You're not staying with me and my daughter at the cottage."

Chase took a step toward her, raising his hands when she backed away. "Look, I know you're upset, and I don't blame you. But you need protection, Sadie."

"Call one of your FBI buddies or get Gabe to assign one of his deputies to protect us. I don't care who it is, as long as it's not you."

Before he could respond, she sent him one last killing glare and then stalked out of the office and slammed the door.

"Ouch. If looks could kill, you'd be dead, buddy."

"Thanks to you. That was a bullshit move, Black."

"It was your call, remember? You're the one who blew our cover." He grinned. "So looks like you're staying with Mrs. M, and I'm playing house with Sadie and the demon spawn."

"No, we stick to the plan," Chase said, barely resisting the urge to wipe the smirk from Black's face. "Once Sadie has a chance to cool down, I'll explain to her why it has to be me."

"Let me know when you plan to give her the news. I want a ringside seat."

As the hours ticked by without Sadie responding to his texts or his attempts to call her, Chase debated skipping the last two hours of his shift and heading back into town. He'd manned the visitors' center for the morning, helped rescue two lost hikers by midafternoon, and now was on trail-maintenance duty, so he figured he'd met his park ranger responsibilities for the day.

He glanced at the wildflowers in the meadow as he walked toward the cottage on Willow Creek and wondered if they'd make an acceptable peace offering. But then he remembered the look on Sadie's face seconds before she slammed the office door, and he knew he had to do better. Black would be of no help, and it wasn't like Chase could call any of Sadie's friends to ask for advice. If Chase played it right, her grandmother might have a suggestion. After all, she seemed to believe he and Sadie were dating.

He crossed the dirt road and headed for the rock under the weeping willow. Pulling out his cell phone, he checked the screen. Nothing from Sadie or Black. His partner was ignoring him too. Chase sat on the rock and called Black. He answered on the second ring.

"Seriously, Roberts. I'm working here. I don't have time to respond to your hourly texts. Nothing's changed. She's still pissed at you, and at me."

"Did she at least talk to her grandmother about you renting a room?"

"Oh yeah, she took care of that all right. She told Mrs. M I love to listen to opera, play Monopoly, and watch the Hallmark Channel."

"Sounds like you're lucky she didn't tell Agnes you're also a vegetarian who likes to play hair and makeup," Chase said around a smile.

"Don't even joke about that. I wouldn't put it past her. She's not as sweet as she looks. She has a vindictive streak a mile wide."

Chase would rather her be mean and vindictive than sad and hurt. Although he had a feeling that, under her icy disdain this morning, there'd been a boatload of hurt and betrayal. She'd trusted him.

"I can't wait to see what she has in store for you," Black continued. "I'm guessing she hasn't responded to you yet."

"No, she hasn't." He gritted his teeth. He hated to ask his partner for a favor, but he didn't have a choice. "If you can get her alone, you need to impress upon her how important it is that our cover isn't blown. To that end, I'm the only one who can stay with her without raising suspicions."

"Yeah, yeah, I'll see what I can do."

Chase blinked, surprised. "I expected you to put up more of a fight."

"Well, you're the only one who the members of the Jackson County Sheriff's Department might not consider a deterrent if they wanted to make a move on her. Now I have to go." His partner disconnected.

Despite the sunshine glinting off the creek and warming the place where he sat on the rock, the potential danger to Sadie and Michaela left Chase cold. He leaned against the tree and closed his eyes. They needed to bring in Elijah sooner rather than later. The gurgle of the creek and the chirping of birds alleviated some of the tension in his chest. It made it easier to think, to come up with a plan to bring Elijah in. He'd need Sadie's help to do so.

As he mulled over how to win back her trust, something wet

touched his hand and then the weight of his phone disappeared. "What the...?" He opened his eyes to see a golden retriever grinning at him around his cell phone.

Chase came to his feet slowly so as not to startle the dog. "Okay, come here. Give me back my phone, and I'll give you a treat." He patted his thigh. The dog cocked his head, and Chase could have sworn he was laughing at him.

Chase picked up a stick. "How about catch? You want to play catch?" He threw the stick, but instead of taking the bait, the dog ran alongside the creek. Chase sprinted after him.

"Finn! Come here, boy!" a woman called. She sounded like she was half a mile up the road.

"Over here!" Chase yelled in hopes that the dog's owner would have more luck getting his phone. The dog turned and barreled toward him.

Chase smiled, relieved, and bent to retrieve his phone. "Good boy. That's a good—*ugh*."

The dog headbutted him in the stomach, hard. Chase lost his breath and his balance. Arms pinwheeling, he slipped on green-slime-coated rocks and landed flat on his back in the creek. The fast-moving, surprisingly deep and frigid creek. Finn bounded in after him without Chase's phone in his mouth. Chase might have been relieved if the dog hadn't landed on top of him, pushing him under. From beneath the icy, crystal-clear water, he saw the dog peering down at him. Chase wrapped his arms around the retriever and managed to get himself in an upright position. From the other side of the creek, an older woman frantically waved her arms. "Save him. Please save him!"

Chase didn't know if she was talking about the dog saving him or him saving the dog, but he didn't have time to think about it. The current was pushing them toward a line of boulders jutting out of the creek. Keeping one arm wrapped around the dog's neck, Chase used the other arm to swim toward shore. His

limbs were stiff—numb from the cold—and his clothes were
weighing him down. It wasn't until the dog got in on the act that
Chase made any headway. Finn towed Chase to shore, depositing
him on the rocks before racing to his owner.

"My poor baby," she crooned, then lifted her gaze to Chase as
he dragged himself the rest of the way out of the water. "Thank
you for saving him. I don't know what I'd do without him. How
can I ever repay you?"

There was no way he was going to tell the woman that Finn
had saved him. If it weren't for her dog, Chase wouldn't have
almost drowned. "All in a day's work, ma'am. But I'd suggest
you keep your dog on a leash from now on."

After promising to do as he suggested, the woman set off
with her dog trailing after her. Chase waited until they'd reached
a car parked on the side of the road before going in search of his
phone. It was lying on the grass. Other than some teeth marks
and slobber, it looked none the worse for wear. Apparently,
it was still working, because there was a text from Black on
the screen.

> She's not happy about it, but she agreed to you provid-
> ing her protection. You owe me, partner. Dinner from
> Zia Maria's on Main Street for starters. I've called in
> the order.

An hour later, Chase walked into Zia Maria's on Main Street.
It smelled like heaven and Luciano's, his favorite Italian restaurant in DC. In comparison to the fine-dining establishment he'd
frequented with his grandfather for the past two decades, this
was a tiny hole in the wall with terra-cotta tiles, the candles in
wicker-wrapped Chianti bottles casting a warm, friendly glow on
the red-and-white-checked tablecloths. Two of the restaurant's
ten round tables were occupied by diners.

The men at one of the tables were around his grandfather's age. Chase imagined the judge sitting with them, enjoying the easy camaraderie of lifelong friends, instead of sitting with the residents of the exclusive retirement home where he currently resided.

Chase was his grandfather's only visitor at the retirement home. The judge had devoted his life to his legal career. He hadn't wasted his time making or keeping friends. The couples that his grandparents had socialized with had been more her friends than his. They'd drifted away when his wife died, long before Chase and his brother had moved in with him.

Chase worried how his grandfather was faring without his twice-weekly visits. The judge still refused to take his calls. He'd been angrier about Chase's demotion than he had been.

Chase stuck his hands in the pockets of the jeans that Black had insisted he buy. The other agent had shaken his head when Chase unpacked his suitcase at the no-name motel off the highway where they'd rented two adjoining rooms last week. According to Black, Chase needed jeans to fit in, not suits and chinos.

Chase glanced at the menu written in Italian on two chalk-boards that hung from the redbrick walls to the side of a long line of customers waiting at the counter. The lineup as much as the basil-scented air gave Chase hope that the food would be as authentic as the atmosphere.

"Look, look who it is," a diminutive woman cried from behind the counter, waving the customers in line to the side with a wooden spoon stained with tomato sauce. She wore her dark hair in a bouffant style similar to the one his grandmother used to wear.

He turned to see who she was talking about. There was no one behind him.

"Come, come." She gestured him to the front of the line. "Eh," she said when someone grumbled a complaint. "He's a hero.

Nessa, she say he saved Finn. You know how much she love that dog. Come, come."

Chase apologized to the people in line. Most of them didn't seem to mind now that they learned he'd "saved" the dog. He wondered what they'd think if he told them the truth.

"You're a good boy," she said to Chase, her smile as bright as the sauce splattered on her white apron. "You take care of our Sadie, and now, you take care of Finn. Eh, look at that face." She put down her wooden spoon and reached up to grab his cheeks between her strong fingers. "What a handsome boy." With her fingers still clamped on his cheeks, she turned his face to the customers in line. "Just like a movie star, eh? If I was younger, I'd give our Sadie a run for her money."

She let go of his cheeks and patted his face. "She needs someone like you. A good man." She wrinkled her nose. "The bambina's daddy? He no good." Then the disgust cleared from her expression, and she clapped her hands. "Now, what can Zia Maria get for you? We gotta fatten our Sadie up, eh? Too skinny. It's the depression. It happens after you have the bambino sometimes." She leaned to the side to look past him. "You had it, eh, Nina? You too, Marge."

Apparently, Nina and Marge weren't the only women in the restaurant to have suffered from postpartum depression, and for the next fifteen minutes, every one of them shared their experiences and advice with Chase.

"Ma, you're backing things up," a man called from the open kitchen, sliding a pizza into the wood-fired oven.

"I'll write it all down for you," Maria told Chase, holding up a pencil and pad of paper. "You make her listen. She pretends everything's okay, but we know it's not so. Too proud, that one. She won't even let her friends help. But you, she'll listen to you."

He highly doubted that was the case, but he appreciated Maria's faith in him, just as much as he appreciated her advice.

They were right. Sadie wasn't just exhausted; she was depressed. He hadn't recognized the signs until he heard their stories. It wasn't something the baby books he'd read had touched upon. They were focused on the baby's development, not the mother.

From behind him, a new voice chimed in. "You'll have your work cut out for you, Mr. Knight. Sadie's as stubborn and as proud as her grandmother."

He turned to the woman with the long, straight coal-black hair at the back of the line, recognizing her from the *Highland Falls Herald*. It was the town's mayor, Winter Johnson.

"The mayor is right. Agnes, she's too proud to tell us her store, it is in trouble. It's Elijah's fault. Her grandson," Maria confided to Chase. "He was a sweet boy, smart but not, how you say, smart about the people. Our Sadie and Agnes"—she wiggled her baby finger—"he had them wrapped so tight he say jump, they say, how high."

"Ma." Her son rattled off something in Italian.

"A little like your Marcello, eh, Maria?" an older man at one of the tables said.

"No pizza for you, Ed," Marcello yelled from the kitchen.

Everyone laughed, and Maria waved her spoon at her son. "This is important, Marcello. You want Agnes to lose her store or what?"

"If you keep talking and not taking orders, we'll be in the same boat. Bring it up at the next business-association meeting. Abby will be there. She'll figure something out."

"Okay, okay." Maria shrugged. "What he say, it is true. Abby, she'll know what to do. Mayor, you'll take care of that, eh?" Once Winter Johnson confirmed that she'd put it on the top of that month's agenda, Maria waved Chase off to the side. "I got the order for the store. The nice boy, he said you'd pick it up. I'll make yours. I know what Sadie likes. Better, I know what she needs. You too. Don't worry, Zia Maria knows what you'll like," she said before calling out orders to her son for what sounded like every customer in line.

While he waited for his order to be filled along with everyone else, the conversation turned to the body discovered in the woods. It was a conversation Chase listened to with great interest. His subtle questions eventually steered the conversation in exactly the direction he wanted it to go. The customers began surmising where Elijah was lying low.

"No, he wouldn't go to Sadie's," Maria dismissed a woman's suggestion. "She cut ties with him last summer. The cocaine. Bah. That boy needs a kick in the culo."

"So does Payton. It's her fault he got involved with the gang on Whiteside Mountain in the first place." Nina rubbed her fingers together, the universal sign for money. "She was always after him to buy her things. Never satisfied, that one. She always wanted bigger and better."

"You've had it in for that girl since she broke your boy's heart, Nina," a woman said from one of the tables.

"I agree with Nina," the woman sitting beside her at the table said. "My boy's been friends with Elijah since they were in grade school. That girl's been leading him around by the nose since they got together."

"Word is she has a bun in the oven and Elijah is the daddy," one of the older men said.

Interesting. Chase wondered if Elijah had shared the news with his sister. If he had, it might create an opening for Sadie to get closer to Payton Howard. The more Chase learned about the woman, the more she came into play as a means of bringing Elijah in.

The women in line turned to look at the older man who'd shared the news. "What? I'm just repeating what I heard at Highland Brew," the man defended himself.

"If that's true, he'd better stop hiding out in the woods and get himself a good paying job."

"How's he supposed to do that, Ed? He's got the Whiteside Mountain Gang after him. You ask me, all of us should be praying he stays far away from Highland Falls. We don't need anyone coming into town looking for him."

"They're already too close for comfort if you ask me," Ed said. "What with the dead body in the woods and the shoot-out last night. Heard they came after Elijah."

So it looked like Gabe's effort to keep last night's shooting quiet hadn't exactly panned out. The chief had admitted it was tough to keep anything quiet in the small town. But while Chase wasn't thrilled word had gotten out, he was relieved that Sadie's part in it hadn't appeared to.

"Damn fool," the older man said. "What was he thinking bringing them so close to Willow Creek and his sister's place?"

The older man made a good point. Something Chase planned to bring up with Sadie once she deigned to speak to him again. He figured he'd be waiting awhile.

"That's what I said to my wife just this morning," the man's tablemate agreed. "Elijah's been playing in those woods since he was a little tyke. Aside from his sister, the lad knows more hidey-holes in those woods than all the citizens of Highland Falls combined. The caves south of Honeysuckle Ridge, for one."

Some of the other customers joined in, naming the places where Elijah Gray used to play. The perfect locations for him to lie low. Exactly the information Chase had been hoping for. He repeated the locations in his head as Maria waved him over to the counter.

"You come back for tomorrow's special, eh?" she said after he'd paid.

"If this tastes as good as it smells, you won't be able to keep me away, Zia Maria." Not only for the food but for the gossip as well.

It took another twenty minutes for him to get out of the restaurant. Someone asked if he'd had a Bigfoot sighting yet, which of course he hadn't. How could he, he asked, when they didn't exist? It was something he shouldn't have said out loud, because every customer at Zia Maria's had a Bigfoot story to tell, including Zia Maria.

By the time Chase pulled his car alongside the sidewalk in front of I Believe in Unicorns, Sadie was turning the sign in the window to *Closed*. Their eyes met and held through the glass. She turned away. She might as well have given him the middle finger.

It bothered him that she was mad at him, far more than it should. He couldn't become intimately involved with the sister of their primary suspect, a suspect herself in his partner's eyes. Even if Chase disagreed with Black, it didn't mean he didn't have some suspicions of his own when it came to Sadie, which made his feelings for her more difficult to understand.

But understand them or not, they were there. So maybe it was for the best that she couldn't stand the sight of him. Living under the same roof with Sadie would be easier if she kept her distance.

Chapter Fifteen

♥

Sadie glanced in her rearview mirror as she pulled into her driveway. Sure enough, Michael was right behind her. Chase, she reminded herself on a low growl. Chase Roberts, the man who'd lied to her. An FBI agent who was using her to get to her brother, and she'd named her daughter after him. He wasn't her knight in shining armor after all.

As a heavy weight pressed upon her and the backs of her eyes began to burn, she looked at herself in the mirror. "Do not cry. He doesn't deserve your tears." She glanced at her daughter. "And he doesn't deserve your love, my sweet baby girl." Tears welled in her eyes, threatening to spill over as she remembered her daughter's delighted giggles. Michaela had rewarded Chase with her first smile and her first laugh. He didn't deserve to be given those gifts.

Sadie sniffed back tears, catching movement in her side mirror as she went to turn off the engine. She must have sat there longer than she'd realized. Avoiding the inevitable, she thought, as Chase walked to the front door with a suitcase in one hand and a large take-out bag from Zia Maria's in the other. If she wasn't worried about her daughter's safety, she would have told him what he could do with his protection. Her stomach gurgled. The food he could leave.

"Stay where you are," he said when she got out of the car.

"Unless the FBI teaches you to open a deadbolt..." She swallowed a mortified groan when he opened the door and stepped inside with his gun drawn. She'd left the door unlocked.

Michaela began to fuss in her car seat, and Sadie eased her way around the car to comfort her. As she did, she searched the area. Nothing looked out of place. Then again, what did she know? She hadn't sensed the gunmen's approach last night. She prayed Elijah wasn't hiding inside the cottage. Surely he wouldn't bring danger right to her door. She liked to believe he wouldn't, but he had a long-standing tradition of thinking only of himself.

And soon he'd have a baby to think about. She'd gone back and forth on whether or not to share the news with her grandmother. Late that afternoon, the decision had been taken out of her hands. Babs Sutherland had arrived to congratulate Sadie and her grandmother about the new addition to the family. Sadie had played dumb. But she hadn't pretended to be happy about the news. How could she be?

Her grandmother was another story. It was like Elijah wasn't on the run and in fear for his life and Agnes wasn't months away from losing her business and home. She was already planning the baby shower.

"You can come in now." Chase hesitated in the doorway as if contemplating helping her with Michaela. Something in her expression must have told him she didn't need or want his help, because he picked up the takeaway bag and rolled his suitcase into the cottage.

She opened the back passenger-side door and leaned in to grab the baby bag and slide it over her shoulder before releasing Michaela from her car seat. Her daughter didn't reward her with a delighted gurgle or a happy smile. Instead, she tangled her grasping fingers in Sadie's hair and tugged. Hard.

She let out a loud *ow*, which brought Chase to the door. "What's wrong?"

"Besides you standing in my doorway with a gun in your hand and your suitcase in my entryway? Nothing. Nothing's wrong." She closed the car door and beeped the lock, wincing as she walked up the path with her hair still gripped tightly in her daughter's hands.

He sighed and stepped aside for her to pass him. As she did, Michaela made small grunting sounds, letting go of Sadie's hair to hold out her hands. Sadie looked from her daughter's hands to the object of her ardent desire. He stepped out of reach, his expression blank, but there was an emotion in his eyes she couldn't read. She thought it might be regret.

"I know how you must feel, Sadie," he said as he closed and locked the door. At her raised eyebrow, he lifted his hands. "You're right. I don't have any idea how you feel, but you need to know, I didn't want to lie to you. My partner was against telling you the truth. You heard that yourself." He looked at Michaela, who was still holding out her arms to him. "Can I take her?"

When Sadie hesitated, he said, "Whatever you think of me, you have to know that my feelings for Michaela were real, are real. Michael is my middle name and Knight is my maternal family's surname. If it makes you feel better, I'll go by Michael. I don't care."

"I have to call you that anyway. You're still undercover, remember?" It wasn't just his offer to go by his middle name or that he was, in a way, Michael Knight that made her feel better and hand him her daughter. It was that he'd asked her permission to take Michaela. Drew had only ever pretended to respect her wishes and boundaries.

"Thank you," he said, then held her gaze. "I meant what I said, Sadie. I care about Michaela, and I care about you."

Sadie woke up to sun streaming in her bedroom window and rubbed her eyes. She wasn't dreaming. Shooting up into a sitting position on her bed, she tried to get her bearings. A towel fell off her head and onto the blanket that covered her. She wore a towel and nothing else.

Images of the night before filtered into her brain in vivid Technicolor. Chase with her smiling daughter in his arms, setting the table for dinner. She'd gone to take a shower before they sat down to eat. A long, leisurely, blissfully peaceful shower. She'd been in there so long she'd used all the hot water in the tank. Afterward, she'd gone to her bedroom to change and remembered, as clear as if it were happening right then, lying on her bed.

She'd only meant to take a moment to think through everything Chase and Nate had revealed to her yesterday morning. To go over what Chase had said about caring for her and her daughter, wondering if she should believe him. Or was he just one more man in a long line of them who would break her heart and her trust?

Her brain synapses seemed to be firing on all cylinders this morning. Which would have been a welcome change if her brain didn't choose that moment to point out that there were only two men who'd truly broken her heart—her father and her brother. After that, she'd never let another man close enough to get past her defenses.

She thought over her past relationships. Okay, so maybe the men she'd dated hadn't been worthy of her love. But she really hadn't given them the chance to be, had she? She got a gold star for her ability to sabotage a relationship. Her trust issues when it came to men were deeply entrenched. For the past ten years, she'd been protecting herself and her heart. The only person she'd truly let in was her baby girl.

She blinked. *Michaela!* Sadie threw back the blanket and leaped from her bed. She stopped with her hand on the doorknob. She was naked, and she had a man in her house. A drop-dead gorgeous man she was attracted to. An attraction that hadn't abated even when she found out he'd been lying to her all along.

She ran to her dresser and pulled out the drawers. They were empty save for two pairs of underwear and a bra that had seen better days. She turned to the overflowing laundry hamper. Clothes littered the honey-colored wood floor around the hamper, with more articles of clothing tossed on the blue chair in the corner. Everything she owned was dirty. She eyed the black yoga pants and white T-shirt hanging over the arm of the chair. They'd have to do.

Grabbing a pair of underwear and the bra from the dresser drawer, she hurried to the chair. She sniffed the yoga pants and T-shirt. They didn't smell, and they weren't stained. She remembered why. She'd tossed them there yesterday morning after deciding they weren't work appropriate.

She listened for signs of her daughter and Chase as she threw on her clothes, her stomach doing a nervous dance. The cottage was suspiciously quiet and must have been so for twelve hours, because she'd slept the sleep of the dead. Then again, they could have had a party and she probably would have slept through it.

Overwhelmed with guilt and more than a little embarrassed, she opened her bedroom door and tiptoed across the hall to her daughter's room. At the sight of the empty crib, she whirled around and ran, stopping short when she reached the living room. Chase was asleep on the couch with her daughter on his chest, his arms wrapped protectively around her.

Sadie stood there staring at them with a lump forming in her throat. It was the most beautiful sight she had ever seen. She glanced around for her camera, wanting to capture the moment. It surprised her a little. Up until six months ago, her camera was always close at hand. Photography had been her passion long before she'd gotten into graphic design. But aside from a few photos of Michaela when she was born, Sadie hadn't taken any pictures at all.

In her search for her camera—even her phone would do—her eyes landed on the bottles on the coffee table, the neatly piled sleepers and diapers beside them. She glanced at Chase to see him watching her through bloodshot eyes that made the blue of his irises stand out even more. She winced and opened her mouth to apologize.

He moved his hand to press a finger to his lips and whispered, "She just went back to sleep."

Her daughter's head came up. Chase looked like he wanted to groan but instead raised a hand to Michaela's head and gently pressed it back onto his chest, humming and rocking her as he did so. As soon as he stopped, Michaela's head popped up again.

After the third time it happened, Sadie was barely able to keep the laughter from her voice. "It's okay. We both have to get ready for work anyway."

He turned his head to look out the window that faced Willow Creek. He frowned, raising his arm to glance at his watch. This time he did groan out loud. "How can it be eight in the morning already? I swear I just closed my eyes."

Her daughter shimmied up his chest to suck on his face. "You can't be hungry again." He held Michaela against him while swinging his bare feet to the floor. "You're lucky you're cute," he told her daughter, rising from the couch to hand her to Sadie.

She snuggled Michaela to her chest, relieved when she didn't cry and reach for Chase. "I'm so sorry I fell asleep and left you to deal with her all night."

He rubbed the back of his head. "I don't know how you've been doing this on your own for the past three months and you're still standing. I feel like I could sleep for a week."

"I feel like I've slept for a week, and that's thanks to you. I really do appreciate it, Chase." Thinking of the almost-naked state she woke up in, her eyes went wide and her cheeks heated. "You covered me with the blanket last night, didn't you?"

"Yeah, but I closed my eyes." A touch of color stained his incredible cheekbones.

She didn't understand how he looked as gorgeous as ever with so little sleep. Still... "You were walking around in my bedroom with your eyes closed and my daughter in your arms? You're lucky you didn't trip over anything."

"All right, I had my eyes open for the very reason you just stated. I intended to shut them, but your bedroom is...well, it's a bit of a disaster." He winced. "Sorry. I understand why it is now."

She didn't take offense, because it was the absolute truth. Although she didn't tell him her daughter wasn't the only reason her bedroom looked like it did. She'd never been a neat freak, and her messy habits had only intensified after she'd had Michaela. "No need to apologize. I'm just embarrassed you saw me almost naked."

"You have no reason to be embarrassed. You look amazing. Uh, I didn't mean to say that. Not that you don't look amazing, you do, but it implies that I was staring at you while you were sleeping, which sounds a little creepy. I wasn't. I—" He scratched the back of his head. "I should probably stop talking and grab some sleep. I mean a shower. I'm going to grab a shower." He went to walk away, and Michaela held up her arms.

He sighed and leaned in to take Michaela's hand and suddenly reared back. With a finger under his nose, he said, "Sadie, I don't know what's in her formula but you need to look for a new brand. Someone that little should not smell that bad." He frowned at her. "Can you not smell that?"

She shrugged. "I guess I'm used to it."

"You should get your sense of smell tested. I'm serious," he said when she laughed, sighing when he noticed Michaela had yet to lower her arms. He pinched his nose and leaned in to kiss her fingers. "I can't take you, stinky. I have to have a shower or I'm going to smell as bad as you do," he told her daughter, gagging as he walked away.

Sadie lifted Michaela to smell her diaper. At first, she'd been afraid Chase had been talking about her. "He's right. You are a little ripe. But don't worry. Mommy still loves you." She hugged her daughter tight and headed to the nursery to change her, amazed at how good a little extra sleep made her feel.

Twenty minutes later, Sadie looked up from the drawer she was searching when Chase walked into the kitchen. "Have you seen my cell phone?"

"No. When did you last have it?"

"At the store, but I'm sure I didn't leave it there." She wouldn't, on the off chance Elijah tried to contact her.

"Did you check the diaper bag?" Without waiting for her to respond, he unzipped the quilted pink bag sitting on the island behind Michaela's carrier and dug around inside. He held up her phone.

"Thank goodness," she said, and reached for it.

He didn't immediately let go of the phone. "You haven't heard from your brother, have you?"

"No, and I have a feeling he won't risk getting in touch with me now. Not after the other night. But if you'd give me my phone, I'll check." He handed it back to her. She entered her passcode and opened her phone. She shook her head. "Nothing."

"If you do hear from him, you need to tell me, Sadie."

"I know. I will," she said when he held her gaze as if he didn't quite believe her. She nodded at Michaela, who was sucking on a pacifier, looking from her to Chase as if she sensed the tension between them. "Maybe we should change the subject."

"Sorry, you're right." He smiled at Michaela and leaned down to nuzzle her cheek. "Someone smells good. But what's with the plug in her mouth?" He gestured at the pacifier as he straightened.

"One of Granny's friends dropped it off yesterday. I'm pretty sure my grandmother asked her to. Even though she knows I'm dead set against them. I don't need the added expense of braces down the road, but it seemed to work. Nate suggested we give her a sucker."

"Of course he did." Chase laughed.

Michaela popped the soother out of her mouth to give him a drooly smile. There was no denying he was drool-worthy. The sexy stubble he'd been sporting this morning was gone, and his golden-tanned skin glowed. He smelled incredible too, and the pristine park ranger uniform he wore only heightened his appeal.

Sadie bent to pick up the pacifier off the floor. She sucked on it and then stuck it in Michaela's mouth.

Chase looked from her to the floor. "Are you crazy? Do you have any idea how many germs there are on a kitchen floor?" He took the pacifier out of her daughter's mouth and went to turn on the tap.

Sadie glanced at the floor. It looked pretty clean to her. Much cleaner than it had yesterday morning when she'd left. "Did you wash my floor?"

"Yes." He tested the water coming out of the faucet with his finger. "It really should be boiled, but this will have to do."

She narrowed her eyes, taking in the starched lines of his uniform pants. "You're one of them, aren't you?"

"I'm not sure I know what you're talking about. But if you're asking whether or not I'm looking for your—"

She picked up the slice of cold pizza she'd been eating while searching for her phone and waved it at him, a piece of pepperoni falling on the floor. "No, a neat freak."

He inhaled noisily and bent to pick up the piece of pepperoni. "I'm not a neat *freak*," he said while opening the cupboard under the sink and tossing the pepperoni in the garbage can.

She grabbed his hand when he went to close the cupboard door and looked inside. "Really? You cleaned my cupboard and lined up the cleaning products in order of their height."

"I'm neat, not a freak."

"Okay, I'm sorry I said that. You're not a freak. But you may have a slight problem." He gave her a look, and she pointed her slice of pizza at his pants, being careful not to get any on the floor. "Your uniform looks brand new."

"It is. I had a run-in with Nessa McNab's golden retriever."

She struggled not to laugh. She'd heard all about it yesterday afternoon.

His eyes narrowed. "You already knew."

"About your swim in Willow Creek to rescue Finn?" She nodded. "Yeah, I did."

Michaela spat out her pacifier again. Chase picked it up and turned on the tap. "I don't know why I'm surprised. Everyone at Zia Maria's had too," he said as he turned off the hot water, waving the pacifier to cool it off.

"I bet that earned you some brownie points with Zia Maria. She and Nessa are besties."

He put the pacifier in Michaela's mouth. "It did, but I think I earned more because of you." Her daughter spat the pacifier out. It landed on the counter, which he inspected before sticking it back in her mouth.

Sadie frowned. "What do you mean?"

He kept his gaze on the pacifier, catching it when Michaela spat it out again.

Sadie smiled, nodding at the way her daughter pumped her arms and legs and the smile she directed at Chase. "She thinks it's a game."

He put the pacifier on the counter and took Michaela's hand in his. "You're a smart baby, aren't you?" he said, raising her daughter's thumb to her mouth. She latched on to it immediately, smiling around it at Chase. He shrugged at the face Sadie made.

"It's better than the pacifier. Thumb-suckers sleep through the night at a faster rate."

"Did you read that in your baby book?" she teased.

"I Googled it in the middle of the night."

"I'm guessing by your bloodshot eyes it didn't do you much good."

"It will, eventually." He glanced at his watch. "You should probably get dressed for work."

"I am dressed." At his raised eyebrow, she said, "I'll find something to wear at my grandmother's store." She went to grab the carrier's handle. "You didn't tell me what you meant by earning brownie points because of me."

Shocking—yesterday she probably would have forgotten his comment by now.

He didn't meet her eyes. "They're worried about you, you and your grandmother. Elijah too. Did you know his girlfriend is expecting?"

"He told me the other night. My grandmother knows too. She wants me to reach out to Payton."

"That's a good idea."

"A good idea because she's pregnant with my brother's child, or a good idea because you want me to pump her for information about Elijah?"

"I think you know the answer, Sadie."

"Yeah, I do." She returned the carrier to the island and opened the cupboard, tossing the rest of the pizza slice in the garbage. "And I don't appreciate you asking me to do your job for you. He's my brother, Chase. Is he a screwup? Yes. Was trafficking drugs for the Whiteside Mountain Gang wrong? Absolutely, and there's a part of me that won't be able to forgive him for that. But you didn't see him when those guys were shooting at him. He—"

"They were shooting at both of you, Sadie." Chase shoved his fingers through his hair. "Look, I understand we're putting you in an untenable position. But what if your brother was responsible for Brodie's murder? Would you be as quick to defend him then?"

"He's not. Why are you looking at me like that? I think I know my own brother better than you do."

"According to the ballistics experts, several of the bullets we recovered from the scene are a match to the one that killed Brodie. Your grandmother's gun came back clean. The bullets didn't come from Nate's gun or the other shooters. They were all using high-powered rifles. The bullet came from your brother's gun, Sadie."

Her gun. The bullet had come from her gun. Her legs went weak, and she leaned against the island for support, schooling her features to keep her expression blank. No, it would be better if her face revealed all the shock and panic icing her insides. Chase would expect her to feel both emotions after learning in all probability that her brother's gun was the weapon used in Brodie's murder.

How was this even possible? She hadn't shot anyone, and no one had access to her gun... Wait. She'd left the door unlocked yesterday. It wasn't out of the realm of possibility she'd done the same when she'd first moved back to Highland Falls. But that wasn't when the deputy had been shot. He'd been shot the weekend of her baby shower.

Relief coursed through her, and she opened her mouth to tell Chase the truth, quickly closing it when she remembered a very important fact. She'd brought her gun with her when she'd come home for the baby shower. She'd been worried about Drew. He'd been in a bad place and drinking heavier than usual. Afraid he'd do something stupid, she'd brought her gun to her grandmother's.

Chase reached out to rest a comforting hand on her shoulder. "Are you okay?"

Instead of giving him a negative head shake like her body seemed primed to do, she nodded. "I'm fine, thanks."

She couldn't tell him the truth, not yet. Not until she figured this out.

Chapter Sixteen

♥

Something's up with Sadie, Black. Keep a close eye on her today. Monitor her phone calls as much as possible," Chase said to his partner as he followed Sadie's SUV on the dirt road, scanning for any sign of a potential threat.

"You tell her that it looks like her brother's gun is connected to Brodie's murder?"

"I did. It hit her hard. She went pale and quiet." He followed close behind her as they turned onto the main road. "She says she hasn't heard from Elijah."

"You believe her?"

"Yes, I do."

"And you believe her because you checked her phone, right?" When Chase didn't immediately answer, Black swore in his ear. "Listen, Dudley Do-Right, sometimes you have to bend the law, go against your Boy Scout scruples to solve a case."

"I haven't done so before, and I don't intend to start now."

"I didn't hear you complaining when I put a tracker on Sadie's car."

"I didn't know for certain that you had. But that was different. Sadie was in danger."

She still was, which was probably why Chase hadn't removed the tracker himself. He'd been waiting for her to ask how Gabe had found her. His reason for not telling her wasn't exactly noble. If she removed the tracker, the odds she was holding out on him went up.

"Have you heard from Gabe?" Chase asked, in hopes of distracting his partner. Plus there was something they needed to discuss.

"Yeah, he tried to reach you about twenty minutes ago."

He'd been in the shower, a shower that smelled like wildflowers and Sadie. It reminded him of seeing her on the bed wrapped only in a towel last night. He'd told her the truth. He'd done his best to avoid looking at all that smooth skin still damp from the shower, but focusing on her face hadn't helped as much as he'd hoped. She was a beautiful woman. One he was attracted to despite his best efforts not to be.

The heart wants what it wants, he remembered his mother saying the day their grandfather came to take them away. It seemed to hold true for her. Only she hadn't wanted him and his brother but a man their grandfather deemed dangerous. His grandfather had been proven right three years later.

Chase wondered what the judge would think of Sadie. He brushed the thought and the answer to his speculation aside. He had a fairly good idea what his grandfather's opinion of the Gray family would be. "What did Gabe want?"

"He suggested we bring his father-in-law in on the search, and he mentioned someone else he thinks could be of use to us. Hunter Mackenzie."

"Abby Everhart's fiancé. I don't like the idea of bringing anyone else in on this, but I have too much ground to cover on my own. What do you think?"

"Shocked that you'd ask my opinion."

Chase sighed. "It has nothing to do with you, Black. I'm just used to working on my own." There was another call trying to come through. His boss at the forest service. Chase glanced at the time. He wasn't late.

"So you've decided you trust me, after all. I'd wondered how long it would take."

He didn't, not completely. "Can we get back to the matter at hand? I'm good with Boyd helping out with the search, but I'm concerned Mackenzie might not be able to keep this from his fiancée."

He glanced at the screen when another call came in from the forest service. He really wished Gabe's father-in-law had suggested another job for him.

"Abby and her camera. Yeah, I agree. It's a concern. But Gabe seems to trust him, and I trust Gabe."

"So do I."

"You know, we're actually starting to sound like partners. I think this calls for a celebration."

Chase was surprised to find himself smiling. It seemed like he was beginning to like the guy. "Let's save the celebrating until after we bring in Elijah Gray."

"Yeah, you're right." The tenor of Black's voice had changed. He was thinking about Brodie. Sometimes Chase forgot his partner's personal connection to the case. It was something he needed to remember, for all their sakes.

"Sadie's about two minutes out. I can't stick around. My boss has called twice while I've been on with you."

"Oh yeah, that was something else Gabe mentioned. Looks like you're going to have a busy day, my man. A black bear was spotted in someone's backyard this morning. I hear he's a big mother."

Chase didn't miss the laughter in his partner's voice. "And you thought you got the short end of the stick working at I Believe in Unicorns."

"Looks like I was wrong. Wait a minute, I take that back." Chase saw his partner in the store's display window as Sadie pulled into the parking spot. "I'm stuck with the kid, and she's crying again."

This time it was Chase's turn to laugh.

Sadie had barely been at the store five minutes when her best friends walked in, which meant she couldn't complete the text she'd started to her brother. It wasn't like she could send him a message while Chase watched her every move as they left for work. Pulling off to the side of the road with him following close behind hadn't been an option either.

"You two are out bright and early." Their concerned expressions worried her. "What's going on?"

"What, we can't drop in and say hi to our bestie without a reason?" Abby asked, her red hair pulled up in a high ponytail. She wore a navy-and-white-checked top with white capris and flip-flops, while Mallory wore a flowy, flower-printed sundress that hid her baby bump.

Today's weather was more summerlike than springlike.

"It feels like I haven't seen you in ages." Her gorgeous blond friend gave her a hug and then beamed at Michaela sitting in her carrier on the counter. Her eyes were still red-rimmed from her latest crying jag. "Oh, look at you, beautiful. Do you mind if I take her out of her seat?" Mallory asked.

"No way. You leave her right where she is. She's quiet, and I'd like to keep it that way," Nate answered for Sadie.

"She's been a little fussy," Sadie admitted, giving Nate a quelling look.

Unlike Chase, Nate had no qualms hiding his identity. If it wasn't for Chase, she'd have no idea that every word she spoke was being scrutinized and judged. It was killing her not to let her grandmother in on the secret. The only positive about Nate working and living with Agnes was that he'd keep her safe. Now Sadie had to figure out a way to do what she needed to without him catching on.

Nate put his hands on his hips and looked at her like she'd lost her mind. "A little? The kid never stops crying."

"She's not crying now." She caught the concern in Mallory's eyes and wanted to shoot Nate.

Logically, Sadie knew she wasn't doing anything that contributed to Michaela's fits of temper and tears. Her daughter had colic. Sadie had tried warm water bottles on Michaela's tummy and giving her a baby massage. Everything her doctor in Charlotte had suggested, she'd tried. It didn't matter. She still felt like a failure.

Mallory was anything but a failure. She was a natural mother. Gabe's sons—her stepsons—adored her. A doctor who was a few months into her hospital residency, Mallory would know exactly how to make her own baby girl feel better.

"Sadie, you should have told us. We wouldn't have let you brush off our offers to help. You must be exhausted," Mallory said.

"No wonder you're depressed," Abby added.

Sadie's cheeks warmed. "I'm not depressed. Who said I was depressed?"

At Abby and Mallory's shared glance, Sadie huffed an irritated breath. "That's why you're here, isn't it?"

"No." Mallory grimaced when Sadie crossed her arms. "Okay, it might have played into our decision to drop by. But we're allowed to worry about you. That's what friends do. You'd do the same for us."

"You don't have to worry about me."

"Yes, we do. Having a colicky baby isn't easy, especially when you're dealing with that baby all by yourself," Mallory said.

"Not anymore, she isn't." Nate slung a companionable arm

across Sadie's shoulders. "Her boyfriend moved in with her yesterday. The kid loves him. No accounting for taste, I guess."

Sadie figured Nate's light squeeze of her shoulder was to ensure she didn't deviate from the script.

Abby and Mallory looked from Nate to Sadie, their eyes wide. She smiled. "It was the best sleep I've had in months." Her smile fell. She probably shouldn't have said that, especially with Nate around.

"Okay, well that just surprises me," Nate said. "After all the PDA I witnessed before I kicked the two of you out of here at closing, I expected to hear you didn't sleep a wink. I gotta have a talk with Mikey."

"Wait a minute. You're supposed to be my bachelorette. You can't be my bachelorette if you have a boyfriend, especially a boyfriend who is living with you," Abby said.

So maybe Chase's fake-relationship idea wasn't a bad one after all. Sadie attempted to infuse her voice with disappointment. "I'm sorry."

Nate snorted and then glanced over his shoulder. "I better go check on Agnes. She told me she'd be down fifteen minutes ago."

"I'm confused," Mallory said when Nate went in search of her grandmother. "I didn't know you were even seeing anyone."

"Sadie has post-baby brain, or maybe it's exhausted brain, and you have pregnant brain, Mal. I called you right after I met Michael, remember? The guy who helped deliver Michaela. The guy she's named after."

"Oh, the baby whisperer. Now I remember."

"Obviously we know where your mind is at. I also said he was right up there with Gabe and Hunter in the looks department." Abby sighed. "So I guess the bachelorette event is out. We need to come up with something else. Any suggestions?"

Mallory cleared her throat and nodded. At what, Sadie didn't know.

Apparently, Abby did. "Unicorns. I'm thinking something with unicorns."

"Did that just pop into your head because you're standing in a unicorn store, or did you guys hear the news that my brother has practically bankrupted my grandmother?"

Abby's eyes went wide. "Your brother? We didn't know Elijah was involved. All we heard is that Agnes is months away from losing the store and her home, which, I might add, we didn't hear from you."

"I'm sorry. I would have told you guys but things kept piling on, and I was overwhelmed."

"That's when most people call their friends," Abby said, sounding a little hurt.

But most people weren't getting shot at in the woods or finding out their knight in shining armor was really an FBI agent hunting their brother.

"I get it. I've done the same thing myself. So have you, Abby. It's easier to give help than it is to receive it. But it doesn't make you weak to lean on people who love you." Mallory smiled. "I'm glad you let Michael in. It can't have been easy after Drew."

If they only knew. "No, it wasn't. But he's nothing like Drew, and he's wonderful with Michaela." She glanced at her daughter, who'd been suspiciously quiet. She was sound asleep with her thumb in her mouth. Sadie reached for her phone to take a picture. It was gone. She looked under and around the carrier. It wasn't there.

"What's wrong?" Abby asked.

"I can't find my phone. I was sure I put it beside the carrier." As she was about to go down on her hands and knees to check under the counter, the door chimed, and Zia Maria walked in with a takeaway bag in one hand and Finn, Nessa McNab's golden retriever, on a leash in the other hand.

"I know, I know," the older woman said. "We'll say he's a support dog if someone makes a fuss." She caught sight of

Michaela and made a beeline for her. "Oh, look at her. Such a bella bambina." She put the bag on the counter and let go of Finn's leash, making grabby motions with her fingers as she leaned toward Michaela. Knowing the woman's cheek-pinching tendency, Sadie said, "She just went to sleep. I promise, I'll bring her in to see you this week."

Zia Maria squinched up her face and then raised her hands and backed away from the counter. "Okay, you do that. You and Michael. The food, it's for you and him. He's such a good boy, and so handsome too. Did you like what I sent home for you last night?"

Even though most of the dinner was sitting neatly wrapped in her refrigerator, Sadie said, "I loved everything. You're going to make me fat."

"You need some meat on your bones. The depression, it's making you too skinny. Men like something to grab on to." She patted her own backside and then waved at Mallory and Abby. "Good, you take care of your friend, girls. And don't let her tell you she's *fine*. She's not fine. Too much to deal with on her own." She patted Sadie's cheek. "But don't you worry. We're all gonna help. Abby, the mayor says you have a plan."

Abby gave Sadie a *sorry, not sorry* glance. "I do. I just have to iron out a few details before I unveil it."

"Good. That's good. But I have some news that's not so good. Nessa, she had a bad fall and broke her hip. She's gonna be in the hospital a long time."

"Oh no, what happened?" Sadie asked.

"I like Michael, but it's his fault. He told Nessa she have to put Finn on a leash, and the leash, it wrapped around her feet when they were going for a walk. Finn, he chases the squirrel, and *whoosh*." She lifted her hand and brought it down. "Nessa, she fall. So now, Finn needs a home." She retrieved the dog's leash and handed it to Sadie.

"Oh no, not me. I can't take Finn, Maria. I wish I could but I have too much on my plate as it is."

"I know. It's okay, you'll feel better soon." She tapped a piece of paper stapled to the bag with her finger. "It's a list we make for you. To deal with the depression."

"But I'm not depressed. I'm just... Wait, you forgot Finn," she said when Maria turned to walk away.

"No, I no forget. Michael, he'll take him. He likes Finn, and Finn, he like him. It's a good match, you'll see. Michael, he saved him. You know the saying. If you save a life, you're responsible for it. Finn, he's Michael's responsibility now. All good."

"No, no it's not. Michael moved in with me." She grimaced, preparing for a lecture from Maria. She was old-school.

"Eh, what's a matter with you? Look at Abby, she lives with Hunter a year. Is she married? No. I don't know what's wrong with you girls. Mallory, you talk some sense into these two for Zia Maria." With that, she was out the door.

Sadie turned to her friends. "You guys have to help me out here. Abby, you love dogs."

"Yes, and I have two. Plus you know how territorial Bella is."

"Mal?"

"I wish I could but we have five boys, a dog, and a baby on the way. Plus, there's Finn's reputation. It would put Gabe in an awkward position."

Sadie frowned, looking at the dog sitting at her feet. "What reputation? He seems perfectly sweet."

"Oh, he's charming all right, until he robs you blind," Abby said. "He's a kleptomaniac."

Chapter Seventeen

♥

Chase wiped the back of his hand across his sweaty brow while casting a nervous glance at the rustling ferns to the right of the forest trail. He was positive he'd heard a snake hiss. The six-foot-four, broad-shouldered man walking on the trail ahead of him didn't seem to share his concerns.

But why would he? Less than an hour ago, Chase had watched Hunter Mackenzie coax a black bear out of a hysterical woman's yard and back into the woods. Chase had never been so glad to see someone in his entire life, a life which he now felt he owed to Hunter.

Chase was positive he wouldn't have made it out of the situation alive, and it might not have been the bear that killed him. The bystanders had turned on him when he'd drawn his gun as the bear lumbered his way. They were equally unimpressed, yelling at him to do his job, when Chase ran in the opposite direction after holstering his gun. Any hero status he might have built up by being there for Sadie on the night Michaela was born, he'd managed to obliterate with his ineptitude as a park ranger.

Hunter glanced over his shoulder. "You doing okay? You look like you're overheated." He stopped and turned, reaching in his pack to pull out a canteen. He tossed it to Chase.

"Thanks. I'm not used to a ten-mile hike in this heat." He'd also forgotten his own pack in his car. So much for always being prepared. This case was chipping away at him. He gestured at Hunter's head after taking a welcome drink of water. "The bun's a good idea."

"It's a man bun, according to Abby, and also her idea. I usually just tie it back."

"Ah, a ponytail—mantail," he corrected, not wanting to offend Hunter. Although Chase had a feeling the other man wasn't easily offended. Aside from Hunter being Tarzan of the woods, they shared some similarities. Both of them kept their own counsel, loners who didn't really care about the opinions of others. It was a nice change from his partner.

He noticed the way Hunter was studying him and said, "You think Black would make a better park ranger than me and that I'd do a better job pulling off his gig at I Believe in Unicorns, don't you?"

"I think your partner could convince anyone of anything."

Something in the way Hunter stated the observation had Chase lowering the canteen from his mouth. "You don't trust him."

"No, I don't." He rubbed his bearded jaw. "Gabe told me what went down the other night. How much do you know about your partner?"

Chase hesitated, then decided to go with his gut. He trusted Hunter to keep the information to himself. "Former spec ops with enough experience that he should have been at the scene in time to warn Sadie and get her out of the line of fire—as well as grabbing Elijah."

Hunter nodded. "I thought the same."

"I can't access anything about him between his time in the military and when he became an agent with NCSBI."

"Have you spoken to his superior?"

"No, nor mine." Chase briefly explained their off-book operation and how their partnership came about.

"Are you sure he's still with the NCSBI? Did he offer you any proof?"

"Of course, I'm..." He trailed off, thinking back to their first meeting. Black had never shown him a badge, nor had Chase asked him to see one. Chase's boss had set up the initial meet. He scrolled through his memory of his conversation with his boss back in February.

He hadn't looked him in the eye. He'd stared down at some paperwork, tapping a pen in an irritated rhythm on his desk. Chase had assumed he'd been irritated with him, but maybe it hadn't been about him after all. Maybe his boss was being forced to do something he didn't want to do. He had mentioned Black by name, but now that Chase thought about it, he hadn't come out and directly said he was an agent with NCSBI. He'd just mumbled something about the investigative bureau. Then, when Chase had asked for personal leave two weeks ago, his boss had simply held up his hand to silence his explanation and granted it with no questions asked.

"No, I'm not sure that he is. I can see now that I made the assumption based on my boss's initial involvement." He'd also made the assumption that his new boss was like his old one and wanted to get rid of him, which may actually have been the case. Only his new boss wasn't just bending the damn law, he was breaking it. Now the question was why. "I need to make a call." He reached for his phone.

"You won't get cell service here." Hunter lifted his chin. "We'll have to go back to the road."

"You go ahead, and I'll catch up with you." Chase turned to set off down the path. He didn't want to delay the search for Elijah. He held up his phone, his eyes on the bars in hopes he'd get service sooner rather than later.

"Don't move," Hunter warned from behind him. "It won't—"

Chase looked down. There was a snake—one big mother of

a snake—coiled inches from his booted foot. Chase yelled and went for his gun. The snake lifted its head and reared back to strike.

Hunter shoved him out of the way, which Chase would have appreciated if he'd given him some warning. As it was, his legs weren't exactly steady, and he lost his balance, going over on his ankle before landing hard on the ground. His gun went off, the shot taking out a tree branch and leaves.

Afraid that he'd become prey for the snake or anything else creeping around under the thick undergrowth, Chase jumped to his feet and nearly fell back to the ground. "Son of a...beehive," he cried out, not because he was trying not to offend Hunter by swearing but because there was an actual beehive on the ground. And holy crap, his ankle hurt like a mother. Worse, he was beginning to sound like Black.

A muffled sound caught his attention. He looked over to see Hunter with his hand pressed to his face, his shoulders shaking.

"Could you maybe stop laughing long enough to tell me which way the snake went?" Chase looked around and shuddered.

Trying to appear like he hadn't been laughing, Hunter pointed in the opposite direction, thank God. Chase gritted his teeth as he limped back onto the path.

Hunter cleared his throat but didn't manage to completely clear the laughter from his voice. "You broke your leg."

"No, I twisted it, that's all."

"No, you broke it. That's our story, and we're sticking to it. No offense, but I'm worried you're going to get yourself or someone else killed. You're not cut out to be a park ranger. This will give you an out. It will also give you more time to focus on keeping Sadie and the baby safe."

It was a good point, especially if his hunch about Black was right. "I'm sure no one at park services will complain.

After today, my boss is no doubt looking for an excuse to get rid of me."

Hunter grinned as he bent down in front of him. "Hop on."

"I'm not getting on your back. I weigh two hundred pounds."

Hunter quirked an eyebrow as if his pack weighed more.

"I'd also look like an idiot, and I've already made enough of a fool of myself for one day." As he'd discovered earlier, while he'd never cared what people thought about him before, he did care what Sadie thought of him.

"I wouldn't worry about it," Hunter said as he walked off the path. He retrieved a walking stick and came back, handing it to Chase. "This'll help keep the weight off your foot. I'll call a friend of mine and get one of those boot things for you. Don't worry, you'll just have to wear it when you're in town." He glanced at him as they set off down the path. "I'm assuming you'll tell Sadie the truth."

"Of course. Including about Black, if I find out he's lied to me."

"Good, that's what I wanted to hear. You need her to trust you, and that's not going to be easy. She's been burned too many times."

"You think she's holding out on us about Elijah?"

Hunter shrugged. "He's her baby brother. She's always protected him, no matter how bad he screwed up."

"Trafficking cocaine and killing a law enforcement officer isn't on the same scale as running a pyramid scheme or hacking into the local high school's computers to change a grade." Offenses Elijah had been suspected of but not formally charged with.

"Don't get me wrong," Hunter said. "Sadie cut Elijah out of her life when she found out about the drugs, but now that he's in danger, I can't see her turning her back on him. It's not who she is. She'll have a hard time believing he's capable of murder. To be honest, so do I."

"At the moment, the evidence disagrees with you. You're

letting your connection to the Grays cloud your judgment. I hope Sadie doesn't let her feelings for her brother cloud hers. Otherwise, she could be in a whole lot of trouble."

"If you found out she was helping her brother, you'd arrest her?"

He nodded, ignoring the twisting in his gut. "I'd have no choice. At the time Agnes hid her grandson and Sadie met with him in the woods, they were unaware he was wanted in connection with Brodie's murder. That's no longer the case on Sadie's end. What she does from now on—"

"No one in town knows about Elijah's connection to the murder, so I doubt Agnes does. Sadie wouldn't tell her. She'd protect her."

"That's a decision she needs to rethink, for both their sakes," Chase said. "Sadie agreed to help us. Her compliance is the only thing that stands between her and a jail cell. If she reneges on the deal, I'll have no choice but to arrest her for aiding and abetting."

"That's cold, man."

"It's my job." One he was actually good at. At least he had been, before he'd gotten involved with this case and Sadie. He glanced at the bars on his phone as they stepped into the clearing. "If you'll excuse me for a minute, I need to make this call."

It took a couple minutes for him to be connected to the special agent in charge. As he waited, he glanced at Hunter. He was on his phone too. Chase had sensed Hunter's disappointment in him. It bothered him. He admired the man. He also wanted to trust him. He didn't want to think Hunter would jeopardize the case to protect the Grays.

The last thing Chase wanted to do was arrest Sadie, but the laws were in place for a reason. They were there to protect the public and their safety, to protect democracy. No one was above the law.

Including his own superior, he thought, when his boss's voice came over the line. "Roberts, I thought we agreed there'd be no communi—"

"You have two minutes to tell me exactly who Nathan Black is and what his connection is to you before I go over your head."

His boss swore. "I'll call you back."

Chase brought his phone from his ear to stare at it. He'd hung up on him. Seconds later, his phone rang. He glanced at the screen. "You're calling me from a burner." His voice was tight with barely restrained anger as his suspicions were confirmed.

"I can explain."

"You can try."

"Nate is my brother-in-law."

The tension in Chase's shoulders loosened. He'd been afraid Black had something illegal on his boss and was using it against him. "Be aware that I can and will verify that you're telling me the truth."

"I have no doubt you will. It's one of the reasons I agreed to this in the first place. I knew you'd keep Nate in line."

"Is he an agent with NCSBI?"

"Technically, no. He's on mandatory leave. I'll let him explain why. Despite him being a hothead with no respect for authority, something the two of you have in com—"

"I respect authority but not when someone is using their position to thwart the law."

"I'm not. The operation is off-book to protect you and Nate."

"And yourself." He glanced at Hunter, who'd pocketed his phone. "We can talk more about that at another time. Right now, you're going to tell me everything I need to know about Black. Everything that is relevant to the case."

Five minutes later, Chase disconnected from his boss.

"Did your boss clear up your concerns about your partner?" Hunter asked, gesturing for Chase to go ahead of him.

Chase nodded. "Black is an agent with NCSBI." It was best if no one other than Chase knew of Black's current status. Things made more sense to Chase after talking to his boss. It certainly explained why Black had so easily acquiesced to Chase calling the shots.

"Did he shed any light on the missing information in Black's file?"

Chase should have been more circumspect. It wasn't like him to be so forthcoming with a man he barely knew. His gut may have told him he could trust Hunter, and over the years, his instincts had proved reliable, but he was out of his element here. Which was why he'd felt the need to confide in someone who had a knowledge of not only the area but also the players.

He stopped, turning to face Hunter. "Do I have your word that this conversation goes no further than us?"

Hunter's mouth twisted to the side, and then he nodded. "Yeah."

The fact he'd taken a moment to weigh his answer made Chase feel better. "According to my boss, Black was messed up after returning from Afghanistan." Someone else might have missed it but Chase caught the flicker of emotion in Hunter's eyes.

Chase had looked into him and knew that Hunter would understand what he'd just shared better than most. He'd lost his best friend in a military operation he'd led in Afghanistan. Upon his return to Highland Falls, he'd cut himself off from his friends and family. Then Abby had come into his life.

"He found another band of brothers when he got stateside. He rode with an MC—motorcycle club—for three years until my boss recruited him for an undercover op."

"Why would he choose Nate for the op?"

"His wife threatened to divorce him if he didn't help get her brother out of the life. Black has five older sisters, who, according to my boss, think he walks on water."

"That speaks well of him, at least. But why didn't your boss bring him into the FBI?"

"Unlike his wife and sisters-in-law, he doesn't think Black walks on water. They don't exactly see eye to eye. On much of anything."

"You trust him now?"

"Black or my boss?"

"I'm sensing that's a no on both."

"You have excellent senses." Chase went to walk ahead and then turned back. "Who were you talking to on the phone?"

"I didn't give Sadie a heads-up, if that's what you're worried about. I called your boss, the other one, and told him you broke your foot and would be out of commission for a couple weeks. He told me to tell you to take all the time you need," Hunter said, clearly fighting back a grin. Then he added, "Someone spotted Elijah near Bridal Veil Falls earlier today. It's about an hour from the caves, so it looks like he's on the move."

"Any idea where he's headed?"

"No, but Sadie might."

An hour later, with a blow-up boot on his foot courtesy of Hunter's doctor friend, Chase called Black from his car. "Where are you?" he said as soon as his partner answered.

"Aren't you in a fine mood? I guess I can't blame you. Word of your exploits—"

Chase cut him off. "We need to talk. I'll be at the store in ten minutes. Meet me in the back."

"Don't bother. I'm sitting outside the cottage on Willow Creek. Sadie—"

"Is she okay? What's wrong?"

"Relax, she's fine. Well, sort of fine. She's not impressed with you at the moment so you'd best be prepared. Then again, when I share what I found on her phone, you're not exactly going to be thrilled with her either."

Chapter Eighteen

♥

D o you hear that?" Sadie asked Abby, getting up from the table where they'd been working on a plan to turn around I Believe in Unicorns' fortunes.

"How can you hear anything over Michaela crying and the dog howling?" Abby reached down to pat Finn, who was hiding under the table. "I think it's hurting his ears. I know it's hurting mine."

"I told you leaving her in her crib to cry it out doesn't work. Now maybe you'll believe me." Sadie moved toward the kitchen window, pushing the curtain aside to glance outside. She hadn't been imagining things. Chase and Nate were arguing.

No, she thought, leaning closer to the glass to get a better look. Chase was yelling at Nate. Her mouth fell open when he limped away from the other agent, a blue boot encasing his foot to his calf. Her irritation that she'd been saddled with Finn because of him was forgotten.

She ran to the door, stepping back when he walked inside. "What happened? Everyone said you walked away from the bear incident unscathed." They'd had a lot more to say but she hadn't cared. All she'd been worried about was Chase. Now it seemed she had reason to be.

"I did. I...didn't know we had company," he said, glancing

at Abby sitting at the kitchen table, watching them with interest. "Hey." He nodded at Abby and then gave Sadie a look she didn't understand until he pulled her against him. "You don't have to worry about me, honey. I'm fine." He bent his head and kissed her.

It took a moment for her to realize why he was kissing her— they were supposed to be in love. But her lips were quicker than her brain and got with the program. Not really a surprise since his lips were warm and firm, and he tasted like spearmint gum. There was also the simple fact that she'd wanted to be kissed by him since the moment she'd looked into his kind blue eyes.

Despite there being no tongue and no heat—well, maybe a little heat—she was enjoying the kiss very much. He seemed to be too. His arm wrapped around her, bringing her in nice and close. The kiss hadn't completely wiped out her ability to think. The thought that they were a perfect fit came clearly to mind. Her hearing was another matter. She no longer heard her daughter crying. She heard... Abby clearing her throat.

They both stepped back, Chase shaking his head as though trying to clear it. She was glad she wasn't the only one affected by the kiss.

"Sorry for interrupting. I just wanted to make sure you two remembered I was here. Your welcome-home kiss looked like it was getting a little steamy."

Sadie ignored her friend. "You should sit down, honey." She took him by the arm but he didn't move. Finn had come out from under the table to sniff Chase's boot.

"What's Mrs. McNab's dog doing here?"

"Aww, isn't that cute?" Abby said when Finn stood on his hind legs to put his paws on Chase's shoulders. "He wants to welcome you home too."

Chase's eyes narrowed. "Home? What does she mean home?"

"According to Zia Maria, you've—I mean, we've—inherited him."

"How are you supposed to look after a dog? You're having

a hard enough time…" He grimaced, attempting to push Finn away. "Down."

Sadie crossed her arms. She knew exactly what he'd intended to say, and while there might be some truth to it, she didn't appreciate him reminding her she wasn't exactly doing a stand-up job with motherhood. "I guess you didn't hear me. I said *we*, but I was right the first time. Finn is your responsibility, not mine. We just happen to be living together." Her tone made it clear she might be changing her mind on that.

Her lips tingled, reminding her about the kiss they'd just shared. Clearly, her body was on board with receiving more. Which was a pretty shocking development, considering she'd sworn off men and sex, and had been quite happy about doing so.

"Zia Maria didn't give Sadie a choice, so don't blame her," Abby defended her. "Mrs. McNab broke her hip, and everyone blames you because you told her to put Finn on a leash. Zia Maria's right though, Finn really does seem to like you. Or he just wanted your wallet." Abby laughed when the dog darted away with Chase's wallet in his mouth.

"Finn, stop. Drop it," Chase ordered, and the dog skittered to a stop. In the nursery, Michaela stopped crying. Probably in anticipation of Chase coming to her rescue. Finn cocked his head, looking like he'd made the connection between Chase and the silence that followed. He dropped the wallet, tongue lolling.

"Wow, that's seriously impressive." Abby cast Sadie a *this guy is a keeper* glance. "Maybe you'll be able to break Finn of his kleptomania."

Chase looked up from retrieving his wallet. "He's a kleptomaniac?"

Abby nodded. "He is. He lands himself in doggy jail every second month."

"That's just perfect," Chase said, wiping off his wallet. "Sadie, I need a minute in private with you."

Sadie frowned as he walked past her toward her bedroom. He'd lost the exaggerated limp.

"Go, go." Abby waved her off. "I want to call Hunter anyway."

"I won't be long."

"Take as long as you want. I would if I were in your shoes." She beamed at Sadie. "I'm so glad you finally found your one, sweetie."

"You think I found my one?"

"Don't you? I thought—"

"Yeah, of course I do," she murmured as Chase came out of the nursery with her daughter in his arms. "I just wanted your opinion. You were never a fan of Drew. You or Mal."

"And we were totally right. But just like me and Mal, you had to walk through the storm to find your rainbow. If you hadn't been with Drew, you might not have recognized how wonderful Michael really is. Now go."

A few days ago, Sadie had believed *Michael* was wonderful. That she'd finally found her prince after kissing so many frogs. Only to have him turn into Chase, an FBI agent who believed her brother was guilty of murder. A man who might just as easily believe her guilty of the same crime if he found out about her gun.

She had to find her phone and talk to her brother. Maybe together they could figure out what was going on. Unless she was wrong, and he really was involved in Brodie's murder.

She forced the worry from her face and opened her bedroom door. Chase was lying on his side on the bed with Michaela gurgling happily beside him. The smile he'd been sharing with her daughter disappeared when Sadie walked into the room.

He sat up and held out her phone.

Her legs went weak as she crossed the room to retrieve it. "Where did you find my phone?" Despite her best efforts, there was a nervous hitch in her voice. She prayed her brother hadn't texted her while Chase had her phone in his possession. "I've been looking all over for it."

He didn't let go when she tried to remove her phone from his hand. He held her gaze. "Nate took your phone."

"That's illegal." Her heart jumped to her throat. She'd been about to text her brother when Abby and Mallory walked in, seconds before her phone disappeared. Moments before Nate had gone looking for her grandmother.

"So is aiding and abetting a known fugitive." Chase released her phone and then scrubbed a hand over his face. "I don't agree with what Black did, but I also expected you to be aboveboard with me."

"I don't know what you're talking about. I haven't been communicating with Elijah." She lowered herself to the edge of the bed, wanting nothing more than to open her phone. Instead, she put it on the comforter and reached out to stroke Michaela's soft curls. She wanted to pick her up and run but she'd lost that chance.

"But you were going to. You'd started to text him when you were interrupted. What did you need to talk to him about? You said it was urgent."

Thank goodness she'd had the luxury of twelve hours of sleep. Her brain was actually functioning today. "My brother has men chasing him. They tried to kill him. Of course I'm going to try and contact him." She moistened her lips. "Did he reach out to me? Is he okay?"

Chase studied her face with the same narrow-eyed intensity he had back in February. Only now that she knew who he was, his intent stare felt more threatening than curious.

"Don't hold out on me, Sadie. I can't protect you if you do." He glanced at Michaela, reaching back so she could grab his finger.

He didn't need to say the words aloud. She knew exactly what was on the line. For her brother's sake and for her own, she had to figure out who'd used her gun to murder Brodie, and she had to figure it out sooner rather than later.

"I know." She picked up her phone, rubbing her thumb along

the edge. "What did my brother say?" She steeled herself for Chase's answer.

"He sounded panicked. Worried that you hadn't responded to his messages. Aside from your attempt to reach out to him this morning, there was only your conversation about the meet in the woods on your phone, so I'm assuming you set up another form of communication. Where's your laptop, Sadie?"

"I haven't contacted him yet."

"Because you didn't plan to or you just haven't had the time?"

"I haven't had time."

"We have time now." Finn barked, and Michaela startled. Sadie reached for her, picking her up as Chase got off the bed.

"What happened to your foot?"

"It's nothing, just a minor sprain. This"—he pointed at the boot—"is to give me a believable excuse to get out of working for the forestry service. Now I'll be able to devote every minute of my day to protecting you and Michaela and finding your brother. And dealing with Finn," he added when the dog's barking didn't subside. If anything, it had turned low and menacing.

Chase went to the window, separating the wooden slats with his fingers. He drew back. "We've got company. Come on." He helped her off the bed, keeping his hand on the small of her back as he guided her out of the room. "Abby," he called to her friend, who looked up from bribing Finn with a doggy treat to get him to stop barking.

"Sorry. I don't know what's gotten into him. I couldn't get him to be quiet."

Chase held open the door to the nursery, patting Finn's head when the golden retriever came to sit at his side. "Good boy," he murmured to the dog. Then he said, "I want the both of you to stay in here. Sadie, call Gabe and tell him to get here ASAP. Let him know that two deputies from the Jackson County Sheriff's Department have come to call."

Abby looked from Sadie to Chase. "I don't understand. That's a good thing, isn't it? They're trying to find the person who killed their colleague. He was with the Jackson County Sheriff's Department," she explained to Sadie like she didn't know.

"Two nights ago, there was another shooting in the woods. Luckily, no one was hurt," Chase told Abby, sending a pointed glance at Sadie that she hoped her friend had missed. "But until I know they're actually with the Jackson County Sheriff's Department, we need to be careful."

He unholstered his gun. "Abby, do you know how to shoot?"

Abby stared at him. "You think we're in danger?"

"Better to be safe than sorry."

"She doesn't know how to shoot as well as I do." Sadie handed the baby to Abby and took the gun from Chase. She held his gaze. "Be careful."

Something softened in his eyes, and he leaned in, touching his lips to hers. "You too."

This time it didn't feel like he was playing a part.

Sadie put the gun on the dresser and called Gabe. He picked up on the first ring. "Chase told me to call. Deputies from the Jackson County Sheriff's Department are here." At the sound of a loud knock and then the front door of the cottage opening, her stomach fluttered with nerves.

"I'm on my way. Stay out of sight, Sadie."

"I'm in the nursery with Michaela. Abby's here too." She glanced at her friend when Gabe swore softly before disconnecting. Sadie briefly closed her eyes.

Any hope Abby hadn't heard her slipup vanished when she asked, "Who's Chase? And don't lie to me. There are two deputies at your door, and you and whoever he really is are acting like they're the bad guys."

"I—" Sadie broke off at the sound of Finn barking and Chase saying, "I won't repeat myself again. Lower the gun before I lower it for you."

Chapter Nineteen

♥

The bald deputy with the face of a bulldog sneered at Chase, his revolver pointed at Finn. Chase held his gaze and thrust out his hand, bringing his palm down hard on the gun to lower the muzzle before wrenching it from the deputy's grip.

"What the—" Bulldog rounded on the tall, lanky deputy at his side, who was staring at Chase. "Don't just stand there. Draw on him!"

"I wouldn't advise it," Chase warned, glancing at a snarling Finn. "Now, why don't we try this again. Show me your badges."

"We don't need to show you nothing." Bulldog puffed out his chest, jerking his thumb at himself and the Jackson County sheriff's vehicle pulled halfway onto the grass. "Give me back my gun or I'll charge you with . . ." He trailed off and rubbed the back of his head, shooting his partner a withering glare.

Chase smiled. "That's an arrest report I'd be interested in reading. I'm sure your boss would be too." The guy flushed under his tan. Chase figured it was a combination of anger and embarrassment that he'd so easily relieved him of his weapon.

"Still need to see those badges, boys. Anyone can buy a

couple uniforms and add a few decals to a vehicle. If you'd prefer, I can call the sheriff." Which was his ultimate goal. He wanted to get a read on the man, and these two had just given him an opportunity to do so. Bulldog had also played into his plan to get his prints.

The men shared a look, then shrugged. And that told Chase something else. They weren't here of their own accord. Their boss had sanctioned today's visit.

Chase winked. "Don't worry, I won't tell him you let me take your weapon." He tucked the gun in the back of his uniform pants. "Just until I know you are who you say you are. Can't be too careful these days."

Tight-lipped, Bulldog clenched and unclenched his fists. Chase smiled. He wished he'd try. This was one of the men who'd shot at Sadie the other night, he'd stake his life on it. He wasn't as sure about the baby-faced deputy.

Chase punched in the number to the sheriff's office, noting the baby-faced deputy's frown as he did so. "Never know when you might need to call in the law," he said by way of explanation. As he brought the phone to his ear, he laid a comforting hand on Finn's head. Maybe Mrs. McNab had done Chase a favor after all. He made a mental note to send her flowers.

When he stated his business, the woman who answered put him through. A man's gravelly voice came over the line. "Sheriff here. My girl tells me you have a problem over on Willow Creek."

"I have two men on my doorstep claiming to be your deputies, Sheriff. Just wanted to verify with you. They refused to show their ID. I don't want to get them in trouble or anything. Maybe they're just embarrassed about their photos."

"They're my boys but it sounds like they might be at the wrong address. They're looking to speak to Sadie Gray."

"They've got the right address." Chase dropped the friendly

local yokel act. "So why don't you tell me why you want them to speak to my fiancée?" He'd been about to say girlfriend but went with fiancée instead.

"I didn't know she had herself a fiancé."

They'd assumed she was living out here on her own, Chase surmised when the two deputies glanced at each other, not looking pleased with the news. Chase was even less so.

"But I do know she has a brother." The sheriff's voice had an edge to it now. He'd probably heard the same in Chase's. "He's wanted in connection with the murder of one of my deputies so my boys are going to want to talk to his sister, see what she knows. Then they'll have a look-see around the house and the grounds."

"Sadie won't be able to help you. She cut off contact when her brother got involved distributing drugs for the Whiteside Mountain Gang. They're in your jurisdiction, aren't they, Sheriff?" He didn't wait for the other man to answer, keeping a close eye on his deputies, watching for any telltale signs that would reveal their connection with the gang. "Seems to me you would have rounded them up by now. Might be one of them was involved in your deputy's murder."

The deputies shared a glance and the muscle in Bulldog's jaw bunched.

"You trying to tell me how to do my job, son?" the sheriff asked.

"No, sir. Wouldn't dream of it. I'm just a park ranger."

"Good, good. Now you let my boys do their job, and we won't have a problem."

"You might not have a problem with me, Sheriff. But I'm not sure how the Highland Falls chief of police is going to feel when he hears you're nosing around in his investigation," Chase said, spotting Gabe's truck flying down the dirt road, dust spraying.

"And how's he going to hear that? You planning on calling

him? Because if you are, you might want to have a long think on that plan. We don't take kindly to outsiders messing in our business."

"The thing is, Sheriff, Sadie's already spoken to Chief Buchanan. And you don't have to worry about her brother showing up here. The chief's got eyes on the cottage at all times. In fact, he's pulling up as we speak. No hard feelings though. I don't blame you for what sounded an awful lot like a threat. If I were you, I wouldn't want anyone messing around in my business either."

"What do you mean by that?"

Exactly what you think I mean, Chase thought, but instead said, "Nothing, nothing at all. Here's the chief now. Would you like to talk to him?" His question was met with silence. He glanced at the screen. The call had ended. "I guess that's a no. Hey, Chief. I think these two boys would like a word with you about your investigation into Elijah Gray."

"Is that so?" Gabe nodded as he approached and took in the deputies, glancing to his left when another truck barreled down the road. It was Hunter.

"We're here to talk to Sadie Gray about her brother's whereabouts," Bulldog said with a belligerent thrust of his chin.

The baby-faced deputy stayed quiet, and Chase began to second-guess the interaction he'd witnessed between the two men at the mention of the Whiteside Mountain Gang.

At least he was until Hunter approached. "Dwight, it's been a while." Hunter slapped the guy on the back so hard it sent the lanky deputy a foot forward. "Sorry about that. Sometimes I don't know my own strength." Hunter smiled and cracked his knuckles.

And that's when Chase saw it, the utter contempt and lightning-fast temper flaring to life in the deputy's eyes. Chase was surprised the deputy's baby face remained smooth and complacent. Dwight was like a snake hiding in the grass, blending in until he struck. Right then, he edged out Elijah Gray and went to the top of Chase's suspect list for the murder of Brodie.

"I'm here to pick up Abby. She still inside?" Hunter asked Chase.

"She is. Maybe take Finn with you. I don't want him chasing after the deputies when they leave." He stepped aside to let the other man pass, the tension in his shoulders loosening its grip. No one would get to Sadie and the baby with Hunter standing between them.

"Let Sadie know it's you. She's got a gun, and she's a crack shot." He smiled at the deputies, sliding his hand in his pocket. "Like I said, you can never be too careful these days. And speaking of guns, you probably want yours back." He reached behind him, closing his hand over the butt, making sure the tape he'd palmed stuck. "Sorry, muzzle's caught on my belt loop." He brought his other hand behind him, grunting loud enough to disguise the sound of him peeling off the tape. He palmed it in his left hand and handed the gun back with his right.

Fighting a smile, Gabe said, "You're wasting your time, deputies. Sadie has no idea where her brother is. But now that you're here, you can tell me what you know about the shooting in the woods the other night. I'm having a hard time getting the sheriff to return my calls."

"Sheriff's a busy man," Dwight said with no change to his expression or the inflection in his voice.

"Funny, I got through to him no problem not two minutes ago." Chase watched Bulldog's face as he gripped his gun. He frowned but didn't remove his hand to check the butt. He also didn't holster his weapon. The radio attached to his right shoulder crackled. The same woman who'd answered Chase's call rattled off an address for a drunk and disorderly through the static.

As Chase and Gabe watched the deputies get in their vehicle,

Gabe said, "What do you want to bet the sheriff was calling them home?"

"Definitely calling them to come in, but not to the station. He's not a stupid man. He wouldn't want to risk you following them."

"You're right. I should have paid closer attention to the address."

Chase gave it to him. "But you're not checking it out. It's too risky. You'd be in his jurisdiction, and you'd be showing your hand. Black will go." He brought his phone to his ear and went to hand the piece of tape to Gabe. "Let's see if anything pops on this. On second thought, I'll have my boss run it. Hunter knows Dwight, so it stands to reason he might have someone in your department feeding him information." Chase planned to find out everything he knew about the deputy. "Can you put an officer on Agnes?" he asked Gabe while waiting for Black to pick up.

"I'll take care of it myself." Gabe looked over his shoulder and sighed when Abby and Sadie came into view. "It looks like the gig is up. Have fun with that." He patted Chase's shoulder. "Nice work today, by the way."

Sadie had her laptop open on the kitchen table, waiting for the server to connect to her brother's preferred message board.

Abby leaned over her to check out the screen. "I love when you do your hacker stuff."

Sadie bowed her head. "I'm not hacking anyone. I'm on a message board."

"Right, of course you are." Abby gave her a broad wink, glancing at Chase, who stood with his phone to his ear talking to his boss at the FBI. "It's so cool he's a special agent. No wonder he sucked at the park ranger thing."

They'd had to come clean with Abby. She was too smart and

had already put quite a bit of it together before she'd confronted Chase in the entryway.

Hunter, who was pacing the living room with Michaela in his arms and Finn trailing after him, raised an eyebrow at Abby.

"You know I think you're the coolest man on the entire planet. But I'm just so happy my besties have cool guys of their own." Abby smiled up at Chase, who'd ended his call to come and stand beside Sadie's chair. "If you've never seen Sadie at work, you're in for a treat. You should have seen her go up against Elijah last summer. She hacked into his Bitcoin account and got my money back. He..." She glanced at Sadie, who was giving her *please be quiet* wide eyes, and cleared her throat. "I think I need some water. Anyone else want a drink?" She got up to go to the refrigerator.

"I'm good, thanks," Chase said at almost the same time as Hunter. Then Chase sat on the other chair beside Sadie, nudging the laptop with his finger so he could see the screen.

His thigh touched hers, and she had to control a shiver of awareness. She blamed it on his cologne, vowing to find the bottle and hide the warm, intoxicating scent from him.

"You won't be able to read his message, you know. It'll be in code," she said just as her brother's avatar popped onto the screen. Relief swamped her. He was alive.

Chase placed a comforting hand on her arm, surprising her with how easily he read her. "You need to get him to come in, Sadie."

She nodded and responded to Elijah. She could almost sense her brother's own relief at her quick response.

"Ask him if he has actual evidence that connects the Jackson County sheriff to the Whiteside Mountain Gang and Brodie's murder," Chase directed, not taking his eyes from the screen. Sadie had a feeling he was trying to decode their messages. She wouldn't be surprised if he did, which is why she did exactly as he directed. But her brother's response surprised her. She stared at the screen.

"What is it?" Chase asked.

"He has proof the sheriff is behind the Whiteside Mountain Gang. He recorded him and two of his deputies on three separate occasions. He doesn't have proof they killed Brodie though."

"It's okay. We can work with that. One of them will turn on the others. They always do. For his own safety, he has to turn himself in, Sadie."

Another message popped up on the screen. She read it and covered her face. "Damn it, Elijah," she murmured into her hand. She took a deep breath before facing Chase. "His phone went missing the same night as the drugs. He doesn't know what he did with them. He was drunk."

Chase dragged a hand down his face, releasing a frustrated sigh. "Okay, I guess all we can do is hope that, once he's not in hiding and in fear for his life, he'll remember something."

Someone else popped onto the message board. Sadie didn't recognize their handle. Her brother went dark.

"What happened?"

"I don't know, but I don't like it." She signed off. Her phone, sitting at her elbow, pinged with a text. It was Elijah.

That was one of them on the message board. From now on we're going old-school, Sis. Tomorrow. After sunset. You know where.

"What does he mean?"

"We used to leave messages for each other, kind of like a treasure hunt. That's how he'll communicate from now on. He'll leave one for me tomorrow at Lover's Leap. It was our favorite place to watch the sun set and stargaze."

Chapter Twenty

♥

What do you think about Abby's plan for the unicorn weekend? Do you think it will create enough interest to impact the store's bottom line?" Sadie asked Chase from the kitchen, where she was heating up the dinner from Zia Maria's. Abby and Hunter had left twenty minutes ago.

Chase liked the couple, but he hadn't been sorry to see them leave. He was enjoying the peace and quiet. Abby never stopped talking, and her mind never stopped working. Admittedly, there were pluses to having her creative mind at work on ways to promote I Believe in Unicorns. Abby had come up with the idea to have a weekend in June devoted to the mythical creatures. She'd feature the event, the store, and Sadie's grandmother on her popular YouTube channel.

"It sounded pretty good to me," Chase said. "I'm just a little concerned that people will be in danger if they decide to go unicorn hunting. The woods aren't exactly a safe place these days." He sat on the couch playing with Michaela, lifting her in the air and then bringing her back down on his knees, smiling at her happy gurgle. He glanced at Sadie and saw her smirk.

"Especially for you," she said, her tone amused. "How's your ankle?"

He glanced at his foot propped on a pillow on the coffee table, courtesy of Sadie. "The ice helped. Thanks," he said. Then, feeling the need to defend himself, he added, "I might make a lousy park ranger, but I do all right as an agent."

"More than all right from what I've seen and heard." She glanced over as she placed a plate of lasagna in the microwave. "But do me a favor. Next time you go up against two men with guns, don't go unarmed. You should have kept your gun instead of giving it to me."

"I wasn't overly concerned that they'd pull something in the middle of the day. Besides that, I didn't want them to see me as a threat. If they had decided to do something stupid, I can handle myself."

"Still, I would have felt better knowing you were armed."

"I felt better knowing that you were, and I had Finn." The dog sat on the floor at his feet, his eyes tracking Michaela as Chase lifted her over his head and then back down to his knees. "He likes the baby."

"He also likes her toys." Sadie nodded at a small pile of stuffed animals peeking out from under the couch. "I'll pick him up some of his own tomorrow. Maybe then he won't steal hers."

"I'm not thrilled about you going in to I Believe in Unicorns tomorrow." Sadie planned to work at the store while he stayed at home with Michaela. The officer currently sitting outside in his patrol car would follow her in.

"I know. You've made that perfectly clear. But when this is over, I want my grandmother to still have the store and her home."

"You could just as easily redo the store's website from here."

"Once I take the photos of the inventory, I can. But if we want the unicorn weekend to be a success, we need to spread the word. And the best way to do that is for me and Abby to hang out at Spill the Tea for lunch."

Chase noted the way Sadie wouldn't meet his gaze. "What else are you planning to do?"

"It's really annoying when you read me like that, you know."

"I hear that a lot. It's never distracted me before, and it won't distract me now. So spill."

She grinned, her eyes sparkling. "You're starting to sound like Nate."

Her sparkling eyes distracted him, reminding him of how she'd looked after the kiss they'd shared earlier today in the entryway. He'd been dazed and confused, and more than a little turned on. He'd been as relieved by Abby's interruption as he'd been frustrated.

He focused on Michaela to regain his train of thought, which wasn't his best idea. She was a miniature Sadie, her eyes sparkling, a heart-stealing smile on her face. She'd stolen his heart the day Black had handed him to her, and Chase had the terrifying thought that her mother had too.

Not trusting his voice to remain steady at the realization that he was falling in love with Sadie, Chase raised an eyebrow at her instead. The simple quirk of his brow wouldn't give away that his heart was practically pounding out of his chest.

She sighed. "Okay, so when you were grilling Hunter about Dwight, Abby and I got to talking about Payton. We're going to drop by her place tomorrow."

This was exactly the distraction he needed. He had to stay focused on the task at hand. "No. I don't want you near her."

"But just the other day you told me it would be a good idea to get close to her."

"That was before I knew she had a connection to Dwight." They'd dated in high school.

"It's a small town. Everyone has a connection. If it makes you feel better, I'll bring my grandmother, and Abby can stay at the store. Nate can tag along. Payton could be the key to all of this, Chase. She might have an idea what Elijah did with the drugs."

"If you and your grandmother want to pay her a visit, I'm okay with that, as long as Nate goes with you. He has a feeling your grandmother has been sneaking over there anyway. He's lost track of her twice already."

"Are you serious? How does he lose track...Forget I asked. I should know by now not to underestimate my grandmother. I guess it's a good thing the bank manager froze the store's line of credit."

She'd lost her earlier sparkle. Now she looked like she carried the weight of the world on her shoulders. Her family was draining her, physically, mentally, and, as he'd come to learn, financially. He wished he could step in but it wasn't his place, no matter how he felt about her. He doubted she'd accept his financial help, even if he framed it as a loan. All he could do was help out with Michaela and make sure Sadie got her rest and they were safe—that, and get her brother back in one piece. Before he arrested him, he thought with an inward sigh.

"You can't question Payton about any of this, Sadie. It's too dangerous. Whether you believe it or not, I think there's more of a connection between her and Dwight than we know. I didn't get a good vibe off the guy. You need to stay clear of him."

"But what if she can tell us where Elijah was the day Brodie was murdered? Maybe she can give him an alibi."

"It wouldn't explain why he has the gun that killed Brodie in his possession." Her face lost all of its color. "Sorry, I know how hard this is on you." He stood up, resting Michaela on his hip. "Let's not talk about it anymore tonight. You need a break." He blinked as he got closer to the kitchen. It was an absolute disaster—sauce and dishes everywhere. "How did you manage to make such a mess? All you were doing was heating up the—" Michaela spat up on him, and not just a little spit-up. It was like the scene in *The*

Exorcist. He felt something warm in his hand and looked down. She'd pooped through her diaper too.

An hour later, Sadie was still chuckling at the shocked and disgusted expression on Chase's face. He hadn't appreciated her doubling over in laughter but oh, she had appreciated the release. His comment about her brother and the murder weapon—her gun—reared its ugly, scary head. She pushed the thought aside. She honestly couldn't deal with it tonight.

She went to close the door to the nursery as the bathroom door opened. Chase walked out of the steam-filled room, and her mouth dropped open. He was bare chested, his navy sweatpants riding low on his hips, his feet bare. Maybe it would be better if she dealt with the gun tonight after all. Dealing with Chase looking like this was just as terrifying.

She knew she had feelings for him when he was Michael, but she'd easily dismissed them when she'd learned the truth— okay, not so easily. But the kiss they shared today had made it obvious she had feelings for him, for Chase. And her fear when he stood facing down the Jackson County deputies with nothing more than his big brain showed her just how deep her feelings for him truly were. She was falling in love with him.

Worse, he was beginning to regain his status as her knight in shining armor. She didn't need or want a man to fight her battles; she wanted a man who would be her partner. A man who shared in the care of her daughter when she needed to catch up on some sleep, a man who surprised her by unpacking her moving boxes when she was feeling overwhelmed. A man who looked like he'd walked out of a dream, she thought, as her gaze met his.

His hand stalled in the middle of drying his hair with a towel. He looked around. "Is everything okay?"

"Everything's good." She cleared the breathless quality from her voice. "Michaela went out like a light. I think we might be in for a quiet night."

"Yeah?" He nudged her out of the way to peek into the room. Cast in the glow from the nightlight, her daughter looked adorable in a pink sleeper with her thumb in her mouth. Finn was stretched out on the unicorn area rug beside the crib, his golden head resting on one of the soft dolls he'd stolen.

"Good boy," Chase whispered to Finn, who'd raised his head to eye them. Chase gave Sadie a smile that made her ovaries twitch. "He won't let anyone near her."

Without thinking, she pressed a palm against his hard and muscular chest to move him out of the doorway. His pec flexed beneath her hand, and she slowly lowered it from his chest before she did something stupid like trace his defined muscles with the tips of her fingers.

"We'll wake her up if we're not careful," Sadie said, pulling the door closed, leaving it open an inch in case Finn wanted out. "Your dinner is in the oven."

"Are you going to bed?"

She couldn't tell if he hoped she was or hoped she wasn't. "I thought I'd watch some TV." She couldn't remember when she'd last enjoyed the simple pleasure of curling up on the couch and binge-watching her favorite shows.

"Sounds good." He started to walk away but then turned. "Do you mind if I join you? I wouldn't be offended if you needed some time to yourself. I can eat"—he looked around—"in the spare bedroom."

She held back a smile. "With the rest of my boxes? I don't mind if you join me. I just thought you had to work."

An hour later, from where she sat curled up on the couch, Sadie said, "Are you sure you don't have work to do?"

He grinned around a forkful of tiramisu and put his bare feet on the coffee table. Of course, Mr. Neat Freak had to put the towel he used to dry his hair beneath his feet.

"And miss this? Not on your life." He licked the last bit of chocolate off his fork to point it at the screen. "Why does Darcey let Tom treat her like that?"

It took a moment for her to pull her gaze from his mouth. She'd had a hard time staying focused on the screen, which was telling, because she loved *90 Day Fiancé*. She always felt better about her own romantic failures after watching the show. But tonight, she'd been more interested in watching Chase eat his tiramisu. It was like food porn.

Finally managing to pull her gaze back to the screen, she said, "My guess is she's in love with the idea of love."

"That's not love." He grinned at her. "But the way you're eyeing my tiramisu looks a lot like love to me. Come on, I don't mind sharing. You gave me more than half the container." He leaned forward, picking up a fork from the coffee table. "I even brought you your own fork."

She had to remember how well this man read her. "Of course you brought me my own fork. Heaven forbid you'd have to share yours with me," she teased, in hopes he wouldn't give more thought to the lust he'd seen in her eyes.

"There you go implying I'm some kind of neat freak again. Come here, and I'll prove you wrong." He waved her over with the fork.

"Says the man who cleaned the kitchen after me." She moved to sit beside him. The thinking part of her brain told her she was an idiot, while the emotional part of her brain suggested she forget about the fork and lick the creamy chocolate dessert off his lips.

She leaned in and got an up-close look at the stubble on his chin, his warm, sexy fragrance enveloping her as she opened her mouth to accept the tiramisu from his fork. She hummed around it, as much in appreciation of him as the dessert.

His smile faltered, something that looked a lot like heat

flashing in his eyes. "Beautiful," he murmured, and then blinked. "I mean, the dessert is beautifully made."

"They are," she agreed, looking into his eyes. She shook her head. "I mean, it is."

"So beautifully made you can't think straight." He touched the side of his mouth. "You have some chocolate here."

Kiss it off, she wanted to say, but instead she wiped a finger down the side of her lips. "Did I get it?"

He stared at her mouth. "What was that?"

"The chocolate, did I get it?"

"No. You still have some here." This time, instead of using his own face to show her where, he touched a finger to the side of her mouth. She shivered as he slowly wiped the edge of her lips and then offered the chocolate-coated digit to her. She accepted the offer without hesitation, her brain a lust-fogged mess. She licked the chocolate off his finger as slowly as he'd wiped it off her face.

She pulled back at his stunned expression. It would have been comical if it wasn't the result of something she had done. "What's wrong?"

"Nothing. Nothing's wrong."

As lust cleared from her brain, she connected the dots and groaned. "You were just showing me you got it all, weren't you? You didn't mean for me to lick it off."

"Yeah, but I, uh, liked your idea better. I liked it a lot." He smiled, his cheeks flushed as he drew the throw pillow onto his lap.

From the nursery, she heard a tiny squawk and a low woof. She'd never been happier to hear her daughter. "I should get her." She practically jumped to her feet. In her hurry, she accidentally bumped the plate, and it fell onto Chase's lap. "Good thing the pillow was there."

"Yeah, good thing."

Chapter Twenty-One

♥

The next morning, Sadie pulled her SUV alongside the curb in front of a white clapboard house that had seen better days. "I can't believe you went to visit Payton without telling me, Granny."

"What was I supposed to do? I can't rightly bring you with me when she told me not to, now can I?"

"Why didn't she want you to bring Sadie, Agnes?" Nate asked from the backseat before she could. She'd been warned by both Chase and Nate to let him do the questioning when it came to Payton.

She didn't think this counted. "That's what I'd like to know. I don't even remember her."

"I suspect it's on account of the money. She thinks you're the reason I can't help her out now and again."

"You could have told her the truth, Granny."

"I couldn't tell her it was Elijah's fault. He's the father of her bairn. She might leave him if she were to hear that. Besides, I'm not sure your brother had anything to do with the missing money. Maybe someone hacked into my account."

"Someone did. Elijah."

"Sadie's right, Agnes. You have to stop making excuses for your grandson."

The hard edge in Nate's voice brought Sadie's head up. She glanced in the rearview mirror. His expression was a little scary. Chase might be willing to hear her brother out and see where the evidence led, but Nate had already tried and convicted Elijah.

"It'll be okay, Granny. Everything will work out in the end. I promise. We'll turn things around." Sadie patted her grandmother's hand. She hated to see her upset.

"You're part of the problem, you know. You coddle her, and she's a lot tougher than you think. Devious too," Nate muttered as he got out of the SUV.

Her grandmother frowned. "What did he say?"

"Same thing as me, Granny." Sadie opened her door as Finn bounded out of the backseat.

"Do you want to tell me again why Mikey foisted the dog on us?" Nate patted his pocket. "He stole my keys!"

"Finn, come here," Sadie called after the dog, who had darted away to chase a squirrel. Finn cast her a mournful glance but did as she directed, coming to sit at her feet. "He doesn't have them now. Check under the seats. He likes to hide things. And in answer to your question, Michael wanted me to have company on my way to and from work."

"You're lucky, dog," Nate said, pulling his head out of the SUV. He wiped his keys on his jeans before shoving them in his front pocket and looked around. "Mikey didn't just want you to have company. There are too many places for me to watch on my own. I hate when he's right." Nate glanced at her grandmother, who'd come around to open the trunk. "I've got it, Agnes. That's why you brought me, remember? I'm your pack mule."

"Is that why you're here, laddie? I thought you were Sadie's and my protection."

"Told you she doesn't miss a trick." There was an irritated

but admiring note in Nate's voice. And while his face was stern, Sadie didn't miss the amused glint in his eyes or the twinkle in her grandmother's. Clearly, they liked each other, which was a good thing since they were living together. The thought reminded her of the man currently living under her roof.

They liked each other too. Only in their case, Sadie was afraid of what would happen to their relationship when this was over. She brushed the thought aside and beeped the locks on her fob before tucking her grandmother's arm through hers.

"Let's go welcome Payton to the family." And get an alibi for her brother.

"Your face doesn't look so welcoming, my girl. You were never very good at hiding your feelings." She patted Sadie's arm. "Let me do the talking. I know what I'm about, and I know what Nate's about. Your new man too. I like him even if he is trying to put our Elijah behind bars. He's good for you."

Sadie stared at her grandmother, stunned that she knew who Chase and Nate were.

From behind them, Nate groaned, and it wasn't because of the ten bags he carried. He'd overheard her grandmother.

Agnes grinned. "Never underestimate the blue-haired ladies, laddie."

"All right, Agatha Christie, what's your take on the lady of the house?" Nate glanced at the front window. "The woman who is currently watching us from behind the curtains. Both of you turn around and pretend you're looking for something in the bags. We need to buy some time."

They did as he asked, Finn joining them in the huddle.

"I think she's pulled the wool over our boy's eyes. She's been stepping out on him with another man," her grandmother said, her head half in one of the bags.

"And you know this how?" Nate glowered down at her. "And do not give me some bullcrap story about it being on account of your second sight. Oh yeah, she tried to pull her scam on me," he said at Sadie's questioning glance. "She freaked me out with her creepy monotone voice, but I figured out fast enough what she was up to."

"You didn't fake it?" Sadie asked her grandmother. "You were able to do a reading?"

"Aye, my gift's back online. I'd lost it on account of the stress, I think. I've never been all that good at keeping secrets, especially from you." She gave Sadie an apologetic smile. "I didn't want to worry you. You already had more than your share of worries, thanks to Drew. Good riddance to him, I say."

"Okay, ladies, let's stay on track. This was a surprise visit for a reason. We don't want Payton to have time to hide anyone or anything. Start moving toward the door. Slowly. Agnes, pretend you're having trouble walking." When her grandmother did as he suggested, Nate said, "Now tell me why you think she's involved with someone other than your grandson."

"I saw it with my own eyes. So did Colin. Colin Murphy. He used to be a spy," she said with a proud smile.

"Where and when, exactly, did you and Sherlock witness this clandestine rendezvous?"

"Here. A man visited her twice in the dead of night. I can't tell you when he left. When you get to be our ages, creeping around and staying out of sight is hard on the knees."

"Granny, what were you thinking?" Sadie whisper-shouted. "You—"

Nate cut her off, a muscle bunching in his jaw. "What nights exactly?"

"The night you were spying on me from across the street. You should have Colin teach you the tricks of his trade," her grandmother said to Nate. "He spied you right away. We saw Payton's man sneaking in again last night."

"What?" Nate said at Sadie's accusatory stare. "I thought she was in bed. It's your fault I missed her the first time."

"How do you figure that?"

"Because just before I could investigate the man I now know to be Colin Murphy going up to Agnes's apartment, I got called away to rescue you and your brother."

Before Sadie could warn him not to say anything about the shooting in front of her grandmother, Finn took off barking.

"Great, now he's off chasing squirrels," Nate muttered.

"I don't think so. He has an excited bark when he chases squirrels. That's the same bark he made when the deputies from the Jackson County Sheriff's Department came to the cottage."

Nate shoved the bags into Sadie's arms and took off at a run toward the back of the house.

"Granny, maybe we should—" Agnes was no longer at her side; she was knocking on Payton's door.

"It's me, lass. Granny MacLeod. I've brought Sadie, the bairn's auntie, with me. We've come to help you set up the nursery for the new addition to our family." She glanced over her shoulder at Sadie and winked.

Ten minutes later, after getting no response to her knocking or bell ringing, Granny sighed. "It looks like she's not home."

"Someone was," Sadie said as she retrieved the bags from the doorstep. In the distance, she heard Nate calling Finn. "We might as well wait in the car, Granny." She'd just gotten her grandmother and the packages loaded back in the SUV when Nate appeared at the corner of the house, Finn racing past him with a piece of light-blue fabric hanging from his mouth.

"What have you got there, boy?" She bent to retrieve the piece of cloth he'd dropped at her feet.

"Looks like he might have caught up with whoever left Payton's place in a hurry. It's the same color and fabric as the Jackson County Sheriff's Department's uniforms." Nate put out his hand for the piece of cloth. "I'll send it to my brother-in-law. See if they can get a hit in the DNA database."

"Aren't you glad he came with us now?" Sadie asked, giving Finn a hug.

"Yeah, yeah." Nate grudgingly patted the dog's head. "Good boy." He opened the back door, ushering Finn inside. "Now stay on your own side, and don't even think about stealing my keys or my shades."

As Sadie drove back to the store, her grandmother texted Payton. Seconds later, her cell phone pinged. "She says she's sorry she wasn't there. She had a doctor's appointment. I'll tell her we'll drop by tomorrow if that works for her."

They were still waiting for Payton's response when Sadie pulled into a parking spot in front of the store.

"I think we need an extra incentive," her grandmother said, head bent over her phone. She typed out her message with one finger, grinning at the *whoosh* of her text being sent.

It was a grin that made Sadie nervous. "Granny, what did you do?"

"I told her you want to set up a generous education fund for the bairn."

Nate laughed. "Mrs. M, you missed your calling. You would have made a great agent."

Her grandmother smirked. "Colin tells me that all the time."

An hour later, Sadie walked across the road with Abby to Spill the Tea.

Abby nodded at Sadie's bag from Penelope's Pet Emporium. "Finn is going to be a happy doggy."

Sadie smiled at the couple walking by on the sidewalk, waiting for them to pass to respond. "He deserves a reward. This morning's visit to Payton would have been a bust if not for him."

"This thing with your grandmother and Mr. Murphy is so freaking lit. Can't you just picture the two of them skulking around looking for clues?"

"Yes, and unlike you, I don't think it's cool. I think it's dangerous." But while on one hand she was worried about her grandmother's nighttime escapades, on the other hand, she was relieved. Now that she didn't have to keep Nate and Chase's identity from Agnes a secret, she could find out if her grandmother had any clue who might have taken Sadie's gun back in February.

As they reached Spill the Tea, Sadie said, "No more talking about my grandmother and Mr. Murphy until we've left here."

Abby waggled her eyebrows and opened the door. "No problem. I'm more interested in why you blushed when I asked you how your night went."

"I didn't blush." Sadie's cheeks heated.

Abby laughed. "You're doing it again. Come on, spill the tea to your bestie."

Knowing Abby wouldn't let up, Sadie shared her embarrassing tiramisu moment with her and then opened the door.

"So you, like, licked his finger, or did you suck on it?" Abby asked, following her inside.

Sadie cast a nervous glance at the lunch crowd gathered at the tea shop. "If you ask a little louder, maybe everyone will hear you."

"Sorry." She lowered her voice, sidling in beside Sadie. "So which was it?"

"Licked it like it was my favorite chocolate popsicle."

"What were you licking?" Brooklyn's voice came from behind the small reservation stand. She stood up with a smile and menus in her hand.

Beside her, Abby was having a hard time containing her laughter.

Sadie scowled at her, then smiled at Brooklyn. "It was nothing. Just something stupid."

"Whatever it was, it sounded like you enjoyed yourself,"

Brooklyn said. "Do you want a booth at the back or do you want to sit at the tea bar?"

Sadie looked to where Babs Sutherland was holding court at the tea bar. "A booth would be——"

Babs pinned her with a bright-eyed stare from under her thick, frosted-blue eyeshadow. "Sadie Gray, don't you dare try to sneak away. We've all heard your big news. Come over here and spill the tea. We want the inside scoop."

She might as well get it over with. It was why they were here. "Abby's putting together an amazing unicorn event in June. She'll be sending around advertising options to all the shops on Main Street later in the week. There will be plenty of opportunities for everyone to participate."

Sadie's enthusiastic smile faltered when the women swiveled on their barstools to stare at her. "You guys could create a unicorn tea. Something pink and sparkly would probably work." She was losing them. The women were leaning into each other, whispering behind their hands. "Or you could add those little gold edible things." She cast a *dear Lord, help me* look at Abby.

"Trust me, it'll boost everyone's business, not just I Believe in Unicorns. But let's be honest, it's our civic duty to support Granny MacLeod. This is what small towns are all about, being there for each other in times of trouble. And let's face it, Agnes and her family are in big trouble. They need our help." She made an apologetic face at Sadie.

The last thing Sadie and her grandmother wanted was to be seen as the town's charity case, but right now, she'd agree to just about anything Abby said to take the attention off her. Except Abby's spiel didn't seem like it had gone over any better than hers.

"I'm sure the unicorn event will be a big crowd-pleaser, but that's not what we wanted to hear about. I knew she wasn't much of a romantic," Babs confided to the women at the tea bar. Then she said to Sadie, "The ring, darlin'. We want to see the ring."

"What ring?"

"Your engagement ring, of course!" Babs gave the other women a *see what I mean* look.

"Drew and I aren't together. We—"

"Not him!" Babs waved an impatient hand, her thick, be-jeweled bracelets clinking. "We're talking about Park Ranger Michael. Your knight in shining armor. The man you're living with, you sly devil, you. Getting your hooks into him before my Brooklyn had a chance."

Brooklyn groaned. "Momma."

"What? You're as gaga over him as half the other single girls in town. Although a few of them dropped out of the running after the bear episode." Babs motioned Sadie closer with her long, bright-pink fingernails. "Tea's spilled. Now show us the ring. And don't try and deny it. That sweet boy with the Jackson County Sheriff's Department told us you were engaged when he dropped in yesterday afternoon."

Abby glanced at Sadie, who was standing there in stunned silence, and asked, "What sweet boy would that be?"

"Deputy Dwight, that's who. You wouldn't know him. He grew up here but he lives over in Jackson County now."

At the mention of Dwight, Sadie pushed all thoughts of her supposed engagement aside. This conversation was too important to miss even a single word.

"What a brat, sharing your secret like that," Abby said to Sadie before turning back to Babs. "Did he happen to share any more of my bestie's secrets? If he did, I'm going to have to have a word with him."

"Now that I think about it, he was more interested in what I knew about Sadie's new fiancé. I shouldn't be surprised. Everyone has been coming to me, asking what I know about him. Help a gal out. Tell me everything." Babs propped her elbows on the sleek, white bar and cupped her face in her hands.

"Oh, Momma, stop. They came in to eat. Sadie, Abby, follow me. Sorry about that. You know how she hates to be the last to know." Brooklyn ushered them to a quiet booth at the back of the room. "And about me being gaga over your fiancé, I'm really not."

Sadie ignored Abby waggling her eyebrows at her as Brooklyn continued. "He's just hot, and I'm looking, and he checks all the boxes, if you know what I mean. Except maybe the steady income box. Momma says his boss at the forest service is thinking about firing him. If you ask me, he's lucky he broke his leg." She smiled, placing the menus in front of them. "I'll give you a minute."

"Should I know who Deputy Dwight is?" Sadie asked Brooklyn, hoping to find out what the other woman knew about Dwight and Payton. "Did he date someone we know or—"

Brooklyn gracefully lowered herself into a crouch beside the table. "I hate to tell tales out of school, but I think Payton might be stepping out on your brother."

"Oh, really. With Dwight?"

"Mm-hmm, but I wouldn't worry about it. It's probably just a passing fling on account your brother is on the run from the law. It has to be hard for Payton knowing she'll be raising the baby on her own. I overheard Dwight tell Momma that Elijah would never see the light of day with the evidence they have against him. Momma said, for Payton's sake, you understand, she'd be better off if your brother died. On account of his life insurance and all."

"My brother has life insurance?" Sadie blurted without thinking. But honestly, it was a little shocking to hear Brooklyn talking about Elijah's death like it was already a done deal. Maybe in Dwight's eyes it was, which meant Brooklyn had just revealed another motive. Chase was right. She had to convince her brother to turn himself in.

"I'm sorry. I shouldn't have said anything. But you asked, and I—"

"It's okay. I'm just a little surprised, that's all. Buying life insurance isn't exactly an Elijah thing to do."

"I know what you mean. It's the responsible thing to do, and Elijah was always quick to duck out of any and all responsibility. I guess becoming a parent changes how you look at things. But Payton's a smart girl. She'd want to take care of her baby's future in case anything happened to one of them."

"I'm glad Elijah stepped up. It's just too bad he wouldn't be able to afford a large policy to give Payton peace of mind. *If* something happened to him, I mean. Which it won't. My brother always lands on his feet."

"Oh no, she'd be very comfortable. The policy is for a quarter of a million dollars." Brooklyn waved a hand and stood up. "But you're right. Elijah has gotten out of more scrapes than anyone I know. Although that was because you and Agnes always stepped in. You wouldn't step in this time, would you, Sadie?"

"No. I'm done with my brother."

Brooklyn pressed a hand to her chest. "I'm so glad to hear that. Dwight was saying to Momma how you'd be in big trouble if they found out that you knew where your brother was or were helping him in any way."

Chapter Twenty-Two

♥

Chase followed Sadie and the white horse she led along a narrow trail up Blue Mountain. She walked the path with sure, confident strides in her well-worn hiking boots, clearly in her element. So was the horse. Chase, not so much, although he felt better with Sadie leading the way than going it on his own, much like he had with Hunter.

She dropped the horse's reins to walk to the side of the trail, checking inside a hollowed-out stump. She'd stopped to check for a note from her brother at a couple of places along the way up the mountain. He didn't remind her again that they'd come early for a reason. She'd gone quiet when he'd first told her that he intended to bring Elijah in tonight. She'd wanted to retrieve her brother's note and leave one in its place, asking him to turn himself in.

She glanced at Chase as she returned to pick up the horse's reins. "You okay back there?"

As unhappy as she might be about his plan to apprehend her brother, he was relieved that it hadn't created a rift between them. "Yeah, just trying to keep my distance from the horse. I don't think she likes me."

"It's not you. Granny boards her horses and goat at the mayor's farm. Agnes hasn't been spending as much time with them as she normally does. Myrtle and Millie don't seem to mind, but Lula Belle is younger and loves attention. Don't you, girl?" She patted the horse.

"Is that why you brought her?" He'd been surprised when Agnes and Nate rolled up behind Sadie's SUV with a trailer hitched to Nate's truck. But between getting Michaela settled with her babysitter—specifically his partner, who hadn't been thrilled to be on babysitting duty—and searching for the right way and best time to tell Sadie that her plan and his for this evening were at cross-purposes, Chase had forgotten to ask.

Admittedly, he'd been preoccupied since learning what Agnes had been up to. Sadie too. They were too involved with the case and were putting themselves at risk.

"No. Lula Belle has the starring role in Abby's unicorn weekend. She's our elusive and beautiful unicorn, aren't you, girl?" Sadie gestured at the pack attached to the horse's saddle. "I won't put on her golden horn and the circlet of flowers until I'm ready to do the photo shoot. I'll video her, take some photos, and then Abby will use them to promote the event on her YouTube channel. I thought now was as good a time as any. If anyone sees us, we have a cover story."

"I remember the part about the cover story. I guess I didn't put it together."

Lula Belle nuzzled Sadie's neck, and she nuzzled her back. "Abby started pimping the event on her channel while we were out for lunch. She says her subscribers seem super excited, so maybe she's right. Maybe you will make Granny rich, Lula Belle." Sadie glanced at Chase from under her lashes. She seemed nervous.

Probably because of her brother. Then again, maybe she was beginning to read him as easily as he read her. He couldn't put it off any longer. "About your visit to Spill the Tea. We didn't get a lot of time to talk about it, but we need to."

She nodded. "It would have been helpful to know we were engaged before I had to face Babs and her friends."

"Like I told you, I wanted them to know you were important to me. That they'd have to go through me to get to you. I thought a fiancé carried more weight than a boyfriend."

"I get it, especially when it comes to me. My boyfriends haven't exactly been stand-up guys."

She deserved a stand-up guy, but now wasn't the time to talk about it. After last night, he'd been more than a little tempted to offer himself for the position. To turn his lie into the truth. This morning, he'd had second thoughts. Especially after learning what Agnes and Sadie had been up to. He had to stay focused on the case. Not on a woman who made his heart race and turned his brain to mush.

"At the time I said it, I didn't think Dwight had a connection to the town or to you. The last thing I expected was for him to go to Spill the Tea." The trail widened, and Chase skirted the back end of the horse, looping his fingers through its bridle to bring their walk to a stop. He wanted to see Sadie's face. "I'm worried about you, you and your grandmother. You need to back off and let Nate and me handle it from here on out."

"If it weren't for me and my grandmother, you wouldn't know about Payton and Dwight or the life insurance policy."

"You're right, and I'm not denying the information that you obtained provided us with the biggest break in the case. But you're also smart enough to realize the danger you're in."

"I'm more worried about my brother. It's bad enough that the sheriff and his deputies are trying to pin Brodie's death on him, but to think that they ultimately want to see him dead. Or at the very least, Dwight might..." She trailed off and looked away.

"That has always been their endgame, Sadie. Your brother

knows too much. That's why it's imperative I take him into protective custody until we get everything straightened out."

"I know that now. Convincing Elijah will be the hard part. He doesn't trust law enforcement." She clicked her tongue to get the horse to walk. "My father made sure of that."

Except Elijah had trusted Brodie. Then again, maybe he hadn't. Maybe the deputy had been a means to an end. "Elijah was, what, nine when your father went away?"

"Closer to ten. It took almost a year before they caught up to my father." She glanced at him. "But you knew that, didn't you? You've known all along the part I played in his escape."

"I've known since the day that I met you. It doesn't change how I feel about you." He cleared his throat at what sounded like an admission that he was falling in love with her. At least in his mind it did. Maybe because he was. "I mean, I don't judge you for what you did. You were young, and he was your father. From what I've read about him, he was a brilliant, charismatic man, who manipulated people much older than you. People who were trained to know better."

Two guards had unwittingly aided in Jeremiah's escape from federal prison. Sadie's mother had been waiting for him a mile away. They'd been in a motor vehicle accident just hours after his escape. The couple had been pronounced dead at the scene.

"It wasn't my father," she said quietly. "I did it because of my mother. She begged me to lie for him and to lead the law enforcement officers far from the cottage so he could get away. I didn't know she'd planned to go with him. I should have known though. Granny used to say my mother wasn't just in love with my father, she was consumed by him. She loved him to distraction. I guess she didn't have enough love left over for us."

"My mother was the same," he surprised himself by saying. He only spoke about his mother to his brother and the judge, and it was rare that they spoke about her at all. But he wanted Sadie to know she wasn't alone, so he continued. "Even when my grandfather warned her that he'd petition for custody of me and my brother if she didn't leave the man she was involved with at the time, she chose him. Happily, I might add."

"I'm so sorry. That must have been horrible for you and your brother."

"No more horrible than it was for you and Elijah."

"What about your father?"

"He'd never been in the picture. My grandfather hadn't been either until we moved closer to DC, and then he stepped into the role of father figure." He smiled. "We were lucky he did. I don't like to think where either of us would be right now if he hadn't."

"He must be proud of you."

"Not right now he isn't." Once again, he surprised himself by opening up to her, sharing what happened in DC and how he'd been demoted to the field office in North Carolina. "The judge always had high hopes that one day I'd end up the director of the FBI, or better still, attorney general. In his mind, I've ruined any chance of that happening."

"Don't you have to be a lawyer to be attorney general?"

"I am." He studied her. Something had changed in her expression and not for the better. "What is it?"

Sadie forced a smile. "I just think it's interesting that we were both raised by our grandparents."

She couldn't tell him that everything he'd just shared had dashed the silly fantasy that had been playing in her head. The one where they really were engaged and lived happily ever after, just like in the fairy tales.

He was an FBI agent, a lawyer, a man who lived by the laws he'd sworn to uphold. He'd been demoted because he'd turned in his boss for simply bending the law. He couldn't be with or love a woman who'd broken the law in the past and in the present.

No matter what he said, it was who he was. She didn't want to think how he'd feel when he learned it was her gun in her brother's possession. Something he'd discover within the next hour if Elijah showed. She put that part out of her head. Her brother's safety was her priority.

Chase smiled. "I have a feeling living with Agnes was a lot more fun than living with the judge. He was pretty strict and regimented."

"Granny was the exact opposite. To be honest, sometimes I felt like the parent. But we did have fun. A lot of it. Even if we had too much freedom." She adored her grandmother and would be forever grateful that she'd provided them with a happy home. But there'd been times when Sadie had missed having a mother closer in age to her friends' mothers.

"It sounds like you and your brother spent a lot of time out here in the woods."

She nodded. "We grew up in the cottage on Willow Creek with my parents. My uncle Bryan bought it for my mother but kept it in his name. He didn't like or trust my father." She looked out over the verdant valley, inhaling the sweet smell of wild-flowers, the sharp scent of evergreens, and the clean mountain air. "I've missed this."

"I can see why. It's beautiful. You're—" He closed his mouth and nodded at the pack she was untying from the saddle. "Can I help you?"

"You can take off her bridle and saddle."

He looked from Lula Belle to her, a hand poised in the air. "She won't bite me, will she?"

"No. She has to get used to you anyway."

"Why's that?"

"I need you to take her into the woods. You have to stay out of the camera's range, so you'll need to duck down."

He glanced from Lula Belle's hooves to the woods. "What are

the chances I'm going to meet a bear or a"—he shuddered—
"snake in the woods?"

Sadie held back a laugh. "I checked out the forest service app
before we left, no bear sightings in this area have been reported.
As for snakes, Lula Belle will warn you. She'll know they're
there long before you."

"Then you and I definitely need to become friends, Lula Belle."

By the time Sadie got the video and photos she needed for
Abby, forty-five minutes had passed.

"No snakes or bears, and she only nipped me once," Chase
said as he led Lula Belle out of the woods. "I'd say that calls for
a celebration." He smiled and came to look over her shoulder as
she scrolled through the photos to find the best ones. "They're
amazing. I didn't know you were a professional."

"More a hobbyist than a professional, but thank you."

"If I didn't know better, I'd swear Lula Belle was a unicorn."

"Lighting and filters help. The video turned out well too."
She returned her camera to the case and then held up her phone
to show him. His incredulous smile while he watched the video
made her feel warm and fuzzy inside.

"It's fantastic. You're very talented and have a great eye,
Sadie. You should seriously consider doing this for a living."

"If I could, I would. Photography has always been a passion
of mine. I just don't know how I'd make enough money to
provide a good living for me and Michaela."

"Talk to Abby. I'm sure she can help you come up with
something."

"Maybe I will once this is over."

He glanced at his watch and looked up at the pink-tinged ceru-
lean sky. "We've got about another hour until the sun sets."

Butterflies danced in her stomach, and it wasn't a happy dance.
"We'll saddle up Lula Belle and tie her there." She pointed at a
tree to the left of the path.

"Sure. Where will we be?" he asked as he picked up the bridle.

"Sitting on Lover's Leap." She shrugged at his raised eyebrow. "Abby suggested we take some pictures of us together. She thought it would make our engagement more believable and maybe stop Dwight from looking too deeply into us, especially you."

Until they had enough evidence to arrest the sheriff and his deputies, she and Chase had to continue their fake relationship. Sadie hoped Chase was a good actor, because he wouldn't want anything to do with her once he found out it was her gun involved in Brodie's murder.

"Will she be posting our photos online?" At her affirmative nod, Chase said, "Okay, just as long as I'm not easily recognizable. I doubt anyone will recognize me—it's not like I've been at the field office that long—but better not to take any chances."

Sadie retrieved her camera and the long-range lens while Chase tied Lula Belle to the tree. He fed her an apple and then met Sadie on the rock that jutted out over the valley.

"You're not afraid of heights, are you?" she asked when he hesitated.

"No. I thought I saw something." He pointed across from them into the valley. The part of the forest he was looking at was thick, making it difficult to see much of anything.

She raised her camera, focusing her lens on the area. "I don't see anything."

"Must have been a trick of the light." He sat down beside her. "How are we supposed to pose for our engagement photos?"

"I think Abby wanted something, uh, romantic." She glanced at him. He was staring at her mouth.

He raised his gaze to hers. After what felt like a heated moment, she was surprised to see his lips twitch.

"What? Do I have something on my lips? My teeth?"

"No, I was thinking we missed the perfect photo opportunity last night."

Sadie put down her camera, lifting her phone instead. "Did you really have to mention that? I thought we could pretend it didn't happen."

"You seem nervous. I wanted to break the tension."

"I'm not nervous. We've kissed before."

"I don't think either counts as a romantic kiss." He rested one hand on the rock behind her and then tipped her chin up with the knuckle of his other hand, holding her gaze before slowly lowering his mouth to hers. He kissed her like they had all the time in the world and he wanted to savor and explore every inch of her mouth in exquisite detail.

She melted against him, wrapping her arms around his neck. He made a low sound of pleasure and angled his head, taking the kiss from soft and sweet to hot and deep. She didn't want the kiss to end. She wanted to stay in his arms forever with the light, fragrant breeze ruffling their hair and dancing over their bare skin. She whimpered her objection when he slowly moved back. He leaned in, touching his lips to hers a second and then a third time, as if he didn't want the kiss to end either.

He stroked her cheek and smiled. "You forgot to take the picture."

Did he actually expect her to be able to think when he kissed her like that? "I, uh, thought we'd do a trial run first, and then maybe we could turn around so I'd get a shot of the sky and the valley behind us."

"Should we turn around now, or do you think we need more practice?"

"If we practice any more, we'll miss the sunset." Or melt the rock.

He looked around. "I didn't realize how much time had passed."

She didn't know if that was a good sign or a bad sign.

They resettled on the rock with their backs to the valley.

"Let's try this." Chase scooped her into his arms, positioning her sideways on his lap. "It makes it easier for you to capture the sunset while keeping my face out of the photo."

But it made it really hard to focus. "Good idea," she said instead, and slid her arm behind his neck while holding up the phone with her other hand. "Okay, we'll... What's wrong?" she asked when he leaned in to look at her phone.

"There." He lifted his finger to touch the screen. "Do you see it? It's a flash of light."

Thinking it was Elijah on his way up the mountain, she handed Chase her phone and scrambled off his lap to grab her camera. Chase turned around, trying to magnify the area on her phone. She lifted her camera to her eye and adjusted her lens.

She gasped, handing her camera to Chase. "It's someone from the sheriff's department. I recognize the uniform."

He stretched out on the rock, moving as close to the edge as he could without falling off. She sat there, hands poised to grab him. He moved the camera slowly from the spot where she'd seen the deputy to the left.

He started taking pictures, whispering, "Get down."

She flattened herself against the rock. "Why? What's going on?"

Shimmying backward along the rock, he gestured for her to do the same, helping her to stand once they were shielded from view by trees and bushes.

"Text your brother. Tell him he has a Jackson County deputy about a hundred yards behind him. I can't be sure, but I think there's another one to the left of him. About seventy, seventy-five yards out. Then get on the horse and go. Text Nate the location once you're sure it's safe enough to do so." He looped the camera strap around his neck and then reached for the gun he'd tucked in the waistband of his jeans.

"No. I'm not leaving you." Her fingers trembled on the keys as she texted her brother. "Let me help."

"Knowing you're safe is all the help I need." He framed her face with his hands and kissed her, hard. "Please. I'll be all right." As he went to walk away, he glanced over his shoulder. "Sadie, go now."

"He hasn't read the text." She lifted her gaze from her phone, unable to keep the desperation from her voice. "I need to do something to help. It's better if there are two of us. You can't hold the camera and shoot. I can get a line on their locations and relay it to you. I can tell you the best place to shoot from. I know these woods."

"Okay." He walked back and handed her the camera. "But the next time I tell you to go, you need to go. No questions asked."

"I will. I promise."

He steered her to a boulder between two bushes. "You should be able to see them from here, and you're not out in the open. Turn the ringer off on your phone." Once she had, he called her. "Keep the line open."

She nodded and scrambled to sit on the boulder, raising her eye to the viewfinder. She played with the lens to bring the area into focus. To her left, she heard the snap of branches and the rustle of leaves.

She picked up her phone. "Be careful," she whispered. "There's a drop-off almost in a straight line from where I am. About fifteen yards from me. You won't be able to see it."

"Thanks. Have you got them in sight?"

"No." She lifted the camera again. "Yes. I see them. There's two of them. They must have heard or seen something. They're moving faster." She scanned to the left about a hundred yards and then moved the lens slowly back toward the deputies. She nearly dropped the camera reaching for her phone. "They're almost on top of him." She pushed the words past a sob.

"Give me a reference point. At least fifteen yards ahead of them." His calm, quiet confidence steadied her.

"Okay. A tree. There's a dead tree with its bark completely stripped. You should be able to see it."

"Got it. Now, as best as you can, tell me how many yards Elijah is ahead of them."

"Twenty, tops."

"Another reference point five yards behind him."

She scanned the area. "Nothing. I've got nothing."

"It's okay. You did great. Keep your lens trained on the area around the dead tree and let me know if I'm close."

She'd barely focused on the tree when his shot rang out. One of the deputies had just cleared the woods to the right of the tree. He ducked at the same time Sadie grabbed her phone.

"He's about six feet to the right of the tree."

Another shot rang out. A spray of pine needles flew up at the deputy's feet. He crab-walked backward, waving his hand, warning someone off.

"There's someone in the woods directly behind him."

Chase fired again. She heard the crack of the bullet's impact and then a shout from the direction the deputy had waved. Sadie swung the lens to where she'd last seen her brother. She didn't see him but the movement of leafy branches suggested he was running in the opposite direction of Lovers Leap and the deputies.

She lowered her camera and picked up her phone. "Elijah's gone. He's safe. I think you might have hit one of the deputies." She turned to see Chase standing behind her and pressed a hand to her chest. "I didn't hear you."

He reached back to return his gun to his waistband and then held out a hand to her. "We have to go. How do you think Lula Belle will feel about two riders?"

"You think they'll come up here?"

He nodded. "How fast depends on how badly one of them was injured."

"Maybe they'll think it was Elijah shooting." She thought of the accuracy of Chase's shots. "Forget I said that. My brother could never shoot like you. I don't know many people who can."

"Nate can." He smiled, giving her hand a light tug. "Let's go."

Her phone pinged as they got settled on the horse. After reading her brother's text, she sagged against Chase. "Elijah's okay. He thinks it was me covering him."

"That's good. If he didn't see us, that means they didn't either."

She held up her phone to him. "He's getting rid of his phone. He can't figure out how they found him."

"Ask him if he told Payton or if he's seen her." He reached around Sadie. "Give me the reins."

She texted Chase's question to her brother, sighing seconds later at his response. "He wants to know why I'm asking. I know him, Chase. He won't believe me."

"Tell him for Payton's and the baby's safety, he can't visit, see, or call her until this is over. Stress that it's for her safety."

"That's good. That should work." She texted him. His response was slow in coming. "He says okay."

"Do you believe him?"

"Truthfully? I'm not sure."

Chapter Twenty-Three

♥

Later that same night, Sadie looked up from where she stood ankle-deep in dirty clothes, loading the washing machine, to find Chase leaning against the door frame watching her. "I didn't hear you come in. Did you guys find anything?"

He'd gone with Nate to bring her grandmother home, and then they met up with Gabe where they'd last seen her brother and the deputies from the Jackson County Sheriff's Department.

"It's not easy to search when you're worried about drawing suspicion, but we did find blood on some bushes in the general vicinity where I'd been shooting. We bagged it to see if we get an identification. Although it's not like we can use it as evidence. They'll just claim they were doing their job. But I'd like to find confirmation that there aren't more people involved in this than the sheriff, Dwight, and his partner."

The photos they'd taken hadn't provided definitive proof it was them.

"Did Gabe hear if anyone went to the hospital with a gunshot wound?" Sadie asked.

Chase shook his head. "Not a word."

"Any sign of Elijah?"

"No, which is probably a good thing. It looks like he made a clean getaway. We've been monitoring the sheriff's department dispatch. Seems like all those calls coming in reporting sightings of Elijah have them scrambling." He angled his head. "I'm guessing some of those calls came from you?"

"I might have called in once or twice. Knowing my brother, he probably called in a few times himself."

"It should keep them distracted for a while." He frowned. "You're putting the dark clothes in with the lights."

"Yeah, so? I do it all the time."

"Which is why your, uh, whites look gray." He lifted his chin at the bra and panties in her hand. "And those need to go on a delicate cycle."

"Really? You've washed a lot of women's underwear in your day, have you?"

"No, but I have been doing my own laundry since I was eight, and that's not the way my grandfather taught me to do it."

Any annoyance she felt at having her laundry skills questioned disappeared at the image of an eight-year-old Chase doing his own. "So your grandfather is as obsessive about cleanliness as you."

"Ten times worse." He smiled, wading toward her through the heaps of clothes and snagging the bra and panties from her hand. "Thank you for not calling me, or him, a neat freak." He nudged her out of the way. "I'll finish this up. You should go to bed."

She glanced at her phone. It was one in the morning. "I didn't realize it was so late. Leave it. I'll do it in the morning. Well, after I get a few hours' sleep. You must be tired too."

He looked down at the piles of clothes around their feet. "I'm afraid it will grow."

"Ha ha, funny. It's not that bad." He raised an eyebrow. "Okay, so it's pretty bad."

"Go." He took her by the shoulders, angling her toward the door. "I think better when I'm doing something anyway."

"Are you thinking about the case? Elijah?"

His hands slid from her shoulders, and he nodded. "You said your brother was drunk and couldn't remember what he did with his phone or the drugs."

She crossed her arms and leaned against the dryer. "That's what he said, and I believe him."

"Don't get defensive. I believe him too. But my point is, he's hidden them somewhere. And my guess is he'd stash them someplace that's familiar to him. Somewhere he feels comfortable."

"So what? You're thinking here? Or at Payton's? Whatever you think of my brother—and I'm the first to admit he's done some shady things—I'm positive he wouldn't hide drugs at Granny's apartment or in the store."

"I don't think he'd stash them at your grandmother's either. I also don't think he'd hide them at Payton's. If he had, she'd be aware of it, and we wouldn't be having this conversation. He hasn't hidden anything here. I searched the cottage from top to bottom yesterday."

"Ah, so you didn't just unpack the rest of my boxes out of the goodness of your heart."

He smiled. "Of course I did. But I'm also good at multitasking."

"You're right. You are . . ." She groaned when she realized he was right about something else.

"What is it?"

"The night we were shot at, Elijah had been digging around the rock. He thought he might have buried the drugs there. I'm sorry. I should have mentioned that before now."

"You've had a lot on your mind, and so has your brother. So if we're working off the assumption that Elijah buried the phone and drugs in the woods, can you think of someplace that holds special meaning to him?"

"Only about a dozen. I'll print off a map of the area and

start—" She broke off at the muffled whimpers and low woof coming from the nursery. "Okay, so it'll have to wait until I get Michaela settled."

"It'll keep until morning. You need to sleep, Sadie."

"So do you."

"As soon as I take care of this, I'll go to bed. Trust me, I won't be able to sleep until I get the laundry done. And no, it's not because I'm obsessive-compulsive or a neat freak."

"I wasn't going to say that." She placed a hand on his chest and stretched up on her toes to press a light kiss on his mouth. "I was going to say you're too good to be true. Thank you for protecting my brother tonight, and thank you for taking such good care of me and Michaela."

"You're welcome. But, Sadie"—he smoothed her hair from her face and held her gaze—"just because I protected your brother tonight doesn't mean I'm convinced he had nothing to do with Brodie's murder."

She nodded, afraid that, if she talked, he'd hear the disappointment in her voice. She was a fool to think they could have a relationship with this case and her brother standing between them.

"I'm sorry," he said. "I know that's not what you wanted to hear."

"It's okay. I appreciate you being honest with me." She wondered how he'd react if she were honest with him. If she told him that the gun was hers. She couldn't take the risk, not yet. Not until she figured everything out.

Chase looked like he was going to say something else. She doubted it was something she wanted to hear and used her now-quiet daughter as an excuse to end the conversation. "I should check on Michaela."

Sadie glanced out the passenger-side window as Chase drove back to the cottage. They'd left Michaela with her grandmother and Nate. The tension in the car was as thick as the morning mist blanketing the forest and mountains.

Chase glanced at her. "You're quiet."

"Just tired. You must be too."

"I think it's more than that. Admit it, Sadie. As soon as I told you I was still looking at your brother for Brodie's murder, you shut down."

"No, I... You're right, I did. I'm sorry. It's not easy knowing that you still consider my brother a suspect, Chase."

"Nothing about this case is easy," he muttered, pulling into the driveway. He shut off the engine and turned to her. "I have feelings for you, Sadie. I wish I didn't, but I do. So trust me when I say that the last thing I want to do is arrest your brother for Brodie's murder."

She stared at him, her heart racing.

"I don't know why you look so surprised. I haven't exactly hidden how I feel about you. Even Nate figured it out."

"What type of feelings, exactly? I mean, I know you care about me and Michaela, but that doesn't sound like the type of feelings you're talking about."

"You're really going to make me spell it out for you, aren't you?"

She fought back a laugh—a happy, relieved laugh. She hadn't been imagining things. But Chase sounded so out of his comfort zone that she took pity on him. "No, I'm not going to make you say the words out loud." How could she when she was afraid to say them herself? "I have feelings for you too. But I think you already knew that, didn't you?"

"Yeah, I did. Or maybe I just hoped that you did as much as I hoped that you didn't." He dragged a hand down his face. "If I were smart, I'd take myself off this case."

"Please don't. You're the only one I trust to get my brother out of this alive."

He leaned in to kiss her. "I said if I were smart, I'd take myself off the case. I didn't say that I was going to." His warm, firm lips took her mouth in a ravenous kiss, heat blossoming inside her with every teasing stroke of his tongue. All her worries and fears faded under his expert, sensual attention, the feel of his hands on her waist, his thumbs stroking the sensitive skin just below her breasts.

He slowly eased away, resting his forehead against hers. "This is a bad idea on so many levels, but I can't seem to help myself."

"Good. I don't want you to. I want—"

He stopped her with a finger on her lips. "Don't say it. Not now. We have a lot of ground to cover today."

"Right. You're right." She went to move away but he pulled her back into his arms.

"Five minutes won't make a difference."

Half an hour later, they set off for her brother's favorite fishing spot. She glanced down at their joined hands and slipped on a rock. Chase hauled her against his chest. "Did you do that on purpose?"

"No, of course not. We agreed we'd keep things strictly professional until we got justice for Brodie, and I intend on keeping my end of the bargain."

"Too bad," he murmured, his eyes on her mouth.

"Well, we are pretending we're engaged, so maybe a kiss now and again wouldn't hurt."

"Trust me, it would." He cleared his throat and released her. "But you're right, we do need to act like a happily engaged couple." As he took her hand, he looked around. "A happily engaged couple out for a day of fishing with their dog, who appears to have abandoned us."

They both called for Finn. Over the rushing water, Sadie heard his answering bark. "It sounds like he beat us to the river."

"Did you fish there often?"

"We used to, but I can't remember the last time I was here. Wait, that's not true. I actually do. Elijah and I brought Granny fishing for her seventieth birthday." She smiled at the memory. "It seems so long ago. I forgot how much she loved it. I didn't realize until I moved back how much I've missed out on."

"You didn't make it home much?"

"Often enough. But it wasn't the same. There was always some crisis to manage, with my brother or the store or the apartment." She shook her head. "And here I am again, more of the same. I guess I forget that when I'm out here."

"I can see why. The scenery's incredible. It belongs on a postcard." He glanced at her. "Maybe that's something you could do."

"Sell postcards?"

"I don't know but I think you should do something with your photography. You have a gift, and you're surrounded by the perfect subjects."

She followed his gaze to an eagle soaring overhead. "You know, for someone who professes to be a city guy, you're sounding like you've got a little country in you too."

"Sometimes you have to be taken out of your element to realize what you've been missing." He glanced at her in a way that suggested he wasn't talking about the scenery, and smiled.

As they rounded a stand of trees, an older man hailed them from the shore of the river. He wasn't familiar to Sadie, but then again, they got a lot of tourists in the area.

"Did you happen to see a golden retriever?" the man asked, looking more than a little disgruntled.

"What did he do now?" Chase said under his breath, removing his hand from behind his back.

He'd gone into special agent mode the second the man called out. Abby was right. It was kind of hot.

"He stole my fish," the man said as they approached.

"Sorry, no, we haven't seen one." No way was she admitting ownership of Finn. The man looked seriously disappointed.

"It took me three hours to catch them. Looks like I'll be at it another three. Promised the wife I'd catch tonight's dinner. She'll never let me live it down if I don't."

"Looks like we're going to have company on our *fishing* expedition," Chase said under his breath.

They wouldn't be able to dig until they got rid of the fisherman. He was standing a few yards from where Sadie hoped to find her brother's stash—a ring of rocks with a blackened center where they used to cook the fish they caught.

"Don't worry. I should be able to catch him a couple of fish and send him on his way within the next thirty minutes."

Chase cast her a doubtful look.

"Trust me," she said. She slipped her waders off her shoulder and set her fly rod on the sandy shore. Chase did the same, only he had a shovel too.

Sadie noticed the older man looking at it. "We're planning to have a fish fry. We have to bury the embers when we're done. Can't be too careful. We haven't had rain for a month."

"You sound like you're a local."

"I am." She smiled, pulling on her waders.

"And I'm guessing he's not." The man grinned at Chase, who was studying his rod.

"No, but he's a quick study." Sadie introduced them and then shared some tips with the man, offering him one of her lightweight lures.

"Thank you for coming to my defense, but I have a feeling I'll disappoint you," Chase murmured as he followed her into the water, struggling to keep upright.

He didn't. As she'd suspected after watching him use her camera and ride Lula Belle, all Chase had to do was simply observe someone performing a skill in order to master it. But Sadie had years of practice and knew where the fish were most likely to be. She caught three before her promised thirty minutes were up.

The man beamed at her and then called to Chase, "You're a lucky man, Michael. You'd better marry this gal before someone steals her away."

Chase turned, the sun's rays playing in his honey-blond hair, the sparkling blue waters mirroring the color of his eyes as he looked at her, really looked at her, and said, in what sounded like all seriousness, "I know how lucky I am, sir. And trust me, I won't let anyone steal her away from me."

The older man winked at Sadie. "You got yourself a good one too." He thanked Sadie again for the fish and then walked off whistling.

Sadie picked up the shovel as soon as he was out of view, heading to where she prayed her brother had buried the drugs. She glanced at Chase and smiled, wondering if he'd meant what he said. He sounded like he did, but maybe he was a better actor than she gave him credit for.

She observed the Zen-like expression on his face as he cast out his line. He was hooked, on fly-fishing at least. She wasn't surprised he enjoyed it. She knew he would. He had the kind of personality and temperament that fit well with the sport. She decided to let him enjoy his time on the river. She owed him for everything he'd done for her. Life was so much better with him in it.

She crouched by the circle, moving the rocks to dig under each one. Nothing. She glanced at Chase as she began digging under the charred remains. His gaze was trained on his taut line. He had a fish, and it looked like it might be a big one. Afraid she'd break his concentration, she didn't shout encouragement or suggestions, and went back to digging.

Five minutes later, his happy shout alleviated her disappointment when there was nothing at the bottom of the hole. She'd dug deep enough that she hit water, so perhaps it was better that Elijah hadn't buried the drugs and his phone there after all.

"Sadie, look," Chase called, a gorgeous brook trout dangling from the end of the line. Even more gorgeous was his smile. Surprised when his smile almost immediately disappeared, she followed his gaze to see Finn racing across the shore and then into the water.

"Finn, no! Come here, boy!" Sadie cried, to no avail. The dog leaped out of the water and stole Chase's fish.

It's not funny, Sadie told herself in an effort to quell the laughter bubbling up inside her, but when Finn raced out of the water and dropped the fish at her feet with a doggy grin, she couldn't contain it any longer.

"It's not funny." Chase waded out of the water, glaring at Finn. Then his gaze went to the hole beside her, and he grimaced. "You should have let me do that."

"I didn't mind. You were enjoying yourself, and as you can see, there was nothing to find anyway."

He gave her shoulder a comforting squeeze. "It's only the first stop on your list. We should be able to cover half of them before I have to meet Hunter at the store. We'll head out from there."

Chase and Hunter were driving to Jackson County to follow Dwight and his partner on their shift in hopes of catching a break.

"Boyd's been tracking the comings and goings of the White-side Mountain Gang for the past week and hasn't gotten anything we can use, so he's taking Nate with him tonight. I want you to keep Finn with you," Chase said.

"You don't have to worry about us. I already told Granny to tell Payton we can't make it tonight."

"Thank you for that, and I know you can handle yourself.

But I'll feel better knowing he's with you. Even if it means he gets a reprieve from doggy jail." He looked down at the fish and sighed.

"Don't worry. We'll come back again. Without Finn next time."

"I'd like that. A lot. I really enjoyed myself." He sounded surprised, and then he smiled at her. "Once all this is over, I wouldn't mind taking a walk up to Lover's Leap again to watch the sunset with you."

"I'd like that a lot too." She smiled and wondered if the warm glow of happiness she felt inside was shining from her eyes. Maybe they really did have a chance of a future together.

Chapter Twenty-Four

♥

Sadie blew a raspberry on her daughter's soft tummy, smiling when Michaela rewarded her with the gurgling giggle she usually reserved for Chase.

"Oh my gosh, she's so happy. What happened to our crankypants Michaela? She's a completely different baby." Abby stood beside Sadie at the counter in I Believe in Unicorns, gazing down at Michaela.

Sadie zipped her daughter into the ruffled pink unicorn onesie. "She's started sleeping through the night."

"I have a feeling it's more than that. Her mommy looks pretty happy too."

"Because Mommy has also been getting sleep, hasn't she, sweet face?" She lifted her daughter off the makeshift changing table on the counter and cuddled her to her chest.

"Really? It doesn't have anything to do with the extremely hot special agent residing under the same roof?"

"All right, I'll admit having Chase around has probably made the biggest difference. He's the reason we're both getting more sleep. He's also the reason my house is clean and we have clean clothes to wear."

Abby looked shocked. "He does your laundry?"

"Yes, because apparently clothes are supposed to be separated by color and fabric."

"Can I borrow him?"

"No. He's all ours, isn't he, baby?" she said to her daughter, then shook her head at her grinning friend. "I didn't mean it like that."

"Yes, you did. The Gray girls are falling in love on Willow Creek, and I couldn't be happier for all of you. I just wish you'd gotten a picture of you and Chase at Lover's Leap yesterday."

"Even if I had, you couldn't use it. If Dwight and his partner had seen it, they might have guessed Chase was the one shooting at them."

"You and Elijah were lucky he was there last night. You must have been terrified."

"For Elijah, but not for myself. Not with Chase there. He was calm and completely in control of the situation."

"From what I hear, he was just as impressed with how you handled yourself. Chase was talking about it to Hunter when he dropped you off. He said he couldn't have asked for a better partner. He was also pretty impressed with your photos, which he shared with me."

"He thinks I should try and turn it into a business." Sadie placed Michaela in one of the electric baby swings her grandmother had ordered, despite Sadie putting the kibosh on all new orders.

"He's absolutely right. The photos you took of Lula Belle are incredible. We've already had a big uptick in subscribers. The unicorn weekend is going to be bigger than last summer's *Outlander* event, I can feel it." She glanced around the store and nodded. "Let me think about it. There has to be a way we can use your unicorn photos to generate an income for you."

"I know everyone loves unicorns, but even if I created wall art, it wouldn't bring in enough income to live on."

"Why not? Anne Geddes did it with babies. She sells books and calendars and makes a fortune. You could do the same with unicorns, and you could advertise the store at the same time."

Agnes walked from the hallway into the store with the map Sadie had printed off after she and Chase had come up empty-handed this afternoon. She was hoping her grandmother might provide a clue about where Elijah had buried his stash.

Abby looked from Agnes to Sadie. "I've got it. You can write a children's book using your grandmother's story and illustrate it with photos of Lula Belle the unicorn. She'll become the store's mascot. It'll be great exposure for both you and the store. You can write a series of books and then branch off with Lula Belle merchandise."

"That's a grand idea." Agnes beamed. "Elsa has been after me for years to write the story. You know how much she loves to promote local history and authors." Elsa Mackenzie was Hunter's aunt and one of the owners of Three Wise Women Bookstore on Main Street.

"Perfect. I'll call Elsa, and we'll—"

Sadie had to stop Abby before she got on the phone with Elsa. If she didn't put on the brakes, every member of the Sisterhood would arrive at the store. Honestly, she was surprised neither Abby nor her grandmother had called a meeting of the town's most influential women.

"Hold it. It's a good idea, and I promise I'll think about it once Elijah is..." She couldn't say *back home* or *in jail*, so she settled on: "...safe. Did you think of any other locations than the ones I already had, Granny?"

"No, but I circled the ones that I think are most likely." She handed Sadie the map.

Sadie glanced at the locations her grandmother had circled and held back a sigh. Agnes had circled all nine locations, including the ones Sadie and Chase had already searched.

Sadie put the map on the counter. "If I knew where Elijah had been drinking the night he'd buried the drugs—and, we're assuming, his phone—we could narrow this down. But the only person I can think to get the information from is Payton, and Chase would kill me if I spoke to her."

Abby smiled at her grandmother. "She's in love with him."

"Head over heels," her grandmother agreed. "And it's about time she found a man worthy of her love."

"Hunter agrees with you. He likes Chase, and that says a lot. He thinks he's good for Sadie too."

"Sadie's right here," Sadie said, trailing her finger over the map, location to location, before looking up. "I agree with you though. Chase is good for me. Too good for me."

"Come on, Sadie, don't do that. You're incredible. You are—" Abby began.

"Let me rephrase that. He's good for me, but I'm not good for him." Before either her grandmother or Abby could argue in her defense, she said, "You know Elijah's gun? The one they've tied to the deputy's murder? It's mine. Your gun was jamming, Granny, and I gave Elijah mine. I haven't told Chase."

"But you didn't kill anyone. You were nine months pregnant, and you were at your own baby shower. You have an alibi," Abby protested.

"Not for every minute of every day that weekend, and I don't think they'd consider Granny a reliable witness. Sorry, Granny, but you were hiding Elijah for all those months," she said at her grandmother's hurt expression.

Sadie explained that she couldn't remember if she'd left her gun in Highland Falls in February or brought it from Charlotte when she moved back home, but it had turned up at the cottage a few days before she met her brother in the woods. "If I can figure out who stole my gun, we'll know who murdered the deputy."

"Okay, so it's just the three of us, and each of us would

hide the body for the other if we, say, had to kill someone in self-defense. So this right here"—Abby linked her fingers over her head, making a dome—"is a sacred place where we can say anything and not be judged. I didn't take the gun, and I didn't kill that poor deputy." She gave Sadie a *play along* look, and that's when she realized what Abby was up to.

Sadie's pulse began to race at the thought her grandmother might have had something to do with Brodie's murder. She knew Agnes would do anything to protect Elijah but would she really go that far? "I didn't either. I wouldn't, even to protect my brother."

They looked at her grandmother, who had her head cocked as if thinking over her answer. "Granny?" Sadie said, unable to keep the panic from her voice.

Agnes frowned at her. "You can't be thinking I had something to do with the poor lad's death."

Abby answered for Sadie. "Of course not, but we wouldn't judge you if you did. Under the dome, anything you say is just between us."

Granny waved her hand. "I'd not do such a thing, and neither would our Elijah. I had a hard time convincing him to take my gun." She looked at Sadie. "I was thinking back to Valentine's Day weekend. Elijah had come home a few days before you. He said everything would be all right because the deputy was going to help him."

"Please don't tell me he was in your apartment when I was home that weekend. I know I had pregnancy brain and was sleep-deprived but surely I would have noticed."

"No. He stayed at the cottage that weekend." She tapped her fingers against her lips, and then her eyes went wide. "Wait now. When we came home from the baby shower, I noticed a few things out of place. So did you. You said something about your room being tossed. I passed it off, saying how your room is always a mess."

"And I'd believe that, because it's true. But at the time, I didn't think anything was missing. Was anything missing from the apartment?"

"At the time, I didn't think so either. But later that week, I discovered the emergency money I kept in the orange juice container in the freezer was gone."

"Did you confront Elijah about it?"

She nodded, her reluctance obvious. "I did. He apologized and promised to pay me back. He didn't want to mooch off Payton is what he said."

"But it was fine to mooch off you." Sadie took a deep, calming breath. It wouldn't do her any good to point out her brother's faults to her grandmother. Agnes would just get defensive.

"Okay, so we know that Elijah, and possibly Payton, were in the apartment that night. But why would they take Sadie's gun? More important, how did they even know it was there?" Abby asked.

"I told Elijah. I was afraid he'd try to sneak in while Sadie was here, and she might suspect he was an intruder and shoot him."

"So that leaves us with Elijah and Payton." Sadie narrowed her eyes at her grandmother. She was holding something back. "Granny, what aren't you telling us? Who else was in your apartment that night?"

"Colin might have dropped in for a wee visit while you were sleeping," she admitted sheepishly.

"How long have you been having an affair with Mr. Murphy?"

"It's not an affair. His wife died going on two years ago now. We've been seeing each other since last fall." She smiled at Sadie. "He likes Chase too, and Nate. Although Colin would prefer if he was my bodyguard. He said I wouldn't have been able to sneak out on him. He was a spy, you know."

"Has Mr. Murphy shared his thoughts on who he suspects of killing Brodie?" Sadie asked.

"Oh, aye, he thinks it was Dwight."

"Did he ever think that Elijah might be involved?"

"He did, and he was none too pleased when he found out Elijah was hiding here. He broke up with me, if you must know. But when he heard about the deputy, he came back around. He was afraid they were going to arrest me so he's been working to solve the mystery."

Sadie was beginning to think Mr. Murphy might be good for her grandmother, until Abby said, "Don't get mad at me, Agnes, but Mr. Murphy was in your apartment the night Sadie's gun went missing, so we have to include him on our suspect list. To be honest, if he was a spy like you say, he's the most qualified to pull it off."

Sadly, Abby made a good point. As Sadie knew, her brother didn't have the stomach or the skills to lie in wait and shoot a man who was armed. And while he did have opportunity, Brodie's death made his situation worse. Sadie didn't see Payton as a murderer, but her brother's girlfriend did have motive and opportunity. She also had a connection to Dwight. From the sound of it, Mr. Murphy had both the skills and the opportunity.

"But why would he want Brodie dead?" Sadie asked Abby instead of her grandmother.

"To protect your brother. He knows how much Agnes loves Elijah, and it sounds to me like Mr. Murphy is in love with her. Sorry, Agnes. I just think we need to look at everyone, especially now that we know the gun that killed Brodie belonged to Sadie."

"Aye, but there's one problem with your theory. Colin wanted to turn in Elijah. He only agreed not to if I agreed that I wouldn't give Elijah shelter or money or lie to the police to protect him when he's arrested."

"Once this is over, I look forward to spending time with your Mr. Murphy, Granny. I like the sound of him. I think he's good for you." It didn't escape Sadie that her grandmother had said almost the same about Chase not ten minutes ago.

Agnes smiled. "You'll meet him before this night is over, my girl." Her grandmother walked around the counter, bending to pick up Michaela. "You'll be a good girl for your granny now, won't you, my wee angel? She's a right love now that the fairies have given her back to us," Agnes confided to Abby.

"Granny, how many times do I have to tell you she's not a changeling? She's grown out of her colic, and she's sleeping—"

"I know what I know." Agnes tapped a finger to the side of her head. "If you'd grown up in Scotland like I did, you'd see the truth of what I—she's here now." Her grandmother gave an almost imperceptible nod at the window.

Sadie's eyes went wide. "Granny, I told you to tell Payton we'll have to make it another night."

"I did. I told her you were busy taking photos for the new website, just like you said. But she wouldn't be put off. She must want that money for the bairn something fierce."

"I don't have any money."

"We'll figure something out to string her along. But for now, tell her you forgot your checkbook at home and—"

"Granny, no one uses checks anymore. Everyone does e-transfers."

"No wonder people can hack into bank accounts so easily these days."

Sadie didn't bother responding. Her grandmother wouldn't believe Elijah had hacked into her bank account even if Sadie had photographic evidence, which she didn't.

Agnes continued. "Just tell her the computer is down."

Abby smothered a laugh with her hand.

Payton knocked on the door, her attractive face pressed to the glass. "Go answer the door. Colin will be waiting for you at Payton's house. Don't worry about the bairn. We have it all worked out," Agnes said while giving Payton an enthusiastic wave. "Stall her for five minutes while I get the bairn settled and do a sound check with Colin's listening device. Come, Finn." She patted her leg when the dog moved to sit beside Sadie, growling low in his throat.

Sadie rubbed Finn's head. "It's okay. Go with Granny and look after our baby, boy." As though he understood, he loped after Agnes.

Abby turned slightly so her back was to the door. "Okay, so Finn's reaction to Payton just put her on the top of our suspect list. We have to check out her place. Chase will understand."

"Maybe the top of your suspect list, but not mine. Finn was just being protective," Sadie said through a clenched-teeth smile. Waving at Payton, she held up a finger and then mimed unlocking the door. When she went to dig around in the diaper bag on the counter, she let her hair fall forward. "We can question her here just as easily."

"If she's been up to what we think she's been up to, she's a lot more devious than she looks."

Sadie thought about the life insurance policy. She still had a hard time believing her brother had bought one so maybe it would be worth checking out. "Okay, but we can't be long. Chase said he'd be back within a couple hours. If he finds out—"

"He won't," Abby promised.

Sadie gave her a look.

"Trust me, as much as you don't want Chase to know what we're up to, I don't want Hunter to know either."

Chapter Twenty-Five

♥

Sadie walked to the front of the store and inserted the key into the deadbolt, forcing a smile for the woman she suspected of being in cahoots with the man who wanted to get rid of her brother. She opened the door. "Sorry about that. Granny's big on security these days."

"Me too. I think everyone in town has been on edge since they heard about the deputy's murder. I can't imagine how you feel with it happening almost in your backyard. Then again, your fiancé is living with you, so you're probably not as worried as some of us are." She gave Sadie a sweet smile and tucked a strand of long blond hair behind her ear.

"I'm sure it's very scary being alone and pregnant, not to mention the fact that my brother is the prime suspect." Sadie added plenty of contempt to her voice when she mentioned her brother.

Payton wore a faded jean jacket over a pretty blue maxidress dotted with white flowers. She rubbed her stomach and then lifted her hand to wipe the corner of her eye with a finger. Sadie didn't see any sign of tears but she did see signs of her brother's baby.

"It's been really hard with Elijah on the run. Your grandmother has been so sweet to me. Always calling to make sure I have everything I need." She chewed on her bottom lip, glancing at Sadie from under her long eyelashes. "She mentioned that you wanted to start an education fund for the baby." Payton rubbed her baby bump. Sadie blinked, positive the small mound had shifted to the side.

"I can't tell you how much that means to me. I know Elijah would be as touched as I am."

"You haven't heard from him?" Sadie asked, forcing her gaze from Payton's lopsided baby bump.

"Oh no, he'd never do anything to endanger me or our baby. I know you've had your differences, and he's made plenty of mistakes, but he's a good man at heart."

"So you don't think he had anything to do with the deputy's murder?"

"I hope not, especially for your grandmother's sake. She loves Elijah so much. She'd do anything for him. She hid him, you know. From the police. I hope they never find out. They won't hear it from me." She crossed her heart with her long, white-tipped fingernail and smiled.

Sadie knew a threat when she heard one. If she didn't pay up, Payton was going to tell the Jackson County sheriff that Agnes had been helping Elijah.

"I probably should get home before it gets too dark, so if you have the money your grandmother mentioned . . ." Payton trailed off with a deceptively innocent smile.

"Of course." Sadie turned. "Did you find my phone?" she asked Abby, who'd spent the entire time Sadie was talking to Payton pretending to search her bag.

"Hi." Abby gave Payton a finger-wave. "Sorry, looks like you left it at home again, sweetie. If you think pre-baby brain is bad, wait until you have post-baby brain," Abby confided to Payton. "Poor Sadie, she can't remember anything."

"Sadly, Abby's right. Why don't you go on up and wait for us while I go home and get my phone? Granny's upstairs with the baby. She thought you'd be joining us for tea anyway. I don't have my car so Abby has to drive me."

Abby grabbed the diaper bag and joined Sadie. "I promise we won't be long. Unless Sadie left her phone in the dishwasher again."

As they watched Payton disappear down the hall, Abby whispered, "I so do not buy her sweet-and-innocent act."

"Neither do I, and something tells me she's not pregnant."

"Why would she pretend to be pregnant?" Abby asked, holding the front door open for her.

"What better way to tug on my grandmother's and brother's heartstrings and get them to open their wallets than to pretend she was having Elijah's baby?" Sadie locked the door.

Ten minutes later, they pulled up two houses from Payton's. Sadie dug around in the diaper bag for her phone and set the alarm for fifteen minutes. "We have to make this fast," she said as they quietly closed the doors on Hunter's truck; Hunter and Chase had taken Chase's car.

Sadie and Abby crouched low as they ran across the neighboring lawns to Payton's backyard. "Careful," said a whiskey-smooth male voice in the dark. "Stay a few feet from the house. She's got outdoor security lights."

Once they did as the man directed, he stepped out of the shadows. He was a tall, handsome Black man dressed in dark clothing. He had an earpiece in his right ear.

Sadie offered her hand. "Hi, Mr. Murphy. Thanks for meeting us. Is everything okay at my grandmother's?"

He shook her hand warmly. "It's Colin. And everything's fine. I wouldn't have agreed to your grandmother's plan if I didn't think she and your daughter would be safe. I left the outdoor security lights on. The next-door neighbor will take his dog for a walk in ten minutes. You can set your watch by him, and the dog uses the shrubs near the house to do his business. If the lights don't go on, he might trouble himself to investigate. I've taken care of the alarms inside. I'll stay out here and keep watch. I'll text you if you need to get out of there." At Sadie's questioning glance, he smiled. "I have your number."

"Mr. Murphy—Colin," Abby corrected at his raised eyebrow. "What exactly did you do for a living?"

He winked. "If I told you, I'd have to kill you. Now get going. Split up, and take these." He handed them each a pair of gloves. "If you find anything of interest, take a picture with your phones."

"You've already searched the house, haven't you?" Sadie said.

"I have, but you'd recognize if the male clothing is your brother's better than I would. I took some fingerprints as well." He lifted his chin at the back door. "Time's a-wasting, ladies."

As they headed to the door, Abby whispered, "Way to go, Agnes. That man is hot. He's an older version of Shemar Moore." At Sadie's blank look, Abby whispered, "*Criminal Minds*? *S.W.A.T.*?"

Sadie shook her head as she closed the door behind them and stepped into Payton's kitchen.

"You need to watch more TV, and I should seriously think of doing a seniors' bachelorette event."

Sadie pulled on her gloves. "For now, let's focus on figuring out what Payton is up to. If there were drugs, Colin would have found them already. I'll take the bedrooms and check out the male clothing."

"What else are we looking for?"

"Anything that proves Payton is expecting, any notes lying around, the life insurance policy, and money." Thinking about what her grandmother said about her emergency cash going missing, Sadie walked to the refrigerator freezer and opened it. There were three orange juice containers on the side shelf.

"You don't think—" Abby's eyes went wide when Sadie twisted off the lid of the first container. "How much money is in there?"

"A lot more than Granny's emergency fund."

One of the containers still had the tab intact so she left it alone, opening the other one. Fifties and hundreds were rolled inside. "You count the money, photograph it, then return it to the containers while I check out the back rooms."

There were two bedrooms. One had been converted to a workout room. It looked like it had been recently used—a towel was hanging on the end of a weight bar—and it smelled like a gym. There was also a pink balance ball, light weights, and a stationary bike. Nothing screamed evidence of another man in Payton's life. Her brother liked to work out, and Payton looked like she was in great shape.

Sadie opened the closet door and went up on her toes to pull one of three blue plastic containers off the shelf. Payton was neat, but Sadie couldn't hold that against her. It made her job a whole lot easier, enabling her to quickly rifle through each of the containers, which were filled with receipts and tax returns from previous years. Again, nothing stood out. After she'd returned the containers to the shelf and closed the closet door, Sadie stopped to check the bathroom before heading to the second bedroom.

She crossed to the bathtub, pulling back the shower curtain. The tub sparkled. Containers of shampoo, conditioner, and shower gel were neatly lined up in the back corner. The garbage can was empty. She opened the medicine cabinet beside the sink to find empty shelves except for a bottle of aspirin, a tube of toothpaste, and a toothbrush still in its packaging.

The cupboard below the sink revealed neatly stacked towels and washcloths, extra packages of soap and cleaning supplies, and a blow dryer and curling iron. She pulled open the drawer in the cabinet and found it filled with a large assortment of makeup. The second drawer contained more of the same. Disheartened, Sadie went to head out of the bathroom when she spotted something hanging on the back of the door: a large white T-shirt and sweatpants that looked familiar but they were generic so it was hard to tell.

She glanced at the time on her phone and hurried to the bedroom. She could hear Abby opening and closing cupboards. She must have finished counting and photographing the cash. Sadie walked into Payton's bedroom. No surprise, the room was tidy with nothing out of place. The stark black-and-white color scheme didn't hold any appeal, at least not to Sadie. It wasn't her taste or her brother's. Then again, she didn't think her brother had spent a lot of time here.

She went through the chest of drawers first, carefully lifting up lingerie to check underneath. She spied a twenty-one-day birth-control pill pack and picked it up. It looked like Payton had taken today's pill. Then again, it could have been from months ago. So not exactly a smoking gun. She took a photo anyway and then went through the rest of the drawers, which were neatly filled with women's clothing.

The cupboard held more of the same, including lots of shoes. The fact that there was no maternity wear was interesting, but a lot of women wore what they already owned if it was made of stretchy fabric, so, like the birth control pills, it didn't really shout *faker*.

But the lack of baby books, prenatal vitamins, and baby supplies did. Sadie had begun buying diapers when she hit the three-month mark, and she'd had enough baby books to start her own library. She also took her prenatal vitamins religiously. There were no baby ultrasound photos here either; Sadie'd had hers framed.

She went down on her knees, not expecting to find even a dust bunny under the bed given how tidy Payton was. She was surprised to discover a black duffel bag. It wasn't her brother's. She took a photo of the bag before undoing the zipper. Inside, she found more men's clothing and toiletries. None of it belonged to Elijah. She was sure of it. She took a photo before carefully examining the contents to check for anything that identified the owner. Nothing did. She patted everything into place, zipped up the bag, and put it back where she'd found it under the bed.

She moved to the nightstand and spotted a file folder between the bedside table and the bed. It was receipts for this year, neatly filed, and right there under *L* was a life insurance policy.

Brooklyn had been right. The policy was for a quarter million dollars, to be paid to Payton Howard in the event of Elijah's death. There wasn't a policy for Payton. Sadie narrowed her eyes at the signature. Positive it wasn't her brother's, she took a picture.

After a quick search of both nightstand drawers yielded nothing else of interest, Sadie headed back to the front of the house, where she found Abby on the floor searching under the couch. "Anything interesting?" Sadie asked, scanning the room for the missing baby books and baby supplies. Nothing there either.

"Other than the two thousand dollars residing in each of the orange juice cans, no." Abby sat up and pushed her long, curly red hair from her face. "What about you?"

Sadie told her about the birth control and life insurance policy. "Did you find any prenatal vitamins?"

"Nada. Did you find any vibrators?"

"No." Sadie laughed. "Why?"

"Because unless—"

Colin walked into the house. "Time to leave, ladies. Payton is on her way home. She got a phone call and hightailed it out of there. No idea who from."

They told him what they'd found and promised to send him pictures as they ran for the back door. "Thanks for this, Colin. And thanks for taking care of Granny."

"Trust me, your granny can take care of herself. Now you two get going and be careful."

"You too." Although she didn't think they had to worry about Colin. She ran after Abby. "I wonder who Payton got the call from," Sadie said as she hoisted herself into the truck.

Abby went to start the engine. "I know how you could find—"

Sadie caught a glimpse of an approaching vehicle and pulled Abby down just as lights filled the interior of the truck. She peeked over the dashboard. "It's Payton. She must have broken every speed limit to get here."

"Do you think Colin got out in time?"

Sadie glanced at the backyard. "I think so. He seems really good at what he does or whatever he used to do. She's inside now." Sadie watched as the lights came on in the living room.

"Do you think she saw us?"

"She didn't slow down when she passed. But I think she knows someone has been there."

"Why?" Abby inched up to look at the house.

"Because she's turned on every light. Let's get out of here."

"You don't have to tell me twice." Abby started the truck and turned off the headlights. "Just until we're off her street."

They both released sighs of relief when they turned onto Main Street. "I'm not cut out for this spy gig," Abby said.

"Me neither. From now on, I'm leaving it up to Chase and Nate. And Colin."

"Maybe if you tell that to Chase, he won't want to throttle you. It's what I'm going to tell Hunter."

"Thankfully, we won't have to say anything. We can credit Colin with finding out about the money, the forged life insurance, and the possibility Payton is faking her pregnancy. What's wrong—" She followed Abby's gaze to where Chase and Hunter stood outside I Believe in Unicorns with their arms crossed.

Chapter Twenty-Six

♥

You don't have anything to say for yourself?" Chase asked Sadie once they'd left I Believe in Unicorns in the rearview mirror.

"I tried, but you said not now." He'd said it in a coolly clipped tone she'd never heard him use before. At least not with her. "What good will it do me anyway? You've already tried and convicted me." She crossed her arms and looked out the window.

"So it's my fault now."

"Of course not, but you told Hunter you couldn't have asked for a better partner at Lover's Leap, and today you said you trusted me to look after myself. Neither of which must be true, given how you're acting."

Headlights filled the car, and she glanced over her shoulder. A Highland Falls police cruiser pulled in behind them, flashing its lights twice. Chase raised a hand in acknowledgment. She'd heard him talking to Gabe while she got Michaela and Finn settled in the backseat. He'd requested two cars be placed on surveillance duty tonight at the cottage.

"I couldn't have asked for a better partner, and I do trust you. But obviously, you don't trust me."

"How can you say that? Of course I trust you. I trust you more than I've ever trusted anyone in my life." As the words came out of her mouth, she realized it was the absolute truth. She trusted him, completely. With her heart and her daughter. So why was she holding back a key piece of information? Because she was afraid it would change how he felt about her.

"If you did, you would have done what partners do."

"I've never had a partner before. I don't know what you expected me to do."

"Call me before you and Abby ran headlong into danger."

"I wouldn't have gone if I thought it was dangerous. Colin had our backs, and he'd planted a listening device so he could hear everything that was going on at Granny's."

"You trusted a man you know nothing about."

"Granny trusts him." She briefly closed her eyes as the words came out of her mouth. It was a weak defense. He was right.

"She also trusts your brother and believes in unicorns."

"I knew you were going to say that." She sighed. "I'm sorry, okay. I should have called you, but by the time Granny laid out her plan, Payton was at the store. I had no idea she was going to show up. If she hadn't threatened my grandmother, I wouldn't have gone."

He raised an eyebrow.

"Okay, so maybe I would have. But I don't know why you're so mad at me. Nothing happened. We didn't take anything, we wore gloves, and we photographed the evidence. Really good evidence, I might add. We found all that money. Then there's Elijah's forged signature on the life insurance policy and the fact that Payton might not be pregnant, not to mention it looks like she's playing house with a man who is not my brother."

"I agree. The evidence could be important to the case. There's only one problem. It's an illegal search so it's inadmissible in court."

"Yes, but you can get a search warrant, and then you'll legally find everything we told you was there."

"It won't be there. Someone warned Payton her house was being searched. It's the only explanation for why she left your grandmother's as fast as she did. And she'll know exactly who to point the finger at."

"She didn't see us. I'm sure of it."

"She didn't have to. She's smart enough to figure out you played her. And what she'll do with that information is what worries me."

She leaned back against the headrest. "So I ruined everything, and I put myself and Michaela in danger. Maybe even Abby and Granny."

Gravel crunched as he pulled into the driveaway. He left the car running and undid his seatbelt. Then he turned to face her. "You and Michaela are safe. So are Abby and your grandmother. If there's any fallout from this, we'll deal with it together." He took her hand, giving it a gentle squeeze. "Don't beat yourself up. We may not be able to use the evidence in court, but trust me, we'll find a way to use it."

"Are you just saying that to make me feel better?"

"Maybe a little. But at some point, we'll have to convince your brother Payton has been playing him, and what you found tonight might be the key to doing that. Stay here while I check the house."

She stared at the cottage sitting in the dark on the creek. The shadows from the trees looked menacing now instead of like the old friends she used to climb. Somehow, the enormity of the danger everyone was in hadn't touched her until now. Maybe because her sleep-deprived brain had finally woken up. She startled at the incoming headlights.

"It's just one of Gabe's officers. There's a cruiser in the field on the other side of the creek as well."

She nodded. "Be careful."

He smiled at her warning, no doubt wondering why she hadn't given it the previous times he'd checked the house to make sure it was safe for them. He'd been putting his life on the line for them since the moment she'd met him. She owed him her full and complete honesty. She couldn't hold back to protect herself. He wanted her to trust him. She'd seen it in his eyes, heard it in his voice.

She clenched her fingers when the entrance light went on, slowly loosening the painful grip when the lights came on in the rest of the cottage and Chase didn't call out. It took him longer than usual. He was on edge too. No matter what he'd said, she'd made the situation worse.

She released the breath she'd been holding when he appeared in the open door, safe and oh so handsome. Just like he'd done in the cottage moments before, he'd filled her life with light, sweeping away the shadows of the depression that had held her in its grip for all those long months before and after Michaela was born.

He glanced at her when he opened the car's back door, a frown furrowing his brow as he snapped the leash on Finn's collar before he took off.

"You're on a tight rein from now on, buddy," he informed the dog before coming around to her side. "You okay?"

"I'm good." She'd be better once she told him about her gun.

He handed her Finn's leash. "You take him. I'll get Michaela."

He must have seen the hint of nerves on her face, which was evident from the concern in his voice as he leaned in to unbuckle her sleeping daughter. "Why don't you take a bath and relax? I'll change Michaela and put her down. Your grandmother already gave her another bottle." He handed Sadie the diaper bag.

A long, relaxing bath sounded wonderful but she couldn't put her confession off any longer. "It's okay. I, uh, want to talk to you." Walking into the cottage, she unhooked Finn's leash from his collar.

"Sounds serious," Chase said as he followed her inside. He shielded Michaela's eyes from the light with one hand while closing the door with the other, and then he locked it.

"It is." She took her daughter from him and got a whiff of his cologne. She should be used to his sexy, intoxicating scent by now, but it still had her wanting to bury her face in his neck. And kiss him, she thought as her gaze went to his lips.

She glanced at the living room, thinking of the conversation they were about to have, that they needed to have. The couch was out. They'd shared kisses there. The temptation to do so again and avoid confessing the truth would be too strong. Her gaze moved to the red Adirondack chairs in the glow of the patio light.

"Sadie?"

"Sorry. I was just thinking it's such a nice night we could sit outside and talk. If that's okay, I mean. If you think it's safe."

"It should be fine." He leaned in to kiss Michaela's cheek. A line formed at the edge of his eyebrow when he met Sadie's gaze. "I'll check it out."

"Okay, thanks." Her stomach jittered with nerves as she walked to the nursery with Finn following behind her. Her sleepy daughter didn't fuss when she changed her and put her down. Sadie went to the dresser and turned on the video baby monitor that connected to her phone. They'd be able to hear her through the screen door if they sat on the patio, and of course no one would get past Finn, but these days she wasn't taking any chances.

She went back to the crib, leaning over to stroke Michaela's hair from her forehead. She kissed her temple. "Sweet dreams, baby girl," she whispered, praying what she told Chase wouldn't change everything.

With her phone clutched in her hand, Sadie walked down the hall to the living room. Through the picture window, she saw Chase sitting in one of the Adirondack chairs in the glow of firelight. He'd lit the wood in the fire pit. As she opened the screen door, he leaned over to pull the other chair close to his.

She swallowed the lump in her throat and lowered herself onto the chair, placing her phone on the arm. "It's a beautiful night."

"Are you going to tell me what's got you on edge?"

"Other than me messing up tonight?"

He took her hand and raised it to his lips, kissing her palm. "I'm sorry if what I said upset you."

A heated shiver raced up her spine. It didn't seem to matter whether they sat on the couch or in separate chairs. The temptation to crawl onto his lap and kiss him would be there no matter where they were.

She cleared the nerves from her voice. "You have nothing to apologize for. You told me the truth."

Watching the creek flow over the rocks and the willow branches dip into the moonlight-dappled water, her tension slowly released. She turned her head to look at Chase, not surprised to find his intent gaze searching her face. "I told you that I trusted you, and I do. You might not realize how big a deal that is for me, but I don't give my trust easily." She gave him a half smile. "I can count on one hand the people in my life that I trust. Not one of the men I've been involved with belonged in that rarefied group. Until you." She winced. "I don't mean we're involved like that. I—"

"Yes, we are. You know it, and so do I." He looked out over the creek. "This is new for me too. I've never let my feelings for someone interfere with a case before. I've always put my job before anything else. You and Michaela have changed that, and as much as I've tried to fight it, I can't anymore. I don't want to. So please, don't downplay what this is between us."

"I won't, but after I tell you what I have to, you might not feel the same way."

He went still.

"The gun that you believe killed Brodie is mine. It's not my brother's." She told him everything, including her conversation with her grandmother earlier that evening. She didn't stop to take a breath. When she was finished, he rested his head against the back of the chair and closed his eyes.

She let a moment pass, her heart beating double time against her ribs. "I'm sorry I didn't tell you right away, but I was afraid. And then it just got harder as time passed. I didn't want to risk losing you, us, this."

He turned his head, holding her gaze. "I'm not thrilled that you kept this from me, but I also understand why you did. I am glad you told me now, that you trusted me enough to tell me. I'm not sure if it was your brother or Payton or someone else, but I have an idea how they returned your gun."

"How?"

"The day we met in the meadow. After you—"

"You mean the day you shot that poor little snake?"

"It wasn't little. But yeah, that day. After you left, I came back here to check around. I noticed the sliding door was open."

"I can't believe I left it open." She buried her face in her hands and groaned. "And that wasn't the only time. The front door wasn't locked the day you moved in with me. For all I know, I'd been leaving either the front door or sliding door unlocked since the day I moved home."

"You were exhausted. You had a lot on your plate. It was a simple mistake. I was going to tell you but what you're doing right now, beating yourself up, was one of the reasons I didn't."

"So between me moving here and that day, someone snuck in the cottage and returned the gun?" She shivered at the thought.

"It's not a big window of time. We can check the gas station off the main road. They have cameras, but it's highly probable that whoever planted the gun wouldn't use the main road, and you're pretty isolated out here. But it's one more piece of the puzzle solved. Don't worry, I won't let this blow back on you."

All her earlier worries vanished with his promise. "Thank you."

"Anything else you need to share with me?"

"About the case?"

"That's what I meant but you look as if you had something else in mind," he said when she got off the chair. As she sat on his lap, he added, "Not that I'm complaining."

She kissed him and then drew back to look into his eyes. "I don't want you to sleep on the couch tonight. I want you to sleep with me."

"Okay, I can do that."

"I'm not sure you get what I mean. I've never propositioned a man before so maybe I'm not doing it right. I don't want you to just sleep in my bed."

He blinked, looking surprised. He wasn't as surprised as she was. After having Michaela, she didn't think she needed or wanted a man in her life, least of all for sex.

"Are you sure? I'm good with just holding you and kissing you, honey. I don't want to rush—"

She placed a finger on his lips. "I've never been surer of anyone or anything in my life. But if you aren't—"

He nipped her finger. "You don't have to ask me twice."

Chapter Twenty-Seven

♥

Chase woke up to two sets of beautiful eyes looking at him—baby blue and tawny gold.

Michaela cooed, and Sadie smiled. "Sorry, we didn't mean to wake you."

"I couldn't ask for a better way to wake up." He rubbed his head. "But I didn't mean to fall into that deep a sleep."

"It's not your fault. I'm the one who tired you out." Her mouth curved in a grin.

He laughed, feeling lighter than he had in...he didn't know how long. It was odd given that he was in the middle of a murder investigation with danger closing in around them.

"You did, but that's not something you'll ever hear me complain about." Last night ranked as one of the best nights of his life; the only one that even came close was the night Michaela was born.

He went to turn onto his side to face them but his feet were trapped under a heavy weight. Finn was stretched out on the end of the bed. Chase nudged their self-appointed watchdog with his foot, feeling a little less guilty about sleeping the sleep of the dead. The officers on duty outside helped too.

Finn moved but not without sharing his displeasure with a couple of low, grumbled growls.

Chase leaned in and kissed Michaela on her forehead. "I love waking up to you," he said, and then he kissed her mother's pretty, smiling lips. "And I really love waking up to you, almost as much as going to bed with you." He looked at Finn. "The jury's still out on you."

Sadie stretched lazily. "I wish we could stay here all day."

He knew the feeling. "One day we will."

She held his gaze. "Promise?"

He nodded, realizing he'd begun to think of a future with Sadie and the baby almost from the first day they met. "This will be over soon, and life can return to normal."

"But you and I have never had normal." She smiled down at Michaela and stroked her daughter's cheek. "Are you sure you won't miss DC? It sounded like everything you wanted is there—your grandfather, your job, your career plans for the future."

"They are." And that hadn't changed. "But we can make it work. It's less than a two-hour flight from DC to here. You guys can come stay with me, and I can come back here. Hey." He gently tugged a strand of Sadie's long dark hair to get her to look at him. "There's no guarantee my boss in DC will offer me my old job back."

But if this case and Sadie had taught Chase anything, it had taught him he'd been too rigid. He owed his boss an apology.

"Whatever happens, we'll make the decision together, okay?"

She nodded, looking anything but convinced things would work out for them.

Before he could reassure her, Finn's head went up, and he growled low in his throat. Chase rolled over and reached for his gun on the nightstand.

"I put it in the drawer."

He pulled out the drawer and grabbed his gun, glad he'd at least

put on a pair of sweats before he'd gone to sleep. He walked around
the end of the bed and went to the window, lifting a wooden slat to
look out. "It's okay. Gabe's officer is on it. She's talking to someone. I don't recognize—" The man turned around to look at the
cottage. Chase was wrong. It wasn't okay. It wasn't okay at all.

"Who is it?" Sadie asked, coming to stand beside him with
Michaela in her arms.

"Drew." He released the wooden slat and faced her.

"Drew? As in my ex, Drew?"

He nodded, and her eyes went wide. He put his hands on her
shoulders. "There's something you need to know."

"He's not coming to try and take Michaela from me, is he?"

"No, not as far as I know, but that's not something you need to
worry about. He wouldn't stand a chance in court." Chase didn't
want to do this now but he didn't have a choice. "Sadie, I'm the
reason Drew dropped out of your life."

"What do you mean? You don't even know him."

He came clean, telling her everything he'd uncovered about
Drew and what he'd said to him that night at the strip club.

"You paid him off? You paid him to stay away from his
daughter?"

"I did, but you have to—"

"Do you know how that made me feel? He'd left his own
daughter without a backward glance. Every time I looked at her,
I thought of the day I'd have to tell her that her father hadn't
cared enough to stick around." Like her mother, and his.

"He doesn't deserve her. He was never good enough for
either of you."

"That was for me to decide, not you. You didn't have the right
to make that decision for me."

"Maybe not, but you were in no condition to make it, or to
deal with him. You hadn't read his file."

"You had no idea what I was capable of. You didn't stick

around long enough to find out. I had to deal with a colicky baby on my own. At least if you hadn't scared off Drew, I might have had some help, and I wouldn't have felt like I was a horrible mother or that I couldn't do anything right."

"Yeah? You really think so? Because the guy whose file I read would have only made things worse, not better." He held up his hand when she opened her mouth to no doubt defend the piece of crap who was now knocking on the door. "I'll go let him in. But don't expect an apology from me. All I did was try and protect you and Michaela, and I'd do it again."

He grabbed his T-shirt off the floor and shrugged into it. "I'll be out front if you need me. I wouldn't want to intrude on your reunion." He wasn't just angry or worried about Drew's influence over Sadie. He was afraid he might lose her, her and her trust.

The fact that she stayed stubbornly silent didn't alleviate his fears. If anything, it made them worse. He wanted to hide her and Michaela away.

No, he thought as he opened the door, what he really wanted to do was slam his fist into Drew's smiling face. A smile that fell as his eyes went wide with shock, tinged with what looked like horror. "You." He gasped.

"Yeah, me." Chase grabbed him by his pristine, white button-down shirt and pulled him inside before he broke Chase's cover to the officer standing beside him.

"Everything all right, Michael?" the officer asked him, eyeing Drew with distaste. He'd probably hit on her.

"All good. Thanks for sticking around last night." He reached around to tuck his gun into the waistband of his sweatpants.

"No problem. We're just changing shifts. Another officer will be along any minute now."

"Appreciate it. Thanks again." He closed the door and shoved Drew against the wall, getting in his face. "You hurt either one of them, and I will bury you."

"Chase!"

Sadie stood with Michaela in her arms between the entryway and hall. She wore black leggings and an overlong, black short-sleeved shirt that slid off her shoulder to reveal a white tank top underneath. Chase wanted to grab the throw off the couch and wrap her in it. He didn't want this piece of crap looking at her the way he was now. He shoved Drew against the wall one last time before he released him.

"You can go now," Sadie said with a stubborn tilt to her chin. "I've got this."

Chase walked to her. Closing his fingers around that obstinate chin, he held her gaze. "You're mine, and so is she." He lowered his head and kissed her hard before letting her go to gently cup Michaela's face in his hand. "I've loved her since the day she was born, and that's not going to change, no matter what you decide." He kissed Michaela's head and stepped back.

"What's going on? I thought he was FBI. The officer called him Michael." Drew flattened himself against the wall when Chase walked past him.

"He is an FBI agent. He's undercover as Michael Knight."

"Wait, you named *my* kid after him?"

Chase smiled and closed the door behind him. *Explain that, Sadie*, he thought as he stepped over the flower bed and onto the grass. He looked back at the cottage, wishing he'd left a window open so he could hear the conversation inside. He turned at the sound of a truck headed his way. It was Nate. He pulled up behind a Volvo that had seen better days.

"Who's here?" Nate asked, eyeing the beater with distaste as he got out of his truck and walked across the lawn.

"Drew."

"What the hell? Are you shitting me?"

"No. I wish I was." He shoved his fingers through his hair, blowing out the anger that had led to what felt like an out-of-body experience. He'd never felt that level of anger before or felt so out of control. "I acted like a Neanderthal."

Nate grinned. "Yeah, what did you do?"

Chase told him what he'd said to Sadie, his face warming as he did.

Nate laughed. "Love makes us do crazy things, my man. Bet the guy nearly shit his pants when you pushed him against the wall. You're a scary dude when you lose your cool."

Chase opened his mouth to apologize for how he'd reacted the day he'd found out Nate had dragged him into all of this without going through the proper channels.

Nate raised his hand. "No need to apologize. I get it. You pulled something like that on me, I would have lost my shit too." He glanced at the cottage. "You should have let me bury the guy like I wanted to."

Chase nodded. He'd been thinking the same. "What happened last night? Did you manage to get any intel on who in the sheriff's department is involved with the gang?"

"No, but something's going down tonight. Sounded like whoever is calling the shots is paying them a visit. They were all on edge."

"Did they buy that you had several parties interested in purchasing their product, including yourself?"

"You didn't really just ask me that. Of course they did."

Chase smiled, glad of the distraction his partner provided. "Anyone you think you can turn?"

"Yeah. There's a kid, can't be more than twenty. He's in over his head and wants out. You have anyone that can cover Mrs. M? Other than a cop. We're already stretching the Highland Falls Police Department pretty thin."

"Yeah. Colin Murphy."

"Mrs. M's paramour. You know anything about the guy?"

"My bet's former CIA. I ran a background check on him and

hit nothing but firewalls. Last guy I ran that had as many was former CIA. I'll talk to him first, see what vibe I get, but he handled things well last night." He filled Nate in on what went down at Payton's place and what Sadie and Abby found. Then he told him about Sadie's gun.

"I can't leave you kids alone without all hell breaking loose. Looks like I was wrong about Elijah. Almost feel sorry for the guy. So you think Dwight turned Payton against Elijah?"

"It's looking that way. When you factor in Sadie's suspicions about Payton's pregnancy, you have to wonder—"

Nate held up a finger. "Hold that thought." He brought his phone to his ear and answered, "Hey, Gabe." He rolled his eyes. "It's for you. You're not answering your phone. Again."

It was sitting on the nightstand. Beside a bed in which he'd shared an incredible night with a woman who'd kicked him to the curb to talk to her ex. He took Nate's phone. "Hey, Gabe, I'm putting you on speaker."

"Sadie around?"

"Nope. She's canoodling with her ex," Nate said. "Ow. Shit, that hurt. What is your fist made of, reinforced steel?"

"Shut up, Nate." Chase shook out his hand. He could say the same about his partner's shoulder. "Don't worry about Drew. I have it covered."

"I hope you do because that guy is a douche," Gabe said.

"Agreed. What's going on?"

"Brooklyn Sutherland dropped by the station a couple of minutes ago to talk to me."

"Is that the blond babe from Spill the Tea?" Nate asked.

"Tell me why you're my partner again?" Chase held up his hand when Nate opened his mouth to no doubt list his sterling qualities. "Go ahead, Gabe."

"Brooklyn's worried about Sadie. Her mother seems to think the Jackson County Sheriff's Department has a warrant for

Sadie's arrest. I'm looking into it, but I wanted you to be pre-pared in case there was some truth to the rumor."

Gabe had barely gotten the words out when they heard it—the sound of sirens headed their way. "I think we just got our proof," Chase said, his voice a hundred times calmer than he felt. "Nate, get out of here."

His partner's face hardened. "They're going down, and they're going down tonight. If you need me, call." He took off for his truck at a run.

"I know what you're thinking, Chase. If it was Mal, I'd be thinking the same. Don't do anything stupid. Let them take her."

"To hell with that." He nodded at Nate as he peeled out, heading in the opposite direction of the Jackson County Sheriff's Department.

"Listen to me. This is the break we were looking for. Sadie won't be alone. I'll be there before they get a chance to book her. It'll give me the opportunity to nose around without drawing suspicion. I've already called Eden Mackenzie. She's a lawyer. She can handle herself, and the sheriff."

"Okay. There's something you should know." He told Gabe about the gun.

"All right. If the gun is listed in the arrest warrant as probable cause, they'll have shown us their hand."

Two county sheriff vehicles pulled behind Drew's car. "They're here."

"Keep it locked down, buddy. She'll be back before you know it," Gabe said.

Chase walked into the cottage at the same time the three men climbed out of their vehicles. Dwight and Bulldog had brought reinforcements—the sheriff.

From where he awkwardly held Michaela on the couch, Drew cast a nervous glance at Chase. Sadie's hands were poised as if worried Drew would drop her daughter while Finn sat beside the couch on alert.

Sadie glanced over her shoulder, straightening at what must have been the panicked look on his face. He was having a difficult time keeping it together no matter what Gabe said. "Chase, what's wrong?"

He walked to her and took her in his arms. "You need to listen to me. The Jackson County sheriff has a warrant for your arrest."

She backed away, her face stricken.

He put his hands on her shoulders and brought his face close. "You need to go with them. You'll be out before you know it. Gabe is headed there with a lawyer. They—"

"Wait. What's going on? What is she being arrested for?" Someone pounded on the door. Drew jumped, startling Michaela. Finn looked from Drew to the door and growled.

"Jackson County Sheriff's Department. Open up. We have an arrest warrant for Sadie Gray for the murder of Deputy Brodie Davis."

Drew's eyes nearly popped out of his head. "Murder? You're wanted for murder?"

Chase strode to the door. Opening it a couple of inches, he propped his foot against it in case they tried to rush in. "Let me see the warrant."

The sheriff, a tall man with a black cowboy hat perched on his head and bushy, steel-gray sideburns reaching to his square jaw, handed the paperwork through the door. His smile didn't reach his eyes. Dwight and Bulldog stood behind him. "You have five minutes to produce Ms. Gray."

"Fifteen. She has a three-month-old daughter who requires her mother's attention before you haul her off on your made-up charges." He would have made it longer but Gabe was probably on his way. Chase slammed the door in their faces.

He scanned the arrest warrant, taking note of the judge

who'd signed off on it. Sadie's gun was listed as the suspected murder weapon. They had a copy of her registration. They'd also included charges of aiding and abetting for the shooting of the deputies in pursuit of Elijah. They hadn't included breaking and entering. They didn't need to, and they wouldn't want anyone looking too closely at Payton Howard. They wouldn't know that Sadie and Abby had taken photos of the evidence.

Drew got up from the couch and handed Michaela to Sadie, who was standing where Chase had left her, looking shell-shocked. "I didn't sign up for this. I'm not getting stuck with the kid if you go away for murder."

Chase tossed the arrest warrant on the table and went to Sadie. "Sit down, shut up, and don't move, Drew." Chase guided Sadie to a chair. Once she sat down, he crouched in front of her, placing a hand on her bouncing knee. "I know this is scary, but I promise you that everything will be okay."

"You were right," she whispered, looking down at her daughter in her arms. "He doesn't care about her. He's only here because he wanted to borrow money. I thought if he held her, spent some time with her..." She lifted a shoulder and raised her tear-filled eyes. "I wish you were her father."

"I am, in every way that counts." He took Michaela from her. "You knew that, didn't you, sweetheart? It just took your mommy a little longer."

Sadie brought her hand to the side of his face. "No, I knew it too. I was just afraid to trust my feelings for you. I love you."

"I love you too." He brushed his lips over hers, stood, and held out his hand. "Come on. Let's get this over with." They walked down the hall to the nursery. He settled Michaela in her crib, tucking the blanket around her and turning on the unicorn mobile. Finn sat down beside the crib. Chase crouched and rubbed his golden head while Sadie kissed her daughter good-bye. "Good boy. Keep her safe."

He straightened and went to Sadie. "Sorry, honey. But you need to go." He took her hand and led her out of the nursery. He felt her pulling back as they reached the door. "You've got this."

She let go of his hands to wipe at her damp cheeks and then nodded. "I've got this."

Her chin went up, and he smiled. "Yeah, you do." He opened the door. "Back off."

The three men retreated a few feet, and then the sheriff read Sadie her rights. As he did, her chin trembled as she struggled not to cry.

"The cuffs aren't necessary," Chase said between gritted teeth when the sheriff produced them.

"You going to tell me how to do my job, son?" The sheriff motioned for Sadie to turn around.

When the sheriff clamped the cuff on her wrist, Sadie winced, and Chase stepped forward. "One mark on her, one hair out of place, and I'll bury you under lawsuits so deep you'll never see the light of day." His heart raced at the thought of her alone with any one of them on the drive to Jackson County.

"Boys, did that sound like a threat to you?"

"Sure did, Sheriff, sir," Bulldog said, while his partner remained silent. Dwight's cold, calculating stare didn't leave Chase's face.

A Highland Falls police cruiser pulled up. An officer got out. He made Nate look like a little girl. He sauntered over, his hand resting on the butt of his gun. "Got a call that you were planning on arresting Ms. Gray in connection with *our* murder investigation. Guess you forgot to give Chief Buchanan a courtesy call."

"Things moved fast, son. Couldn't risk her hightailing it out of here like her brother."

The officer nodded. "Yeah, that's what the chief thought. He'll meet you at your office."

"That's not necessary," the sheriff sputtered.

"Take it up with the chief. I'll be transporting Ms. Gray to Jackson County." He moved to Sadie's side, gently gripping her arm. "Chief's concerned for her safety...on account of your vehicle's shocks. That was your defense on the latest lawsuit filed against your department for police brutality, isn't it?"

The sheriff's face went red, and not with embarrassment. He was furious he'd been outmaneuvered. "Boys, lead the way. I'll follow." He turned to Chase. "You and I aren't finished here, son. Not by a long shot."

Bring it, Chase wanted to say but instead he leaned in to kiss Sadie's cheek. He moved his lips to her ear. "Don't say a word. We'll have you home in no time." He lifted his head and met the officer's eyes, taking his measure. "Thank you."

"It's all the chief's doing, but I'm happy to be of service." He glanced at the sheriff, who nearly ripped the door off his cruiser. "Don't underestimate him. He's a snake."

Sadie smiled. "You don't have to worry about Ch—Michael. He knows exactly what to do with snakes. Don't you, honey?"

He'd never admired her more than in that moment. "I really do love you, Sadie Gray."

But as much as he knew she wouldn't break and that she had Gabe looking out for her, the officer was right. Chase didn't trust the sheriff, or his deputies. As Gabe's officer settled Sadie in the back of his cruiser, Chase brought his phone to his ear, waiting for his boss's assistant to put him through. He didn't bother with niceties. "The Jackson County sheriff just arrested Sadie. I don't want her to spend a minute longer in there than she has to."

"I'll see what I can do."

"That's not good enough." He let the threat linger in his voice.

"All right. All right. You're as bad as my brother-in-law."

"I'll take that as a compliment." He disconnected and called his grandfather. "Judge, don't hang up. I need a favor."

"You back in DC or still swimming in that backwater?"

"I've got a bunch of dirty cops." There was nothing his grandfather hated more than dirty law enforcement. "They've just arrested a woman who is integral to my case." If he told the judge what Sadie meant to him, he'd make sure she never got out. "I need her released, and I need her released now." He gave him the information he'd need, including the name of the judge who signed off on the warrant.

"I'll be calling my marker in on this one, son. I want you home. I haven't eaten anything half-decent since you left."

"I miss you too, Judge."

His grandfather snorted and disconnected.

Through the door, Chase heard Drew shrieking and Michaela wailing. He retrieved his gun and flung the door open, shaking his head at the sight that greeted him. Drew had been trying to escape out the screen door, and Finn had grabbed him by the seat of his pants.

"Remember how I told you the jury was out on you, boy?" Chase said to Finn as he walked over to pat the retriever's head. "Decision's in. I love you too."

He shook his head at himself. He'd probably said "I love you" more today than he had in his entire life.

Chapter Twenty-Eight

♥

The moment Gabe turned his SUV onto Willow Creek Road, Sadie had to stop herself from jumping out and running home. The fear that had held her hostage for the past several hours disappeared knowing that within minutes she'd be with Chase and her daughter. This nightmare of a morning would be behind them.

Except it hadn't all been a nightmare. There were moments of exquisite beauty, moments she'd cherish for the rest of her life. Like waking up to Chase sleeping beside her with Michaela between them and Finn stretched out on the end of the bed. It had been a snapshot of the family she'd always wanted and dreamed of.

When her heart was breaking over Drew's rejection of Michaela, Chase had put it back together again with his declaration that he was her father in every way that mattered. Sadie hadn't thought it possible but his love for her and her daughter had somehow healed the lingering hurt of her mother's rejection and abandonment—a hurt that Sadie acknowledged had played a hand in her poor choices of the past. She hadn't felt worthy of the love of a good man or trusted that every man she met didn't have an agenda. Until the gorgeous man throwing open the cottage's door had come into her life.

"Sadie, wait—" Gabe began.

She jumped out of the SUV before Gabe had pulled completely to a stop, running around the front of the vehicle to throw herself into Chase's arms. He held her in his strong, protective embrace, kissing her with a passion that matched her own.

Gabe cleared his throat, reminding them that they weren't alone. Chase eased her away from him to search her face and then her arms. His jaw hardened as he took her hands in his and examined the thin red lines encircling her wrists.

She squeezed his hands. "I'm okay. Thanks to Gabe, and Eden. She never left my side."

Chase released her hands to put his arm around her shoulders. "Thanks for everything you did, Gabe. You have good people working for you."

"They were impressed with you too."

"Yeah, I didn't have much choice but to tell them I was a special agent when I brought Drew in. He would have blown my cover as soon as I took the gag out of his mouth."

Sadie blinked. "You gagged Drew?"

"He's lucky that's all I did to him."

"You sure that's all you did?" Gabe's lips twitched as if he were holding back a grin.

"Okay, so I brought him to town in the trunk." He looked at Sadie and shrugged. "I didn't want him anywhere near Michaela. Even the trunk was too close. I brought her to your grandmother's. I know you want to see her, honey, but right now it's the safest place for her. Colin's there, and so is Finn." He glanced at Gabe. "We have to keep Drew locked down until this is over."

"I can hold him for forty-eight hours but even that will be pushing it."

"If we have to, I can bring charges against him to keep him there. Legit charges," he said at Gabe's raised eyebrow. "But right now, he's the least of our concerns. There's been an uptick on Google searches of Michael Knight and Nathan Black. I'm worried Nate's cover has been blown. I haven't been able to reach him."

"I'll get Hunter and Boyd to head over the mountain to check out what's going on at the Whiteside Mountain Gang's camp. But the searches aren't our only problem. The sheriff wasn't happy the DA cut Sadie loose. You have friends in some pretty high places to get her off that fast. But it won't deter the sheriff for long. Best guess, we have twenty-four hours to get something on him that will stick or he'll come after Sadie again. And, if I'm not mistaken, you."

Gabe smiled, looking happier than he should, given the news he'd just delivered. He pulled a piece of paper from his pocket and handed it to Chase. "As tough as this morning was for you and Sadie, this just might make it worth it."

"What is it?" Sadie glanced at what looked like a hand-written note.

"Just before you were released, the dispatcher asked me if I wanted a coffee. I was about to say no, but something about the way she was looking at me made me say yes. When she handed me the coffee, she slipped me that note."

"Don't trust the sheriff or his deputies. They're dirty. Meet me tonight at Dot's Diner at nine o'clock," Chase read, and then looked at Gabe. "Are you sure she's not setting you up?"

"She could be, but I don't think so. She was scared. And it wasn't just her. I could feel the desperation in the air as soon as I walked into the station. If she does have intel that can bring the sheriff and his deputies down, I think others will follow her lead."

"Make sure you take backup just in case," Chase said.

"You sound like my wife." Gabe smiled, then grimaced. "Who is not happy with me at the moment. She knows something's up. Do me a favor, Sadie, don't take her calls."

"I can't do that, Gabe. You know what Highland Falls is like. She's probably heard that I was arrested. She'll be worried."

"Yeah, you're right. And it's gotten a whole lot worse since Spill the Tea opened. Just keep your conversation brief. Don't give her a chance to question you. The woman is too smart for her own good, and mine."

"I'll keep it short. I'll pretend Chase and I are busy making up for lost time." She grinned up at him.

"On that note, it's time for me to say goodbye." Gabe shook Chase's hand and then pulled Sadie in for a hug. "You did great today. Stay safe and keep an eye out for the sheriff and his deputies." He walked to his SUV and opened the door. "Call if you need me. One of my officers will be here to cover you within the next twenty minutes."

As Gabe's SUV faded from view, Chase said, "I wish we had time to make up for the last three hours you were out of my sight, but we don't. We need to find your brother's stash in case Gabe's lead doesn't pan out."

"We'll be together. That's all that really matters."

He took her hands and raised them to his lips, kissing the abraded skin that circled her wrists. "You've ruined me for any other partner, Sadie Gray."

An hour later, Sadie stood at the edge of Deadman's Gorge with her partner looking on. He wasn't as happy with her now as he had been earlier.

"Are you crazy? Get away from there. It's not safe."

"It just looks that way from where you're standing." She put her hands on her hips. "You told me you weren't afraid of heights."

"I'm not, but I'm also not stupid. You're standing on shale. It's unstable."

"Elijah and I came here all the time when we were younger, and nothing ever happened to us."

"Your parents were idiots." He walked carefully to her side. "Sorry, but they were." He looked around. "I don't like this. We're out in the open."

"I know. But it'll just take me a minute to check if he hid his stash here." She stretched out carefully on her stomach, ignoring Chase's muttered curse. He fisted his hand in her T-shirt but otherwise didn't try to stop her. She reached over the ledge, feeling around in the deep crevice between two boulders. She had just gotten her hand in as deep as it could go when, around the other side of the gorge to the right of them, there was a mini-rockslide.

"We need to get out of here, and we need to get out of here now," Chase whispered, yanking her to her feet by the back of her T-shirt without warning.

She was about to give him crap when she realized the urgency. The rockslide hadn't been a natural occurrence. Someone was on the other side. Chase grabbed her hand and ran, bending over to pick up their packs without stopping.

As they reached the tree line, Sadie glanced over her shoulder and blew out a breath, tugging on Chase's hand to get him to stop. "It's okay. It's not a someone. It's a something."

He stopped and turned, shielding his eyes with his hand. "Is that a mountain lion?"

"No, it's a bobcat."

"Good. I like the sound of a cat more than a lion." His eyes narrowed. "You've scraped your arm." He opened his pack, taking out a first aid kit. "Sit on the rock, and I'll clean the wound."

She didn't think it was necessary but did as he directed. She could use a rest. She'd barely been able to keep up with him, and it had nothing to do with his longer legs. "How are you not even winded after running that fast and that far?"

"I run every day, or I did when I was in DC." He crouched in front of her with a disinfectant wipe in his hand. "It'll sting a bit."

"Not any worse than coming up empty-handed again does. I don't know where else to look."

He gently dabbed at the scrape. "We'll go back to the cottage, get something more substantial to eat than a couple of granola bars and fruit, and regroup. Something might come to—"

"The cottage. We haven't searched the grounds. It's the only place I can think of that we haven't looked."

He wrapped the used wipe in plastic and returned it to the first aid kit. "Don't worry about it," he said as he placed the kit in his backpack. "It's not the end of the world if we don't find it." He told her about Nate and the young man who wanted out of the Whiteside Mountain Gang and then reminded her about Gabe's meeting with the dispatcher tonight.

"You're worried about Nate."

"I am. Someone's looking into us, and if the sheriff and his deputies didn't have a problem taking out Brodie, they won't have a problem taking out Nate."

"Or you."

"Nate doesn't have a partner looking after his back. I do." He smiled and helped her to her feet. "Now let's go find your brother's stash. We can celebrate with tiramisu later."

"Nice. Did you get lasagna or pizza?" Her stomach growled in anticipation.

He grinned. "Neither. I'm making it my business to expand your very limited palate."

"Ugh, don't tell me you ordered something with smelts or snails." She wrinkled her nose.

"Trust me, you'll love it." He kissed the tip of her nose. "I also brought Finn and Michaela to see Nessa."

"That was sweet of you," she said as they took the shortcut through the woods to the cottage.

"I have to admit I had an ulterior motive. Now that I think about it, I probably should have asked you. Are you interested in keeping Finn?"

She pressed a hand to her chest. "I didn't even think about Nessa wanting him back once she's finished rehab. Does she?"

"She did. But for a price and visiting rights, she agreed to let us adopt him. Zia Maria put in a good word for us, but Michaela was the clincher. Nessa thinks every child needs a dog."

"So we're the proud owners of a kleptomaniac." She laughed at the face he made. "Don't worry. I'm sure he'll grow out of it."

"I'm not so—" He broke off, putting out his arm to hold her back.

"What's wrong?"

"I heard something. It sounded like a door closing." He lowered his arm, retrieving his gun from the waistband of his jeans. "Stay here. I'll check it out."

"Wait," she whispered, grabbing his arm. "If you think someone's at the cottage, I'm coming with you." Sound traveled, and other than the cottage, there was nothing around them for miles.

"It's safer for you to stay—"

"What if I was wrong? What if it wasn't a bobcat? I'm safer with you."

He looked around, then nodded. "Okay. But stay behind me."

They continued walking through the trees in silence. Every few minutes, Sadie glanced behind her. As they reached the edge of the meadow, they had a clear view of the cottage.

"Someone's been inside, and Gabe's officer isn't here."

"How do you know someone's been inside?" she whispered.

"I wedged a piece of yellow paper at the base of the door. It's on the front lawn." He scanned the yard. "But they're not in the house any longer." He nodded at the weeping willow tree.

Someone was hiding behind it. Someone who was wearing a familiar camo jacket.

"Elijah!" She raced past Chase, running through the meadow.

"Damn it, Sadie." Chase grabbed her before she reached the gravel road, shoving her behind him.

Her brother came out from behind the tree with his hands up, the fingers of his right hand closed around her gun in a white-knuckled grip. He was unkempt and looked exhausted, and defeated. "I know who you are. Let my sister go. It's me you want, not her. She had nothing to do with it." His gaze moved from Chase to Sadie. "I'm sorry, Sis. I never meant for this to blow back on you."

"You heard that they arrested me, didn't you? That's why you're here." And this is the reason she'd gone to him that night in the woods. Deep down she'd known that the baby brother she loved was still inside there somewhere.

"Yeah, and I know he's FBI." His face hardened. "I'm sorry, Sis. But he's been playing you to get to me."

"Elijah, he's the reason you're still alive. It wasn't me covering you from up on Lover's Leap. It was Chase."

He lowered his hands, looking confused. "Why?"

"Before I tell you," Chase said, "I need to know if you're the reason we no longer have a Highland Falls police officer sitting on the cottage."

He nodded. "I put out an all-points bulletin on their radio. Pretty sure they're all on Honeysuckle Road right now looking for two armed and dangerous men who robbed a convenience store."

Chase pulled out his phone, no doubt to text Gabe, telling him to call off the search. "I also need you to confirm that you didn't blow my cover or my partner's to anyone else."

"You were the one doing the searches on Chase and Nate?" Sadie asked.

"Of course I was, but someone else must be too if you picked up on it."

She sighed. "It's true. He is that good."

A fleeting smile crossed her brother's face before he returned his attention to Chase. "So why am I supposed to believe you're not playing my sister to get to me?"

"First, because I'm in love with her, and she's believed in your innocence all along. And second, it's become evident that the sheriff and his deputies were behind Brodie's murder and that they've used Ms. Howard against you."

"What are you talking about? Payton wouldn't turn on me. She loves me. We're having a baby together."

"Chase could have handled that better, but it's true." She glanced at Chase. He shrugged, and then he lowered his arm to let her go to her brother. But he didn't lower his gun and remained very much on alert.

"I'm sorry." She hugged her brother before stepping back to show him the photos on her phone. She explained everything they had uncovered that night at Payton's and what had come to light in the interim.

Her brother stared at the screen. When he finally lifted his gaze from her phone, he looked heartbroken. "So there never was a baby?"

"I'm sorry, Elijah, but I honestly don't think that there was." She didn't tell him it was for the best, not now. He wasn't ready to hear it.

He sat down on the rock under the willow tree and buried his face in his hands, just like he used to as a little boy when he was upset or things didn't work out...

"Elijah, I think I know where you buried the drugs and your phone."

He scrubbed his face and looked at her. "Where?"

"There." She pointed at the rock.

It took them less than fifteen minutes to discover that she was right, but they didn't have time to celebrate.

The sheriff stepped out from behind the cottage with a menacing grin, his gun in his hand and his black cowboy hat pushed back from his forehead. "Now what do we have here?" He slanted a glance at Chase. "Drop your weapon or I'll shoot your girlfriend and then I'll shoot you."

Chase slowly lowered the gun, but the sheriff was distracted by her brother and didn't notice that Chase hadn't straightened. His fingers were a hair's breadth away from his weapon. Elijah dove for the gun behind him on the ground.

The sheriff scoffed. "We know your sister is the only one who knows how to shoot so don't even bother trying to play—"

Chase shot the gun from the sheriff's hand. The man bellowed, clutching his bleeding fingers. "You'll pay for that, you son of—"

Chase walked over and kicked the sheriff's gun out of reach. Then he pulled his wallet from his back pocket, flipping it open to show the sheriff his badge. "What was that you were saying?"

The sheriff went pale, and Chase gave him a lethal smile. "I thought that might shut you up." He glanced back at her. "Sadie, grab his gun and then call Gabe. Tell him to come in quiet. Elijah, pick up your sister's gun."

She didn't understand why he was acting like they still had something to worry about, and then it came to her. Dwight and his partner might not be far behind.

Chapter Twenty-Nine

♥

Eight hours later, Chase looked up from fastening the tabs of his bulletproof vest to find Sadie watching him from the couch in her grandmother's living room. "I'll be fine, and so will your brother."

"I know you will." She glanced at Elijah, who was being helped into his bulletproof vest by Mr. Murphy in the kitchen, with Agnes sitting at the table looking on. Michaela was sleeping in the back bedroom with Finn on guard. "I'm just not sure my brother will."

She got up from the couch and came to Chase, smoothing her hands down the front of his vest. "He didn't say it, but I know he's hoping that Dwight and his partner don't show tonight. He'll be devastated if they do. It'll be the final proof that Payton betrayed him."

Dwight and his partner were in the wind, which was why Chase had come up with the plan to smoke them out. Twenty minutes ago, Elijah had called Payton. He'd told her he was turning himself in and wanted to see her before he did. He asked her to meet him at the rock at ten o'clock. It had taken some convincing to get him to make the call, but he'd bowed to his sister's and his grandmother's pressure. Chase had been relieved they backed him. He was using Elijah as bait after all.

"I know. I'll keep an eye on him." Chase shrugged on his

black FBI windbreaker. "I have a job for you." He reached for her laptop on the bookcase.

She frowned. "What do you want me to do?"

"I want you to do a deep dive into Payton. Check to see if she has any bank accounts or Bitcoin accounts that we're unaware of. I cleared it with my boss. Our tech guy isn't as good as I hear you are." He smiled at the stunned expression on her face.

"You're serious?"

"I am, and I wish I could stick around to watch you at work, but we have to get going. Just promise me that if she has any money in her account, you'll leave it there."

"I promise. I'll behave."

Chase's phone pinged in his pocket. He took it out and glanced at the screen. "Gabe brought the dispatcher into protective custody until Dwight and his partner are arrested."

"Did she give him the evidence you need to put them away?"

"And then some. But she can't tie them to Brodie's murder." He leaned in and kissed her. "We've got to go. Gabe is waiting for us."

Fifteen minutes later, Chase sat in the passenger seat beside Gabe, staring at his phone.

"Still no word from Nate?" Gabe asked as he shut off his headlights, pulling onto a deserted side road. He parked his personal vehicle under a tree.

"Nothing. Hunter and Boyd see anything?"

"Nate's truck is there but they haven't seen any sign of him." He gave Chase's shoulder a reassuring squeeze. "He'll be okay. He's good at what he does."

"So are Dwight and his partner." Chase got out of the truck and opened the back door for Elijah, trying to put his worry for his partner out of his head. It wasn't easy. He had a bad feeling.

Sadie's brother glanced at him, and Chase forced a confident smile. "You'll be fine. You have four of us watching your back. Your guys see anything yet?" Chase asked as they met Gabe at the back of the vehicle. Gabe had two of his officers guarding the perimeter of the rock. They were out of sight and wearing night vision. They'd been at the location for the past two hours.

"Nothing yet." He glanced at his phone. "They've spotted us. We've got the all clear. Elijah, you start walking. Don't look back. We'll be right behind you. Just act like you're on your own. If you hear an owl, it's one of my guys letting us know we've got company."

The kid looked like he was going to wet his pants. "This is a good thing you're doing, Elijah. Your sister and grandmother are proud of you." Chase smiled when Elijah's chin went up. He had his sister's stubbornness. "I'm not going to let anything happen to you. Sadie would never forgive me."

"Yeah, she would. She's in love with you."

"She loves you too. They both do. Now get moving so we can get home before your sister eats all the tiramisu."

The kid grinned. "Or gets hack happy." He held up a hand. "Kidding. She's good, almost as good as me, but she plays by the rules. Always has," he said, and then headed off through the woods. Like his sister, he knew his way around.

Chase's estimation of Elijah had gone up a lot when he'd been willing to sacrifice himself for Sadie. Now Chase just had to keep him safe and then find his partner.

Half an hour after they'd gotten into position at the rock, Chase found his partner. Dwight and Bulldog dragged Nate through the woods, dropping him when they reached the clearing. Nate landed on his hands and knees. Chase let out the breath he was holding when he stayed that way. He would have breathed a lot easier if Dwight didn't have his gun aimed at the back of Nate's head. Chase was a good shot, but he couldn't risk that Dwight got off a shot before Chase took him out.

"Come out, come out wherever you are," Bulldog called to Elijah, who was crouched behind the rock. The glow from the campfire he lit illuminated his hiding spot.

"If you don't, your grandmother's friend is dead. You wouldn't want to upset your granny, now, would you, Elijah?" Dwight cocked his gun.

"You're going to kill us both anyway," Elijah said, his voice going in and out. "Just like you killed Brodie."

Son of a—Elijah was on the move.

Bulldog laughed. "That wasn't us. Ask—"

"Shut up and go drag him out from behind the damn rock," Dwight muttered.

An owl hooted. More company. Damn it to hell. Elijah broke into a run through the trees. Chase clocked one of Gabe's men to his right, going after him. They didn't realize Elijah wasn't on the run. He was creating a diversion, and Chase prayed it worked.

"Go get him!" Dwight yelled.

As Bulldog went to run past him, Chase stuck out his foot, bringing it up to connect with the deputy's knee. He fell heavily. Chase slid back behind a tree.

"What the hell happened?"

"I tripped over a rock. I think I broke my knee."

"Do I have to do everything by myself? Get back here and watch him. I'll get Gray."

"No need. I've got him," a woman said. Elijah walked into the glow of firelight, Payton following behind with a gun pointed at his head. His vest wouldn't save him now.

Chase didn't see any other choice. Gabe and his other officer were in position, hidden behind trees on either side of Dwight. The officer who'd gone after Elijah was heading back but was still too far away from the sound of it. Chase clamped his hand over Bulldog's mouth and put the muzzle of his gun in his ear. "Get up, and don't make a sound," he whispered.

"What are you doing here?" Dwight asked Payton.

"Making sure you don't screw up again."

"It was you," Elijah said, a tremor in his voice. "You killed Brodie."

"You didn't give me a choice. You were going to ruin everything." She looked at Dwight and nodded at Nate. "Do it."

"FBI, drop your weapons." Chase walked Bulldog in front of him, swinging his gun in Payton's direction. Her eyes narrowed as her expression hardened. He couldn't see the gun—her right hand was in shadows—but he knew she had no intention of dropping her weapon. He had to take the risk.

"Elijah, get down!" Chase yelled and took the shot. Elijah dropped to the ground. Payton cried out and staggered backward. The bullet had hit her in the upper arm. Nate took advantage of the distraction and came to his knees, knocking Dwight's gun hand to the side. Gabe and his officer ran up behind Dwight. "Drop your weapon."

He complied, but it wasn't over yet. Payton hadn't lost her grip on her gun. She snarled at Elijah, cursing at him for ruining everything. Covering the bleeding wound with her left hand, she raised her gun. Chase took another shot, this time aiming for her hand, which he could now see without Elijah shielding her. The bullet hit her hand. She screamed and fell to her knees, the gun dropping to the ground. She picked it up with her left hand. Chase shoved Bulldog away from him and moved in, his gun raised. The other officer broke through the woods and rushed Payton. Elijah tried to scramble away, his eyes never leaving Payton's face.

It was like it happened in slow motion. Elijah tripped on a rock, and he put out his hand, tilting toward the fire. "Elijah!" Chase ran to Sadie's brother, pulling him from the fire. He rolled Elijah on the ground to smother the flames. He heard Gabe radioing for the paramedics who were on standby just minutes away.

Sadie sat on the right of Elijah's hospital bed while her grandmother sat in a chair on his left. Hunter and Abby were spending the day with Michaela and Finn at the cottage.

It had been five days since Elijah had fallen into the fire. Chase's quick actions had prevented him from being burned too badly. Still, he would need another round of skin grafts on his left hand and leg. He would have been recovering at home if not for spiking a fever late last night. He was on an IV drip to combat the infection.

Payton was in a hospital room around the corner, under guard. The sheriff, Dwight, and his partner were in jail. The Whiteside Mountain Gang had been rounded up, and today they'd learn what the future held in store for her brother.

"I thought Chase said he'd be here by noon." Elijah had been cracking jokes twenty minutes ago, but he'd been growing quieter as the minutes ticked by. Chase was to deliver the verdict. Both he and Nate had talked to the DA on Elijah's behalf. Nate should probably have been in the hospital himself after the beating Dwight and his partner had given him, but he refused, signing himself out against the doctor's advice.

"It's only five after twelve. Both Chase and Nate have been swamped with paperwork and debriefs." Sadie could attest to that. She'd barely seen Chase.

Which might have been why she practically swooned when he walked into Elijah's hospital room moments later. He wore a black suit and white shirt and looked even more handsome than the day they first met. Nate followed him into the room, his face battered and bruised. Her grandmother lit up when they walked in. Chase was a hero in her eyes, and she couldn't be happier for Sadie. But she had a soft spot for Nate. She treated him like another grandson. Yesterday she'd overheard Nate teasing Chase that Granny liked him best.

Chase walked over to Sadie and kissed her. "Where's Michaela?"

"Abby and Hunter are watching her. I thought it might be best to leave her at home today."

He smiled, but it didn't quite reach his eyes. Oh no, she thought, he had bad news for Elijah.

"Just in case you're going to haul her uncle away in handcuffs," Elijah quipped, but he looked nervous.

"No cuffs, buddy. Hotshot got you sprung." Nate grinned when Chase gave him a look.

"Really? You're not yanking my chain, are you?" her brother asked Nate but his gaze went to Chase.

"No, he's not. The charges against you are being dropped. Your cooperation and agreement to testify in court played in your favor, as did your role in helping us capture Payton and her partners."

"I still can't believe she played me like that. She was actually going to shoot me." He grimaced and looked at his grandmother. "I'm sorry I dragged you into all of this, Granny. I promise, as soon as I can, I'll get a job and pay you back."

They'd learned her grandmother had been right after all. Her bank account had been hacked, but not by her grandson. He'd been going to. He was no choirboy. He'd had her account open on Payton's laptop but had second thoughts at the last minute. Elijah and Payton had gotten into a fight, and he'd gone to the kitchen to grab a beer. When he'd returned, the laptop had been closed, but Sadie had uncovered proof in her FBI-sanctioned deep dive of Payton's finances—and the money that she'd stolen from their grandmother.

Elijah glanced at Sadie. "And no more get-rich-quick schemes. I'll work three jobs if I have to."

"How about one job that pays well and you get to do something you love?" Chase said, reaching inside his jacket to pull out some papers.

"Like hacking? I'm joking," he said to Sadie and her grandmother.

"I'm not. My boss at the North Carolina office has offered

you a position as their tech expert, which does involve a legal form of hacking at times." He handed Elijah the offer.

"Seriously?" He scanned the paper and looked up. "Whoa, that's wicked money."

"Benefits too."

"The one drawback is my brother-in-law is your boss, but I'll teach you how to handle him," Nate said.

"And I get to work with you too, right?" Elijah asked Chase, who'd become his hero.

Chase rubbed the back of his head, sending Sadie an apologetic glance. "I'm afraid not. I've been transferred back to DC."

Sadie stared at him, reeling from shock. "What? Why didn't you tell me?"

"I didn't find out until an hour ago. Let's go somewhere and talk." He held out his hand. "Congratulations, Elijah. You're going to do great."

Sadie rested her back against the wall outside her brother's room and crossed her arms. "You could have called me."

"I wanted to see you when I told you." He rubbed her arms. "Come on, honey. We talked about this. You knew it was a possibility."

He was right. They had, and she did. But she'd become convinced he wouldn't leave them, especially when he'd bought them a dog. "When do you leave?"

"Tonight. I'm sorry, I tried to push it back a couple days, but I'm hitting the ground running tomorrow morning."

"You're excited to get back to DC, aren't you? I can hear it in your voice."

"About the job, yes. Leaving you and Michaela, no. Come with me. I'll buy your tickets right now." He pulled out his phone.

"I can't leave Granny and Elijah. And Abby's already had to postpone the unicorn event. I have to help—"

He gently pressed his finger to her lips. "You don't have to explain. I'll come back whenever I can. We'll make this work. I promise."

Chapter Thirty

♥

Six weeks later

Sadie stood in the meadow across from the cottage with Abby. It was a glorious summer afternoon with not a cloud in the sky. Butterflies flitted among the flowers, and children's excited voices filled the air. It was exactly the kind of day they'd been praying for to wrap up the We Believe in Unicorns event.

"That settles it," Abby said, looking at the groups of family and friends milling around the pastel-striped tents set up in the meadow. Each of the tents flew a unicorn flag, while flags of Scotland dotted the gravel road that was lined with cars. "We Believe in Unicorns is officially an annual event. Gotta give the people what they want, and they really want to celebrate Scotland's national animal. Next year, it will be even bigger. We'll start working on it next week." She grinned at Sadie. "You better work out your finger muscles so your hand doesn't cramp up on you when you're doing all your book signings next year."

"All my book signings? I thought we agreed I'd do one book a year and just do a book signing during the Unicorn Hunt."

"I didn't want to stress you out. You were on a tight deadline with this one, and to be honest, I wasn't sure it would be any good."

"Hey." Sadie laughed, acting offended. She really wasn't. She'd shared Abby's worries at the beginning of the project. The turnaround time had been incredibly tight. But it'd been good for Sadie. She'd had fun, and working on the book had helped fill her nights now that Chase was hardly around.

"I know. I never should have doubted you. You're incredibly talented, and the book turned out amazing. I really do think you can make a good living from this."

"I do too. And the best part is that it doesn't feel like work at all."

"Great." Abby grinned, patting Sadie's shoulder. "Then you won't complain when I tell you I want you to write three books a year, plus do a calendar."

"Are you my manager now?"

"Yes, I am. You might be a photographer extraordinaire with a magical flair, but, sweetie, you suck at self-promotion."

Sadie couldn't argue with that. "Okay, you're hired."

Mallory walked across the meadow toward them, looking beautiful and very pregnant in her sky-blue sundress. "Final tally is in," she said when she reached them. "Congratulations, ladies, your event was a huge financial success."

"Yay!" Abby cheered. "I knew it would be. What did we rake in? Is it enough to wipe out I Believe in Unicorns' debt?"

"That and then some. Except Agnes has other plans for the money. Do you know what she wants to do with it, Sadie?" Mallory asked.

"I do, and I think it's a wonderful idea." Sadie turned to Abby. "Granny's asked Gabe if he can rename Project HOPE 'Project Brodie,' and he agreed. She's donating the money to the program. Nate and Chase are going to match it. Chase offered to clear Granny's bank loans but she wouldn't let him. She went with Elijah to the bank, and my brother set up a repayment plan with Mr. Teller. When they eventually get the money that Payton stole from Granny, they'll make a lump sum payment." Sadie had been proud of her brother and her grandmother.

"Oh, wow, that's amazing on all counts. I bet Nate was touched that your grandmother did that for his friend."

"He was. Brodie did a lot of work in the community with young offenders, helping to turn their lives around."

Abby got a look in her eyes that both Sadie and Mallory were familiar with, which is probably why they said at almost the same time, "What are you thinking of doing now?"

"I'm going to do a story about Brodie on my channel, and we can promote the project at the same time. Do you think Nate would let me interview him?" she asked, her eyes going to the man who was holding court with several of the single women in town.

"If you hide his identity."

"Is he going undercover again?" Mallory asked.

Sadie nodded. "He's determined to find the person who was responsible for getting the drugs into the hands of the Whiteside Mountain Gang. Chase is worried about him. He—" She broke off to smile at Mallory's stepson Teddy, who ran toward them with Finn on his heels.

"Mom, the twins are finding all the rainbow poop, and it's not fair for the little kids."

Along with the golden alicorn—unicorn horn—they'd hidden boxes of jewel-like candy, because, according to Sadie's grandmother, unicorns pooped rainbows.

"I swear those two can sniff out candy from a mile away." Mallory shielded her eyes and smiled. "Look, Daddy's solved the problem. He's got your brothers helping the kids ride on Lula Belle the unicorn."

"Hey, Teddy, how would you like a clue where the golden alicorn is?"

Abby shrugged at Mallory's and Sadie's "Abby!"

"I'm not telling him where it is. It's just a clue. He'll have to figure it out on his own. Besides, I think we made it too difficult. They should have found the alicorn by now." Abby pulled a piece of paper from the pocket of her white capris and handed it to Teddy.

"Thanks." He grinned, waving the paper as he ran off.

Suddenly, Abby pulled Mallory in front of her. "Oh no. Hide me."

Mallory looked at an approaching group of older women. "Thanks for thinking I'm big enough to hide you, but if you think you can escape Elsa and the Sisterhood, think again."

"Watch me." Abby took off for the cottage.

"What's going on?" Sadie asked as she watched their friend sprint across the gravel road.

"Elsa is sure Abby's pregnant, and she's been pressuring her and Hunter to set a wedding date. But rumor has it—a rumor that's been circulating at Spill the Tea, thanks to Babs—that Elsa has already set a date for them."

"Do you think Abby's pregnant?"

"I think she might be." Mallory smiled and rubbed her baby bump, slanting Sadie a look.

"Don't even." She laughed. "Michaela's just turned five months, and Chase and I are living in different states."

"Of course, you're right. How are you doing, really? I mean, you look incredible, and you seem happy."

"I'm good. Really good, actually. Don't get me wrong. I miss Chase like crazy, but we're making it work." She moved her head from side to side. "Sort of. It's easier for me than it is for him. He's the one making all the sacrifices. The poor guy is exhausted. Last weekend when he was here, I woke up to find him asleep at the kitchen table. He had the keys of his laptop imprinted on his cheek. He tries so hard not to let work interfere with his time with Michaela and me that he stays up half the night to keep on top of things."

"That's not good."

"I know. It was the same when we went to visit him a couple of weeks ago." She smiled, thinking of walking into his gorgeous condo and discovering he had a nursery set up and decorated for Michaela just like her room here. He'd done it all on his own.

"Would you ever consider moving to DC? Please say no. I know it's selfish, but we'd miss you. A lot."

"I'd miss you guys too." She looked around at the cottage, the mountains, and the forest, at her friends and family in the meadow. "I'm happy here. Happier than I've ever been, and I'd love Michaela to grow up in Highland Falls. But for Chase's sake, we can't keep going the way that we are. I planned to talk to him about it this weekend but he got a break in his case and couldn't get away."

"Are you sure about that?" Mallory nodded at a drop-dead gorgeous man in a black suit and white shirt carrying a gigantic stuffed unicorn. Chase stood at the end of her driveaway surrounded by Zia Maria and her friends. "Go." Mallory smiled, waving Sadie off.

Zia Maria and her friends dispersed as Sadie wove her way through the parked cars. Chase met her halfway and pulled her into his arms, the unicorn squished between them. They both went in for a kiss and ended up kissing the unicorn instead.

"I need to get rid of this. Where's my girl?"

"She's with Granny and Colin. They took her for a walk." She tugged on the unicorn's horn. "Don't tell me this is a five-month birthday present."

He grinned. "Of course it is. I can't let it go by without marking the occasion."

"You're going to spoil her. Besides, having you here is the best present of all." She cupped the side of his beard-stubbled face with her hand, taking in the dark shadows under eyes that were bloodshot. "Chase, you're exhausted. You should have come next weekend."

"And miss your big event? Not on your life. How did the signing go? Did you sell out?"

"Yes, probably because someone in DC ordered two cases of books."

"Who ratted me out?"

"Babs."

He rolled his eyes. "I hope your brother knows what he's getting himself into."

Much to everyone's surprise, her brother and Brooklyn were dating. Sadie thought it was a little fast, but who was she to judge? "I'm more worried about you, Chase. You can't keep this up."

He looked around. "Is there somewhere we can talk privately?"

Her heart gave a nervous thump, which was silly because she knew he loved her as much as she loved him. "I'd say the cottage but Abby is in there hiding out from Elsa." At his quirked eyebrow, she said, "I'll tell you about it later."

She glanced at the yellow rowboat floating on the creek. With Abby's help, Sadie had decorated the front of the boat with flowers for a photo shoot. Lately, parents had been asking her to take professional photos of their children so she'd taken advantage of the opportunity today.

"I have the perfect spot." She took him by the hand and led him around the back of the cottage.

He spotted the boat and smiled. "You're right. It is perfect." He left the unicorn on the seat of the Adirondack chair and then shrugged out of his jacket, leaving it on the arm. They walked hand in hand to where the boat sat bobbing on the creek. Chase let go of her to tug on the rope that was attached to the willow tree, bringing the rowboat to shore. He helped Sadie in, waiting for her to get settled before joining her. The boat rocked, throwing him off balance.

"Careful." She grabbed his hand.

Chase stretched out beside her and brought her close. "Thanks for saving me." He kissed her temple and then tipped his head back, the sun's rays dancing on his handsome face. "I've missed this. I don't get outside much in DC."

"You don't get out at all." She stroked his face. "I really am worried about you. Did you wrap up the investigation?" She knew from what little he could tell her that it was a big case, a career-making case.

"I did," he murmured, sounding like he was seconds from falling asleep.

"That's great. I'm sure your boss was thrilled."

"He might have been more thrilled if I wasn't offered his job."

"Chase, that's amazing. It's exactly what you've been working toward."

"It was." He took her hand in his. "I turned them down. I can't do this anymore."

"No, you can't give up the opportunity because of us. We'll move—"

He shook his head. "My career used to be my life but it isn't anymore. You and Michaela are. I want to make a life with you here. I requested a transfer, and it's been granted. With a little help from Nate. My boss, his brother-in-law, wasn't happy that I'd left them as soon as DC came calling. I can't say I blame him."

"Are you absolutely sure this is what you want?"

He cocked his head. "Are you?"

"Yes, a thousand times—"

"Hold that thought." He reached into the pocket of his pants and pulled out a small blue box, opening it to reveal a gorgeous, sparkling diamond ring. "Sadie Gray, the love of my life, will you marry me?"

"Yes, a thousand times over." He slid the ring onto her finger. She held it up and the diamond caught the sun's rays, a rainbow of light dancing around them. "It's beautiful, just like you. I adore you, Chase Michael Roberts, and so does your daughter." As they leaned in to kiss, a cheer went up from the bushes across from them.

Abby popped out with a huge grin on her face and her camera in her hands. "Yay! You're getting married! Congrats, and thanks for taking the pressure off me. Now go back to what you were about to do. I need to get a shot." She held the viewfinder to her eye. "Oh my gosh, you would not believe how gorgeous you guys look right now. I'm captioning it 'Falling in Love on Willow Creek.' Thanks!" She blew them a kiss and darted off through the trees.

"That woman is—" Chase began, only to have Abby pop out of the bushes again.

"Sorry, guys. And I do mean that. But we need your help. Finn just stole the golden alicorn from Teddy, and Teddy's upset he can't make his wish." Abby's mouth fell open, and they followed her gaze.

Finn broke through the trees with the golden alicorn in his mouth, making a beeline for the boat. Chase came to his feet and held up his hands. "No, Finn, don't—"

Finn leaped through the air and landed in the rowboat, dropping the alicorn at Chase's feet. The boat rocked violently. Chase lost his balance and fell over the side of the boat. He landed in the creek, spraying Sadie with water.

Dripping wet, she leaned over the side of the rowboat and offered her hand to Chase while struggling to contain her laughter.

Chase grinned up at her and took her hand. "My lady in shining armor, here to save me again."

"It seems only fair. You've been my knight in shining armor since the first day we met."

For a bonus story from Debbie Mason, please turn the page to read "A Wedding on Honeysuckle Ridge."

It's autumn in the cozy little town of Highland Falls, and for Sadie Gray, it's the most romantic time of the year, not to mention her life. After all, she's engaged to brilliant and gorgeous FBI agent Chase Roberts. But when Sadie and Chase start planning to say their "I do's" on a reality TV show, Chase's grandfather goes from disapproving to full-on Wedding Sabotage Mode. Can Chase and Sadie find their way back to each other . . . before their wedding turns into a happily never after?

FOREVER

A Wedding on Honeysuckle Ridge

DEBBIE MASON

A Highland Falls Novella

FOREVER

New York   Boston

Chapter One

♥

Sadie Gray stood at the front of the Blushing Bridal Boutique filming a segment called Say Yea or Nay to the Dress for her best friend's YouTube channel, *Abby Does Highland Falls*. Their mutual best friend Mallory was the MC for the event.

It wasn't a role Mallory was comfortable with. She was eight months pregnant, and being the center of attention on camera wasn't exactly something she enjoyed. But her six-year-old stepson Teddy, who was one of Abby's biggest fans, had won her over. Looking adorable in a black tux, Teddy stood beside Mallory to the left of the dais in front of a packed house.

The women filling the rows of white chairs had their paddles at the ready—*yea* on one side, *nay* on the other. So far none of the dresses had gotten more than a smattering of yeas. Sadie didn't think it had anything to do with the dresses. Abby, the bride-to-be, looked like she was going to a funeral instead of shopping for her wedding gown. When Abby had first begun planning her wedding, Sadie had assumed her lack of enthusiasm was because she was pregnant and had morning sickness. But lately, she'd begun to worry something more was going on.

Raised whispers coming from behind the backdrop drew the

audience's attention. The shop owner—who had gone to considerable expense and effort to create a fabric wall that resembled barn board decorated with autumn leaves and pumpkins, the words *Fall in Love* just above where Abby should be standing but wasn't—shot a nervous glance at Mallory, who in turn shot one at Sadie.

Sadie reached behind her for her phone on the counter and started "Isn't She Lovely" by Stevie Wonder over from the beginning, raising the volume in hopes of distracting the audience from whatever was going on backstage.

Mallory bent to whisper in Teddy's ear. The little boy nodded, disappearing behind the backdrop. Moments later, he returned with Abby clutching his arm.

She wore an organza mermaid wedding gown with a ruffled skirt, which wasn't much of an improvement over the high-neck metallic lace dress she'd appeared in ten minutes earlier. They were beautiful dresses; they just weren't Abby.

Mallory gave Abby an encouraging smile while reading from the notes the shop's owner had given her. Then she said, "Okay, ladies and gentleman, are we saying yea or nay to the dress?"

Teddy was the only one who gave the dress a yea, which wasn't a surprise. He'd voted the same way for every dress. But their audience didn't just let their paddles speak for them; they began explaining in detail why they'd voted nay.

Sadie didn't know who looked more defeated, Abby or the shop owner.

At the chime of bells, Sadie turned to see her cousin, Elliana MacLeod, maneuvering a stroller inside. Sadie stopped filming and hurried over to hold open the door.

"Sorry, someone was missing her mommy." Ellie grinned down at Sadie's seven-month-old daughter who babbled up at her from where she sat strapped into the stroller. The words were barely distinguishable except for one that sounded a lot more like *dada* than *mama*. It wouldn't surprise Sadie if her daughter's first word was *dada*. Not only did Chase spend an inordinate amount of time teaching her the word, but Michaela had rewarded him with her first smile and giggle too. "And her daddy," Ellie added.

Sadie missed Chase as much as her daughter did. He'd once again flown to DC to check on his grandfather. It was his second trip in the past seven weeks. Sadie waited for the shoe to drop each time he came home, positive his grandfather had convinced him to give up on the life he was building in Highland Falls with her and Michaela and return to DC.

"Mommy misses Daddy too, baby. But he'll be home tomorrow afternoon." Sadie leaned in and kissed her daughter's rosy cheek. She looked adorable in a pink faux-fur vest, gray-and-white-striped top, pink leggings, and gray baby boots. "And it looks like Auntie Ellie took you shopping again."

Ellie had come home two weeks ago to help her maternal grandfather run the Mirror Lake Inn.

"I hope you don't mind but I couldn't resist. They were unveiling their new fall line at Cutie Patootie when we walked—" Ellie broke off at Abby's raised voice, narrowing her violet eyes at Sadie's best friend standing on the dais. Ellie's grimace seemed to validate everyone else's opinion of the dress.

"Okay, I get the picture, ladies. I think we're done for the day." Abby hiked up the wedding gown and tromped offstage.

"Wait! You have to pick a dress," the shop owner called after Abby. "I won't have enough time to order yours in before the wedding if you don't find something soon."

Abby and Hunter were getting married on October twenty-third, less than a month away.

"That's fine." Abby smiled before disappearing behind the backdrop.

The shop owner stood wringing her hands, shooting a *do something* look at Mallory, who in turn shot one at Sadie.

Obviously sensing that Sadie was at a loss for what to do, Ellie patted her shoulder. "Don't worry, I'm sure I can find Abby a dress she'll fall in love with."

Sadie's cousin reached back to twist her long, raven-black mane into a ponytail as she walked toward the wall of wedding gowns. Removing a clip from the pocket of her brightly colored ankle-length sweater, Ellie pinned her hair on top of her head, clearly focused on the task at hand. Sadie's cousin owned Custom Concierge, a personal shopping company she'd founded in New York years before.

Blushing Bridal's owner hurried over as Ellie flicked through the dresses with an expert eye. "We're closed at the moment, but if you come back later, say, in an hour, I'm sure I can find you some—" the owner began.

"Lena, she's not looking for a wedding dress for herself. Her fiancé left her at the altar in May," said Babs Sutherland, the owner of Spill the Tea, shrugging in response to the women hissing at her to be quiet.

Sadie stared at her cousin. Ellie hadn't said anything to her about a broken engagement or a wedding, and they'd once been as close as sisters. It couldn't be true. But when Sadie's gaze landed on their grandmother looking sheepish in the front row, she had a feeling that it was.

Ellie's exclamation of delight drew Sadie's attention from their grandmother. Her cousin was working a blush-colored lace dress free from among the frothy white gowns. Ignoring the shop owner's moue and negative head shake, Ellie held up the dress, gave what looked like a satisfied nod, and made a beeline for the back of the store. She slowed to cast a disappointed look at their grandmother.

So Granny had spilled the beans after all.

Which was odd. Her grandmother didn't like to gossip, especially about family. But if Agnes hadn't told Babs, then how...?

Sadie sighed. How indeed. Her grandmother had the second sight, a gift that she couldn't really control. If she'd taken Ellie's hand when she'd stopped in at I Believe in Unicorns, her grandmother's store on Main Street, Agnes wouldn't have been able to keep from blurting out whatever she saw in front of customers. She went into a trance-like state when foretelling someone's future.

"It looks like your great-granny is in hot water with Auntie Ellie," Sadie murmured as she crouched beside the stroller. "And it looks like Mommy is going to be up late editing today's video for Auntie Abby's channel. Let's just hope Auntie Ellie picked a winner."

Michaela took her fist from her mouth, offering Sadie a drooly smile before responding with a minute-long commentary in baby speak. Sadie laughed. "I think your daddy's right. You're going to talk as much as your Auntie Abby."

Her daughter validated Chase's predication by babbling non-stop for another few minutes, and, as Sadie so often did, she responded as if they were having a real conversation. "I agree. You are a very lucky girl to have so many amazing women in your life, including your Auntie Abby. I just wish she was a little more excited about her wedding."

"I don't think that's going to happen," Ellie said, coming to crouch on the other side of the stroller.

"Why not? What did she say?" Sadie asked her cousin.

"She didn't have to say anything. Her first marriage ended in disaster, so she's obviously afraid of making the same mistake."

"Hunter is nothing like Abby's first husband. He adores her, and she adores him. They're perfect for each other." The couple had been living together for more than a year at the farm on Honeysuckle Ridge.

"And that's why she doesn't want to get married. She's afraid if they do, it will change everything."

"But that's crazy. It's just a piece of paper."

Ellie shrugged. "Fears are rarely based on logic."

Sadie frowned, wondering if her cousin might be projecting after what Babs had revealed about Ellie's disastrous trip to the altar.

"It has nothing to do with me," Ellie said as if she had somehow read Sadie's mind. "And before you ask, I don't want to talk about it."

At that point, Sadie was barely listening to her cousin. She was stuck on the thought that Ellie had been able to read her mind. She leaned in to her cousin. "You didn't just put two and two together, did you? You didn't just sense that Abby's scared because her first marriage didn't end in a happily-ever-after. You read her mind."

"I don't know what you're talking about." Her cousin avoided meeting her eyes, busying herself straightening Michaela's vest. "Mommy's being silly, isn't she, sweetheart?"

"No. Mommy isn't being silly. I know you, Ellie, and I know when you're hiding something from me. Granny always told me I didn't have to worry about inheriting her gift. She said the oldest MacLeod granddaughter would—"

Sadie was cut off by a cacophony of women's voices yelling at her to start the music. "We're not done talking about this," she told her cousin.

Shuffling through the playlist on her phone, Sadie swapped out "Isn't She Lovely" with Marvin Gaye and Tammi Terrell's rendition of "Ain't No Mountain High Enough" in hopes that the change of music would bring about a change in the result. She thought it was a good sign when Michaela started moving to the music in her stroller. Sadie got up and retrieved her video camera, turning it on just in time to capture Abby walking out from behind the backdrop.

Abby had barely taken her place on the dais when Teddy's paddle went up and he shouted, "Yea!"

He was right. Abby looked gorgeous in the lace wedding gown. The dress, warm beige with a hint of peach, complemented her best friend's pale skin and long, curly red hair rather than washing her out like the white wedding dresses had. And while the other dresses had overpowered her petite frame, this one fit both her figure and her personality to perfection.

Smiling at Teddy, Mallory opened her mouth to read from her notes, but before she got out a single word, every member of the audience echoed Teddy's yea.

"Yay!" he cheered, grabbing Abby by the hand. And for the first time that day, the bride-to-be smiled. A real smile that lit up her face and grew wider when Teddy started swinging her arm and dancing to the music. The entire front row got to their feet, clapping and waving their paddles. Within seconds, everyone in Blushing Bridal was singing and dancing to "Ain't No Mountain High Enough."

Sadie smiled as she captured the moment on video, her heart overflowing with love for her friends, her family, and her hometown.

"Turn off your camera and join in," her cousin said, dancing past her with Michaela in her arms.

What the heck, Sadie thought. She had more than enough footage. She turned off the camera, set it on the counter, and danced her way to her cousin's side.

Chapter Two

♥

The women in Blushing Bridal were still celebrating Abby's wedding dress pick fifteen minutes later when Sadie's cell phone rang. She glanced at the screen, and her heart thumped an excited beat. She shook her head at her reaction to seeing Chase's incoming FaceTime call. Honestly, the way her heart raced you'd think she hadn't spoken to him in a month instead of a mere fifteen hours.

"Hey," she said, unable to keep her smile from spreading into an ear-to-ear grin when his gorgeous face appeared on the screen. Obviously, she had no shame when it came to the man. She was totally out there with her feelings for Chase, which was a new experience for her. And every once in a while, it gave her pause. Like now. Because the smile he offered in return was strained by comparison. "What's wrong?"

"I can hardly hear you. Where are you?"

Okay, so maybe she was overreacting. "Just wrapping up at Blushing Bridal. Abby said yes to the dress. Give me a sec."

"Is that Chase?" Zia Maria asked. Sadie barely got out a yes when her phone disappeared from her hand. Zia Maria—the owner of the best Italian restaurant in North Carolina—and her friends adored Chase almost as much as Sadie did. While he was passed among the older women, Sadie strapped Michaela into the stroller, placed the video camera and a Blushing Bridal bag with her earlier purchase in the storage basket, and then went to open the door.

"Everything okay?" her cousin asked, coming to hold the door for her.

"Yeah, just a little loud for a FaceTime call." She glanced over her shoulder. "Would you mind rescuing Chase from Zia Maria and her friends and bringing me my phone?"

"Sure. No problem."

When Ellie brought her phone outside a few minutes later with a worried expression on her face, Sadie thought her initial impression that something was wrong had been right. Which might have been why her first words to Chase were "Are you not coming home?"

"Hang on a minute, honey." The screen went dark.

"I'll take Michaela for a walk," her cousin whispered.

Sadie nodded and sat down on the brick window ledge, worrying her bottom lip between her teeth as she watched Ellie push the stroller up the sidewalk. The orange, yellow, and red pattern in her cousin's sweater matched the autumn leaves on the stately trees that lined Main Street. Sadie huddled deeper in her sage-green chunky knit sweater, feeling chilled despite the midafternoon sunshine warming her face.

"Sorry about that." Chase rubbed the back of his head, an action that usually meant he was nervous or about to deliver bad news.

"So you're not coming home?" She briefly closed her eyes at the plaintive note in her voice. She sounded like a clingy, whiny woman.

"Actually, I'm home now. I got in twenty minutes ago." She noticed the yellow door behind him. He was standing outside the cottage on Willow Creek.

A relieved breath whooshed out of her, and then she realized why he was acting a little weird and winced. Chase was compulsively neat, and she was habitually messy. "Okay, I can explain the mess in the kitchen. Zia Maria gave me her recipe for tiramisu, and, surprise, I made it for your welcome-home dessert. But I had no idea it would take that long to make, and I had no time to clean up." If she hadn't used cottage cheese instead of ricotta in her first attempt, the dessert wouldn't have taken her so long to make, but she wasn't about to share that with Chase. "I had to be here at eleven. Plus, you weren't supposed to be home until—"

"You made me tiramisu?" He gave her a smile that made her ovaries twitch. But then his smile went from downright sexy to strangely wistful, and her twitching ovaries froze.

"Chase, what's going on? You're making me nervous."

He frowned. "Why are you nervous?"

"Oh, I don't know. Maybe because your grandfather has been trying to break us up from the moment you told him we were engaged." The judge, as Chase referred to his grandfather, blamed Sadie for his grandson refusing the high-profile position he'd been offered with the FBI in DC.

"Right. I see where you're coming from."

Just this once, she wished he'd lie to her. Tell her that she was overreacting or imagining things. It wasn't easy knowing that one of the most important people in her fiancé's life disapproved of her.

Chase leaned back and opened the door. "Give me a minute, and I'll be right with you."

"I bet Finn was happy to see you." At Chase's grimace, she laughed. "What did he steal this time?" Finn, the golden retriever they'd adopted in June, was a canine kleptomaniac.

"Um, I wasn't talking to Finn. I was talking to the judge."

Sadie slowly came to her feet. "Like on Zoom, right? Because you would not bring your grandfather—your grandfather who is even more obsessively neat than you are—home without warning me."

"I'm sorry, honey. I didn't have much of a choice. He—"

"Chase Roberts, you get in that cottage right now and shut the door to our bedroom." Her mind raced, making it difficult to remember the state of the other rooms. "The laundry room and bathroom too."

He pressed his lips together, his eyes dancing with amusement. At any other time, she would have taken pleasure in those dancing blue eyes, but not today. "Don't you dare laugh at me. This is serious. He already hates me and thinks I've ruined your life." She wrapped an arm around her waist, glancing at the traffic crawling along Main Street to hide how much it upset her.

"Hey, look at me."

When she returned her gaze to that handsome face she'd never tire of looking at, he said, "I don't care what he thinks. You and Michaela are the best things that ever happened to me. I love you."

She sighed. She knew he did. He never gave her any reason to doubt his feelings for her and Michaela. "I love you too. I just wish you would have given me some warning."

"I didn't know he was coming. Honest, I didn't. We had a...difference of opinion, and I decided to come home early. I didn't realize he was on the plane until we were disembarking."

"He wanted you to stay in DC, didn't he?"

"He did. I know the timing isn't great, but in the end, this might be for the best. He's lonely, and he's not getting any younger. Who knows? Maybe Highland Falls will win him over."

"You're thinking of moving him here?" Her voice went up an octave, garnering the attention of several women leaving Blushing Bridal. Sadie gave them a bright smile and friendly wave while moving farther along the sidewalk.

Elsa Mackenzie, the owner of Three Wise Women Bookstore, frowned at her. "Are you all right, Sadie?"

"I'm great. Really, really great." She kept that bright smile plastered on her face. "Thanks for taking part in Say Yea or Nay to the Dress. I should have the episode online tomorrow morning so be sure to check it out."

"We wouldn't miss it. I hope you got my best side," two of the women said at almost the same time, laughing as they went their separate ways.

With her smile still firmly in place, Sadie returned her attention to Chase. She wondered if she should apologize for the panic he'd undoubtedly heard in her voice. It was his grandfather they were talking about, after all.

"I'm sorry, honey," Chase said. "I know the last thing you need right now is to deal with my grandfather on top of everything else. If you want, I can check and see if they have a room available at the Mirror Lake Inn."

"For him or for me?"

He smiled. "The only place you're staying is here with me."

His feelings for her were evident in his words, in that slow, seductive smile he only ever shared with her. Ellie was right. Just like Abby's, Sadie's fears had no basis in reality. Nothing the judge could say or do would change how she and Chase felt about each other. "Your grandfather is staying with us too."

"Are you sure? Because I—"

"Of course I am," she said with as much enthusiasm as she could manage with her nerves doing a panicked dance in her stomach. The plan she had to welcome Chase home would have to go on the back burner. The cottage wasn't all that big, and the walls were pretty thin. But the judge was Chase's family. The man who'd raised him. "It's the perfect opportunity for your grandfather to get to know me and Michaela better." The perfect opportunity for Sadie to win him over. If she didn't, then surely her adorable daughter would.

Except...the judge wasn't exactly the grandfatherly type, as their one and only visit to his retirement home had proven. There'd been no oohing and aahing over Michaela. So maybe her daughter, who was as messy as her mother, wouldn't win him over. But thanks to Chase, Sadie had inside information on the judge that at the very least might soften him up. He loved Italian food as much as his grandson did. "I'll stop by Zia Maria's and pick up something for dinner."

"Okay, as long as you're sure..." Chase broke off with a wince. "I'd better go. It sounds like the judge and Finn aren't bonding as I'd hoped."

So she wasn't the only one with a plan to win over Jonathan Knight. If Chase's plan wasn't working out, she wondered what that said about the chances hers would.

"Everything okay?" her cousin asked.

Sadie startled. Lost in thought after Chase had disconnected, she hadn't heard Ellie approach. She turned to smile at her cousin and Michaela. "Everything's fine. Chase is home."

"You know I can see through you, don't you? And no, it's not because I've inherited the MacLeod curse."

She found it interesting that her cousin referred to their grandmother's gift as a curse but let it go. Ellie had always known when Sadie was pretending everything was fine when it wasn't. "This is me trying to channel my inner optimist. Chase's grandfather is with him, and he's not exactly on board with our relationship."

Ellie laughed. "You don't have an inner optimist. You're the most pessimistic person I know."

"And you're the most optimistic person I've ever met so tell me everything is going to be all right, and I might believe you. At least I'll try to." Her cousin grimaced, and Sadie's stomach dropped to her toes. "Tell me the face you just made has nothing to do with Chase and me."

"Sorry. I'm usually better at keeping my feelings to myself. I tend to let my guard down around people I love. When I retrieved your phone, Chase's grandfather was standing behind him. He was thinking of ways to—"

"I knew it! You did inherit Granny's gift."

"Shh," Ellie hissed, shooting a panicked glance up and down the sidewalk. "The last thing I need is for anyone to know, especially my parents."

"So it's true."

Ellie sighed. "Yes, and obviously it's not only my feelings I can't keep to myself when it comes to you. I'm sure everything will be fine but you need to watch out for Chase's grandfather. He's here to break you guys up."

Even though her cousin wasn't telling her anything she didn't already know, Sadie's shoulders sagged in defeat. "Is there any chance you might be wrong? He was on the phone, and it wasn't like you could touch him."

"Unlike Granny, I don't need to have physical contact to read someone. I wish I did. At least it would be easier to control. It really is a curse, Sadie. I wouldn't wish it on my worst enemy."

She doubted her cousin had any enemies. Ellie was the kindest person Sadie had ever met. "Does Granny know?"

"No." She tilted her head to the side. "Maybe. But I don't think she'll say anything. She knows how my parents would react."

Sadie's aunt and uncle weren't the most open-minded or accepting people. When they'd first learned Agnes had the second sight, they'd been horrified. They'd dragged her to psychiatrist after psychiatrist, threatening to have her committed if she didn't stop. So Sadie understood why Ellie wouldn't want them to know.

She gave her cousin's shoulder a reassuring squeeze. "I promise, no one will hear about it from me. But I'm sorry it feels like a curse and that you're the one who has to bear it, Ellie. If there's anything I can do to make it easier for you, just tell me."

"I will." Ellie leaned in and gave her a quick hug. "I've missed you, Sadie."

"I've missed you too. It's nice to have you home."

Her cousin glanced at her phone. "Speaking of home, I'd better get back to the inn." Ellie kissed Michaela on the top of her head and then set off down the sidewalk. Turning as she reached the stoplight, she called out, "I'll get a room ready for Chase's grandfather. Just in case."

Chapter Three

♥

You know what your problem is? You have a hero complex," Chase's grandfather said from where he sat at the opposite end of the couch from Finn, a pillow in his hand to shoo the dog away if he dared to come close. "The only reason you're with this girl is because you think she needs saving."

"If you knew Sadie, you'd know how far that is from the truth," Chase said as he leaned against the island in the kitchen, keeping an eye out for Sadie's SUV.

"I don't have to get to know her, nor do I wish to. The investigator I hired provided enough information about Sadie Gray and her family that I know exactly the type of person you've gotten yourself mixed up with. You've thrown away everything you worked for to play house in this shack in the woods."

Chase ground his back molars together to keep from saying something he couldn't take back. He knew why the judge was lashing out at Sadie. In his grandfather's mind, she *had* ruined Chase's career, but more importantly, she was the reason Chase had left DC. The judge was old and lonely. The reminder helped Chase rein in his anger but not the need to set his grandfather straight. He opened his mouth to do just that but apparently the judge wasn't finished making his case.

"She's manipulating you, my boy. She's no doubt put those hacking skills of hers to good use and discovered my net worth. Now she's just biding her time until I die. She'll be in for a shock when she discovers I disinherited you. You'll not get a single penny of my estate if you stay with her."

"Sadie wouldn't hack into your finances." He didn't bother denying that she had the ability to uncover any and all of his grandfather's secrets. Like her brother, Sadie had inherited their late father's talents. Only, unlike their father, Sadie and Elijah Gray used their tech skills for the greater good. At least now her brother did. "She doesn't care about your money, and neither do I."

"I find that hard to believe. You always had a taste for the finer things in life." His grandfather looked around the cottage, his upper lip curling in distaste. "Obviously, that is no longer the case."

Chase had spent the first eight years of his life going to bed hungry, never knowing where his next meal would come from. All that had changed when his grandfather took custody of him and his younger brother. But those early days had left a mark, and Chase had worked hard to ensure he'd never go hungry again, no matter what life had in store for him. Except the small fortune sitting in his bank accounts—thanks to his baby brother's investment acumen—hadn't filled the void. Sadie's love for him had, and he wouldn't let anyone, not even the man who'd raised him, damage what they had together.

At the sound of a vehicle coming down the gravel road, Chase pushed off the counter. "If you were anyone else, I would have thrown you out for what you said about Sadie, Judge. But I love you, and I understand what this is really about so I'm giving you one more chance. Don't make me regret it."

He saw a flicker of fear flash in his grandfather's eyes before he covered it with a contemptuous snort. "Or what? You'll throw me out? Choose a woman you've known for seven months over me, the man who raised you?" The judge gave his head a bitter shake. "I'm disappointed in you. I thought you were smarter than this. But I guess you are your mother's son, after all."

Chase's cheeks burned as if his grandfather had slapped him. They rarely talked about his mother, the judge's daughter. Twenty-four years ago, his grandfather had given her an ultimatum—either leave the man she lived with at the time or he'd have Chase and his brother removed from her care. His mother had chosen the man over her sons. Three years later, the judge's prediction that Chase's mother's involvement with the man would lead to her death had proven correct. He'd killed her in a drunken rage.

Chase held his grandfather's gaze. The old man had the good grace to look contrite. It didn't matter. Chase wasn't about to let him hurt Sadie like he'd hurt him. "I'll book you a room at the inn. You can stay there tonight, and I'll drive you to the airport tomorrow."

"You said the girl…Sadie," his grandfather corrected at Chase's pointed stare, "was picking up food for our dinner. It would be rude for me to leave before we ate."

"She'll get over it," Chase said as he walked to the front door.

"Wait!"

Surprised at the pleading note in his grandfather's voice, Chase turned.

"You said you'd give me a second chance. I'd like to stay." His grandfather stood, glancing from Finn, who was watching him warily from the other end of the couch, to the kitchen. "At least for dinner."

Chase gave him a curt nod and opened the door. From where she sat behind the wheel of the SUV in the driveway, Sadie looked at him, her warm smile turning into a frown when she got out of the car. As Chase walked toward her, he worked to clear the anger at his grandfather from his face. It wasn't as difficult as he thought it would be. Then again, he shouldn't be surprised. Sadie had that effect on him. His life was so much better with her in it. He took her in his arms and bent his head to kiss her, the last of his anger fading away at the feel of her soft, welcoming lips beneath his.

She brought her hand to his cheek, breaking the kiss to search his face. "Are you okay?"

"I am now." He turned his head to kiss her palm. "I've missed you. And you too," he said when Michaela started babbling and clapping her hands in the backseat.

"Dada, dada."

His jaw dropped. "Did you hear that?" Without waiting for Sadie's response, he jogged around the SUV and opened the back passenger-side door. "You missed your dada, didn't you, my sweet girl?" He kissed her button nose while getting her out of the car seat, scooping her into his arms. "Can you say dada? Come on, say it again for me. Dada."

She gave him a drooly smile and patted his cheeks. "Dada."

His chest got tight, and his throat clogged with emotion. He'd had a similar reaction the night he'd helped bring Michaela into the world. She'd captured his heart the moment he'd first held her.

He cleared his throat. "That's right, my brilliant baby. *Dada*. Get out your phone, honey. We need to record this," he said to Sadie, who'd come to stand at his side.

Sadie didn't want to burst Chase's bubble but it had sounded more like *blah blah* to her. She lifted her phone, suppressing a laugh as she filmed Chase encouraging Michaela to say *dada* again. Seconds later, the urge to laugh gave way to an emotion that blurred her vision. She switched from video to photo, capturing the two people she loved more than life itself.

The sunlight glinted off Chase's honey-blond hair and her daughter's auburn curls, the two of them smiling at each other with the forest of autumn-colored leaves in the background. Sadie picked out a frame and matting for the photo in her mind. She'd give it to Chase for Christmas.

"Did you get it?" Chase reached for her phone. He frowned when she handed it over. "Are you okay? You're not upset she said *dada* first, are you?" he asked, looking a little guilty.

"No." She laughed out loud this time, taking Michaela from him so he could watch the video. "It seems only fair since you've spent every waking minute coaching her."

"I haven't spent...okay, so maybe I have." He grinned, his brow furrowing as he watched the video. He brought the phone to his ear. "Something must be wrong with your sound card. It sounds more like *blah blah* than *dada*."

"I'll have a look at it later. We should probably get inside before your grandfather wonders what happened to us." She forced a smile, reaching past him for Michaela's diaper bag. The disgruntled look Chase shot at the cottage didn't help combat the nervous flutter in her stomach. "What's wrong?"

He kissed the top of her head. "Nothing." But the smile he offered her seemed as forced as her own. He closed the back passenger-side door and then opened the front passenger side, retrieving the takeaway bag from the seat. "Smells great. What's this?" he asked, tucking their food under one arm to pick up the bag from Blushing Bridal Boutique.

"Don't—" She sighed when he looked in the bag, and his eyes went wide. "It was another welcome-home surprise, but it'll have to wait a few days until your grandfather leaves." Thinking of Chase's plan to move the judge to Highland Falls, she grimaced and opened her mouth to correct herself but didn't get a chance.

"Days? Are you kidding me? No way I'm waiting that long to

see you in this, babe." He lifted the barely-there red lace negligee out of the bag and waggled his eyebrows. "I'll take the judge to the inn as soon as we've eaten. And Mommy will put you"—he gently tapped a finger on Michaela's nose—"into bed as soon as Daddy steps out the door."

She knew she should leave it alone. She was totally on board with his plan, but she couldn't help feeling Chase was keeping something from her. "I thought we agreed your grandfather was staying with us."

"He'll be more comfortable at the inn. We're not really set up for guests."

It was true. But Chase's unwillingness to meet her gaze said the change of plans had nothing to do with their lack of space.

"Let's get this over with," he said, confirming her suspicions.

She didn't like to see him this way—tense and angry, no doubt worried how he was going to keep the peace between her and his grandfather. "Hey." She reached for his hand when he went to open the door. "Don't let your grandfather's feelings for me cause a rift between you. I understand where he's coming from. I can stand up for myself. You don't have to protect me."

"I know you can. But you shouldn't have to."

"Maybe I won't. Maybe we'll have a perfectly delightful dinner together."

He made a face. "Don't hold your breath."

An hour later, as they sat around the dinner table, Sadie wished she'd kept her mouth closed. Either Chase was taking her at her word or he didn't realize that his grandfather's smiling face and congenial manner were a ruse. She'd spent the entire dinner tiptoeing around the conversational minefields the judge set up for her.

"So when's the big wedding?" he said with a smile, and then winced as if he'd mistakenly stepped on the biggest mine-field of all.

Sadie wasn't buying it. The judge had an agenda. She could tell by the speculative glance he cast in Chase's direction.

"We haven't decided on a—" Sadie began, looking at Chase to help her out. But he was imitating an airplane with Michaela's rubber spoon, trying to get her to open her mouth.

"I shouldn't have asked. You'll have to forgive an old man for wanting to see his grandson happily married before he dies."

Sadie caught Chase's broad shoulders rise and fall on a sigh and waited for him to say something. But all he did was make the sound of an airplane sputtering in a death spiral before crashing it into Michaela's bowl of rice cereal—much to the delight of her daughter, who giggled.

While the two of them laughed and smiled, Sadie was left to reassure Chase's grandfather. "I'm sure that's not something you have to worry about, Jonathan. Chase and I just haven't gotten around to talking about wedding plans. Have we, *honey*?" She wondered if the man she loved picked up on the *help me out here* in her voice.

"No, we haven't," Chase said, getting up to walk to the refrigerator.

Sadie stared at him. Did he think that was helpful? He could have been a little more enthusiastic.

"I've made a mess of it, haven't I? I hope you'll accept my apologies, Sadie. The last thing I want is to create problems between you two."

As if she'd believe that, Sadie thought, while her gaze remained on Chase.

The judge leaned toward her and patted her hand. "I'm sure it will be different for the two of you. He was much younger when he asked Gwen to marry him."

"Gwen?" She realized her mistake as soon as she blurted the woman's name. She should have simply smiled and talked about it with Chase later. Instead, she'd given the judge the opening he'd obviously been looking for.

"Oh my, I seem to have put my foot in my mouth again. Sorry, my boy. I'd assumed you would have told Sadie about Gwen. She played such an important role in your life. His first love, you know. They met at Yale."

"It was a long time ago, Judge. I'm sure Sadie isn't interested." Clearly uncomfortable with the conversation, Chase squeezed the banana puree he'd retrieved from the refrigerator into a bowl for Michaela with a little more force than was necessary.

But he was wrong. Sadie was very much interested in this woman who'd obviously been important to him. A woman she'd heard absolutely nothing about. "Of course I am. Please go on, Jonathan."

Chase's grandfather dabbed at his mouth with a napkin. "It's probably best if I stay quiet. I wouldn't want my grandson tossing me out on my ear. I simply thought it would help for you to have some context as to why he might be dragging his feet on setting a wedding date. He's good at proposing, just not so good on the follow-through."

"Gwen and I weren't compatible. We were also too young. I have no problem setting a wedding date with Sadie. Like she said, we just haven't had time to talk about it."

"Not compatible?" The judge threw his napkin on the table. "I've never met a more compatible couple. You were both brilliant and ambitious, a power couple if I've ever seen one. Gwen was very disappointed that you turned down the promotion with the Washington bureau, my boy. But I'm sure you already know that. The last time Gwen and I were out for dinner together, she told me she'd called you and tried to change your mind. Gwen's with the DOJ," he explained to Sadie. "She helped Chase out on his last investigation. On the quiet, of course."

"I didn't realize you and Gwen saw each other socially," Chase said, spooning the banana puree into Michaela's mouth.

"We see each other more often now than we used to. She

knew how difficult it was for me when you left and visits me once a week. She's a very thoughtful woman." The judge smiled. It was a *cat's got the cream* smile if Sadie had ever seen one.

Chase gave a noncommittal grunt while still avoiding her gaze burning a hole in the back of his white shirt.

Sadie's smile was so forced it felt like rigor mortis had set in. It took a moment for her to unclench her teeth. "How nice."

"Oh my, it appears I may have given you the wrong impression, my dear. My grandson is as loyal as they come. He'd never think of stepping out on you with another woman, no matter the temptation."

Sadie was tempted to dump the last of her pasta on the older man's head.

Before she had a chance to formulate a more appropriate response—with words instead of actions—Chase swiveled in the chair with an incredulous expression on his drop-dead gorgeous face. "What are you even talking about, Judge? Of course Sadie knows I wouldn't cheat on her."

Chase was smart—brilliant, in fact—but sometimes, like in this instance, he was clueless.

Chapter Four

♥

Sadie stifled another jaw-cracking yawn while she waited with Mallory for Bliss, the owner of Bites of Bliss on Main Street, to get organized for today's cake tasting at the bakery.

"That's your third yawn in the last five minutes. It's either my company or Chase must have really loved his welcome home surprise from Blushing Bridal," Mallory said with a teasing grin.

Sadie lowered her voice. The bakery was long and narrow and already crowded with people wanting to take part in the Say Yea or Nay to the Wedding Cake segment for Abby's YouTube channel. "It's not you, and my welcome home surprise didn't go according to plan. I mean, Chase liked what he saw of the lingerie in the bag but I didn't get a chance to model it for him. He got called into work on his way to the inn to drop off his grandfather, and I stayed up half the night cleaning the cottage while I waited for him to come home."

Binge-watching the latest British crime drama on Netflix was typically her stress-busting activity of choice but dinner with the judge had left her feeling inadequate, like she and Chase weren't as compatible as she thought. Certainly not as compatible as he was with Gwen.

She must have made a face at the thought of the other woman because Mallory said, "I'm taking it dinner with his grandfather didn't go well."

Sadie was a private person. Even with her closest friends, she wasn't as forthcoming as they were. But in this instance, she really wanted a second opinion, so she shared the judge's bombshell about Chase's ex-fiancée with Mallory. Sadie was probably worried about nothing, but if anyone could alleviate her fears, it would be Mallory.

"What did Chase say? Did he tell you why he's never mentioned Gwen? You'd think she'd have come up before now, especially since they'd obviously been working together in Washington this summer."

Okay, so maybe sharing was overrated. Mallory seemed as concerned about Chase's relationship with Gwen as Sadie was. "We didn't have a lot of time to talk about it. I was asleep when he got home, and he had to go into work early this morning. But it probably wouldn't matter if we'd had the entire morning to talk. When I brought it up, he got the same look on his face that he does when Granny talks to him about unicorns and fairies or when I try to explain why Darcey still has feelings for Tom on *90 Day Fiancé*. Chase honestly doesn't understand what I'm concerned about. He says he loves me, and that's all that matters."

"He does have a point. It's obvious to everyone how much he loves you."

The tension in Sadie's shoulders released. Maybe sharing wasn't overrated after all. Or so she thought until Mallory added, "But now that his grandfather knows Chase kept his relationship with Gwen a secret from you, he'll bring her up at every opportunity in hopes of driving a wedge between you."

"I said the same thing to Chase but he just doesn't get it. He said the only way the judge could drive a wedge between us is if we didn't trust or love each other as much as we do. To his way of thinking, Gwen is about as much a nonissue as Drew." Drew was Sadie's ex and Michaela's biological father.

"I guess I can see where he's coming from. I mean, you, me, and Abby didn't exactly go into our relationships without some baggage. For that matter, neither did Gabe, Hunter, or, obviously, Chase."

"You're right, and maybe I'm just imagining Gwen was Chase's perfect match because of what his grandfather said."

Sadie smiled at Bliss, moving aside so she and her other baker could get by with the tray of cake slices. Abby's wedding cake choices had come down to the top three vote getters: chocolate with salted caramel frosting, ginger carrot with buttercream frosting, and spiced pear with honey-caramel frosting. The winning design had already been chosen by Abby's social media followers, and Bliss had assured Abby she could make the design work for any of the flavors. It would be a three-tier cake decorated with ruffled frosting, muted flowers, and wispy grasses.

"I swear I could eat that entire tray of cake by myself." Mallory rubbed her baby bump and smiled. "Good thing I have an excuse." She gave Sadie's shoulder a comforting squeeze. "Now put Chase's grandfather and Gwen out of your mind and enjoy—"

"Who's Gwen?" Abby asked as she left a group of women to join them.

Before Sadie could get the words "nobody important" out of her mouth, Mallory said, "Chase's ex-fiancée."

Her eyes going wide, Abby looked from Mallory to Sadie. "I didn't know Chase had an ex-fiancée."

"It's not im—" Sadie began before Mallory chimed in.

"Neither did Sadie. Chase's grandfather brought her up last night after asking Sadie and Chase when they were getting married. He thinks Gwen is the reason they haven't set a date."

Sadie stared at Mallory. "That's not what I said." She felt like she was in a game of telephone where everything got mixed up and blown out of proportion. "Anyway, we have an episode to film. We can talk about this later."

She nudged Abby toward the table at the front of the room where they'd set up a laptop for the twelve lucky subscribers from *Abby Does Highland Falls* to join in on Zoom for the tasting. They'd shipped their boxes of cake to them a couple days before.

Abby dug in her heels. "Hang on a minute. This is too important."

"Trust me, it's not. But your wedding is, and so is this episode. You don't want to disappoint your fans, do you?" Sadie shot Mallory a *now look what you've done* glance. They'd talked about Abby's lack of enthusiasm for her own wedding just yesterday. Their best friend was looking for any excuse to get out of finalizing her wedding plans.

Abby blinked and then got a smile on her face that made Sadie nervous. "I know exactly how you can shut down Chase's grandfather's plot to break you guys up. Set a wedding date."

"Sure. We'll get right on that. Tonight, in fact," Sadie said, knowing that Abby wouldn't be satisfied with half measures or open-ended promises.

At the sudden gleam in Abby's green eyes, Sadie braced herself for whatever her friend had come up with. Because that was definitely an *I've got the best idea ever* look in her eyes. Sadie should know; she'd seen it many times before. "How about October twenty-third?" Abby grinned.

"Sounds perfect. I won't have to think of anything. I'll just borrow all your ideas and decorations. But it won't be October twenty-third next year, it'll be October twenty-second."

"I wasn't talking about next year, silly. I was talking about this year." Abby grabbed Sadie's hands. "Say yes, please say yes. It'll be perfect."

Say no, say a hard no, Sadie told herself. She had problems saying no, especially to Abby. "Abs, I love that you want us to have a double wedding." After what her psychic cousin had said, Sadie hoped something hadn't gotten lost in translation and that Abby wasn't planning a bride switcheroo. "Maybe if it was, say, eight months away," Sadie continued, "I'd think about it. But it's in a few weeks' time."

When the excitement in Abby's eyes faded and she got a dejected look on her face, Sadie blurted, "I'll talk to Chase," kicking herself as soon as the words came out of her mouth. She couldn't help it. Abby had to look like the happy bride-to-be that her subscribers, not to mention half the town, expected. Sadie would find a way to let her down gently later. They had a week before they filmed the Say Yea or Nay to the Wedding Menu segment.

Abby's face lit up. "Really?"

"Yes, really. Now go before Bliss bites her fingernails to the quick." Sadie nodded at the bakery's owner, who stood behind the comfy, white high-back chair they'd brought in for the occasion. It went perfectly with the bakery's robin's-egg-blue decor.

Abby gave Sadie and Mallory exuberant hugs before winding her way through the tables, greeting the audience effusively.

"Someone is in a much happier mood than they were yesterday," Mallory observed as they made their way to the table to the right of Abby's. Sadie stopped at the tripod first to check the angle of the camera, which she could pause and start with a remote control. That way she could enjoy the tasting too.

She waited until they got settled at their table to share her concerns with Mallory. "You don't think that was a play by Abby to get out of her wedding by making me the bride-to-be, do you?"

Mallory frowned, turning in her chair to look at Abby, who was welcoming everyone to the cake tasting. "No, I don't think so. I mean, she hasn't exactly been acting like the Abby we know and love, but I'm sure she's just nervous. A lot of brides get pre-wedding jitters."

"Did you?"

Mallory smiled. "No. But our wedding was spur of the moment. It was just me, Gabe, the boys, and a couple of witnesses on the beach." Gabe had proposed when they were on vacation with their sons at spring break. "Abby's basically having a wedding with millions of people attending, even if the majority of them will be online. That would make me nervous too."

"Because you don't like to be the center of attention. But Abby thrives on it."

At that moment, Abby turned the laptop, introducing everyone in the bakery to twelve of her super-fans, who'd won the chance to take part in the cake tasting. Concerned that the angle of the camera might not capture the fans' faces, Sadie got up from the chair and hurried over to the tripod, apologizing to the women sitting at the surrounding tables as she did so.

Abby smiled. "Hey guys, let's put our hands together for Sadie. She's the one who makes the magic happen behind the scenes."

Everyone in the bakery and on-screen clapped, and Abby led them in a cheer for her. Sadie smiled her thanks and gave a little wave. When the clapping and cheering died down, Abby grinned and said, "I have some super exciting breaking news for you guys, but I might need some help from you to make it happen."

Abby's announcement was met with shouts of "What is it? What do we need to do?"

Sadie glanced up from the viewfinder to find Abby looking at her with her eyebrows raised. *No*, Sadie mouthed, shaking her head, only to find that the audience's attention was now on her too.

Babs Sutherland waved a hand. "I know, I know. Sadie set a wedding date!"

"No. Sadie has not set a wedding date," Sadie said, thinking she was going to kill her best friend when the audience began shouting their suggestions on the best time of year for her to get married.

Abby put her fingers between her lips and whistled loudly. The room went quiet. "Okay, so as you can see, my bestie isn't totally on board with sharing our news just yet. So it's up to us to convince her that October twenty-third would be the absolute perfect day for her to get married."

"We're going to have a double wedding!" several older women cried, including Babs.

Sadie bowed her head. It felt like she was on a runaway train that she had no chance of stopping. She looked up to have her worst fears confirmed. Babs's fingers were flying on her phone. By now, the owner of Spill the Tea had no doubt texted the news to anyone who wasn't at the bakery. Which meant that the news would spread throughout the entire town of Highland Falls and beyond by tonight.

Abby must have picked up on Sadie's panic because she once again whistled for quiet. "Let's not put the cart before the horse. Sadie needs to talk to her fiancé first. Although why he wouldn't want to marry this incredible woman as soon as possible is beyond me."

Sadie could say the same about Abby, who'd been dragging her heels about setting a wedding date with Hunter, who was an amazing man. In the end, it had been Hunter's aunt, Elsa, who'd forced the issue, setting the date for the couple. Sort of like Abby was doing for Sadie.

At that moment, she had a better understanding of how Abby must have felt. Just like Elsa, Abby probably thought her wedding-date intervention was in Sadie's best interest. If it served to shut down the judge's plot to break them up, she supposed there might be merit to the plan.

It wasn't like Sadie didn't want to marry Chase or hadn't given it some thought over the past few months. An image of her walking down the aisle toward Chase appeared before her eyes, and Sadie found herself smiling.

"Do you see that? I think we might be winning her over, guys," Abby said.

Damn it. "No, I just—"

"Okay, no pressure, sweetie. Well, maybe a little pressure. But just in case you're doing this, you need to pick a cake too so get over here."

Sadie narrowed her eyes as she made her way to Abby's side. "You said 'in case you're doing this,' not 'in case we're doing this.' This would be a *double* wedding, wouldn't it?"

Abby waved her off. "Of course, of course," but she wouldn't meet Sadie's gaze.

"Abby—" Sadie began, only to have Abby ignore her and turn a radiant smile on Bliss. "Let's give a big round of applause to Bliss for hosting the sampling and making the cakes." Abby clapped and cheered along with the audience. "You'll all be happy to know that Bliss has each of the cakes available for sale and to order," Abby said once the appreciative noise had died down. "So let's show her our thanks and support by buying everything she has in stock. Now, everyone ready? Forks up. Let the sampling begin!"

In between sampling the cakes, Sadie lifted her phone to film the audience. She blinked at the number of text messages on her cell. She'd asked everyone to turn off the sound when they'd first arrived, and she'd done the same. If her grandmother needed her, she would send someone to get her. They were only a couple stores away.

She took a few minutes to film the live and online audiences' enthusiastic responses to the cakes and went back to finishing up her own. All three were amazing, but it was the chocolate cake with salted caramel that won Sadie over. So much so that she was tempted to lick the plate.

She leaned back in her chair and whispered to Bliss, "Can you reserve one of these for me?" She pointed to her empty cake plate.

Beside her, Abby laughed. "It looks like Sadie's made her pick. Let's see if you guys agreed with her. Which cake did you pick for Sadie?" The majority of people held up the number one.

"It wasn't hard. She looked like she was having an orgasm when she was eating it." Babs laughed.

Sadie's cheeks heated. "Thanks, Babs."

"Don't even think about editing that out," Abby said. Then she asked the audience, "I'm having a hard time deciding between cakes two and three, so help me out, guys. Which one did you pick for me?"

Cake number three—spiced pear with honey-caramel frosting—won out for Abby.

"Perfect, and I'll take one to go, Bliss." Abby glanced from cake number two to Mallory, who got a nervous expression on her face.

Sadie understood why when she got a look at the gleam in Abby's eyes.

"I've just had a brilliant idea. Mallory, get up here." Abby leaned over to pull another chair beside her.

"It's okay. I'm good right here," Mallory said.

"Please, for me." Abby fluttered her eyelashes. When Mallory didn't look like she was going to move, Abby started chanting, "Mallory, Mallory," and the rest of the audience joined in, clapping when Mallory finally complied.

"I'm already married and almost nine months pregnant, so don't even think about—" Mallory began as she lowered herself into the chair.

"But *we* weren't at your wedding," Abby said, putting an arm around Sadie's shoulders and bringing their heads together. "And neither were your other friends and neighbors. Come on, what do you say? It'll be perfect. You and Gabe can renew your vows."

If the town of Highland Falls had been excited about Abby's wedding, they were over the moon at the idea of three best friends getting married together. Even Sadie found herself getting a little caught up in the excitement of the moment, cheering when Mallory reluctantly agreed. And then Sadie remembered. She had to consult the groom.

Chapter Five

♥

How are you going to break the news to Chase?" Mallory said from between her teeth, her face frozen in a strained smile that Sadie imagined mirrored her own. As the audience filed out of the bakery loaded down with boxed cakes, cookies, and cupcakes, shouting their congratulations as they left, they took their contagious excitement with them, leaving Mallory and Sadie to brood over the situation they found themselves in.

"I have no idea. I'm still trying to figure out when I agreed to it. I'm positive I said I'd think about it," Sadie said.

"It might have been how you reacted not only to the cake but the wedding talk. You looked like you were into it, even more than Abby."

"I guess I got caught up in the moment. Everyone was happy and having fun...It was contagious."

"You can't back out. You're the reason I agreed to do it. Well, you and Abby. All for one, and one for all, right?"

Sadie laughed despite the nervous jitters in her stomach at the thought of telling Chase what she'd done. "So we're the Three Musketeers now?"

Mallory grinned. "The boys were watching the movie with Gabe when I left."

"I wondered where Teddy was."

"Nothing interferes with father and sons' movie day."

"At least you know Teddy will be thrilled you and Gabe are renewing your vows."

She nodded and then made a face. "I'm pretty sure Gabe won't be."

"How are you going to break the news to him?" Sadie asked. She could use some inspiration.

"I'm not sure, but I think I'd better figure it out fast," Mallory said, giving a finger-wave to someone in the bakery window. "Same goes for you."

Sadie turned, groaning at the crowd outside that included a reporter and photographer for the *Highland Falls Herald*. "I knew the news would go viral as soon as Babs got out her phone, but I thought we might have at least a few hours' reprieve." She pulled her cell phone from the back pocket of her jeans. "I'd better give Chase a heads-up." She needed to let her family know too, but it wasn't their reactions she was worried about. They'd all be thrilled, especially her grandmother.

Abby hugged Bliss and then came over to join them, waving at the crowd. "Oh my gosh, look at how excited everyone is." She frowned. "Everyone but you guys. What's wrong?"

"What's wrong? We've just agreed to get married—in Mallory's case, remarried—and our grooms have no idea that we'll be dragging them to the altar in a few weeks' time."

"Right." Abby grimaced and nodded at the door. "It looks like they might have some idea what's going on."

Chase held the door open for Sadie's grandmother, who pushed the stroller into the bakery, followed by Teddy and Gabe.

"Is it true?" Teddy asked. "Are we getting married again?"

Sadie didn't hear Mallory's answer. Her grandmother had

given her a hug while declaring it was the best news she'd heard since Sadie and Chase had gotten engaged. Michaela, picking up on the excitement, squealed and clapped her hands.

Chase and Gabe, who'd become good friends while working on Sadie's brother's case last summer, stood shoulder to shoulder at the door—their arms crossed, heads cocked, and eyebrows raised.

"Aww, look at how gorgeous you guys are. My subscribers are going to love—" Abby began before Sadie and Mallory cut her off, saying at almost the same time, "I can explain."

"You go first," Sadie said to Mallory.

"Thanks a lot," Mallory murmured.

"Coffee and cake are on the house," Bliss said, casting a nervous glance at the silent and serious men blocking her door.

"Bring me a piece when you're done. I have to get back to the store," Agnes said. She patted Sadie's cheek with a fond smile and then kissed Michaela goodbye. She said something to Chase and Gabe on her way out the door that made both men sigh.

"That's a great idea. You guys can try your wedding ca…" Abby glanced from Sadie and Mallory to Gabe and Chase. "Okay, so maybe I'll just —" She groaned when Hunter opened the door, nudging Chase and Gabe to either side so he could stand between them. The three men shared noncommittal grunts she assumed were their version of *hey*, as well as similar *what the hell is going on?* expressions on their faces. Hunter had also bonded with Chase last summer, and Gabe the summer before.

"It's Abby's fault," Sadie blurted under Chase's penetrating stare.

Mallory nodded. "She made us do it."

"Hey, what happened to all for one and one for all?" Abby protested. She must have overheard Sadie and Mallory's earlier conversation, which wasn't a surprise. Abby had a severe case of FOMO—fear of missing out.

"It's true, Dad. Abby's real nervous about her wedding, and it'd make her feel better if she had her friends getting married with her." Teddy looked around at the adults. "Did I say something wrong?"

"No, of course you didn't," Abby said with a strained smile.

Hunter moved to his fiancée's side, lifting her chin with his knuckle to get her to look at him. "Is that why you've been acting weird these past few weeks? You don't want to get married?"

"I never said I don't want to get married. I just..." She lifted a shoulder. "It's been a lot, that's all."

"You didn't say you *wanted* to get married either." Hunter rubbed his head. "Neither did I, for that matter. I guess we just let Aunt Elsa ride roughshod over us and gave in."

Abby's eyes welled with tears. "You don't want to marry me?"

Hunter held up his hands. "No, that's not what I said. I'm good with whatever you want, babe. It's not a big deal."

Sadie winced, glancing at Mallory who did the same. This was going downhill fast.

Abby wiped at her eyes with angry swipes. "A wedding isn't a big deal or marrying me isn't a big deal?"

Hunter glanced at Chase and Gabe as if looking for guidance. *Good luck with that*, Sadie thought. "I think we should all sit down and have some cake," she suggested.

Hunter pulled out a chair for Abby, who took a seat and crossed her arms. Hunter sighed and took the chair beside her. Teddy dragged Michaela's stroller beside his chair, leaning in to say in an overloud whisper, "I don't know what all the fuss is about. Weddings are fun."

"Unless the groom doesn't want to marry you," Abby muttered.

Hunter said, "I didn't say that."

Taking a seat beside his wife, Gabe said, "Don't look at me. I already did the deed."

Mallory raised an eyebrow. "Really? You already did the *deed*?"

Gabe scooped up a forkful of cake and shoved it in his mouth.

"I didn't say anything," Chase said when Sadie shot him a look. "I didn't even know you wanted to get married."

Sadie held up her hand, the gorgeous diamond engagement ring he'd given her sparkling in the sunlight shining through the bakery window. "I said yes, didn't I?"

"Well, yeah, but every time I brought it up, you said we had lots of time." He cocked his head. "This doesn't have anything to do with Gwen, does it?"

"Of course not. Why would you even think that?"

"Maybe because she's all you wanted to talk about this morning."

"Who's Gwen?" Hunter and Gabe asked at almost the same time.

"Chase's ex-fiancée, who I knew nothing about until his grandfather brought her up last night." She glanced at the time on her phone. "Aren't you supposed to be bringing him to the airport?"

"He heard that we were getting married and decided not to leave."

So instead of the wedding thwarting the judge's plan as Abby had suggested, it sounded like it might have had the opposite effect, and he was going to up his game. Abby grimaced and mouthed, *Sorry*, while Mallory reached across the table and patted Sadie's hand.

"So was he happy about the news? I imagine he must be. He certainly was all about us setting a date last night," Sadie said.

Chase ran a finger under the collar of his white dress shirt. "I'm sure he will be. He was just a little surprised."

"And what about you? How do you feel about us getting married on the twenty-third?"

He hesitated, glancing from Hunter to Gabe. "Ah, good." He must have read something on her face because he added, "Really good?"

She wondered if he heard the question in his own voice. From Gabe's and Hunter's pained grimaces, they certainly had. A call coming in on her cell phone saved her from responding. It was her cousin.

"Hey, Ellie. I'm guessing you heard our happy news." She shot Chase a pointed glance. Obviously he got her meaning because he rubbed the back of his neck.

"I did, but that's not why I'm calling. The judge just booked a room for someone named Gwen. I got the feeling she and Chase shared a past. I hate to tell you this, but I think he's trying to stop your wedding."

"He'll have to get in line. His grandson is doing a good job of that all by himself."

"Okay, that doesn't sound good. Listen, I'll spend some time with the judge. Maybe then I'll have a better idea what's really behind this. I'll call you once I do, and we can take it from there."

As soon as Sadie disconnected, she pulled up WhatsApp and shared Ellie's news with Mallory and Abby. Seconds later, both women stared at her, their mouths hanging open.

"Is something wrong?" Chase asked.

"Other than the men we love not wanting to marry us, you mean?" Abby said, pushing back her chair. "But don't worry, we can have perfectly wonderful weddings without you guys. We'll just marry ourselves, if we have to. Come on, ladies, we need to pick out your dresses asap or they won't be in on time."

Chapter Six

♥

Chase stared out the bakery window at the three women and his daughter heading down Main Street. "What just happened?"

"You messed up," Teddy said around a mouthful of cake.

"He's right," Hunter said. "What were you thinking not telling Sadie about your ex-fiancée?"

"It was years ago. Long before Sadie and I ever met," he said defensively, at a loss as to why everyone was making an issue of it. To his way of thinking, what Hunter said was worse than an old girlfriend slipping Chase's mind. "At least I didn't say getting married wasn't a big deal."

Teddy nodded. "Yeah, that was pretty dumb."

Gabe grimaced. "I'm not crazy about you using the word dumb, son. But in this instance, you have a point. He's right, Hunter. Pregnant women are extremely sensitive. You have to choose your words carefully."

"Whoa, you're really lucky Abby and Mom aren't here, Dad. You'd be in bigger trouble than you already are."

"Okay, would someone like to tell me what I said that was so wrong?"

Hunter and Chase pointed at Teddy. "He'll tell you."

"Before or just now?" Gabe's son asked.

"All right, I get your point. I was being insensitive to Mom's feelings when I said I'd done the deed. But the whole renewing-the-vows thing caught me by surprise. I can see it if we've been married for years but—"

"It's not like it was a real wedding. You only did it because you found out about the baby," Teddy said.

Gabe looked stunned. "Is that what your mom thinks?"

Teddy shrugged. "I don't know. That's what some of the boys at school said to Dylan," he said, referring to his eleven-year-old brother.

"Is that so, and who would those boys be?"

"It's okay, Dad. Oliver took care of them." Oliver was Mallory's sixteen-year-old stepson.

"But you guys know that the only reason I married Mallory is because I love her, right?"

"Sure. But love is a verb, Dad. Without action it doesn't mean anything."

Gabe narrowed his eyes at his son. "Have you been reading your mother's romance novels?"

"Maybe." Teddy grinned and then said, "We did a class project on love in February. That's where I learned about love being a verb and stuff."

"Okay. So, Teddy, what do you think we should do to make this right?" Chase asked.

"You're asking a six-year-old for relationship advice?" Hunter said, then winced. "No offense, Teddy."

"None taken," Teddy said amicably.

"Teddy might be six but he seems to have more insights into Abby, Mallory, and Sadie than we do. I don't know about you two, but I'm open to any help I can get," Chase said.

"I'm almost seven but I don't really know much about kissing-and-making-up stuff. I don't have a girlfriend. If me and my friends hurt each other's feelings, we just say sorry and then we go and play. Maybe you should read my mom's romance books."

Gabe ruffled his son's hair. "Maybe we should."

Or talk to Teddy's teacher, Chase thought. But surely between the three of them they could figure this out. After all, Hunter was former special forces, Gabe was chief of police, and Chase was an FBI agent. They'd worked a high-profile case together last summer and had a successful outcome. This was really no different.

"We need to approach this like we would any other case. First, let's identify the crime and the players." Chase was used to having a board and photographic evidence when presenting a case, so he moved the three cake slices to the center of the table to represent the unhappy women in their lives. "Because of our ineptitude"—he gathered up three coffee cups and lined them up to the side of the plates—"we've given Sadie, Mallory, and Abby the impression that we don't want to get married on the twenty-third."

The laughter Hunter was obviously trying to hold back came out in his voice. "I'm beginning to understand why you didn't think it was necessary to tell Sadie about your ex-fiancée."

Chase wasn't sure what Hunter meant by that, but at least Hunter now understood where Chase had been coming from. However, it wasn't Hunter he needed to convince. But if they could solve this problem, Chase was positive everything else would fall into place. "We need to stay focused. It all comes down to convincing Sadie, Mallory, and Abby that we're on board with their wedding plans. Now we just have to figure—"

"But are we on board with all of us getting married on the twenty-third?" Gabe said, moving one of the coffee cups out of line. "Mallory, Abby, and Sadie are smart. If we're just going through the motions to make them happy, they'll see right through us, and we could wind up making things worse."

"You have a point." Chase nudged the coffee cup Gabe had moved back in line with the others. "So I guess the question is: Do our reasons for not getting married on the twenty-third outweigh our objective to make the women we love happy? I can only speak for myself, but I don't have an issue with it. If Sadie wanted to get married today, I would."

"I guess my only issue is that Mallory and I are already married," Gabe said. "I thought it was a nice wedding, private and kind of romantic. But after what Teddy said, maybe I was wrong. So yeah, I'm good with whatever makes Mallory happy."

"Honestly, since all this wedding crap began, Abby hasn't been happy. She hasn't been acting like herself. But if the three of them getting married on the same day makes her happy, I'm game," Hunter said.

"Good, so we're all agreed." Except Chase felt like he was missing something. He went back over each of their responses to his question, and then his gaze went to the slices of cake. He picked up his fork, using it like a pointer. "Cake is beautiful. It smells amazing, tastes even better. Eating cake is an emotional experience." He moved his pointer. "Coffee cups are solid, stoic, and—"

"Are you going somewhere with this?" Hunter asked.

Chase looked up to see the two men and Teddy watching him with their brows furrowed.

"Sorry, I tend to talk through a case."

"You were talking about cake and coffee cups," Gabe pointed out.

"Yes, and now I know what's wrong with our plan."

Hunter scratched his head. "I didn't know we had one."

"That's true too. But now we do. When I went over our responses, I realized we were making the same mistake. We were willing to go through with the wedding, not because we necessarily want to but because Sadie, Mallory, and Abby do.

We want to make them happy, which is a noble reason. Except they're the cake and we're the coffee cups. We need to become the cake. We need to become as invested in the wedding as they are. If they sense a lack of enthusiasm on our part, they'll assume we don't want to get married, and we'll be back to square one. And, as we've seen, square one is not a good place to be."

"So how do you propose we become invested in the wedding?" Gabe asked.

"We need to learn everything we can about weddings." Chase Googled *wedding planning*, scanned through several links, found what he was looking for, and sent the page to Gabe and Hunter.

They went line by line through the list together. "Already have the venue," Hunter said. "We're having it outside at the farm so we don't need to decorate."

"I'm not sure that's true," Gabe said. "Mal loves to decorate."

Chase pulled up Abby's social media and checked out her upcoming events. "They're voting on the decor next week so we should probably put together a few ideas."

"Pumpkins," Teddy said. "You have to have pumpkins."

"Okay, sounds good," Chase said, and checked the box.

"Music is taken care of. My brother's band, Culloden, will be playing," Hunter said.

"Would that be the same brother that had me chasing a nonexistent moose down Main Street?" Chase asked. Hunter's brother was with the forestry service, and Chase had done a stint as a park ranger when he was undercover last summer.

Hunter laughed. "Yep, one and the same."

Gabe chuckled and then looked back at the list. He made a face. "Flowers? We're not choosing flowers."

Chase and Hunter agreed and crossed it off their lists.

"There's no beer on here, just soda and wine. How about a taste testing at Highland Brew? Anyone else up for that?" Hunter asked.

"Put me down," Chase said.

"Me too," Gabe said.

Teddy raised his hand. "Me four."

Gabe laughed. "Good try, honey, but we're doing a men's night out."

Chase looked at the next line. "Tuxes and colors? I don't know about you guys, but I vote for a simple black tux."

"No way, you're both wearing kilts like me. Chase, you're a Roberts, your grandfather's a Knight. You've probably got Scots in your line somewhere. Same goes for you, Buchanan. Besides, even if you didn't have a drop of Scottish blood in you, you live in Highland Falls so you're an honorary Scot now at the very least."

"Wedding planning isn't as difficult as I thought it would be," Chase said, holding up his phone. "We've pretty much completed the list. Cake's next." He glanced at the plates on the table. "We could get this one done right now. Bliss." He waved over the bakery's owner. "Have Sadie, Mallory, and Abby picked out their wedding cakes?"

"Yes." She cast a nervous glance around the table. "Is there still going to be a wedding?"

"Of course there is. Why would you think there isn't?" Chase asked, surprised at her question.

"The reporter from the *Herald* called. He seemed to be under the impression the wedding was off."

"I don't know why." Although he could guess. Earlier, they obviously hadn't looked like happy couples about to get married. But that was about to change. "We can't wait for the big day, can we?" he said to Gabe and Hunter.

Hunter, who was digging into a piece of cake, gave Bliss a thumbs-up.

Around a mouthful of cake, Gabe said, "Can't wait." Then he added, "This is really good."

"I'm glad you like it, especially as it's the cake Mallory picked. In fact," she said with a smile, "you've all chosen the same cake as your brides-to-be did."

Chase shared a *we're good* grin with Hunter and Gabe. "Would you mind showing us what the cakes will look like?"

"Oh, they're all the same. I'll just change the flavor for each of them."

"That sounds great, but would it be possible for us to choose our own cake designs? It'll be a little more personal then." She seemed to be hesitating so Chase added, "As you can see, we're all excited about the big day and want to be as involved as possible."

"Right. Of course. I'll, um, get you the book, and you can choose what you'd like."

It took them almost an hour to decide. Hunter overruled Abby's design choice, proclaiming it too girlie. He wanted more of a woodsy feel, which he felt suited them both better. The white frosted cake would be decorated with leaves, ferns, and feathers, and would sit atop a wooden platter that Hunter would make.

Gabe, with help from Teddy, picked an elegant cake decorated with gold-speckled accents and fall-colored roses, while Chase went with something called a semi-naked cake that was wrapped in branches. It had an outdoorsy feel that he thought would appeal to Sadie but was more delicate than Hunter and Abby's.

Bliss proclaimed their choices spectacular and went to make up their bills. Before she did, they each took a photo of their cake.

"I'll admit I had my doubts, but I enjoyed that. I actually feel part of the wedding now," Hunter said.

"I think we did good. Now to see what our brides-to-be think," Chase said. "And yes, I know Mallory is already your wife, Gabe, but let's just go with that."

"It's a good idea, Dad. Mom never really got to do all the fun stuff, and now she can."

Gabe scrubbed his face. "I really messed up. We'd both had big weddings before, and I just thought . . . Maybe this is a good idea after all. I don't want Mallory to feel like she missed out."

"It's going to be the best wedding ever!" Teddy proclaimed.

"Yes, now we just have to convince our brides-to-be that we're as excited about the wedding as they are, or they might go ahead and marry themselves," Chase said.

"Is that really a thing?" Hunter asked.

"If Abby mentioned it, it probably is," Gabe said.

Chase Googled *marrying yourself*. "Gabe's right. It's a thing." He looked up from the screen. "Should we do an in-person cake reveal? They're just up the street."

"You can't see their dresses. It's bad luck," Teddy said.

"Right, the dresses. Should we offer some suggestions?" Chase asked. Even though Sadie would look beautiful in anything she wore, he wanted her to know he was invested.

"Abby already bought hers," Hunter said.

"Okay, well, we could pay for them then," Chase suggested.

"Money doesn't buy love. My teacher said so," Teddy informed him.

"We just bought the cakes so I don't know if that argument holds water," Chase said, sounding a little defensive. He couldn't afford for this to go wrong. "But what you said about you and your friends was a good idea, Teddy. We need to apologize for earlier, and then we should probably ask them to marry us again. They seem to have forgotten we asked when we put a ring on their fingers."

"And I actually put a wedding ring on Mal's."

"Dad."

"Yeah, yeah, I remember. It's a do-over. Maybe you two should take a page out of my book and start fresh," Gabe said to Chase and Hunter.

Chase nodded. "I'll Google *best wedding proposal ideas*."

Chapter Seven

♥

Sadie, Abby, and Mallory sat on the plush pink chairs in Blushing Bridal, sipping nonalcoholic champagne from crystal flutes. Lena, the owner, had taken one look at them when they walked in and offered them a drink. Sadie could use a shot of the real deal but didn't think it was fair to Mallory and Abby. Michaela sat in her stroller beside her, eyeing them cautiously over the bottle of apple juice she had in her mouth.

"Everything's okay, baby." Sadie leaned in and kissed her daughter's hand. "I think she picked up on the tension at the bakery. I imagine Teddy did too. Poor little guy. Sorry about that, Mal."

"What are you apologizing for?" Mallory said. "I was the one who overreacted. I knew what Gabe meant. I felt the same way, more or less. So I don't know why it bothered me as much as it did."

"I'm sure Gabe understands you're more emotional right now. It's not like he's a newbie at this," Sadie said, and then sighed. "I, on the other hand, don't have an excuse for snapping at Chase. It's no wonder the poor guy was surprised. He's brought up setting a date a couple of times."

"I wouldn't worry about it, Sadie. Chase is a smart man. I'm sure he wasn't surprised by your reaction. Not with his grandfather trying to break you guys up," Mallory said.

"Except he has no idea how far the judge is willing to go. But Chase was right. I let my worry about Gwen goad me into agreeing to the wedding. And that's a terrible reason for getting married."

Beside her, Abby sniffed, swiping at a tear that rolled down her cheek. Sadie wrapped an arm around her shoulders. "Don't cry, sweetie. I'm sure just like Chase and Gabe, Hunter understands what set you off. Your hormones are all over the place, and you've had a lot on your plate."

Abby shook her head. "No. You heard him. He doesn't want to marry me. He said so himself."

"No. What he said was that his aunt steamrolled you guys into setting a wedding date. But, Abs, be honest. Is it any surprise that Hunter might think you don't want to get married? You haven't exactly been acting like a happy bride-to-be."

"Sadie's right, sweetie." Mallory looked around. It was just the three of them. "You can tell us anything, you know. Nothing you say will go further than here. Do you want to get married?"

Abby chewed on her bottom lip and then shook her head. "I love Hunter with all my heart. I just don't want to marry him."

"Because you don't think he's your one?" Sadie asked, looking for an opening to get at what Ellie sensed was the real reason that Abby didn't want to get married.

Abby's eyes went wide. "Oh my gosh, how can you even say that? I thank God every single day that Hunter's in my life, that he loves me. He means everything to me, absolutely everything." Her eyes welled with fresh tears. "I knew this was going to happen. I knew the wedding would ruin everything."

"Abs, Hunter isn't Chandler," Sadie said, referring to Abby's first husband. "He adores you. You guys are perfect together.

And a wedding and a piece of paper aren't going to change how much you love each other."

"How can you say that? It already has. Hunter doesn't want to marry me."

"Take it from me, as someone who has 'done the deed,' as my husband says, not once but twice: the love you and Hunter have for each other doesn't go away just because you get married. Over time and with life's ups and downs, your love evolves. In most cases, it gets stronger. But sometimes, like with you and Chandler, you discover you weren't meant for each other after all."

"Chandler did the deciding, not me. Things changed between us right after the wedding. It was like I couldn't do anything right in his eyes from that day on. The more time he spent with me, the more he realized I wasn't what he wanted. He…he fell out of love with me. And now it's happening again. This wedding is changing everything."

"Unlike with Chandler, you and Hunter have been living together for more than a year. Up until you started planning the wedding, I've never seen you happier. The same goes for Hunter. Everyone says so," Sadie said.

"You see, even you can tell that the wedding has ruined everything."

"Um, no. What I think is that you've been acting like it will. You're creating a self-fulfilling prophecy, and you really have to stop that, sweetie. This isn't good for you or the baby, or for you and Hunter." Sadie took Abby's champagne flute from her and put it on the table. Then she took Abby's hands in hers. "It's time for you to put your past with Chandler behind you. It has nothing to do with your relationship or future with Hunter. You—"

"Actually, I don't think that's true," Mallory said.

"See?" Abby said. "I told you. Even Mal agrees with me."

"No, I don't. I think Sadie made a good point about you creating a self-fulfilling prophecy because you're scared. But you gave Sadie and me some really good advice not that long ago."

"I did?"

Mallory smiled. "You did. You told us that we had to go through the storm to find our rainbow. Chandler was your storm. Hunter, he's your rainbow."

"He is," Abby whispered. "He really is." She closed her eyes and bowed her head. "I've messed everything up, haven't I?"

"If you have, so have we," Sadie said. "But that's okay. We can make things right, because we were lucky enough to fall in love with amazing men who love us too. This was just a blip."

"You're right." Abby wiped her eyes. "But my blip was bigger than your blips. I need to do something special to make it up to Hunter. I've been acting like a crazy person these past few weeks. A witchy, hormonal crazy person."

"So," Sadie asked tentatively, "is the wedding still on?"

"Yes. I mean, I think so. If that's what Hunter wants." She looked from Sadie to Mallory. "What about you guys? I kind of steamrolled you into agreeing to get married on the twenty-third, just like Elsa did to me and Hunter." She held up her hand. "Before you answer, I want you to know that today was the most fun I had planning the wedding. There's nothing I'd love more than for the three of us to get married on the same day. And it has nothing to do with the number of views and subscribers for my channel going through the roof."

"I'm sure." Sadie laughed. "But I'm game if Chase is."

Mallory rolled her eyes. "That's as romantic as Gabe saying we did the deed." She smiled. "But if Gabe is good with it, so am I."

"Yay!" Abby pulled them in for a hug.

Michaela, who'd dozed off, jerked awake and started clapping.

"Oh my gosh, we have to get her a dress too. We'll have to call Cutie Patootie." Abby grinned, hugging them again. "We're going to have a blast. Once we get Hunter, Gabe, and Chase on board, that is."

The three of them turned as the bells over the door chimed, watching as a stream of women filed into Blushing Bridal. The majority of them were members of the Sisterhood, a group of the town's most influential women. Sadie, Abby, and Mallory were also members.

Before they could ask what was going on, Hunter's Aunt Elsa said, "I just got off the phone with that new reporter at the *Herald*. He said the wedding is canceled."

Abby blinked. "What? Where did he hear that?"

Babs, who was not a member of the Sisterhood, said, "That's what I asked him when he called me for a quote. I'm the *Herald*'s go-to person for the inside scoop, so you can imagine my surprise when he scooped me. Anyway, he said that his source was a close family member."

"Don't look at me," Elsa said. "I've been campaigning for this wedding since the two of them moved in together. Long before I found out about the baby."

"It wasn't me," Sadie's grandmother said. "I've got my dress picked out, and Colin is renting a tux as we speak." Colin and Agnes had been dating for several months and seemed to be serious.

"Since it wasn't Chase, Hunter, or Gabe—" Sadie began.

"Remember our blip? We can't know that for sure." Abby slumped in her chair.

"Yes, we can. Reporters use precise language. He would have said it was one of the grooms, not a close family member," Sadie said. "And I bet I know exactly who he got the quote from." Just as she was about to text her cousin, Ellie rushed into the store.

Her cousin looked from the crowd of women to Sadie, Mallory, and Abby. "You already heard."

"That the *Herald* is reporting our wedding is canceled? Yes, we heard. I was just going to text you to see if the judge had talked to the reporter," Sadie said.

Ellie wrinkled her nose and nodded. "He did. But don't worry, he didn't say anything about Gwen."

When several of the women, including her grandmother, asked who Gwen was, Sadie groaned. Ellie filled them in. Much to Sadie's surprise, all the women, with the exception of Babs, considered Gwen a nonissue. The same couldn't be said for the judge.

"We need to get him on board," Elsa said, and the other women agreed.

"Sadie, do you know why he has a problem with you?" asked Winter Johnson, the mayor and one of the founding members of the Sisterhood.

"I think I might be able to shed some light on that," Ellie said. "The judge hoped that Chase would marry someone like his grandmother. He credits her for his successful career."

"Ah, I see." Elsa nodded. "So that's where this Gwen person comes in. She lives in Washington and has the connections the judge believes his grandson needs."

"Yes, and the judge believes that one day Chase will regret giving up his chance of having a high-powered career," Ellie said.

"If you ask me, the judge should take a good long look at his life. His fancy career didn't seem to make him a happy man. His wife and his grandson did."

Sadie smiled at her grandmother. It was just like Agnes to get at the heart of the matter.

"All right, ladies. We have our work cut out for us and not a lot of time," Elsa said. "The judge needs to get a life. We need to find him a place to live and some friends, and a new love interest wouldn't hurt either."

"Jonathan seems happy at the inn, and I'm more than happy

for him to stay there. He's company for my grandfather," Ellie said.

And Sadie was sure her cousin could use the guaranteed income from the room rental. Ellie's grandfather had let the inn fall into disrepair. It was a bone of contention between Ellie and her mother, who wanted to sell the inn.

"All right, we have a place for the judge to live for now, and a friend, but I think we can hunt him up some more. So now we just need a love interest. Any suggestions?" Elsa asked.

"Don't look at me," Sadie's grandmother said. "I'm already taken."

"What about Zia Maria?" Ellie suggested. "The judge loves Italian food."

"Perfect. Now girls, pose with your champagne flutes in the air, and I'll take a photo and send it to that reporter." Elsa held up her phone and then lowered it. "Since the reporter's quoting Chase's grandfather, maybe we should get the grooms in the picture."

"I think we'd better talk to them first," Abby said. "We had a small...really small"—she pinched her thumb and forefinger together—"disagreement earlier at the bakery. We just need to sort a few things out."

Several phones started pinging with incoming texts. Ellie looked up from her screen and grinned. "I think Mallory and Gabe's disagreement is all sorted. I've just had a special reservation made for this evening that I should go and take care of."

"Really?" Mallory ducked her head with a smile, her cheeks pink.

Agnes looked up from her phone. "And it looks like my little sweetheart is spending the night with me. Seems Chase has plans for you, girlie."

Her grandmother's news burst the bubble of worries and fears that had been growing in Sadie's chest since they'd left the bakery. She felt like she was floating. But the smile that was spreading across her face fell when Abby, who was staring at her screen, began crying.

"What's wrong?" Sadie and Mallory asked at almost the same time.

"Hun...Hunter canceled the cake my subscribers picked." She held up her phone. "He picked this one instead." She was crying so hard that it was difficult to make out what she said, but it sounded like Hunter was also going to carve the cake stand. "He...he really does want to marry me." Abby's phone pinged two more times, and she hiccupped on a laugh. "Chase and Gabe picked yours too." She turned the screen to show Sadie and Mallory, and then pulled them in for a hug. "They really do want to marry us."

"Why are the three of them carrying on like that?"

"Pregnancy hormones," the mayor said. "I cried at the drop of a hat."

There were murmurs of agreement, and then Babs said, "Wait a minute. Sadie isn't pregnant, is she?"

Chapter Eight

♥

Chase began to second-guess his wedding proposal idea the moment he saddled up Lula Belle. The white horse belonged to Agnes and played the starring role in Sadie's children's book series, Lula Belle the Unicorn.

After several tries, Chase had managed to attach the gold unicorn horn but his attempt at weaving wildflowers into the horse's mane and tail had only served to irritate Lula Belle. Chase and the horse were already on shaky ground so he didn't think it was in his best interests to further tick off Lula Belle, especially since he was a novice rider.

From where he now sat on the horse in the meadow, half-hidden by a tree, Chase watched for Sadie's SUV. His phone pinged with an incoming message. Lula Belle shook her mane and then went back to beheading the yellow flowers in the meadow. Chase gingerly adjusted the unicorn horn that had slid over her eye before retrieving his phone from the back pocket of his jeans.

He opened WhatsApp and checked out Hunter's latest text, smiling at the photo of Bella and Wolf, the couple's dogs. Bella, a tiny Yorkshire terrier, wore a pink frilly dress with a sign around her neck that read *Marry Me*. Beside her, Wolf, a white dog who was actually part wolf, wore a tuxedo with a sign around his neck that read *On October 23*.

Above the photo, Hunter texted:

She said yes.

Chase replied with a thumbs-up and a smiley-face emoji. Seconds later, Gabe did the same.

Gabe followed up with a photo of a bed covered in red rose petals and then a selfie of him and Mallory sitting at a small table on a balcony, enjoying a candlelight dinner with a view of Mirror Lake in the background. From the smiles on the couple's faces, Mallory had said yes too. Which Gabe confirmed seconds later. Both Chase and Hunter responded with thumbs-ups and smiley-face emojis.

They were followed by a text from Hunter:

Seriously? Emojis? How about 'You rocked it'? Or 'Best proposals ever'?

Then another text from Hunter:

Sorry. Abby got hold of my phone.

Chase laughed and texted Abby's suggestions to both Hunter's and Gabe's phones, adding fireworks and a couple of confetti horns. Then he typed, *Still waiting for my bride-to-be.* Raising his hand, he took a selfie of himself sitting on Lula Belle. Seconds after he'd posted the photo to their group chat, he received a line of laughing/crying emojis from each of his friends.

Lose the shirt, Fabio.

Chase glanced down at the white Henley he wore and typed, *Who's Fabio?*

How should I know? That was Abby again. Please keep your shirt on.

Then Gabe wrote:

A male romance-novel cover model. But don't listen to Abby. You're going to rock your proposal, Chase.
Just FYI, I do not read romance novels. That was Mallory.

Chase typed, *This is a private group chat. Keep your phones with you at all times.* He added a wedding chapel and a bride emoji so Hunter and Gabe would get his point. They were using the group chat to discuss their wedding plans.

At the sound of a car driving down the gravel road, he looked up from the screen. It was Sadie. He stuck the phone in his back pocket and gathered up the reins. "Okay, Lula Belle. It's showtime." He gently nudged her sides with the heels of his hiking boots to get her moving as Sadie's SUV approached. "Come on, girl. Stop eating. We're going to miss our window of opportunity." He tugged on the reins, and Lula Belle stamped her right hoof without lifting her head.

Sadie's SUV drove by.

Chase opened the saddlebag and pulled out an apple, leaning over to give Lula Belle a look at what he had in his hand. She gave the apple the side-eye.

"You want it, girl. You know you do." He drew his arm back and pitched it a solid ten yards in a straight line down the meadow. "Yes," he said when the horse lifted her head. But his *yes* quickly turned into a *no* when Lula Belle took off at a gallop instead of the easy trot he'd envisioned.

They passed Sadie's SUV. Chase, who was hanging on for dear life at that point, didn't dare raise his hand to wave. "Whoa, Lula Belle. Whoa." He tugged harder on the reins. The landscape whizzed by. "I said whoa, not go!" he shouted, as they raced past the cottage.

Up ahead, a downed tree loomed in their path. Chase frantically tugged on the right rein to get the horse to change direction before it was too late. A sharp whistle rent the air. Lula Belle stopped short less than a foot from the tree. Chase slid sideways off the saddle.

Heart hammering, Chase was pulling himself upright when Lula Belle started moving again. He was relieved she appeared to be heading back the way they'd come, but he was ready for the ride to end. "Whoa, girl. Whoa. Stop!" he shouted when she shot off at a gallop. Hanging sideways off the saddle, wildflowers slapping him in the face, Chase made out the woman he loved running toward them.

"Lula Belle!" Sadie called, and then whistled.

The horse came to a dead stop. Chase slid the rest of the way out of the saddle, landing flat on his back in the meadow. Breathless, Sadie ran to stand over him, phone in her hand, tears streaming down her face. She dropped to her knees at his side. "Honey, are you okay?"

He raised a hand to her face. "Other than a little battered and bruised, I'm fine." His ego was certainly battered and bruised, but he doubted the rest of him was.

Her shoulders were shaking, and that's when he realized the tears on her face weren't from fear but from laughter. If there was any doubt, the gurgle in her voice when she confirmed that he was all right alleviated it. She must have called emergency services.

"You can cancel the ambulance."

She lay down beside him on her back and held up her phone.

Gabe and Mallory and Hunter and Abby appeared in boxes on the screen. They were laughing hysterically.

"Best proposal ever, bro," Hunter said, swiping tears from his face.

"No way anyone will top that," Gabe said.

Chase stabbed the phone with his finger, ending the call.

"I'm sorry but I had to call them. It was just too—" She broke off when Lula Belle came over to nuzzle his cheek, her unicorn horn falling off her head and onto his face.

Chase sighed, turning his head to look at Sadie, who buried her face in his chest, no doubt in an attempt to muffle her laughter. She raised a finger. "Just give me a minute to get—"

"I was going for a romantic proposal, you know. Not one that would send you and our friends into fits of laughter."

Lifting her head from his chest, Sadie smiled and wiped the tears from her face. "I'd take an unforgettable proposal over a romantic one any day of the week. Besides," she said, pressing a sweet kiss to his cheek, "you did romantic the first time."

"Are you forgetting I fell out of the rowboat?"

She pressed her lips together, her eyes sparkling with amusement. "Don't make me laugh again. My stomach muscles can't take it."

"You're so beautiful." He took her hand, pressing a kiss to her knuckles. "Especially when you laugh."

"You're the only man who's ever made me laugh, Chase. I'm happier with you in my life than I've ever been or than I ever thought I could possibly—"

"Hold that thought." He released her hand and pushed himself to his feet. Hiding his pained grimace, he did his best to walk to Lula Belle without a limp.

"You are so hurt," Sadie said, getting up to come to his side. She wrapped her arm around his waist. "Let's get you to the cottage and get some ice on your ankle."

"We can't. You'll miss the best part of my proposal."

"Better than you riding Lula Belle?"

"Yes, especially considering how that turned out."

"How was it supposed to turn out?"

"After I wowed you with my equestrian skills, I was going to sweep you off your feet and onto the back of Lula Belle, and we were going to ride to Blue Mountain and—"

"Watch the sun set over the valley. Oh, Chase, that was an extremely sweet and romantic idea." She wrapped her other arm around him and tipped her head back. "But you didn't need to propose to me again. You have nothing to make up to me for. If anything, I'm the one who should be going all out with a romantic proposal after the way I acted. I'm really sorry, you know."

"You have nothing to apologize for. But I wouldn't say no to you making it up to me tonight. Say in that little red number you bought from Blushing Bridal." He waggled his eyebrows.

"Oh, Mr. Roberts, you can count on getting very lucky tonight."

An hour later, Chase sat with Sadie on the rock that jutted out over the valley. At least this part of his proposal had gone as planned.

Sadie sniffed as she looked through the photo album. "How did you manage to put this together so quickly?"

"I was going to give it to you for Christmas but I thought you might need something other than words to convince you how good we are together." He turned the pages of the photo album, stopping at one Abby had taken. It was the day he'd proposed to Sadie in the yellow-flower-bedecked rowboat. "What you said in the meadow, it's the same for me, Sadie. I never expected any of this: falling in love with you, becoming a father, leaving Washington to move here. You've changed my life..." He gave her a rueful grin. "Honestly, I don't think I had a life until you."

"Now look what you've done. You've made me cry." Blinking back the tears in her eyes, she put down the photo album and framed his face with her hands. "Thank you for today, for your proposal, for this gift. It couldn't have been more perfect."

He turned his face to kiss her palm and then leaned to the side to drag the saddlebag toward him. "There's something else." He pulled out a rolled piece of paper tied with a pink ribbon and a blue velvet box, handing the paper to Sadie first. "I pulled some strings. I hope you don't mind."

Sadie frowned as she untied the ribbon and unrolled the paper. Her gaze shot to his. "Is this what I think it is?"

"If you think it's Michaela's adoption papers, it is."

"Take it, take it." She shoved the paper into his hands. "I'm going to cry all over it and ruin it." She covered a sob with her hand, shaking her head. "I didn't think we needed a piece of paper to prove that you're Michaela's father. You've been more of a father to her than her own since the day she was born. But this..." She pointed at the paper. "It's important. For Michaela. She'll know that you wanted her, that you've made her your own. Thank you for loving her as much as you do. Thank you for—"

"Stop," he said, wiping the corner of his right eye. "You're going to make me cry."

She took his hand and gave him a watery smile. "You cried the day she was born. You didn't think I noticed but I did. I fell a little bit in love with you then."

"Thank God Nate didn't notice. He never would have let me live it down," he said, his voice still gruff with emotion. Nate Black had worked with him undercover last summer. They'd had a rocky start, but now they were as close as brothers.

"I'll let you in on a little secret if you promise not to tell him. Nate cried too."

"Yeah?" He pocketed the blue box, deciding he'd give it to Sadie the night before the wedding. They'd cried enough for one day. His cell phone pinged with an incoming message and then kept pinging. So did Sadie's.

"Michaela's fine," he said, knowing what she was thinking because it had been his first thought too. "Your grandmother texted us fifteen minutes ago." He didn't want anything to intrude on their night together but he glanced at his screen. The first line of the message had him opening the text. He rubbed the back of his neck. "Babe, is there something you want to tell me?"

She frowned and opened the messages on her phone. "I don't believe it." She turned to him. "I'm not pregnant. It's just a big misunderstanding. Abby, Mallory, and I got a little emotional at Blushing Bridal, and someone assumed I must be pregnant too." She sighed. "Babs. It's probably all over town by now."

"That's a given," he said, wishing he hadn't opened the message from his grandfather. It was putting him in a bad mood, which probably came out in his voice. "Just so you know, no one would have been happier than me if you were pregnant. But I'm just as happy to wait another year." This, at least, was something he and Sadie had talked about, and he knew they were on the same page.

"Who texted you?"

"No one important." He put down his phone and wrapped an arm around Sadie's shoulders. "And we have a sunset to enjoy." His phone rang. He hit Decline. Seconds later, it rang again.

"It's your grandfather, isn't it?" Sadie sighed when he nodded. "Take his call, Chase. I bet he's heard the latest gossip and thinks I'm using my supposed pregnancy to trap you into marriage."

She was probably right but he wasn't about to let his grandfather ruin their night. "I'll call him in the morning," he said and went to decline the call.

But Sadie was faster and grabbed his phone. "Hi, Jonathan. It's Sadie." She paused and then said, "He's busy at the moment but I have a feeling I know why you're calling and wanted to set your mind at ease." She frowned. "I'm sure I can if you'd just hear me out."

Chase retrieved his phone and whispered, "Trust me, you won't get a word in when he's on a roll." Then he said to his grandfather, "It's me, and you should know better than to listen to small-town gossip. Sadie isn't pregnant, but even if she...Oh, so now you think she's faking her pregnancy because of Gwen? Honestly, I don't know how...What do you mean you invited Gwen to Highland Falls?"

Chase glanced at Sadie, and she made an apologetic face. She must've known. "This has to stop, Judge. I love Sadie, and I'm marrying her. And if you don't cancel Gwen's visit, I will," he said, and disconnected.

"Sorry, I forgot to tell you about Gwen. It's kind of why Abby, Mallory, and I left the bakery the way that we did. Ellie called to give me a heads-up that your grandfather booked a room for her at the inn."

"So I was right. Gwen's the reason you want to get married."

"No, of course not...Okay, so maybe she was in the beginning. Abby thought if we set a date your grandfather would realize he couldn't use Gwen to come between us. Obviously, that didn't work. He just upped his game."

Chase put his phone down and took her hand in his, rubbing her engagement ring with his thumb. "There's nothing I want more than to marry you, Sadie, but if the only reason you agreed to this is because of my grandfather and Gwen, I think we should hold off," he said, struggling to keep the disappointment from his voice.

"It may have started out that way, and then I got caught up in the excitement and I wanted to make Abby happy. But all that changed when I was at Blushing Bridal, thinking about how I'd messed up at the bakery and about how much I love you." Sadie took his hands and brought them to her cheeks. "There's nothing

I want more than to pledge my love to you in front of our family and friends, so please, will you marry me?"

"Nothing would make me happier than to marry you." He waggled his eyebrows. "Except maybe seeing you in that little red number from Blushing Bridal."

She grinned, settling herself between his legs and resting her back against his chest. "We have a sunset to watch first."

"You're right, and I have a grandfather to shut down." He reached for his phone.

"No, don't." She covered his hand with hers. "We might as well deal with this head-on. Tell your grandfather you've had a change of heart, and Gwen is welcome to come for a visit. That way he'll see there's nothing between you and her, and he'll let it go."

Chapter Nine

♥

Thirty minutes into their lunch date with the judge and Gwen at Zia Maria's on Main Street, Sadie was kicking herself for not letting Chase cancel Gwen's visit two days ago. The sophisticated blonde was as beautiful and as brilliant as Sadie had feared she would be.

As much as Sadie didn't want to admit it, she could see why the judge believed Chase and Gwen were the perfect match. Not only were they both gorgeous, they looked fantastic together, and they were finishing each other's sentences within minutes of sitting down at the table. They knew all the same people and clearly had a long history together.

Sadie tuned back into their conversation when Gwen reached over and smoothed a wayward lock of Chase's hair with a familiarity that caused Sadie to tighten her grip on the knife in her hand. Sadie never ate pizza with a knife and fork, but moments before, as she'd lifted a slice to her mouth, she'd caught the judge and Gwen sharing a raised-eyebrow glance.

"Oh, darling, you're too modest," Gwen trilled. The woman had an annoyingly shrill voice, which seemed only fair considering everything else about her was perfect. "They never would have solved that case without you."

Okay, no one was prouder of Chase's accomplishments than Sadie. He was brilliant, his IQ was off the charts, and he probably did have the highest case clearance rate of anyone at the FBI. He'd caught not one of America's Most Wanted but two, for goodness' sake. But seriously, was that all these people could talk about?

Sadie glanced at Chase. He appeared as uncomfortable with Gwen's praise as he had been the last twenty times the woman and the judge had regaled Sadie with stories of his brilliance.

Thinking it was time for a subject change, Sadie said, "So, Gwen, how are you enjoying your time in Highland Falls?"

"I only arrived last night so I haven't had much time to take in the sights," she said with a patronizing smile.

Right. Sadie should have come up with something else. But it's not like she could ask about Gwen's job. They'd already heard ad nauseam how important she was to the Department of Justice. Maybe Sadie should have asked her how she was able to take time off to visit.

"But honestly"—Gwen reached for both the judge's and Chase's hands—"if not for my two favorite men, I wouldn't be caught dead in this backwater." Gwen released their hands to bring her own to her mouth. "I apologize, Sadie. That was rude of me. I'm sure it's a lovely little town. It's just that I much prefer big-city living." She turned to Chase. "You were always the same, darling. You can't tell me you're actually happy living here."

Chase smiled, the kind of smile that crinkled the fine lines at the corners of his eyes. It was the first time he'd truly smiled since they'd sat down at the table, Sadie realized. "I'm happier than I've ever been, actually. I've become a fan of small-town living, especially this town. Then again, I might be slightly prejudiced." He turned his breath-stealing smile on Sadie. "After all, I found the love of my life in Highland Falls."

The judge cleared his throat, effectively ending the smile Sadie and Chase shared. Chase leaned in to kiss her cheek before turning back to his grandfather and Gwen. "Loves of my life, I should say. I'm sorry you weren't able to meet our daughter, Gwen. She's not at the pasta-eating stage yet."

"Unless you blend it for her," Sadie reminded him. "And turn her spoon into an airplane."

Chase laughed. "She loves that, doesn't she? We really should have brought her with us, honey. It's never too soon to introduce children to the pleasures of dining out."

His grandfather harrumphed. "I, for one, would disagree. There's nothing more annoying than having a fine meal interrupted by a whining and crying child."

Chase's gaze narrowed on his grandfather. "Michaela doesn't whine or cry at dinner time. She loves to eat, as you saw for yourself, Judge."

"Perhaps. But that infernal airplane noise you make while feeding her is just as annoying."

Afraid the lunch was on a death spiral that would bring Chase and his grandfather's relationship down with it, Sadie intervened. "Well, it's a moot point. Michaela couldn't come even if we wanted her to. Ellie took her to Cutie Patootie to look for her dress," she reminded Chase.

"Was that today?" At Sadie's nod, he heaved a disappointed sigh. "I thought we were taking her. Ellie's not choosing the dress for her though, right?"

"No. She's just putting a couple options on hold for us. She was worried their new holiday line would be picked over if we waited another day." She patted his hand. "Don't worry, Daddy. You'll get to have your say."

Gwen tilted her head to study Chase as if he were an alien

from outer space. "Do you always involve yourself in the choice of Sadie's daughter's clothes?"

"*Our* daughter," he corrected Gwen. "And no, I don't. But this dress is special. It's for our wedding, and I want to be involved."

"Really," Gwen said in a disbelieving tone of voice.

"Oh yes, Chase is *very* involved," Sadie said. "He chose our wedding cake design, and yesterday he and his fellow grooms-to-be had a meeting with the florist."

"Now, honey, I told you, we didn't have a meeting with Winter. She's the mayor and owns Flower Power on Main Street," he explained to his grandfather and Gwen, who were staring at him with almost comical expressions of horror. "We just happened to be walking by and noticed her window display. All we said was that adding the feathers and ferns to the bouquets of garden roses, dahlias, and peonies would go well with our ideas for the wedding decor."

"Funny, that's not what I heard. Winter told Abby the three of you had actually ordered more garden roses, dahlias, and peonies than would fit in her coolers." And as much as they were happy that the men wanted to be involved, they hadn't expected them to take over.

"We might have gotten a little carried away," he said with a sheepish grin. "You're not mad, are you?"

"No, not at all. But you might want to talk to Abby before you change anything else. Her subscribers have been helping plan the wedding. They're really invested."

Chase frowned. "No more invested than we are. Surely they'd understand if we tweak a few things."

"I'm sorry," Gwen said. "I don't mean to interrupt your scintillating conversation, and please don't be offended, Sadie, but I feel this must be said. Chase, I'm worried about you. I find all of this remarkably unlike you. In a matter of months, you've moved from the city you love—and your grandfather, I might add. You accepted a job that effectively takes you out of the running for either directorship of the FBI or attorney general, career aspirations that you've had for as long as I've known you. My God, you ended our engagement because I refused to sign on with the FBI." She held Chase's gaze. "I thought you'd eventually come around. I was willing to wait. Had I known that—"

"I don't know what's brought this on, Gwen." The castigating look Chase sent his grandfather said otherwise. "But you know as well as I do that your decision not to join the FBI had nothing to do with our breakup. I'd realized I was marrying you to make my grandfather happy, not me. Besides, we're too much alike. We would have driven each other crazy."

Covering Gwen's hand with his, Chase gave her a gentle smile. "I'm sorry. This really isn't the place to have this conversation. But you're right, I'm not the same man you remember. This past year, thanks to Sadie and Michaela and the people in this town, I've discovered what really matters. I hope one day you will too."

Zia Maria rushed through the door, stopping short at the sight of them. Her hand went to her hair, which she'd obviously had freshly done.

"Why did you not tell me you come for lunch today?" Maria said as she approached their table.

Sadie and Chase had decided to keep their lunch date with the judge and Gwen between them and made the reservations in another name. They'd known exactly what would happen if anyone in town had found out about it.

"I would have made you something special." Maria glanced at the judge's plate. "Ah, now you have good taste. Just like your grandson. Did you enjoy your linguine di pesce?"

The judge nodded. "I must admit I was pleasantly surprised at the caliber of your cuisine. My only criticism is that the tiger shrimp were somewhat overcooked."

Maria crossed her arms. "You say my Marcello cooked the shrimp too long?"

"Don't be too hard on your son. No one else but me would notice. I'm somewhat of a connoisseur when it comes to Italian food, you see," Jonathan said, completely misreading the situation. No one but Maria criticized her son.

Chase, who by now knew Maria as well as Sadie did, intervened. "My meal was perfection, Maria. The gorgonzola cream sauce…" Chase brought the tips of his fingers to his lips and kissed them.

"Ah, you are such a good boy." She came over and pinched Chase's cheeks. "Look at that face. So handsome," Maria said. Then she glanced at Gwen. "And your carbonara, did you enjoy?"

"Very much, thank you. It was excellent," Gwen said, her voice subdued.

Obviously, the lunch hadn't gone as either Gwen or the judge had planned.

Maria looked at Sadie's plate and slapped her palm to her face. "Pepperoni pizza. Madonne! You have the taste buds of a teenager." She flicked Chase's shoulder with her finger. "What are we going to do with her?"

"I wouldn't change a single thing about her, Zia Maria." Chase turned a heart-melting smile on Sadie. "She's my perfect match."

Chapter Ten

♥

Three days after their lunch date, Chase and his grandfather were still not talking. The only positive that came out of it was that Sadie no longer worried about Chase's ex-fiancée. She'd actually felt sorry for the woman when they'd said their goodbyes. It had been obvious the judge had gotten Gwen's hopes up. In the end though, it wasn't only the other woman's hopes that had been dashed. According to Ellie, Chase's grandfather was barely eating and moped around the inn like he'd lost his best friend.

Sadie glanced at Chase as she buckled Michaela into her car seat. As much as he tried to hide it, she knew it bothered him that he and the judge were on the outs.

"Did you mention the tasting tonight at Highland Brew to your grandfather?" Sadie asked casually. "I'm sure he'd enjoy hanging out with you guys."

"He won't be here. His flight leaves at three," Chase said, and slid behind the wheel.

Sadie kissed Michaela. "Be a good girl for Daddy," she said before closing the door and rounding the car to come to Chase's side.

He was meeting Hunter, Gabe, and Gabe's sons at the tailor's to pick out their kilts, after which they'd head to the pumpkin patch at Owen Campbell's farm.

"I'm sorry, honey. Maybe he'll be back for the wedding."

Chase shrugged. "It's probably for the best that he isn't. I don't want anyone to ruin our special day."

"How could anyone ruin our wedding when you and your fellow groomzillas have thought of everything right down to the smallest detail?" she teased in hopes of distracting him from his disappointment that not a single member of his family would be attending.

The night before last, his brother had called to give his regrets. He had a conference that same weekend. But no matter what Chase had said after ending the call, he'd been disappointed. So disappointed that Sadie had been tempted to go bridezilla on both his brother and his grandfather. It didn't matter that Chase was a treasured member of their family as far as her grandmother and brother were concerned. Or that he'd grown incredibly close to Gabe and Hunter. Chase's grandfather and brother were important to him, especially the judge.

Chase raised his hands from the wheel, his lips twitching at the corners. "I had nothing to do with the candy apple stand. That's all on Gabe. But in his defense, he was under a lot of pressure from his sons. The twins are addicted to candy."

Sadie knew this to be true. She'd witnessed the twins' candy addiction firsthand. "Actually, I was thinking of the menu change you guys tried to sneak through. Abby and her subscribers weren't impressed."

"Again, that wasn't on me. But I think Hunter is right. A couple guy-friendly appetizers couldn't hurt, could they? I mean, who doesn't like grilled chicken wings and nachos?"

"Abby's subscribers?" She kissed his cheek. "Don't worry though, I defended you in our *Abby Does Highland Falls* video chat."

"You mean your What Are the Groomzillas Up To Now?

segment." He gave her a raised-eyebrow look, but the amusement in his eyes gave him away.

Sadie laughed. "You wouldn't believe how popular that segment was. It's gone viral."

Michaela banged her bottle on her car seat. "Dada, dada."

"Okay, sweetheart, we're going," Chase said to Michaela before returning his attention to Sadie. "And we'll see you later." He curved his hand around her neck and drew her in for a kiss.

Which might have gone on longer if their daughter didn't start banging her bottle again. Sadie withdrew her head from the window, blowing a kiss to Michaela as she did so. "You two have fun," she said, adding as an afterthought: "And no more tweaks to the wedding plan." Her eyes narrowed at the blank expression on his face. An expression she'd come to think of as his *I'm up to no good* tell. "Chase, I'm serious."

"Have I told you how much your serious expression turns me on?"

"Not in the last thirty minutes."

He grinned, calling out his open window as he backed out of the gravel drive, "Check your file before you go shopping. I sent you a few more wedding dress ideas."

She bowed her head. Between Ellie, Abby, Mallory, and Chase, she had at least eighty wedding dress suggestions already. They were right though. She had to get on that today. Mallory had decided on her dress a few days ago.

However, as Sadie stood at the open door to the cottage, waving until Chase's car faded from view, wedding dresses were the last thing on her mind. She kept seeing Chase's face the other night when he'd told her no one from his family would be attending the wedding.

At least he had Nate. But then she remembered, Chase wouldn't have Nate at his side. The NCSBI agent worked undercover more often than not and couldn't afford to be seen by millions of people. It could be dangerous to him and the people he loved.

Sadie pulled out her cell phone and called Abby. There must be something they could do to ensure that Nate could take part in the ceremony. Five minutes later, she disconnected from Abby, who'd promised to figure something out. But she'd sounded far less optimistic than she usually did when coming up with a plan. If Nate's attendance wasn't a guarantee, Sadie had to somehow get Chase's grandfather and brother on board.

Sadie walked into the cottage, glancing at Finn, who looked forlorn. "Don't worry, boy. They're coming back to get you for the trip to the pumpkin patch," she said, and headed for her bedroom to get dressed. Her grandmother and Ellie were meeting her at a bridal boutique in Jackson County in an hour.

As Sadie pulled a cream-colored sweater over her head, an idea came to her. Ten minutes later, she hugged Finn goodbye, locked the cottage door, and headed for her SUV.

Sadie glanced at the time and called her cousin. "Hey, Ellie, can—"

"Thank goodness, I was just going to call you. The judge is leaving, and there's nothing I can do to stop him. Trust me, I've tried."

"I know, but do you think you can stall him? I'll be at the inn in fifteen minutes."

"I'll do what I can. But his bags are packed and waiting at the door, and he just called an Uber."

"Cancel his ride and hide his bags."

Twelve minutes later, Sadie pulled into the parking lot at the inn. She spotted the judge on the dock, his hands clasped behind his back as he stared out at the crystal-blue lake. The anger Sadie had been nursing on Chase's behalf left her as she made her way across the damp grass and down to the dock. The judge looked dejected and incredibly sad.

"Jonathan," Sadie said as she approached him.

Beneath his dark suit, the judge's shoulders rose on a sigh. "If you've come to talk me out of leaving, it won't do you any good," he said without turning.

"I was hoping we could talk, just for a few minutes." When he glanced at her over his shoulder, she gestured to the Adirondack chairs. "Please. Come sit with me."

"I don't have long. My driver should be here any minute now." He raised an eyebrow. "I'm taking it you're the reason Ellie canceled my first ride and hid my luggage."

"I plead the Fifth," she said, in an attempt to lighten the mood.

It didn't appear to work. He took the seat beside her, folding his hands neatly in his lap, looking every inch the Superior Court judge that he used to be. Sadie's stomach danced with nerves.

She stiffened her spine. This was too important to Chase for her to cave under the older man's steely gaze. "I know I'm nothing like the woman you'd hoped Chase would marry, but I'm also not the woman you seem to think I am."

His only response was to stare at the waves lapping against the dock.

Sadie soldiered on. "Chase and I didn't have the best examples when it came to our parents. But we were both blessed to be taken in and raised by grandparents who loved us, and who we respected and loved—love—in return. Despite what it might feel like right now, Chase loves you, Jonathan. He loves you very much."

Again, he didn't say anything, but Sadie caught the softening in his expression. "And while you and I have our differences, there are a couple of things we do agree on. We both love Chase and only want the best for him."

He turned his head. "And you think that's you."

"Me and Michaela." She nodded. "Yes, I do. I didn't feel that way in the beginning though. At least about myself. I didn't

think I was worthy of his love. But Chase convinced me otherwise." She took the photo album Chase had made for her and
offered it to the judge.

He tapped the album's cover. "And this is your evidence?"

"Yes. As a mother, I would protect my daughter with my
life. You've been a father to Chase, as well as a grandfather, so
I understand where you're coming from. But as parents, all we
really want is for our children to be happy. Isn't it?"

"I thought he was," the judge murmured, and opened the
album.

As he slowly paged through the photos, she told him when
and where each one was taken. When he reached the last page,
she took out her phone, pulling up some of her favorite photos
of Chase. "I took this one a few weeks ago. He's become quite
the fly fisherman."

"My grandson fishing? I never would have believed it if I
didn't see it with my own eyes."

"I don't think he could either." She smiled, bringing up a
photo of Chase laughing with his head thrown back at a bonfire
with Gabe and Hunter, another of him playing fetch with Finn in
the meadow at sunset, and one of him dancing with Michaela in
his arms under the harvest moon at last month's Fall Festival.

"I've never seen him so happy. I thought I had, but I hadn't."

At the touch of sadness in his voice, Sadie decided to lighten
the mood and played videos of Chase trying to teach Michaela to
say *dada*. She ended with the video of Chase's botched proposal
on Lula Belle the day before. The judge laughed almost as hard
as Sadie.

As he dabbed away his tears of laughter with a hankie, Sadie
said, "I know all the changes Chase made this past year have
been difficult for you to understand and accept. But none of them
had anything to do with how he feels about you. He worries
about you, you know. He wants you to move to Highland Falls."

She tentatively reached out to cover his hand with hers. "I'd like that too. I want you to be part of our family, Jonathan."

He rubbed the corner of his left eye with his hankie and then cleared his throat. "I loved my wife. She was the best thing that ever happened to me. She was my best friend, the best life partner that I could have asked for."

"You must miss her."

"I do, very much so." He handed her back the album. "She'd be disappointed with how I've behaved this past week. I'm sorry for how I've treated you, Sadie. I was rude and unkind."

"Thank you. I'm sorry too. I should have come to you sooner. My only excuse is that planning this wedding has taken over my life."

"And not only yours from what I understand," he said with a touch of amusement in his voice. "Ellie was watching What Are the Groomzillas Up To Now? on your friend's YouTube channel the other night and asked me to join her. It was... enlightening."

Sadie smiled. "Living here has been good for him. Maybe it would be good for you too. The seniors in Highland Falls are very active in the community. I don't know if you've heard from the mayor yet, but she mentioned that an opening is coming up on the town council, and she thinks you'd be a perfect fit."

"I've heard from quite a few people in town, actually. Some with very interesting proposals." His smile faded, and he looked down at his hands. "Only I'm not sure Chase wants me to stay here any longer." He held up a finger when Sadie went to protest. "I know that he did. But he was also very clear that he wanted nothing more to do with me if I hurt you."

"Trust me, he wants you here. We both do. And as much as I'd like to sit here all day and enjoy the view, we have things to do."

"We do?"

"Yes. You need a tux if you're going to be in the wedding party, and I think you should go to the pumpkin patch with the groomzillas. I don't trust them not to change our wedding decor to pumpkins and bales of hay. And there's the beer tasting at Highland Brew tonight. You definitely don't want to miss that. Plus, who knows what those three will get up to? I need you to keep them in line, Jonathan. You have a way about you that I think they'll respect."

"My wife would have liked you, Sadie. Just now, you reminded me a little of her."

"That's the nicest compliment you could have given me. Thank you." Her phone pinged, and she glanced at the screen. "Oh no, I forgot I was supposed to meet my grandmother at the bridal shop."

"I thought you would have bought your dress by now."

"You and everyone else. I haven't found the one I want yet. They're all so fussy and frilly. I just want a simple dress with elegant lines."

"I may have what you're looking for. I've kept my wife's wedding gown. It's very much like you described, and you're a similar size. If you'd like, I can have it sent to you."

Her throat tightened, and it took her a moment to get the words out. "I...I'd be honored."

"You're not going to cry, are you?" he said with a touch of alarm in his voice.

"No." She sniffed. "I'm..." Despite her best efforts, she cried, throwing her arms around the judge. "Thank you. Now our wedding really will be perfect."

Chapter Eleven

♥

Sadie, Abby, and Mallory learned the hard way that weddings are never perfect. Something invariably goes wrong. In their case, it wasn't the groomzillas taking over the wedding planning, it was the weather. Fifteen minutes before they were set to walk down the aisle, the skies opened up, the storm providing a light-and-sound show they could have done without.

Luckily, their guests and the other members of the wedding party made it into the barn in time and were relatively dry. The bales of hay their grooms had substituted for chairs didn't fare as well. Now that the storm had passed, there was a mad scramble to set up the chairs that the men had stored in the barn.

Abby had already canceled her subscribers' online viewing of the wedding, so the big screens hadn't been set up. She hadn't canceled only so that Nate could participate in the wedding. She'd done it for all of them. She wanted their actual wedding day to be special and private. No one had been happier with her decision than Hunter.

Her subscribers had been pretty good sports about it. Probably because Abby had promised she'd host an After the Wedding episode with the groomzillas in attendance—something she conveniently forgot to mention to Hunter, Chase, and Gabe.

As the first strains of Israel Kamakawiwoʻole's "Somewhere Over the Rainbow" drifted through the screen door and into the farmhouse, Abby turned to Sadie and Mallory. "I love you guys. You've turned a special day into an unforgettable one. I—"

"No. No more," Sadie and Mallory said, waving their hands in front of their faces. "Don't say anything else. You'll make us cry," Sadie added, close to tears. She'd already cried once today when she put on Chase's grandmother's dress. It was an antique-lace V-neck sheath wedding gown with three-quarter-length sleeves and a gorgeous rose sash adorned with pearls, crystals, and rhinestones. She couldn't have envisioned a more perfect wedding dress.

Abby's twin sisters opened the screen door, looking beautiful in their pumpkin-colored bridesmaid dresses. "Come on, Abs. It's time."

Abby took a deep breath and smiled. "Here we go." Her mother and stepfather joined her on the porch, handing her Bella. Wolf was standing with Hunter, along with his brother.

As they began walking down the steps together, Mallory's father came to stand with his daughter. "Are you ready, honey?"

Mallory, who looked stunning in a pale peach wedding gown, gave her father a watery smile and nodded. Her father surreptitiously wiped at his eyes, as emotional as his daughter. It was the first time he'd walked Mallory down the aisle.

"Look, look, here she comes!" Teddy cried as Mallory and her father walked down the steps. Snowball, the family's tiny white dog, barked, making the five boys standing with their father laugh.

As Sadie's grandmother and brother came to take their places on either side of her, Ellie, looking beautiful in her pumpkin-colored bridesmaid dress, handed Michaela to Sadie. In the end, it hadn't been Sadie or Ellie who'd picked Michaela's outfit, it had been Chase. She looked adorable in the creamy tulle dress, the sash and the bow in her hair the same plaid that Chase wore.

Finn, Nate, and Chase's grandfather were his groomsmen. Sadie smiled, thinking back to the moment she'd dropped off Jonathan at the tailor's. Chase had been as happy as she had known he would be. Although the judge hadn't been as good at keeping the groomzillas in line as Sadie had hoped. Owen had delivered a wagonful of pumpkins to the farm early this morning.

As Ellie walked ahead of them down the leaf-strewn aisle, Agnes leaned in to Sadie. "Look at Nate. He can't take his eyes off your cousin." Sadie's grandmother adored Nate and treated him like a grandson. She'd also been trying to set him up for the past three months so Sadie thought she'd better warn Ellie and Nate.

But then Chase turned to watch her walk down the aisle and thoughts of anyone else but him scattered. He looked beautiful in his black jacket, white shirt, and plaid bow tie that matched his kilt. But it was his smile that stole her breath. She blinked her eyes, afraid she'd cry. The last thing she needed was mascara running down her cheeks. Just when she thought she couldn't hold the tears back any longer, Michaela saved the day. She yelled, "Dada, dada" and reached for Chase, making grabby hands.

Everyone laughed, including her grandmother and brother, who leaned in to kiss Sadie's cheeks. "I love you, girlie." "I love you, sis."

"Love you too," she said, once again struggling to contain her tears as she went to stand with Chase.

"Hi." She smiled.

"Hi." He grinned, bending down to kiss both her and Michaela. "You're so beautiful," he whispered in Sadie's ear.

"So are you," she whispered back.

"I love you."

"I love you more."

"Okay, you two," Abby called over. "The sooner the mayor marries us, the sooner we get to the fun part."

The mayor stood in front of a wooden arch draped in peach- and cream-colored roses and rust-colored vines. The flowers looked a little worse for wear after the storm but were still beautiful and smelled divine. Sadie cast Winter an apologetic glance.

The mayor gave her a *no worries* smile and began the ceremony. They said their vows together. Chase interrupted them in the middle of the ring exchange. "I need a minute." He crouched beside Finn, taking a blue box from the pocket of the plaid tux the golden retriever wore. Straightening, Chase opened the box to reveal a tiny diamond ring on a delicate chain.

"Oh, Chase," Sadie murmured.

"I wanted Michaela to have something special to remember today."

"She has you." Sadie sniffed, helping him fasten the chain around Michaela's neck and then kissing him. "It's beautiful."

"Thanks a lot, Chase," Abby said. "Now you've made us all cry."

"I'm not crying," Hunter said.

"Neither am I," Gabe added.

"You kind of are, Dad. So are you, Hunter," Teddy said.

The judge blew his nose and then shrugged as he tucked his white hankie in his breast pocket. "There's nothing wrong with a man shedding a tear or two on a special occasion such as this." He winked at Sadie. "I've gained a granddaughter and great-granddaughter, after all."

Chase wiped at his eyes, sharing a laugh with Sadie when Nate did the same.

"Hurry up and marry them before they flood us all out, mayor," someone called from the back row.

They were all still laughing when Winter declared them husbands and wives. "You may now kiss your brides."

Gabe and Mallory's boys started groaning seconds into their kiss, Wolf started howling minutes into Hunter and Abby's, and Nate told Sadie and Chase to get a room.

But when Sadie's grandmother cried, "Look, look," they all broke their kisses to follow the direction of Agnes's pointed finger. And there, over the farmhouse, was a gorgeous double rainbow.

Standing in the circle of Chase's arms and holding Michaela close, Sadie caught her best friends' eyes and shared a smile. Mallory and Abby nodded, believing, like her, that it was a sign. The three of them had each gone through a storm and had come out the other side to be blessed with the men they had just married.

About the Author

Debbie Mason is the *USA Today* bestselling author of the High-land Falls, Harmony Harbor, and Christmas, Colorado series. The first book in her Christmas, Colorado series, *The Trouble with Christmas*, was the inspiration for the Hallmark movie *Welcome to Christmas*. Her books have been praised by *RT Book Reviews* for their "likable characters, clever dialogue, and juicy plots." When Debbie isn't writing, she enjoys spending time with her family in Ottawa, Canada.

You can learn more at:
AuthorDebbieMason.com
Twitter @AuthorDebMason
Facebook.com/DebbieMasonBooks
Instagram @AuthorDebMason

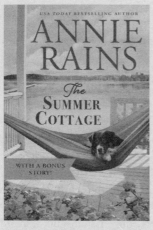

THE SUMMER COTTAGE
by Annie Rains

Somerset Lake is the perfect place for Trisha Langly and her son to start over. As the new manager for the Somerset Cottages, she's instantly charmed by her firecracker of a boss, Vi—but less enchanted by Vi's protective grandson, attorney Jake Fletcher. If Jake discovers her past, she'll lose this perfect second chance. However, as they spend summer days renovating the property and nights enjoying the town's charm, Trisha may realize she must trust Jake with her secrets...and her heart. Includes a bonus story!

FALLING IN LOVE ON WILLOW CREEK
by Debbie Mason

FBI agent Chase Roberts has come to Highland Falls to work undercover as a park ranger to track down an on-the-run informant. But when he befriends the suspect's sister to get nearer to his target, Chase finds that he's growing closer to the warm-hearted, beautiful Sadie Gray and her little girl. When he arrests her brother, Elijah, Chase risks losing Sadie forever. Can he convince her that the feelings between them are real once Sadie discovers the truth? Includes a bonus story!

A WEDDING ON LILAC LANE
by Hope Ramsay

After returning home from her country music career, Ella McMillan is shocked to find her mother is engaged. Worse, she asks Ella to plan the event with her fiancé's straitlaced son, Dr. Dylan Killough. While Ella wants to create the perfect day, Dylan is determined the two shouldn't get married at all. Somehow amid all their arguing, sparks start flying. And soon everyone in Magnolia Harbor is wondering if Dylan and Ella will be joining their parents in a trip down the aisle.

FRIENDS LIKE US
by Sarah Mackenzie

When a cancer scare compels Bree Robinson to form an *anti*-bucket list, she decides to start with a steamy fling. Only her one-night stand is Chance Elliston, the architect she's just hired to renovate her house. Bree agrees to a friends-with-benefits relationship with Chance before he returns to the city at the end of the summer. But as their feelings for each other grow, can she convince him to risk it all on a new life together?

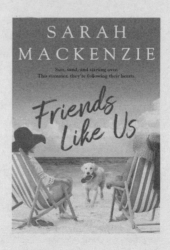

SUMMER AT FIREFLY BEACH
by Jenny Hale

Hallie Flynn adores her aunt Clara's beautiful beachside house, yet a busy job and heartbreak over the years have kept her away. But when her beloved aunt passes, Hallie returns to fulfill her final wish: to complete the bucket list Hallie wrote as a teenager. With the help of her childhood friend Ben Murray, she remembers her forgotten dreams ...and finds herself falling for the man who's always been by her side. But to have a future with Ben, can Hallie face the truths buried deep in her heart?

ONCE UPON A PUPPY
by Lizzie Shane

Lawyer Connor Wyeth has a plan for everything—except training his unruly mutt, Maximus. The only person Max ever obeyed was animal shelter volunteer Deenie Mitchell. But with a day job hosting princess parties for kids, the upbeat Deenie isn't thrilled to co-parent with Max's uptight owner...until she realizes he's perfect for impressing her type-A family. As they play the perfect couple, it begins to feel all too real. Can one rambunctious dog bring together two complete opposites?

Discover bonus content and more on
read-forever.com

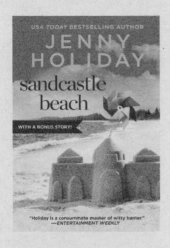

"Holiday is a consummate master of witty banter."
—ENTERTAINMENT WEEKLY

SANDCASTLE BEACH
by Jenny Holiday

What Maya Mehta really needs to save her beloved community theater is Matchmaker Bay's new business grant. She's got some serious competition, though: Benjamin Lawson, local bar owner, Jerk Extraordinaire, and Maya's annoyingly hot archnemesis. Turns out there's a thin line between hate and irresistible desire, and Maya and Law are really good at crossing it. But when things heat up, will they allow their long-standing feud to get in the way of their growing feelings? Includes the bonus story *Once Upon a Bride*, for the first time in print!

DREAM SPINNER
by Kristen Ashley

There's no doubt that former soldier Axl Pantera is the man of Hattie Yates's dreams. Yet years of abuse from her demanding father have left her terrified of disappointment. Axl is slowly wooing Hattie into letting down her walls—until a dangerous stalker sets their sights on her. Now he's facing more than her wary and bruised heart. Axl will do anything to prove that they're meant to be—but first, he'll need to keep Hattie safe.